Dear MVP, You're Ice Cold

Seattle Havoc Hockey Romance

Vivian Wood

Copyright © 2026 by Vivian Wood

All rights reserved. No part of this publication may be reproduced, distributed, or transmitted in any form or by any means, including photocopying, recording, or other electronic or mechanical methods, without the prior written permission of the publisher, except as permitted by U.S. copyright law.

For permission requests, contact Vivian Wood via www.vivianwoodwrites..com.

Without in any way limiting the author's [and publisher's] exclusive rights under copyright, any use of this publication to train generative artificial intelligence (AI) technologies to generate text is expressly prohibited. The author reserves all rights to license uses of this work for generative AI training and development of machine learning language models.

This book is a work of fiction. While this story is set in several real locations, all characters, incidents, and events are entirely fictional. References to real places, businesses, or institutions are used for setting only and are not intended to represent or depict actual people, events, or endorsements. Any resemblance to actual persons, living or dead, or to actual events is purely coincidental.

Book Cover © 2026 by Najla Qamber Designs

Seattle Havoc Roster

In case you haven't read a Seattle Havoc book or you just need a refresher, here's the hockey team and everyone who appears in this world.

CURRENT ROSTER

Hunter Huxley (#47) - Right Wing (*Dear #47, You're the Worst*)

Silas Huxley - Defenseman (*Dear MVP, You're Ice Cold*)

Alexander Thorne - Co-Captain, Center (*Dear Hotshot, I Hate You*)

Beckham "Beck" Tate - Co-Captain, Defenseman

Grayson Reed - Left Wing

Jett Huxley - Goalie

Mason Decker — Defenseman

Moose Taggert — Right Wing

Jamie Proulx — Center

Shane Villareal — Defenseman

Connor Li — Left Wing

Theo Kozlov — Center

TEAM STAFF

Juliet Monroe - Head of PR (*Dear #47, You're the Worst*)

Scout Nash — Athletic Trainer (*Dear MVP, You're Ice Cold*)

Mollie Tate - Junior Social Media Manager (*Dear Hotshot, I Hate You*)

Ivy Prescott - Crisis Communications Lead

Jessa Laramie - Lifestyle Coordinator & Café Barista

COACHING & MANAGEMENT

• **Coach Damian Cross** - Head Coach

• **Jared Duke** - General Manager

• **Ryan Haart** - Assistant Coach (*Say Yes to the Nemesis*)

CONNECTED TO THE HAVOC WORLD

Wren Haart - TV Producer, married to Ryan Haart (*Say Yes to the Nemesis*)

Calla Rustin - Bakery Owner, married to Jay Rustin (*The Accidental Honeymoon*)

Jay Rustin - Lifestyle Ambassador (*The Accidental Honeymoon*)

Chapter One

Scout

Taking a part-time gig as the Seattle Havoc's unofficial den mother means I know who's allergic to peanuts, who left their wallet in the weight room, and who needs new laces before warmups. It also means I've learned the first rule of caring for professional hockey players: they're essentially very large, very expensive toddlers who lose everything and need it fixed yesterday.

When my alarm goes off at 5:47 AM, my phone is already buzzing with seventeen missed texts. Seventeen. Past-Scout, the one who cheerfully handed out her cell number insisting "text me anytime!" was an optimistic idiot. Present-Scout would like to throttle her.

I've been on the Havoc payroll for six months since my ex-husband Enzo decided to trade in our marriage for a carousel of Instagram models. The one good thing he left me? This job. And despite the fact that these overpaid man-children treat me like a combination personal assistant, fairy godmother, and emotional support human, I'm keeping it.

As I scroll through the messages, the clock mocks me. Jessa wants oat milk lattes from the café that's twenty minutes in the opposite direction. Juliet needs copies for some Very Important Meeting. A rookie lost his AirPods, which has somehow become my problem.

Juliet handles player relations, which means she puts out fires before the whole organization burns down. PR crises, player meltdowns, media scandals. When a Havoc player screws up, Juliet makes sure it doesn't end up on ESPN. She's also part of the Coven, Jessa's nickname for a witchy little group of women who actually keep this team functional.

But back in reality, I'm a personal assistant, not a metal detector. Though at this point, I should probably add it to my resume. *Scout Nash, Professional Stuff Finder.*

I drag myself out of bed and into yesterday's jeans. Since the divorce, I've been living with Jessa, who took pity on me when I showed up with two suitcases and the kind of desperation that says, *this is my last option before I have to move in with my father*. Jessa is bubbly, brilliant, and has inexplicably decided I'm worth keeping around despite my tendency to sing to my houseplants and do yoga in the middle of the living room at odd hours of the day.

Every day, I try to prove she made the right call by bringing home flowers or making her favorite lemon bars. It's either that or actually talk about my feelings, and we both know that's not happening.

This is what I do. I keep things running smoothly. Someone has to make sure the world doesn't implode, and apparently that someone is me. It's easier this way. If I'm busy solving everyone else's problems, I don't have time to think about my own.

Win-win. I just need an attitude shift. I can make today a great one, as long as I'm willing to ignore the shitty Seattle winter and the heinously early start time.

Getting coffee and pastries at the café is a breeze.

Heading to the practice arena is pretty easy, although the traffic is already fairly hellish by the time I arrive. My fingers are icy from the January cold and my phone won't stop pinging with new requests. I distribute the lattes and pastries first, mostly because Jessa texted three crying emojis and I'm not heartless. Then I head to the copy room with my list of tasks, ready to power through my never-ending list of to-do items until lunch.

The copy machine hums and spits out stack after stack of paper. Media packets for tomorrow's press conference. Practice schedules color coded by position. Travel itineraries for next week's road trip. I've highlighted each player's schedule in a different color because it makes things easier to read at a glance. Yellow for forwards, blue for defense, green for goalies.

Nobody told me to do these errands. I'm doing them of my own volition to be helpful. And because I was married to a hockey player for several years, I know as much as anybody that they work hard on the ice and then take a mental vacation when you hand them any kind of paperwork. If you color-code things for athletes, the chances that they'll actually read it and not just toss it are greatly increased.

I'm gathering the papers into neat stacks when Juliet appears in the doorway. She moves so quietly that I don't notice her until she's right there, watching me work.

"Scout," she says.

I jump, straightening up too fast, and the papers slide. They scatter across the floor in a rainbow of highlighted sheets. "Sorry, sorry." I drop to my knees and start gathering them.

Juliet crouches down beside me, her movements precise and efficient. She picks up a handful of schedules and studies them. "When did you do all this?"

"Last night." I reach under the table for a runaway packet. "It's not a big deal."

"It is a big deal." Her voice is gentle but firm. "You're not paid to color code schedules at midnight. The team has money. We can hire more help." She pauses, her dark eyes searching my face. "I know we don't know each other that well, but I can see that you're smart. Too smart to be running errands forever, Scout."

Heat crawls up my throat. I try to laugh it off, make it sound light. "I didn't get a kinesiology degree to be a professional copy maker, but it pays the bills while I figure things out."

Juliet stills, her gaze on me. "Kinesiology?"

"From UW." I gather papers faster, not meeting her eyes. "I was pre-physical therapy track after..." I trail off because the end of that sentence is too complicated.

After my mom died, but before I married Enzo and let him convince me I didn't need a career. She doesn't need to know all of that. Juliet's extremely nice and a consummate professional. This is work, not a therapy session.

"That doesn't matter now," I say instead.

"Are you interested in working with the players?"

"I would love that." I blush. "I mean, that's what I studied in school. Soft tissue issues, mobility problems, recovery setbacks. I geek out on that stuff."

"So why are you in the copy room? Why not apply to work with the trainers?"

"Oh, you know." I wave away my embarrassment. "Life got in the way of getting my certifications. So for now, I'm just the team gopher. And I teach yoga classes here and there. Those are so much fun."

Juliet purses her lips. "But you're qualified to be helping injured athletes recover? That's what you want to be doing?"

Is my face on fire? Sure feels like it. I look down at Juliet, the sassy brunette with a take-charge attitude I would kill for, and I swallow.

"Yeah. That's my goal. Mobility work, basic athletic training, yoga certification. But I'm not a licensed PT. I didn't finish the program."

Juliet's eyes narrow. She asks carefully, "Do you mind if I ask why not?"

The question lands like a punch. I sit back on my heels, still holding a crumpled schedule. "Like I said, life happened. First my dad needed someone to stay with him after my mom died. And then my ex and I got married, and he didn't want me to work." I shrug, trying to make years of regret sound casual. "I left the work force before I ever really entered it. And now... I'm here."

"It sounds like you just need a little help getting to the right job." She stacks the last of the papers and presses them into my hands, her grip firm. "Think about what you'd actually want to do here if you could use your training. We'll talk about it the next time I see you."

"Okay," I say quietly. "Thanks, Juliet."

"Of course. I love helping women reach their potential." She gives me one more brief smile, something knowing and sad in her eyes, then walks out.

When she looks at me like that, is she seeing a young divorcée? A meandering soul? A lost little girl? It doesn't matter because I don't want to see myself from the outside.

I already know that my life is screwed up.

I stay on the floor for another minute, surrounded by highlighted schedules and half-formed dreams. Then I stand up, smooth my team polo, and get back to work. That's what I do. It's all I know how to do.

The rest of the morning passes in a blur of tasks. I find the rookie's AirPods in the locker room, reorganize Juliet's filing system because someone messed it up, answer countless emails and confirm reservations. When it gets near lunch time, I order lunch for a sponsor meeting.

By two o'clock, my feet hurt and my stomach is growling. I'm heading to the break room for a granola bar when I turn a corner and walk straight into a wall.

Except it's not a wall. It's Silas Huxley.

The papers in my arms jab into my ribs. I stumble back a step, looking up and up until I find his face. He's massive. Six foot eight of muscle and silence, standing there in training gear that somehow looks both casual and severe. His dirty blond hair falls past his chin. His blue-gray eyes are both unfathomable and unreadable at once.

He's the one hockey player on this team that I do have some history with. *Unfortunately*.

"Sorry," I blurt out, already moving to squeeze past him.

He doesn't say anything. He doesn't move either. No, he just stares down at me with that blank expression that gives away nothing.

Is he angry? Annoyed? Even a little acknowledgment that I'm a human being standing in front of him would be a positive note at this point.

I edge sideways. My shoulder brushes his arm and something electric shoots through me, quick and unwelcome. I don't look back as I hurry down the hallway. My skin prickles like I've stepped from a sunbeam onto a vast, icy hockey rink.

I've worked for the Havoc for a while now. Of all the players that I deal with on a daily basis, only Silas Huxley still unsettles me. He's the team's star defender, quiet and intense. The kind of player who racks up points without saying a word. Off the ice, he's a ghost. He shows up, does his job, and disappears. No drama, jokes, or warmth.

Just cold, controlled silence.

And I can never tell if he still hates my guts or if he's forgotten me entirely. He doesn't talk or smile, not even with his teammates. He's a mystery, and not one that I should find intriguing.

I shake off the feeling and focus on my tasks. When my shift finally ends, I check my phone and find a text from Jessa.

JESSA

Coven meeting at The Secret History tonight. You're coming. No excuses.

The Coven is Jessa's nickname for the girls that work for the Seattle Havoc team. I stare at the message, already thinking of reasons to say no. Truthfully, I hate bars. The noise and the crowds put me off. And the way laughter bounces off walls while I sit in the corner feeling invisible is almost shameful. But… Jessa asked.

I've learned that saying no to people who care about you is harder than just showing up.

ME

Thanks for the invite! I'll be there.

The Secret History sits on the ground floor of the Sinclair, the luxury condo building where most of the Havoc players live. The team owns the building and subsidizes rent, which explains why a bunch of twenty-somethings who get paid to hit people with sticks can afford waterfront real estate.

The bar is all dark wood and mood lighting, the kind of place that smells like expensive whiskey and poor decisions. Music plays low. Conversations hum. I slip inside and head straight for the back room reserved for team personnel.

Juliet handles player relations, which means she puts out

fires before the whole organization burns down. PR crises, player meltdowns, media scandals. When a Havoc player screws up, Juliet makes sure it doesn't end up on ESPN. She's part of the Coven, Jessa's nickname for our little group of women who actually keep this team functional.

The women have claimed a corner booth. Juliet sits on one side looking like she's about to negotiate a hostile takeover in her navy bodycon dress. Jessa wiggles in her seat wearing a cardigan with tiny embroidered cherries and grinning. Ivy Prescott, the teams's crisis communications director, nurses a martini with the expression of someone who deals with hockey player drama for a living. Mollie Tate gestures wildly while explaining something, probably another viral TikTok idea. She's the Havoc's newest hire and her bouncy Gen Z energy is nearly irresistible.

I slide into the booth next to Jessa, and she immediately wraps an arm around my shoulders.

"You came!" she says, beaming.

"You guilt tripped me," I reply, but I'm smiling.

"Someone had to. Tell me you weren't going to spend another night mooning around, sighing and petting your houseplants."

"They get lonely!" I protest, giggling.

The Havoc players are scattered throughout the room like very large, very expensive lawn ornaments. Hunter Huxley leans against the bar with a scowl that could curdle milk. His brother Jett argues with the bar owner Olivier about the playlist. Together with Silas, they make up what the press calls the Brothers Grimm. Big, muscly hockey players with bad attitudes and even worse tempers.

Currently the Brothers Grimm are down one grim brother, but Hunter and Jett are doing their best to radiate *don't talk to us* energy.

Grayson Reed sits alone in a booth looking like he's hoping to become invisible through sheer force of will. I relate. Beck Tate, the team captain, talks quietly with a rookie near the pool table.

No sign of Silas. Shocking. He treats team gatherings the way vampires treat sunlight. And yes, I'm embarrassed that I noticed his absence. He's just... intriguing. He's like a really grumpy puzzle I want to solve.

Ivy Prescott runs crisis communications. She's seen every stupid thing a hockey player can do and has a PR strategy for all of it. Right now she's drinking a martini like water and looking exactly like someone who spent the day convincing a twenty-three-year-old not to post shirtless gym selfies with questionable captions.

The women talk and laugh. Jessa slides me a glass and the pitcher of something that looks like lemonade. Margaritas, my nose informs me. Juliet shares a story about a disastrous press conference. Mollie shows us a TikTok of the players attempting a dance challenge with all the grace of newborn giraffes. Ivy rolls her eyes but she's smiling.

"You're mopey." Jessa nudges me. "Are you okay? You're usually sunny all the time."

I paste on a smile, not telling her that most of my sunniness is fake. *Fake it 'til you make it.*

"It's been a really long day. Tomorrow will be better."

"Hm. You know what? We need to make a list. A sexy list."

"Of what? Like… positions I've done it in?" I cringe. I've only ever been with one guy, my ex. And he mostly liked sex to be vanilla, missionary, and less than five minutes.

"A list of everything you're going to do this year. I don't mean goals, I mean all the naughty, selfish things you want to do for yourself." She pulls a pen from her hair like it's been waiting there for exactly this moment. She drags a napkin across the table. "This is the post-Enzo Scout list. The… umm… the Naughty Girl Scout List."

"Jessa," I protest. "What do I need a list for?"

But she's already writing.

"Kiss a stranger," she says, scribbling it down. "Wear red lipstick every day for a week. Dance on a table. Have morning sex before coffee."

"You're ridiculous," I say. But her words bring a smile to my lips.

"Ridiculousness can save your life," Juliet replies, leaning in. "Come on. What do you want to do? Seriously, let's drink more margaritas and come up with a really dirty list."

I purse my lips then shrug. "Okay. Let's drink a little more first."

Jessa's eyes dance. "That's my girl."

Twenty minutes later, we have a list scrawled on the back of a blank sheet of paper borrowed from Juliet's attaché case.

The Naughty Girl Scout List

- Wear red lipstick every day for a week
- Dance on a table
- Download a dating app and actually swipe
- Have morning sex before coffee
- Try a toy with someone watching
- Fall asleep still sweaty and tangled up with him
- Confess my fantasies to a complete stranger
- Sleep naked and not feel weird about it
- Figure out what my body actually likes in bed
- Send a nude without apologizing for it
- Sext until the phone dies
- Let someone go down on me until I cry
- Give a blowjob and take control until he begs
- Ride someone's face just because I want to

• Have sex against a wall, messy and desperate
• Let someone tie my wrists and take whatever they want
• Watch myself in a mirror while he's inside me
• Let a man talk filthy to me without flinching
• Get fucked on the kitchen counter
• A finger up the butt (on either person)

"This list just gets hornier as it goes on." I frown down at the paper.

"So what?" Jessa giggles. "It's great. A girl should have big plans in life."

"It feels like asking a lot. How am I supposed to find a guy to try all of these things with?"

"No one ever said you had to find one guy to try these out with." She squints, then points to an item. "You should see what's out there. You said you hadn't set up a Twinge account. So maybe start there. That would be a good first item to cross off."

"Yeah." I exhale, feeling pleasantly buzzed. "I could do that."

"You sure?"

"Yeah. It's probably the easiest thing on the list." I wrinkle my nose. "Don't kill me, but I think I need to crash. How are you still upright? You were up before me."

Jessa shrugs. "I only sleep four or five hours a night. Should I grab my coat and walk you home?"

"No, you stay. I'm going to be unconscious the second I hit my bed anyway." Walking the fourteen blocks home will help me sober up. Plus, it's the only hard cardio I get besides running around the arena all day. I'd rather eat cinnamon rolls than spend my life in a gym.

I hug Jessa goodbye and thank the other girls for having my back. Then I head out into the rain, letting the cold wake up my brain.

The walk home is peaceful. Seattle at night is all glowing windows and wet pavement. My boots splash through puddles and I don't even care. I've got a pocket full of filthy goals and just enough tequila in my system to believe I might actually accomplish some of them.

Mmm, a cinnamon roll would be excellent right about now.

In my apartment, I shake the rain off my pink shell jacket and put my boots on the rack by the door. Then I change into my favorite black yoga pants and an oversized Havoc hoodie. After pulling on my coziest socks, I smooth the list out on the kitchen counter. The ink has bled a little, but the words are still clear.

The Naughty Girl Scout List stares up at me, daring me to actually do something about it.

I think about all the years I spent making myself smaller for Enzo. Playing hostess. Laughing on cue. Pretending his constant absences didn't bother me. He called my degree a waste. Got me a part-time job where he could keep tabs on me. He might have loved me, but only the version that stayed quiet and useful.

Screw that.

My phone sits on the counter, the Twinge app I downloaded three weeks ago just sitting there. Unopened. Judging me for being a coward.

Well, not anymore.

I tap it open and spend a few minutes uploading photos and answering inane questions. Then I start swiping.

Faces blur past. Guys holding fish. Guys with dogs. Guys whose profiles mention craft beer and hiking like it's a personality. Honestly, I have no idea what my type even is. I was twenty when I started dating Enzo, completely dazzled by his looks and money and attention. I just said yes the first time he asked me out and didn't question it for six years.

So now what? I swipe almost indiscriminately. Tall, short, whatever. Photos of abs. Photos of travel. Photos that are definitely someone else's photos.

Then I stop. One profile catches my eye. Grainy photo from the neck down showing a truly impressive number of abs. The next is a blurry shot of a tall guy on a plane, staring out the window. The caption reads, "Seems like I'm always at an airport."

About to swipe left, I catch the profile bio.

Don't like small talk. Just looking until I'm not. Numbers make more sense than people.

Weird. Blunt. This is probably a bot trying to scam me.

I look at the abs photo one more time and think, *screw it. My hormones can make this decision.*

I swipe right.

The app pings immediately. *A new match!*

My heart jumps. I tell myself it doesn't matter, but I open the message anyway.

STATMAN12

You don't look like you belong here.

I stare at it. Rude. Presumptuous. Somehow, it's exactly what I needed.

YOGA4LYFE

And yet you messaged me first.

He's online, because he writes back in under a minute.

STATMAN12

Exactly.

Heat skims under my skin. Not fear or obligation. Something wilder.

Another message appears. Then another. The conversation flows easy and sharp. He's not trying to be nice or asking me to take care of him. He's just... talking to me like I'm interesting.

The rain taps against my window. My phone lights the dark kitchen with squares of possibility.

And for the first time in months, I feel awake.

Chapter Two

Silas

I wake before the sun slips up from the horizon. The world is still. It's the only time life makes sense to me. I feel like I can breathe without feeling like something's pressing on my chest.

The silence fills my whole body with peace.

I grab my phone off the nightstand. I look at First National, my investment portfolio, and my money market account. Same ritual every morning, same ritual every night. All the numbers sit exactly where I left them.

As long as my numbers are a few pennies more than the last time I check, I can convince myself that everything is fine. Most people would call this paranoid. I call it necessary when your own mother tried to steal everything you earned.

I start my morning by dropping to the floor beside my bed. Pushups until my arms shake. Sit-ups until my ribs burn. Pull-ups on the bar mounted in my doorframe until my grip starts to fail. The old injury in my right shoulder, a consequence of a run-in with an opposing enforcer, flares hot and angry. But I don't listen.

The pain doesn't get a vote. It never has.

My condo looks like a locker room. Everything is in its place. Protein shake bottles line the counter in perfect rows. Meal prep containers stack in the fridge. Chicken, rice, broccoli. Same thing every day. The knives in the block all face the same direction. My shoes sit squared by the door.

I eat my prepared meal, heated in the microwave, while I'm standing at the kitchen counter. It's the same meal I eat every day, so I don't think about it, don't even taste it really. Instead, I work on a Sudoku puzzle on my phone. Dropping numbers into their allotted spaces, neat and predictable. True.

Numbers never look at me with soft green eyes and ask for parts of myself I don't know how to give. Scout Nash slips into my head anyway.

I add a 9 to my Sudoku puzzle, determined to pay attention. But I quickly realize that I haven't gotten the last few numbers in this row right. Does the 9 go at the end of the row or in the middle? Damn it.

It's ridiculous. It's all Scout's fault, really. I tell myself I'm not thinking about her, but there she is. Arms full of schedules and coffee cups, dark braid slipping loose, smile too bright for six in the morning. She's always running somewhere, always helping someone, always making herself useful.

I remember the time she asked me out. Eight years ago, back when she and I were both U of W students. She approached me in the parking lot after practice, cheeks flushed, words tumbling out fast. She was gorgeous, even though she was dressed down in a pair of stretchy black yoga leggings and an oversized sweatshirt that said Juicy. Not a hint of makeup, her voluptuous curves calling to me.

She looked like a ripe peach, begging to be plucked from

a tree and devoured whole. And she was offering me the first bite.

Like a complete idiot, I told her no. I had reasons, of course. Hockey came first. Focus. No distractions. No complications.

They all sound like excuses now, standing here alone in my silent kitchen, eating nuked chicken at five in the morning. I'm a coward. Scout figured that out back then. Soon after, she did a disappearing act, dropping out of school. I told myself it was fine, because Scout has been nothing but icy to me ever since I turned her down.

But last night, when I saw her photo on Twinge, I had to swipe right. Because, what if...?

Pretty curls, grippable hips, those tight black yoga pants and tantalizing crop tops. Scout's my fantasy, come to life. Always has been.

To my surprise, she swiped right on me too, even though my profile is just a shot of my abs and a couple of lines of bio designed to keep me anonymous.

Yoga4Lyfe. How fitting that she would call herself that. We exchanged a few lines of meaningless chatter before she stopped answering. And I spent the next few hours gripping my dick in one hand and my phone in the other, flipping through the photos she posted while I jerked off, over and over.

God, I'm such a fucking creep.

The morning air is brittle, cold and damp and relentless. January in Seattle feels like being inside a freezer while you're soaking wet. Though I'm used to it, I still have the yearning for sunlight like all Pacific Northwesterners. By February, I'll actually look forward to flying into Phoenix and Houston just for the sunny winter skies. It's always so gray and drizzly here.

The practice facility smells like cold metal and rubber when I walk in. The scent hits me first, then the quiet. I'm always the first one here. I like it that way. No voices or expectations. Just the hush of the ice and the hum of the building settling around me.

I head straight to my stall in the locker room. My sticks lean against the wall in perfect order, tape spiraled on each one. I check my laces, pulling them tight the same way I have since I was fourteen. My helmet visor gets polished with the microfiber cloth I keep in my bag. My phone goes face down on the shelf in my locker so the screen can't light up and distract me.

The room fills one by one.

Jett shows up first, all broad shoulders and movie-star grin, chirping at a rookie like he's already in mid-conversation. His hair looks like he just ran a hand through it and called it styling. Beck Tate walks in next. He's sharper, his jaw set as he mutters about traffic and curses when his skate lace won't stay flat. My brother Hunter prowls through after him, all dark intensity and tightly wound muscle, eyes flicking like he's waiting for someone to start something. And then there's Grayson Reed, leaning against his stall with careless grace, curls messy, tan coat hanging open, smirking at whatever's on his phone.

The noise swells and fades around me, but I stay quiet. I absorb it without giving anything back. That's what I do. I watch. I listen. Filing everything away in the organized drawers of my mind.

Then Enzo Morelli walks in. I stifle a groan.

The guy might be my agent, but he's not particularly likeable. Wearing a pin-neat blue suit and tie, his dark hair is slicked back, his smile as sharp as razor wire. For a former hockey player, he's awfully pretty. Too good-looking for me to trust him, that's for sure.

When Hunter took him on as an agent, Jett and I did, too. But I have always felt this hostility toward him. After I turned Scout down, he swept her off her feet and married her within a few months. I was forced to watch them together, especially after their relationship had lost its shine. Enzo made me a lot of money, but my stomach turned every time I saw him slipping a pretty girl his phone number or hiding lipstick stains on his collars.

Not only did he take someone I wanted, but he didn't treat her right. It was sickening to watch.

I sigh as Enzo slips in, late as usual. Enzo's suit fits like it was painted on. His laugh carries across the locker room, too loud, too practiced. He shakes hands with one of the assistant coaches, then slaps backs with a sponsor who's touring the facility. He's all performance and charm.

He's back in his old stomping grounds, doing deals and putting his greasy palms all over any player who will look his way. The *motherfucker*.

It makes him an ideal agent. Enzo has made me a lot of money since he signed me in college. He scores big deals and those deals come with fat checks. Doesn't mean I have to like the guy, though.

Just outside the doorway, I see a flash of curly hair and hear a melodic laugh, the sound sliding down my spine like a thousand tiny bells rung in harmony.

Enzo's head jerks because he hears Scout as I do. He smiles as he starts moving toward the staff station where Scout is working. And I follow him.

Damn if I'm going to let him mess with her. I don't give a fuck who he is. He's been coming around the arena more since Scout officially divorced him. I think he's here to keep tabs on her, not monitor the hockey players who he's supposed to be worried about.

Fucking *asshole*.

"Hey, Silas," Coach Ryan calls. "Can we talk about the Buffalo game?"

He comes up and pulls my attention. Scout moves away, Enzo slipping out the door toward her. In a second, they are both out of sight.

"One sec. I'll be right back," I promise. "I just have to grab something."

Or kill someone, I think.

I brush past the doorway, pausing, cocking my head. There are low voices coming from the narrow corridor behind the training room. Following the sound, I steel myself for a confrontation.

Scout's pressed against an equipment cart, juggling a clipboard and a bundle of lanyards. Enzo leans on the edge of the cart like it belongs to him. His voice pitches low, intimate in a way that makes my jaw lock.

"You should quit while you're ahead, bella. This place isn't for you. You look like a volunteer who wandered in and got lost."

Scout's smile stays fixed on her face, but I see her knuckles go white on the clipboard. The plastic creaks under her grip. She doesn't answer him. It's the silence that gets me. The way she just *takes* it.

I want her to fight back. Or maybe I want to pound my agent into the ground so she never has to fight with him again. Either way would be fine by me.

Enzo's back is toward me, so he doesn't see me as he leans in. "I want you gone."

Scout's lips part but no sound comes out. Her eyes are

wide, her breathing too fast. She's scared of him. My hands tense, forming fists.

"Why are you here, Enzo?" My voice comes out flat and cold. Enzo straightens and turns, that billboard smile spreading across his face. There's no evidence that I startled him, but Enzo doesn't ever show much of anything on the surface.

"Ah, Huxley." He holds up his hands like I'm the one being unreasonable. "I was just talking to my wife. What are you doing here? Try not to look like you're plotting murder, huh? Sponsors don't love that energy."

"Ex-wife," Scout corrects. "Very ex."

He laughs, looking at me like we're old friends sharing a joke. My eyes harden.

"Sure, bella. Whatever you say." Enzo edges closer and Scout takes a half-step back. That fucker.

I growl, "Enzo, she obviously doesn't want to talk to you. You shouldn't be back here anyway. Go rub elbows with rich sponsors like you're paid to do."

"You're prickly, aren't you?" His smile sharpens at the edges. "She's my ex-wife, not your problem."

The words land like a blade between my ribs. I don't flinch or react in any way. I just stare at him until his smile wavers at the corners. He pats my shoulder like he's patting a dog and drifts off down the hallway, still grinning at anyone who'll look his way.

Scout keeps staring down at her clipboard. Her throat works like she's swallowing something sharp. She doesn't lift her eyes.

"You shouldn't let him push you around," I say.

It comes out wrong, like a rebuke. I meant it to sound protective, but I hear criticism. She flinches and my chest tightens.

"Is that all?" Her voice is clipped, tight. "I'm working, Silas."

Shit. Scout is responding to me like I'm Enzo. I shouldn't be here, either.

I nod once and walk away because I don't know how to fix the raw thing in her expression. I don't know how to fix anything. It's obvious by now that I only know how to break things.

Scout looks broken enough already.

By the time I get back into the locker room, it's empty. I can hear the distant echoes of the announcer, getting ready to call us out onto the ice. I hurry to pull on my skates and curse myself. I already got distracted and the game hasn't even started yet. Not a good sign.

I make it out just as the announcer is calling me out onto the ice. "Anchoring the blue line for your Seattle Havoc, six-foot-eight of pure shutdown power. Give it up for #12, Silas Huxley!"

Once I'm on the ice, I feel steadier. With all the drama, I nearly forgot that we're playing a game against the Anaheim Voltage, a team that we usually have no trouble trouncing. The cold air bites sharp in my lungs. My skates bite into fresh ice. The puck ticks clean against my blade. Here, things make sense.

There's order. There's control. There are rules that don't change.

For the first few minutes of the game, the Havoc look good. Our team captain, Alex Thorne, wins a clean faceoff. Beck hammers a perfect dump-in along the boards. Hunter pins a defenseman and forces a turnover. A Voltage player tries a tricky move to get around me, but I block him with my body, using my left shoulder to check him aggressively into the boards. Thorne seals the wall on defense. For just a breath, I almost believe we might actually be okay this season.

Then the wobble creeps in.

I always feel it first when the team starts to slide. It's like the ice tilts under my skates.

Kozlov, a vet who should know better, mishandles the puck on the blue line. It bounces out to center ice. Connor's stick is a beat too slow on a lift. Jett, our starting goalie, saves it at the last second. Everybody breathes, like we're saved.

But I don't. I file the mistakes away. They make little red marks on the map in my head.

I push my body harder to cover other players' gaps. I make faster crossovers. Stick in every passing lane. I clear the crease until my shoulder screams in protest. Hunter takes a stupid retaliatory penalty after a clean hit. Of course he does. Two minutes shorthanded.

I block a shot with my ribs and stay on my feet even though my breath disappears. We kill the penalty. My chest still burns.

The unraveling keeps coming. Grayson screams obscenities at a linesman and costs us a whistle. Jett tries to walk the puck through three defenders instead of just clearing it to safety. The bench swings from rage to silence and back again. Beck mutters curses under his breath like they might tilt the ice in our favor.

Hunter paces, jaw working, ready to snap at anyone who gets close. He's a fucking hothead and even marrying his pretty little wife Juliet has only taken so much off the edge of his rage. Connor Li and Shane Villareal, two of our best rookies, watch Hunter and seem to shrink into themselves.

I catch sight of Enzo in the stands during a line change. He's shaking hands with sponsors, laughing too loud, playing to the crowd. I don't look directly at him, but I feel his presence like a weight. The whistle blows and I can't wait to get off the ice. Anything that takes me away from him is worth it.

I know I need to think about finding a replacement for him, but that's low on my list. Too many other things to deal with at the moment.

Then I spot Hunter and Juliet near the tunnel.

They're not doing anything dramatic. Hunter's hand just rests at the small of her back, protective and easy. Juliet leans into him like it's the most natural thing in the world. They fit together like puzzle pieces, as though they were designed specifically for each other.

Something twists hard in my gut.

My brother doesn't know how fucking lucky he is. I'll never be soft enough, open enough, or good enough for someone to lean on like that. The thought sits heavy in my chest as I vault back over the boards for my next shift.

By the third period, the math in my head has already written the ending. Our possession is slipping. Scoring chances are bleeding away. We're going to lose.

And we do.

The buzzer makes it official. Three to one. Another loss to add to the pile.

The locker room mood is sour the second I step into it. Hunter slams his stick into the wall hard enough to crack the composite. Jett mutters to himself; he's always taken losses harder than anyone else on the team. Beck strips tape off his stick like he's skinning something. Grayson laughs too loud at nothing and no one joins him.

Then comes the silence, thick and suffocating. Normally, it's my friend. But not right now.

I strip off my pads, hang my jersey, and take a shower hot enough to sting. Putting on my suit, I make sure I'm gone before the trainers finish cleaning equipment. The rot in the air makes me want to choke.

The tunnel is mostly empty when I walk through. Scout's crouched by an equipment cart, her braid half undone, cross-checking itineraries on a clipboard. Her eyes look raw and red-rimmed.

I should keep walking, but my feet don't want to comply. They stop without consulting me and my mouth opens to speak before I can shove the words back in. "Why are you crying?"

It comes out like an accusation. I didn't mean it that way, but that's how it sounds.

She freezes, her back stiffening, but she doesn't look at me. "What do you care?"

I stuff my hands in my pockets. "Is this about Enzo? You shouldn't let him get to you. He's a bastard."

Her mouth trembles. Fresh tears slip down her cheeks anyway. She ducks her head. I take a step closer without thinking about it. The scent of eucalyptus and something floral clings to her. Lavender, maybe. It knocks loose the careful order in my head.

Before I can stop my hand, I almost reach out to touch her shoulder. My fingers twitch with the need to make things better. But of course, I don't. I can't. The wall inside me holds.

"Don't cry over him," I say. "He's not worth the mud on the bottom of your shoes."

The words come out rough and wrong. She snaps upright and her clipboard smacks into my chest. Her green eyes pierce me and hold me in place.

"I'm not crying over him." Her eyes shine, fierce and humiliated at the same time. "Not everything is about my ex-husband."

She walks away fast, leaving me like a gawping idiot, standing there like an idiot and watching her go.

Jett appears just as she disappears around the corner. He raises his eyebrows at me. "What'd you do?"

"Nothing."

"It didn't look like nothing."

I stare down the empty hallway, but Scout is gone. With a sigh, I turn to my brother. "Mind your own business."

"You're such an ogre." Jett smirks and claps my shoulder. "Try not to terrify the staff, Silas. We need them."

Jett's grin fades. "Mom called again."

I strip off my jersey. "I didn't answer when she called from the state pen."

"Me either," Hunter says from across the locker room.

"I can't believe that she still thinks she'll get one of us to listen to her bullshit. She stole so much from all of us. Not just money, either," Jett says.

"She was a pretty shitty mom," I chime in.

"I think we can all agree on that," Hunter grumbles.

Pulling his duffel bag over his shoulder, Jett says, "Last one there buys drinks."

He heads out, still grinning. I'm about to follow when I spot a cluster of reporters near the exit. One of them catches sight of me and his eyes light up like he's found prey. My jaw tightens. I can feel the questions coming already. Pointed jabs about my penalties, about being past my prime, about the team falling apart.

Hunter materializes at my elbow before I can make a mistake. He's solid. Steady.

"Keep walking," he says, his voice low. "Don't give them anything."

My fists curl at my sides. "They're going to ask about the penalties."

"Let them ask. You don't owe them answers." Hunter's hand lands on my shoulder. "Come on."

The tension in my chest eases by a fraction. I nod once. Hunter steers me toward the player exit, away from the cameras and the questions that would've made me snap.

I'm grateful for him. I don't say it out loud because I don't know how, but I feel it.

The drive home is silent. At home, I ice my shoulder and pull up a Sudoku puzzle, but the numbers blur together.

Scout's face keeps appearing in my head. Her tears. The sad look on her face when I tried to reassure her.

My phone lights up on the coffee table. The dating app notification glows. **Yoga4Lyfe.**

I set it face down without opening it.

Hockey comes first. It always has and it's not changing. Scout is Enzo's ex-wife, which makes her off limits for about a dozen different reasons.

And there's the fact that I don't do relationships.

So why does my shoulder ache less than my chest right now?

Kids wait by my car. Six or seven of them wearing Havoc jerseys that swallow them whole, clutching Sharpies and programs.

I should walk past them.

A little girl at the front has her arm in a cast. She looks at me like I'm supposed to matter.

"Can you sign my cast?"

Her voice comes out small. Hopeful. It pisses me off.

I crouch down. "What happened?"

"I fell playing hockey. Like you."

Something twists in my chest. "Hockey's hard."

"I know. But I'm not quitting."

"Good." I take the Sharpie and sign her cast carefully. "Don't quit. Wear your pads next time."

She beams like I just handed her the Stanley Cup. The other kids swarm forward with programs and jerseys. I sign everything they shove at me even though my hand cramps.

When the last one runs off, I stand up and catch Scout watching from across the lot.

I shove my hands in my pockets and walk past her. Whatever she thinks she figured out about me? I'm delighted for her to be wrong.

Chapter Three

Scout

My arms are full again. Story of my life. Four coffees rattle in a cardboard tray balanced on my left hand. Practice schedules press against my chest. A roll of hockey tape is wedged between my elbow and ribs because someone asked for it and I've already forgotten who.

I'm basically a walking supply closet at this point.

The Havoc hallway hums with post-loss tension. Skates scrape concrete. Voices echo. The stench of sweat and rubber permeates everything. Hockey pads get this uniquely awful smell, collectively a truly terrible stench that's stomach-churning. Everywhere that a door can be propped open with a huge fan has one full blast, blowing the smell around so that it's somewhat tolerable in the locker rooms and gym.

The locker room has a certain *we lost and everyone's pissy about it* vibe going on. Hunter Huxley paces like a caged bear with a grudge. Beck Tate mutters curses while ripping tape off his stick like it personally offended him. Jett Huxley barks orders at rookies. Grayson Reed laughs too loud at nothing until Beck tells him to shut the hell up.

Connor Li tapes his stick in silence, probably wishing he could teleport somewhere else.

Same, Connor. Same.

Juliet Monroe is the only thing keeping this powder keg from exploding. She moves through the room with her clipboard, smoothing tensions like some kind of hockey whisperer. The giant sapphire on her ring finger catches the light every time she gestures, which is often.

She's married to Hunter "the Chainsaw" Huxley, and somehow they work. Tiny, composed Juliet and her massive, scowling husband. I've watched them together when they think no one's looking. The way she whispers in his ear and he softens against her like warm butter.

That used to be me and Enzo. Or at least, I thought it was. Turns out what I had was a cheating husband and what Juliet has is actual love.

The difference is pretty stark.

I shake off the thought and get to work. Coffee delivery time. I slide into the locker room unnoticed, which is my specialty. Being helpful without being seen. It's basically my superpower.

"Here you go," I say to the room at large. "Good luck tonight. You'll destroy them."

Most players don't even look up. I'm furniture to them. The Coffee Chair. The Schedule Table. Very useful, totally invisible.

Except Connor, who glances up and mumbles, "Thanks, Scout."

I beam at him like he just handed me a Nobel Prize instead of two words of basic human decency. Pathetic? Maybe. But I'll take what I can get.

I slip out before anyone can see me having feelings about it.

I'm halfway down the corridor when I hear footsteps behind me. Heavy and purposeful. I glance back and catch Hunter's eye. He gives me a slight smile, the kind that reminds me of the big brother I never had. His expression makes me feel safe for just a second. Juliet trusts him. I've come to trust Juliet. Therefore, I innately trust this massive goliath she calls her husband.

Hunter's gaze shifts past me and his face hardens.

"Silas," he calls out, voice carrying down the hall. "Quit."

I don't hear a response, but I feel the weight of eyes on my back. My spine straightens. I know that Silas is staring at me. Too many times in the past few weeks, I've felt the weight of that stare.

I don't know what he could possibly want with me. Silas has made it crystal clear that I'm not important. What does Hunter want him to quit?

I can't begin to guess, so I keep moving.

Near the training room, I spot Connor again. He's rolling his shoulder, wincing like something hurts. The movement is stiff and compensating. I recognize it immediately. Tight pec minor, probably from overuse. I've seen it a hundred times in textbooks and clinical observations before I dropped out of studying kinesiology.

"Hey." I set down my stack of schedules on a nearby bench. "Your shoulder okay?"

"Me?" Connor looks surprised that I'm talking to him. It's almost as if he wasn't as tall, ripped, and dreamy-looking as the rest of his team. His shyness must be a rookie thing. "Yeah, it's just... I don't know. It feels like my shoulder is stuck or something."

"Can I take a look?"

His brows shoot up, but he nods right away. "Sure, yeah."

I step closer, pressing my fingers just below his collarbone. I feel the knot immediately, hard and angry under the skin. "You're tight here. It's pulling your shoulder forward and making your rotation feel locked."

"Can you fix it?"

I hesitate. This isn't my job. I'm not a member of the medical staff. I'm not even supposed to be touching players without supervision. But he's looking at me like I might actually be able to help. And it's been so long since anyone looked at me like that.

"Sit," I say. "Please."

He does. I guide him through a doorway stretch, talking him through the position until he feels the pull in the right spot. Then I grab a lacrosse ball from the equipment bin and show him how to do a pec release against the wall. His relief is immediate.

"Holy shit," he breathes, rotating his arm. "That's so much better."

"Keep doing that twice a day. And make sure you ice your right upper quadrant after practice." I'm already gathering my things, cheeks warm with something that feels like pride. "You should probably tell the trainers if it doesn't improve, though."

"Thanks, Scout. Seriously. You're a lifesaver."

I beam at him again, that small glow of being useful spreading through my chest. Using what I actually know instead of just fetching coffee and making copies feels good. Then I turn and nearly run straight into Juliet.

"Oh!" I smile at her, tucking a strand of my hair behind my ear. "Sorry. I know that I'm supposed to go grab lunch for the office soon. Do you need me to go now?"

Juliet studies me for a long moment, her expression unreadable. I feel like I'm about to get into trouble.

"Walk with me," she says. She's already moving down the hallway, her high heels clicking.

My pulse jumps as I fall into step beside her. Did I overstep? I'm not medical staff. Maybe I shouldn't have touched Connor. Shit. I shouldn't have given him advice without clearing it first.

"Juliet…" I start as we reach the elevator bank. "If I'm overstepping…"

"Not at all. In my office, please." She guides me inside and presses a button. "I would just prefer a little more privacy when we talk. People are so nosy here."

"…okay?" I say. I'm not sure what that means.

The elevator doors open and it's only a few steps down the hall until we reach her office. She ushers me in and closes the door. Double shit. She must be about to ream me out. I wince, rushing to explain myself.

"If this is about Connor…"

Juliet interrupts me, cutting off my explanation with a wave of her hand.

"I'm not trying to get you in trouble, Scout. How long have you been doing that?" Juliet asks.

I'm impossibly confused. "Doing what?"

"Soft tissue work. Mobility assessments." Her voice is calm, curious rather than accusing. "I saw you with Connor."

"Ah." My throat tightens. "Like I said, I studied kinesiology in school. I know some things. I was just trying to help. I'm so sorry if I overstepped."

She leans against her desk, arms crossed, studying me like I'm a puzzle she's trying to solve.

"You also teach yoga, right?"

My cheeks warm. "Yeah. I haven't led a class in a while, but that's part of my kinesiology practice. Very… holistic."

She pushes her cheek out with her tongue, studying me as

if seeing me for the first time. "So tell me. If you could design a program for this team, what would it look like?"

"Oh, easy." The words tumble out before I can stop them. "Mobility Mondays. Twenty minutes post-practice of targeted work based on position and common injury patterns. Hip flexors for forwards who need speed. T-spine mobility for shooting mechanics. Shoulder capsule work for injury prevention." I'm talking with my hands now, gesturing to my body as I talk about each part like I'm presenting to a class. "We could track baselines, measure range of motion improvements. I'd tie it directly to on-ice performance metrics."

Then I stop, breathless, heat flooding my face. "But that's... I mean, I'm not qualified. I'm not a licensed PT. I didn't finish the program."

Juliet's mouth curves into something that might be approval. "You seem to know more than most of these players do about their own bodies. And right now, we're hemorrhaging games to soft tissue issues and fatigue penalties. I don't know if you keep up with the staffing around here, but we lost two of our best trainers this year to retirement and maternity leave." She straightens, picking up her tablet. "So I would like you to write up your program. Scope, key performance indicators, risk mitigation. Show me what it would actually look like."

My heart hammers against my ribs. "You're serious?"

"I'm always serious about winning. And if this keeps even one player out of the medical bay, it's worth exploring. I happen to be married to a particularly injury-prone player. Anything to keep him off the IR list helps." She glances at her tablet, then back at me. "Send me a proposal. I'll take it to the coaches."

"Juliet, I..." My voice catches. "Thank you."

"Don't thank me yet. You have to convince Coach Cross

first." But there's warmth in her voice. Her approval makes my chest swell with something dangerous. *Hope.*

I float out of her office with my mind already spinning. Plans and metrics and proof. Structure and purpose to my life. The chance to actually use my brain for something that matters instead of just making myself useful in ways that anyone could do.

I round a corner and nearly collide with Jamie Proulx.

He's a rookie defenseman, maybe twenty years old. Way too young for me, but already a good-looking go-getter. Like I said, this whole team is handsome.

I, on the other hand, am a new divorcée at twenty six. I have almost nothing in common with Jamie except that we both live in Seattle and work for this team. His hair is still damp from the shower. He's got that wide-eyed eager look that all the new guys have before this league chews them up. He shifts on his feet, scratching the back of his neck like he's gearing up for battle.

"Uh, hey, Scout," he says. His voice cracks a little, which makes me feel ancient. "You want to grab dinner sometime? There's this place by the pier that does really good..."

My feet stop moving. Heat climbs up my throat. *Oh god.* He's a kid. Sweet, but still a kid. And I'm standing here in my team polo with coffee stains on the sleeve, feeling older than dirt.

"Jamie, that's really kind of you," I start, trying to keep my voice gentle. "But I can't. I'm sorry."

His face falls. His ears turn red. "Oh. Yeah, sure. I just thought... you know, that you're so... never mind."

My eyebrows knit. "Never mind?"

"Proulx." The voice booms down the hallway like a shotgun blast. A voice I'd know anywhere.

Silas.

He appears suddenly, filling the corridor with his presence. The tallest guy on the team. Broad shoulders. Gorgeous, eerie eyes. That same unreadable expression that makes me feel like I'm being catalogued and filed away in some drawer.

Silas isn't exempt from the team's good looks. If anything, he's hotter than the rest of the team, if hotness and surliness can be the same thing.

His stare locks on Jamie. "Quit harassing her."

Jamie blinks, startled. "I wasn't..."

"She works here," Silas says. His tone is as frosty as a frozen lake in January. "She's not here to entertain you."

My pulse jumps. "Silas, it's fine. He was just..."

"It's not fine." He doesn't look at me or even acknowledge that I spoke. His gaze stays pinned on Jamie like a physical weight.

Jamie stammers. "I didn't mean... I just thought..."

"Really," I try again, desperate to stop whatever this is. "It's okay..."

Jamie's eyes dart between us, panic creeping into his expression. "I didn't realize you two were... you know..." He swallows hard. "I thought..."

"Oh no." My stomach drops. "We're not..."

Before I can finish the sentence, Silas's hand fists in Jamie's jersey and shoves him back a step. Not hard enough to hurt, just hard enough to prove he could if he wanted to. His voice drops to something lethal.

"Apologize. Then leave."

Jamie's face goes crimson. He mutters a rushed apology to me without meeting my eyes, then bolts down the hallway. His sneakers squeak against the tile.

Silas stands rigid in the middle of the corridor. His chest rises and falls like he just finished a shift on the ice. His jaw is tight. He doesn't look at me or say a word. My lips part, but no words come to mind. Silas has that effect on me, turning my brain to mush.

"Sorry about the kid," he grumbles.

Then he turns and stalks away, shoulders stiff, leaving me pressed against the wall with my heart racing. My cheeks burn.

What the hell was that?

I stand there for a full minute, trying to process what just happened. Silas Huxley, who barely acknowledges my existence most days, just scared off a rookie who asked me to dinner. My pulse is still pounding, my skin too hot.

Why would he do that?

I don't have answers. And standing here trying to figure things out isn't helping me any. So I do what I always do… I get back to work.

I duck into the staff lounge to catch my breath and reorganize my stack of schedules. I'm fumbling with papers when Melanie Greene sweeps in like a force of nature. She's the wife of Jimbo Greene, the owner of the Seattle Havoc. I haven't seen her around since I started working here. But she was always nice to me when Enzo played for her husband's team.

Melanie is all pearls and perfume, her smile warm enough to soften the whole room. She spots me immediately.

"Scout Morelli!" she exclaims, arms out, drawing me into a hug before I can dodge. "It's been ages, sweetheart. How's Enzo doing? I heard he's making some serious deals for our boys now."

I freeze. My breath catches in my throat. My old name hits me like a slap across the face and I can't focus on anything else.

"Actually..." I force the words out, giving her a wobbly

smile. "My last name is Nash. Enzo and I divorced last year. I have been working here while I figure things out."

Melanie's smile shifts into something softer, almost maternal. She pats my arm like she's confiding secrets. "Oh honey. Well, you're better off, then. And it's obviously his loss. Enzo's always been a bit of an asshole, hasn't he? I hope we'll see more of you now that you're free of him."

I force a smile even though my stomach twists. "Thank you. That's kind."

She nods, satisfied with herself, and glides out of the lounge. Her perfume lingers in her wake, sweet and cloying.

I grip the schedules so hard the edges curl.

Everyone here still remembers me as Enzo's wife. That's all I am to them. Not Scout Nash, kinesiology graduate. Not Scout Nash, a caring friend. Just Enzo's ex, still hanging around, making herself useful until someone tells her to leave.

Except maybe Juliet. Juliet saw me help Connor. She asked for a proposal. Maybe she sees something in me that I'd almost forgotten was there.

The rest of the day blurs together. I track down missing foam rollers for the equipment manager. Getting down to work, I update travel itineraries for the road trip next week. Then I make sure the rookies know where the bus leaves from.

And of course, I keep smiling until my face hurts.

But my mind keeps spinning back to Mobility Mondays. Scope. Key performance indicators. Risk mitigation. Proof that I'm more than just coffee runs and sympathy.

I work late. By the time I get home to the tiny apartment I share with Jessa, my feet ache and my smile feels permanently fixed in place. Jessa's door is closed, which means she's either asleep or not here. The smart thing would be to collapse on the couch and watch mindless television until I fall asleep.

Instead, I open my laptop.

Mobility Mondays call my name. I work until almost nine building the proposal. I pull up research studies on mobility work and injury prevention, create templates for tracking range of motion improvements, design sample stretches tied to specific game situations.

Hip openers for wingers. Thoracic rotation for shooters. Shoulder stability for defensemen.

By the time I save the file, my eyes burn and my back aches from hunching over my keyboard. But my chest feels light. Hopeful. It feels better than I did last night, that's for sure.

I should sleep. We have a big game tomorrow, so I need to be at the arena by six tomorrow morning. But instead of closing my eyes, I open the dating app.

A message waits for me, timestamped from an hour ago.

STATMAN12

Still awake?

My pulse jumps. I type back quickly.

YOGA4LYFE

Just finished working on something. You?

He gets back to me right away. A little chill runs down my spine, thinking how StatMan might have been waiting around to hear from me.

STATMAN12

Can't sleep. My mind won't shut off.

YOGA4LYFE

I know that feeling. What's keeping you up?

STATMAN12

Just life. I worked out pretty hard today so I should be dead asleep. But my brain is an asshole sometimes.

Something in my chest twists. I curl up on my bed, laptop balanced on my knees, and type.

YOGA4LYFE

I get that. My brain likes to whir like an overheated computer sometimes. Especially when I care about something.

STATMAN12

Like work? Or something else? Do you like your job?

I stare at the question. Three months ago, I would have said yes automatically. I'd have convinced myself that making coffee runs and fetching equipment mattered because it helped people.

Now I'm not sure what the answer is.

YOGA4LYFE

Sorry, this isn't a very sexy conversation. I'm in a mood, I guess. We should talk about something else.

STATMAN12

Why?

Not every interaction with me has to be sexy.

YOGA4LYFE

You're very sweet. But you're also just a stranger who is probably online right now because you're horny. You're looking for someone interested in talking about their fantasies, not complaining about their life.

STATMAN12

Don't put words in my mouth, sweetheart. Just because I'm horny doesn't mean I'm shallow.

I pause, my cheeks heating.

YOGA4LYFE

You're right. I shouldn't assume. But I'm done complaining, anyway.

STATMAN12

So what do you want to talk about?

YOGA4LYFE

Something sexy. I want to feel like I'm desired.

STATMAN12

I've seen your photos. You're unbelievably hot. I bet you have to pry men off with a crowbar.

YOGA4LYFE

You're just saying that to get in my pants.

STATMAN12

Nah, I don't think I am. I bet every time you walk down the hall, men turn and stare at you. They think about what it would be like to kiss you, to feel your soft curves pressed against them, to slide a fist in your hair and tug you closer.

My mouth opens in surprise.

YOGA4LYFE

No one thinks about me. I promise you that.

STATMAN12

Yes, they do. Maybe all they can imagine is how sweet you would be the first time they got you naked and tasted you. I bet that men think about you when they're alone in the dark, jerking off, moaning your name. Wishing that they had your hot pussy to sink their cock into.

Never in my life has a man talked dirty to me. Certainly not as explicitly as this man. My cheeks must be glowing right now, they're so hot.

YOGA4LYFE

Do you think about that when you're alone in the dark?

STATMAN12

I've been thinking about it all night, sweetheart.

YOGA4LYFE

Do you.. um... touch yourself?

STATMAN12

Yes. I look at your photos and picture you sucking my dick. Or sometimes I picture you riding my cock. How you would moan. How your cheeks would flush. You would take every inch of my fat dick. I'd stretch you out, be more than you could handle. But you'd do it for me because you're such a sweetheart. Wouldn't you?

Jesus. I'm so turned on by his words that I have to press

my thighs together, shift against the couch to try to ease the pressure that is already building there.

STATMAN12

Tell me that you would, sweetheart.

YOGA4LYFE

Yes, I would. I'd take everything you gave me.

STATMAN12

That's right, you would. You seem like a good girl to me. And good girls get everything that they want. I'd fuck you until you saw stars. I'd whisper dirty words in your ear. And I'd make sure that you came at least three times before I finished.

He's trying to kill me. I suck in my bottom lip, rolling onto my stomach, texting furiously.

YOGA4LYFE

I've never... uh... done that.

STATMAN12

What? Been given multiple orgasms?

YOGA4LYFE

I didn't realize that women could have that.

STATMAN12

With the right man, they can. And I'd never leave you unsatisfied, sweetheart.

YOGA4LYFE

I think we should meet.

Not right this second. But soon.

When he doesn't answer, I figure he's gotten carried away with the fantasy, that he's breathing hard and stroking his cock in the dark. I wait a minute, then text again.

YOGA4LYFE

I have to go to sleep. Goodnight, StatMan.

I put my phone down, the dirty talk swirling in my brain. Could this guy really make me come more than once? My experience with Enzo taught me to feel lucky if I managed to come at all. Maybe I'd just never had this with the right person.

A tingle of excitement runs up my spine. Then my phone lights up.

STATMAN12

Goodnight, Yoga Girl.

I stare at the message for a long moment. Sure, he probably has a ton of girls that he talks dirty to. But right this second, I don't care. I want to feel special.

Desired.

I set my phone on the nightstand and pull the covers up. I fall asleep with a smile on my face.

Chapter Four

Silas

Do you think about that when you're alone in the dark?

Yes. That's all I think about these days.

I shake my head and refocus. It's game day. I shouldn't have stayed up texting Scout last night. But I would've missed that conversation… and damn, was it ever worth it.

I'm tired today, but I'm not sorry.

"Huxley!"

I jerk up from my thoughts as I huddle on the bench in the locker room. Coach Ryan's giving me an intense look that's just short of anger.

"Pay attention." He points and snaps at Coach Cross, who's been talking for a while now. The older, dark haired man arches a brow.

"Can I go on, Silas? No running stats or doing Sudoku while I finish."

He knows me too well. Usually, those are my go-tos for when I'm bored. Now I'm too busy imagining a naked Scout. God, I can't think about that right now. I refuse to get hard in the locker room like I'm a fucking teenager.

"Sorry," I mumble. "I'm paying attention."

Coach Cross sends me a heated look, but he turns to the rest of the locker room. "As I was saying. Tonight, no dumb penalties against Chicago. Stay out of the box. Play your lane."

He taps the board once with his marker and looks right at me. I nod. I mean it when I nod.

The locker room hums around me while I go through my rituals. I tape my sticks the exact same way I always do. Heel to toe. No gaps in the spiral. Laces pulled tight until my fingers ache. Finger tape snug but not cutting off circulation. My right shoulder aches under the pad, a steady pulse that asks for attention and gets none.

The Chicago Flames come in loud during warmups. They always do. Their captain glides past our line with a grin that shows too many missing teeth. One of their wingers drifts close and taps my shin pad with his stick.

"Old school, Huxley. All meat, no mind."

"Fuck off," I growl.

His chirps are just noise. I refuse to make room in my already crowded brain for that bit of static. I skate my lines and keep my eyes on the ice instead of giving him the satisfaction of a response. I count the turns from the half wall to the blue line. Ten in rhythm. My lungs feel clean. The ice feels good under my blades.

For just a second, I think tonight might actually go our way.

Then the puck drops and hope dies fast.

Our first touch dies on a Flames stick. They cycle clean through our zone like we're standing still. Hunter tries to jam the puck loose with a hit that makes the glass pop and shake. The puck squirts to the weak side. Our winger's late by a full step. I take the passing lane, stick in it, body square, shoulder burning in protest. Our team clears it.

The play's ugly but effective. Now, the chirping starts in earnest.

The Flames bench becomes a chorus of cheap praise and cheaper shots. I let it run off me like water. I remember the number in my head.

Zero retaliations. That's the goal. That's what Coach asked for.

Jett's in the goal and I do my best to stick to him like glue. Five minutes into the first period, their center runs a lazy screen in front of Jett and clips my skate with his stick. He makes it look like an accident. He turns with wide eyes and an innocent shrug when I glare at him. I see red for one heartbeat before I swallow it down. Then I shove him once to clear the crease.

Legal. Clean. Within the rules. He winks at me like we're sharing a joke. I have the urge to bash his face in.

Next shift, he clips me again. Blade to my ankle bone. Pain shoots up my leg, sharp and bright. Without thinking, I snap my stick down on top of his with a crack that's louder than I meant it to be.

Whistle.

Slashing. God damn it.

My feet are already moving toward the penalty box before the call fully sinks in. I sit. I stare at the clock and count to one hundred in sets of four. The Flames score and the crowd groans around me. My jaw goes tight enough to make my teeth ache.

Coach Cross doesn't look at me when I come back to the bench. He looks past me. That's worse than yelling. It's *so* much worse.

I tell myself it's fine. I build a wall inside my chest and

lean on it. Next shift I keep everything simple. Glass and out. Body first. No extra shove. No retaliation.

They want discipline? I can be disciplined. I've done it my entire life.

The Flames make it hard, though.

They finish every hit with an extra push. They whisper in my ear during scrums like they're reading lines off a script written specifically to fit every sore spot I have.

"You're just a machine, Huxley."

"Too slow, Ice Man."

"He's too fucking dumb to keep his line."

One late puck after the whistle slides near my skate. I sweep it back to the ref with more force than necessary. He points at me. Warning. I nod and skate away, focusing on the only things I can control.

We get a scoring chance in the slot and whiff it completely. The puck bounces over our forward's stick. Momentum goes, thin as paper. On the next rush, I flatten their winger at the blue line just as the puck leaves his stick.

The hit's perfect. Textbook. The crowd roars its approval.

Legal. Beautiful. I feel steady for one breath.

Then the Flames grinder skates behind me late and barks, "There he is. The Ice Man finally showed up."

I turn with my stick too wide. My hip clips him. Not hard. I *barely* make contact.

Whistle.

Interference. Two more minutes. God *DAMN* it.

My mind blanks for half a second. I shouldn't have given the ref the angle to make that call. I sit in the box again and watch the Flames score again. Two goals on my penalties in one period. Fuck. I stare at the ice through the scratched plexiglass and taste metal.

Between shifts, Jett tries to spark energy in the room.

Beck bangs the boards and yells about the next shift being ours. Hunter paces and mutters threats under his breath. Decker stands near the bench talking to the rookies, trying to keep their heads in it. Coach Cross is ice at the whiteboard, drawing plays with sharp, angry strokes.

The third period's a long, slow tilt toward the wrong end of the scoreboard. We chase. The Flames keep the puck between the dots and get under our team's skin with their constant chirping. Hunter tries to drag us back with a fight that the ref kills before it begins.

The clock bleeds away. Fuck, fuck, double triple fuck. We push hard and get nothing for it.

The final horn sounds like a door slamming shut.

The locker room after is a meat locker. No one speaks. Gear drops into piles on the floor. Showers hiss in the background.

Coach Cross stands in the doorway and looks at each of us like he's counting heads after a fire. He doesn't say a word. He doesn't have to.

We all heard him before the game. And then we all ignored him in a dozen small ways. Fuck, that loss smarts.

I strip out of my gear fast and get out before the media can swarm. The tunnel's cooler and quieter, just the echo of my footsteps against concrete.

Scout's at an equipment cart outside the exit. Headset around her neck, media packets in her hands. Her curly hair is in that same braid that's always coming loose. She's wearing black leggings that make her ass look amazing. I force my eyes up before I get caught staring.

I already know I'm too volatile to stop.

She looks down, her eyes on the floor until she senses me coming. Only then does she glance up.

Her eyes, normally a peaceful green, widen when she sees

me. Fuck, I love the way her eyes take in my chest, my arms, my height.

"You can't take that bait," she says quietly. She's not quite looking at me, like she's talking more to herself than to me. "They set the trap every time and you keep walking into it."

The words slide under my skin sideways. It sounds so simple when she says it. It's as though I chose to feed the machine that's eating our season alive. Like I wanted to cost us the game.

The heat in my chest flashes bright and angry. I grab at the only defense I have left. "Stay in your lane, Scout."

The words come out sharper than I mean them to. Colder. I watch her flinch like I just slapped her. Her eyes go wide for a second before she blinks hard and looks away.

"Right," she says. Her voice is flat, careful. "Sorry."

She gathers her packets and walks past me without another word.

"Shit. Sorry. Scout…" I don't make any move to follow, though. She's not my girl. If she were, I would let her down, again and again.

Besides, hockey comes first. It has to. It's the only real thing that I have.

When I get there, the press corral outside the locker room is a feeding frenzy. Microphones push toward me like a tide trying to drown me.

"Are you too slow for this league now, Silas?"

"Two penalties that changed the game. Do you regret them?"

"Is the Havoc locker room lost?"

My answers come out terse. "No. We play as a unit. I take responsibility for my minutes on the ice. We'll fix it for next game."

And on and on. Juliet does her best to deflect questions

where she can, but I deserve hard questions after that shit show I just put on out there. That was trash.

The thing is, I'm only twenty-six. The youngest Huxley brother. I should have at least four more years on the ice, maybe more. But Jett and Hunter don't have my shoulder injury. Or my groin injury. Or my knee injury that keeps coming back, season after season, slightly more painful every year.

That's why focus matters. I can't waste time on distractions. I spend every available calorie either playing my heart out, practicing to play hard, or resting. No time for anything in between, no matter how pretty or sunny my latest distraction might be.

In the parking lot, the wind cuts through my suit like the fabric doesn't exist. I sit in my car and don't turn the key right away. Instead, I just stare at my hands on the steering wheel. My knuckles are scuffed from the game. The finger tape imprint's still visible on my skin. My right shoulder burns and pulses under my jacket like it wants to remind me of every wrong angle I chose tonight.

I run the game back in my head, shift by shift. The slash. The interference. The crease clear that started everything. The hit that felt clean and perfect. All the small, jagged moments that turned the whole thing sideways.

None of it gives me what I want. A reason that doesn't sound like ego and control and fear.

Scout's voice won't leave my head. *You can't take that bait.*

I think about the Flames bench and their chirping that felt scripted specifically for me. Machine. Too slow. One step from the injured list.

I think about how good it felt for one heartbeat to cut that winger in half with a legal hit. Then I think about how fast everything went sideways when I played like a hammer that only knows how to find nails.

It's pouring rain as I drive home without music. The silence feels appropriate, like a punishment I deserve.

At my apartment, I take a shower hot enough to turn the bathroom into a steam room. I still feel cold when I step out. Icing my shoulder, I open my laptop to watch the game film. I scrub through clips until the screen becomes a smear of gray and red jerseys.

Rubbing my hand across my mouth, I let out a frustrated groan. Nothing makes sense. Every decision I made looks worse in replay.

My phone lights up on the arm of the chair. A message preview glows from the dating app I shouldn't have opened in the first place.

YOGA4LYFE

Rough day?

One line. Simple. But it slides through my chest like a hand that knows exactly where every bruise is.

I should ignore it, put the phone down, and go to bed. If I had any sense, I would try to sleep off this disaster of a game.

But of course I don't.

I type out an answer that's darker than I mean it to be, then delete it. I try again with something cleaner.

STATMAN12

You could say that. Work didn't go well.

YOGA4LYFE

Want to talk about it?

STATMAN12

Not really. I just want to forget it happened.

YOGA4LYFE

I get that. Sometimes the best thing to do is let the day end and try again tomorrow.

Her words are simple but they settle something in my chest. I lean back in the chair, phone in my hands, ice pack slowly warming against my shoulder.

STATMAN12

How was your day?

YOGA4LYFE

Mixed. I did something I'm proud of. Then someone reminded me why I don't put myself out there very often.

STATMAN12

What happened?

YOGA4LYFE

I tried to help someone that's a little cranky. And then I got told to stay in my lane. It sucked.

The words hit me like a punch to the gut. My hands go still on the phone. That's what I said to Scout. Those exact words. *Stay in your lane.*

STATMAN12

That's harsh. Were you actually overstepping?

YOGA4LYFE

I don't think so? I just pointed out something obvious that they couldn't see. But maybe I should have kept my mouth shut.

STATMAN12

No. If you saw something, you should say it.

YOGA4LYFE

Even if the other person doesn't want to hear it?

I stare at the question. I picture Scout's face when I snapped at her and the disappointment she clearly felt. Man, I feel like a fucking asshole. It takes me half a minute to come up with a reply that doesn't worsen that feeling.

STATMAN12

Even if they don't want to hear it, you should tell them. Especially then. Sometimes we can't see our own blind spots.

YOGA4LYFE

That's generous of you. The person I tried to help didn't think so.

STATMAN12

Maybe they will eventually. Sometimes it takes time to see things clearly. Maybe they had a bad day.

YOGA4LYFE

Maybe. They always seem to have bad days.

Ouch. It hits like a blow to the throat.

STATMAN12

Are you talking about me now?

YOGA4LYFE

Hah. Are you someone who makes things harder for yourself?

STATMAN12

Apparently, yes.

Yoga4Lyfe

Then I guess I am 😉

The winky face makes me smile despite everything. The loss, the penalties, and the fact that I hurt Scout's feelings for no good reason.

We talk until my eyes start to blur with exhaustion. She tells me about working on a project that might change things for her professionally. I try to tell her about the pressure of work. Keeping it light, knowing I can't get too specific without outing myself as a hockey player. Instead, I talk more generally about performing when everyone's watching, waiting for you to fail.

She doesn't try to fix me. I appreciate that she doesn't offer empty comfort or tell me everything will be fine. She just listens through the screen.

Yoga4Lyfe: You should get some sleep. Tomorrow's a new day.

STATMAN12

Until it's the same day again.

YOGA4LYFE

Wow. That's bleak.

STATMAN12

Sorry. I told you work didn't go well.

YOGA4LYFE

It's okay to have bad days. Just don't let them define you.

STATMAN12

Easier said than done.

YOGA4LYFE

Most good things are.

I stare at those words for a long time. Most good things are hard.

STATMAN12

Goodnight, Yoga Girl.

YOGA4LYFE

Goodnight, StatMan. Be kind to yourself tomorrow.

I close the app and set my phone down. The ice pack has gone warm against my shoulder.

I should have kept my mouth shut with Scout instead of snapping at her for trying to help. She was right. I took the bait. Again.

Tomorrow I'll do better.

Chapter Five

Scout

I wake up to my alarm at 5:30 AM and immediately regret being born. Why did I stay up until 3 AM sexting a stranger? Oh right. Because he might be hot and I have terrible impulse control.

My eyes feel like someone rubbed them with sandpaper. I need coffee before I can form complete thoughts.

I stumble to the kitchen and start the pot brewing. While it gurgles, I check my phone. Three texts from Jessa asking if I'm alive. One email from Juliet.

My stomach flips.

Scout, just wanted to remind you about the proposal. It could be a really exciting addition to the team. Let me know if you need any resources or access to medical files. - J

Two weeks. I have two weeks to prove I'm more than a mobile coffee cart. Two weeks to convince coaches who barely register my existence that I actually have a brain.

No pressure.

The coffee finishes and I pour a cup, dumping in enough oat milk to make it barely qualify as coffee anymore. My hands shake a little. Lack of sleep, obviously. Not terror. Definitely not terror.

I take my coffee to my bedroom and open the proposal document. In the harsh light of morning, it reads like a fever dream written by someone with imposter syndrome and a thesaurus problem.

This needs a complete rewrite. I need to sound confident and professional. Someone who deserves to be in that room.

Fake it till you make it, right?

A knock on my door makes me jump. Jessa pokes her head in, concerned.

"Are you okay? You look like death."

I smile. "Thanks. That's exactly the look I was going for."

"Seriously, did you sleep at all?"

"Define sleep." I gesture vaguely at my laptop. "I was up late... working."

Working is code for *sexting a man I've never met while questioning all my life choices*, but Jessa doesn't need those details.

Her eyes flick to my screen. "Is that for the Havoc?"

"Maybe." My cheeks heat. "Juliet found out about my kinesiology degree. She asked for a mobility program proposal."

"Scout! That's amazing!"

I downplay it. "It's just a proposal. They might hate it."

"Or they might love it and you'll finally get to use that expensive degree." She grins. "Either way, don't work yourself to death before lunch."

"Right back at ya!"

I shower fast and throw on my uniform. Black yoga pants. Gray team polo. Hair in a braid that's already staging an escape attempt. Minimal makeup because I'm too tired to care about looking human.

I grab my bag, my travel mug of coffee, and head out.

The drive to the arena's quiet this early. The sun hasn't fully risen yet and the streets are mostly empty. I count red lights out of habit. Five between my apartment and work. The same as always. The predictability's comforting.

When I arrive, the parking lot's nearly deserted. Just a few cars belonging to early staff and maybe one or two players who couldn't sleep. I recognize Silas's car in his usual spot, perfectly centered between the lines. Of course he's here.

He's got this stubborn streak that pairs well with his self-denial. His strict routine, his devotion to being first at the rink every single day, his near-obsessive relationship with preparation. These things make up the core of who he is. I've watched him arrive before dawn for months now, always the same time, always the same parking spot.

Most people would call it discipline. I think it's closer to fear of what happens if he stops controlling everything.

But I don't want to think about Silas right now. Then I'd have to remember the way he looked at me last night after the game. Cold and dismissive. *Stay in your lane.* Like I'm a child who needs to be reminded of her place. *Ugh.*

I push through the staff entrance and head to my tiny office. It's more of a closet with a desk, but it has a door that closes. And right now, that's all I need. I drop my bag and pull out my laptop, opening the proposal document with a sick feeling in my stomach.

The introduction's weak. The methodology section's incomplete. The budget projections are based on guesswork because I don't actually know what anything costs. I have no idea how to make this sound professional when I feel like a fraud.

My phone buzzes. A message from the dating app.

STATMAN12

Good morning. Did you sleep at all?

I stare at his message, taking my time before answering.

YOGA4LYFE

A little. You?

STATMAN12

Not much. My stupid brain won't shut off.

YOGA4LYFE

What's it saying?

STATMAN12

I'm not good enough, I'm failing.
Everybody's laughing at me. The usual.

My chest tightens. I know that voice. It's the same one that's been screaming in my own head since I woke up.

YOGA4LYFE

Those thoughts are liars.

STATMAN12

Knowing it and believing it are different
things.

YOGA4LYFE

Yeah. They really are.

I want to say more, to tell him I'm sitting here staring at a half-finished proposal and wondering if I should just give up now before I embarrass myself. That feels like too much vulnerability for someone I've never met.

STATMAN12

What are you working on today?

I hesitate. My fingers hover over the keyboard.

YOGA4LYFE

A project that might change things for me professionally. Or it might blow up in my face. Hard to tell which yet.

STATMAN12

Tell me about it.

So I give him the basics. Not the whole story, just the outline.

STATMAN12

Sounds important.

YOGA4LYFE

It is. That's what makes it terrifying.

STATMAN12

What's the worst that could happen?

I stare at the question. The worst that could happen? They say no. Coach Cross tells me to stick to coffee runs and copies. I prove to everyone, including myself, that I don't actually have anything valuable to offer.

Worse, I stay invisible forever.

YOGA4LYFE

They say no. Then I'm back to square one, except now I know for sure that I'm not good enough.

STATMAN12

Or they say yes. And you get to do
something that matters.

YOGA4LYFE

That's a nice thought. Not sure I believe it.

STATMAN12

I get that. For what it's worth, I think you
can do it.

YOGA4LYFE

You don't even know me.

STATMAN12

I have strong intuition. You're good people,
Yoga Girl.

His words settle warm in my chest, but they don't quiet the panic. I thank him and close the app. I need to work. I need to make this proposal something I'm not ashamed to present.

Sighing, I force myself to focus. StatMan might be nice, but he doesn't pay my bills. I'm deep in a section about injury prevention when my door opens without warning. I jump and nearly spill coffee all over my keyboard.

Juliet stands in the doorway, perfectly put together as always. "Morning. Didn't expect to see you here this early."

"I'm always here early." I close my laptop quickly, paranoid she can somehow see how bad the proposal still is. "What can I help you with?"

"Walk with me." Again, she's already moving. I have to scramble to follow, even though she's a tiny woman and wears four inch heels. She struts like she owns the building, like everywhere she goes is a catwalk. I envy her confidence.

We head through the empty hallways toward the training facility. The lights are still half off and our footsteps echo.

"So, regarding Mobility Mondays. I forwarded you some injury reports from last season. Soft tissue issues, missed games, recurring problems. Use them for your proposal."

"Thank you. That's really helpful."

"Also, Coach Cross agreed to meet with you. Next Tuesday at ten a.m. Preliminary conversation about your program."

My heart stops. "Next week?"

"Too soon?"

"No. No, I can do it." My voice sounds strangled.

Juliet stops walking and turns to face me. Her dark eyes are sharp and assessing. "Scout, I'm giving you this opportunity because I think you have something valuable to offer. You need to act like it."

"I know. I will. I just..."

Her expression softens. "You just what?"

I swallow hard. "What if I'm not ready? What if I mess this up?"

"Then you'll learn from it and do better next time." She tilts her head, her eyes kind. "For what it's worth, I don't think you're going to mess it up. I am worried about you walking in there apologizing for breathing. You have to believe in yourself. You need to tell them how you're going to revolutionize their hockey program and save them money. At the moment, you seem... unsure of yourself."

The words sting because they're true.

"I don't mean to do that," I say.

"I know you don't." Her voice softens slightly. "You have a degree from a good school. Right?"

"Right." I nod nervously. "Not the certifications, though. Or any relevant experience whatsoever."

She squeezes my hand. "You have knowledge these players need. Stop acting like you're lucky anybody lets you in the building. Start believing you belong here. You're a badass bitch, Scout."

I bark a laugh. "That's easier said than done."

"Most worthwhile things are." She checks her tablet. "I have to meet with Ivy. Keep me posted on your progress. And remember that you're better than you think you are."

She walks away, leaving me standing in the dim hallway with my heart pounding and my stomach churning.

I head back to my office and stare at the proposal. Tuesday. I have less than a week to make this perfect. I'll have to sound confident when I feel like I'm drowning. I'm convincing coaches who barely remember my name that I'm worth listening to.

By the time other staff start arriving, I've rewritten the introduction four times and I hate all of my attempts. My coffee's cold. My back hurts from hunching over the keyboard. My eyes burn.

My phone buzzes. Jessa asking if I want lunch.

JESSA

Want lunch?

ME

Can't. Too much work.

JESSA

You have to eat, Scout.

ME

I'll grab something later.

I don't grab something later. I work through lunch, through the afternoon, through the early evening when most people go home. And I'm still there when the parking lot empties and the building goes quiet around me.

My phone buzzes again. The dating app.

STATMAN12

How's it going?

YOGA4LYFE

Not great. Everything I write sounds terrible.

STATMAN12

I'm sure it's not as bad as you think.

YOGA4LYFE

Maybe.

STATMAN12

Take a break.

I stare at his message. He's probably right. I've been staring at the same paragraph for twenty minutes and it feels like the words are written in Greek. Stopping feels like giving up.

YOGA4LYFE

What do you do? When you're stuck like this?

STATMAN12

Honestly? I keep pushing until I break. It's not healthy but it's all I know how to do.

YOGA4LYFE

That's terrible advice.

STATMAN12

I know. That's why I'm telling you to do something different. Take a break. Watch a movie. Cook some dinner. However you disassociate the best.

YOGA4LYFE

You first.

STATMAN12

Fair point. I'm not really any better.

Eventually he tells me he has to go. He has an early morning tomorrow. I reluctantly close the app and look at my proposal one more time. It's still not good enough. It might never be good enough.

I'm too exhausted to keep working.

I save the document and pack up my things. The building's dark and quiet when I leave. My car's one of three left in the lot.

Jessa's asleep by the time I get home. That's fine by me because I don't need her seeing me spiral. Food seems challenging at this late hour, so I eat handfuls of sugary cereal straight out of the box. It's not the best food for me and contributes no protein or fiber to my diet. But it's satisfying in a soul-deep way.

I should work more on the proposal. Or maybe I can practice what I'm going to say. Whatever I do, it should be something productive.

Instead I curl up on the couch and open the dating app again. My brain isn't working, so I barely know what I'm typing. He already said he was going to bed, so I'm just talking to no one.

YOGA4LYFE

I made it home. I'm still freaking out but at least I'm freaking out somewhere comfortable.

I use the camera to send a selfie of myself on the couch. The lighting is terrible, but that's okay. I don't want him to see the bags under my eyes or judge my wild hair. It just feels right to send a quick snap.

Hell, maybe he'll start getting comfortable and send something back.

A minute goes by. I put the phone down because even my sometime-sexting buddy deserves a little downtime. I sigh. *Should I just go to bed?*

When my phone lights up, I pounce on it. It's a message from him. My chest fills with warmth.

STATMAN12

That's progress. Sort of.

YOGA4LYFE

Thank you for talking me off the ledge tonight.

STATMAN12

Anytime. We disasters have to stick together.

YOGA4LYFE

Goodnight, StatMan.

STATMAN12

Goodnight, Yoga Girl. Talk to you tomorrow.

Chapter Six

Silas

Superstition is a funny thing. I don't believe in demons. I've never been religious. But I believe that somehow my fate will change if I don't practice certain rituals before every game. I'm cold and logical to a fault, but I have to follow these stupid rules I've made for myself because…

What if they are the difference between me killing it on the ice and a shutout loss?

I lace my left skate, then the right, then redo the left because the knot sits wrong. God forbid that I tie my laces wrong or tape my stick differently. I'm too superstitious for my own good.

Sitting in the locker room, I try to soothe myself. Game day rituals matter. The order is a big deal. The process needs to be done in a certain way. If I do everything right, in the right order, we win. That's not superstition; that's fact proven over hundreds of games.

Though I try to tune it out, noise builds around me in layers. Beck raps his stick on the floor in a steady beat, his own pre-game rhythm that drives me crazy. But I'd never tell him to stop. What if he needs it to play his best?

Jett flips a puck into the palm of his glove, over and over. Hunter paces with his headphones on, shoulders loose, eyes already focused. He's listening to something aggressive, probably death metal, getting his head where it needs to be.

My left shoulder aches under the compressive sleeve. It always aches before we play the North Carolina Hurricanes. They're dirty players, every last one of them. They run traffic through the crease like it belongs to them. They crowd the goalie and count on the refs to swallow the whistle because they play every game like it's playoff-style hockey.

I stretch my shoulder joint until it pops. The pop doesn't bring any relief, though. My shoulder throbs, but I've played through worse.

Coach Cross steps into the middle of the room, using two fingers to whistle. The locker room falls silent. His voice stays flat, controlled, the way it gets when he's expecting a war.

"Here's what I want to see. Start on time. Pucks deep. Own the net front." He pauses, eyes scanning the room. "They'll try to bully the crease. We don't get pushed around in our barn."

His gaze finds me, holds a second longer than everyone else. He knows my shoulder's bothering me. He also knows I'll play through it. That's what I do.

Coach Ryan follows him, tapping the doorframe twice. "Let's go to work."

I stand, grab my helmet, and bump knuckles with Jett. He shoves my shoulder like a brother, not a goalie. His shove is harder than usual, making sure I know he's counting on me.

"Keep my porch clear," he says.

"Keep your rebounds playable."

He grins. "Done and done."

We hit the tunnel and the air thins out. The crowd on the other side sounds like a thunderhead about to break. We step into the light and the whole building jumps to its feet. Seventeen thousand people screaming for blood. Our blood or theirs. It doesn't matter as long as someone bleeds.

Warmups are muscle memory. Edge checks along the boards, hip turns to loosen up. Short passes at the blue line to get our hands warm. The ache in my shoulder throbs with the vibration of every pass. I ignore it, push through.

We skate out for the announcer introductions followed by the national anthem. Then the puck drops and the Seattle Havoc *fly*. The crowd roars so loud it feels like the air shakes. I take a hit along the boards, absorb it, and reset. We hold off their first surge, then the next. Hunter forces a turnover, Reed fires low, and their goalie kicks it wide.

The rebound rolls to the corner, and I race back to kill a two-on-one. I drop to one knee, knock the pass aside, and Jett covers the loose puck. Whistle.

I stay focused on my job. Block shots. Clear bodies. Protect Jett.

There's someone new on the opposing team. #18, Evan Malinsky. He's replacing their usual right winger, a guy who's been on and off the injured list for two years. Malinsky is young, spry, and aggressive. He makes it clear from the jump that he's ready to toss gloves and brawl.

Hunter whistles at me, using two fingers to gesture to Malinsky. We've had all of our lives to develop a wordless code, so I know that I should watch Malinsky so that the rest of the team can operate more efficiently. Fuck yes, I can help with that. I love a mission.

I make my entire job to check, block, and frustrate #18. And it works. Every shift I'm on the ice, I follow him around, acting like I was put on this earth to be in his fucking way. Malinsky tells me to fuck off more times than I can count, his face getting redder and redder every time I check him into the boards.

He doesn't even handle the puck much because I ride him so hard. None of his teammates will pass to him. By the second period, Malinsky's hits grow heavier. I'm playing this one-man game of keepaway.

My shoulder throbs after he slams me into the boards, but I push through it. Pain is part of the job. I call out coverage when I can, keeping my stick low, closing lanes.

Then everything slows down. A deflected shot lands in the slot, and Jett sprawls to smother it. The puck slips free and rolls toward the post. Malinsky cuts across the crease at full speed, stick down, eyes locked on the rebound. Jett's still prone, glove out of position. He's wide open. I don't think, I just lunge.

I push off hard, crossing the paint and getting between Malinsky and Jett. Malinsky can't stop and doesn't bother to try to blunt his trajectory. He barrels right into me and his impact hits me like a runaway train. My right shoulder is pulled down into my chest. My helmet toward my collarbone. And then, without warning, there's the screaming red goalpost.

Something cracks as I hit the metal. Pain floods down my right arm, white-hot and blinding. My fingers go numb. I stay upright long enough to shove Malinsky off Jett, using the last of my energy, then I drop to the ice.

The whistle screams. The crowd roars. Hunter slams Malinsky into the boards before the refs can get there. Beck grabs another player by the collar. The officials pull everyone apart.

Fuck, I'm in pain. I try to get up, only to have Jett's hand and in the center of my chest.

"Stay *down*," he growls.

I roll my eyes back to see him hovering above me, his eyes flashing. He's fucking *pissed*. The Havoc trainers hit the ice. I wince. There's something wrong with my right arm. I close my eyes and someone presses a gloveless hand to my chest. Someone else steadies my arm, moving it very slightly. I can't help the yelp that escapes me. The world narrows to lights and noise. I hear my name, a voice saying not to move. I can't breathe past the fire under my ribs.

Fuck, I'm in pain.

They strap me down, keep my shoulder still, and wheel me through the tunnel. The crowd noise fades behind me. As soon as we're in the tunnel, the medics give me something that spreads through my veins like a slow-burning fire and steals my consciousness.

When I stir, I feel the pain first, flickering to life before I even open my eyes. *Fuck*, it hurts.

White. Ceiling tiles. Curtains. A sheet rough against my legs. I blink until shapes form. My left arm's trapped in a sling, heavy and useless. The air smells like disinfectant.

Scout sits closest to the bed, her blonde hair thrown up in a wild bun, her head propped on her hand. Why is she here? Maybe to keep Juliet company.

Hunter leans against the window, his wife Juliet in a seat beside him, their fingers entwined. Jett sits on the couch, ice on his ribs, eyes red. Coach Cross fills the doorway. Coach Ryan stands behind him, his lips pursed, his phone pressed against his ear.

"Okay," I say, or try to. My throat burns and I clear it. "Okay."

Scout startles, showing she had been falling asleep. Relief breaks across her face as she pushes her chair closer until her knees touch the bed. "You're awake."

She leans toward me in my bed, very nearly grabbing my hand. I feel like I'm on acid. Everything has a surreal quality to it. This woman that usually doesn't give me the time of day is looking at me like I just broke her heart.

Huh. I must be on the good drugs.

"Yeah." My voice sounds rough. "What's the damage?"

Ryan answers. "Fracture on the distal clavicle. Torn labrum. You'll need surgery. Rehab'll take months, not weeks."

I take that in and nod once. "Jett?"

"I'm fine," Jett says. He pulls the ice pack away. "Took a knee to the ribs, that's all. You saved me." His voice cracks and he looks away.

Cross steps forward. "You're on the disabled list, effective immediately. We'll fill your spot. You focus on surgery and rehab." He looks straight at me. "You had a choice. You chose to break yourself."

"He was unprotected."

"You could've waited a second and buried him clean." His jaw tightens. "Now I have to replace you. Somehow… I don't know how to do it."

Ryan steps in. "That's enough for tonight." He turns to me. "We'll talk about the next steps after imaging. Rest."

Cross leaves without another word. The room exhales. I try to sit up and immediately regret it. Pain slams through my chest. The world tilts. I grab for the rail and miss.

The pain spreads fast, bright and merciless. I squeeze my eyes shut until it fades. Sweat beads along my hairline. I feel exposed and stupid in a paper gown.

Scout catches me. "Stop. Don't move." She presses me back against the bed, voice trembling. "Stay down, please."

Why is she here again? Touching me, smelling like eucalyptus, tempting me. My head throbs and my shoulder is a bright white point of pain.

"Did, uh…" I scrabble to pull my thoughts together. "Did we win?"

"Yeah we won, asshole," Hunter grunts. "Can you believe this kid?"

"Be nice," Juliet chides. "He's your baby brother."

"We know," Jett says with a sigh. "Our very stupid baby brother."

I ignore them, glancing at Scout. "You didn't have to come."

"Are you kidding?" Scout asks softly. "You scared us."

She fusses with the blanket, smoothing it flat, tucking the corner by my hip. I feel disconnected from my body. Her hands hover above my skin like she wants to fix what she can't.

Juliet and Hunter look at each other but stay quiet. Jett stares at the floor. I push weakly at Scout's wrist. "I need sleep." My voice is low and final.

"Oh." She nods and takes a step back. "Okay. Whatever you want, Silas."

"Whatever… I want…" I echo her words. They bounce around inside my skull. "I wish you would say that to me… some… other time."

Scout's cheeks turn pink. "What?"

"He's high," Hunter mutters. "I'll get the nurse, Silas."

Eventually a nurse swans in with an IV bag, checks the line, and adjusts the drip. "This'll help with the pain," she says. She leaves and the room goes quiet again.

The pain meds hit hard. The room softens at the edges. The ache dulls to a low hum. Scout says something I can't make out. I stop trying to listen. The dark comes fast and I let it take me.

Chapter Seven

Scout

Tuesday morning, I move through the corridor with my tote bag, clipboard tucked against my ribs, headset cord brushing my cheek. I've already solved two fires before coffee. I located a missing mouthguard for one of the rookies. I swapped out an allergy-friendly snack box for another because Shane doesn't like hummus.

After the saga with Silas, reality came back with a vengeance. For one heart-shattering moment, I thought he might not be okay. But he made it through surgery fine. When Juliet left his hospital room, I went with her. It's not like I had any compelling reason to be there. Other than a shared past, one that we definitely don't talk about.

So I went back to work on Mobility Mondays. The world moved on and I have to keep pace with it. By this point, I've drafted so many versions of my proposal I can recite it word for word from memory. It's still imperfect, but it's as good as I'm going to get.

I'm about to enter the coaches' conference room when I spot Silas and Hunter ahead of me in the hallway. Silas's right arm sits in a sling, and he moves with the careful precision of someone trying not to show pain. His jaw's tight, shoulders rigid beneath his dress shirt.

Hunter mutters something and Silas snaps at him. "I said I've got it."

"Asshole," Hunter says. "You had surgery nine days ago. Let me help you."

Silas spots me and his expression hardens. The look he shoots me could slice a lesser woman in two. But I've known this stubborn jerk for years. He's always hostile. You just have to work around it if you want to deal with Silas.

People call him Ice Man, but I've seen glimpses of something else underneath. The way he watches players when they're struggling, mentally noting their weak spots so he can adjust his game to cover for them. How he arrives at the arena before dawn and leaves after everyone else, like hockey's the only thing keeping him upright. He's not cold. He's scared of being anything else.

"Hey!" I say, rushing toward him. "You're already up and around after surgery?"

His expression's flat and standoffish. "Clearly."

"Hey," Hunter says in greeting. "Don't mind him. Were you headed to the coach's office?"

"Yeah. We're supposed to have a meeting at ten."

Silas arches an icy brow. "You must have the wrong time. Cross told *me* to be here at ten."

"Oh!" My cheeks warm. "Yeah, maybe I got the time wrong."

"Dude. Shut *up*," Hunter says, looking at Silas. He sighs. "He's going without pain meds, so he's extra grumpy today."

Silas grunts. "Am not."

I nod. "Right. Well, should we go in? We can figure out who's supposed to be where."

"Great." Hunter checks his watch. "I have to get downstairs. I have a check in with my trainer before the optional skate."

"Good. Stop buzzing around me." Silas waves his hand dismissively.

Hunter loses his temper. "Sure. I normally leave family members who've just had surgery in the fucking hallway like they're garbage."

"I can help!" I jump in. "Since we're both going to the same place."

"Are you sure?" Hunter asks. "He's extra feisty today."

"It would be my pleasure." I smile at Hunter, hoping he can feel my sincerity.

"When my arm's healed, I'm going to kill both of you," Silas says.

"Yeah, yeah." Hunter heads off down the hallway, calling over his shoulder. "Don't threaten anybody else, bro. Text me if you need me, Scout!"

"Traitor," Silas whispers under his breath.

I turn to sweep my gaze over Silas and frown. His chin-length dirty blond locks are unstyled and rumpled, falling across his forehead in a way that would be endearing if he weren't glaring at me. His button-up's misbuttoned and wrinkled, hanging awkwardly over the sling. He's a big guy—six foot eight of muscle and barely controlled irritation—and a very handsome one at that, but hostility rolls off him in waves. Those blue-gray eyes are harder than usual, probably from pain and lack of sleep.

"Let me get the door," I say, reaching past him for the handle.

He jerks away from me like I've burned him. "I don't need help."

The words are sharp enough to cut. His eyes are flat and cold, daring me to argue.

"I wasn't—" I start, but he's already shouldering the door open with his good side, teeth clenched against what must be significant pain.

I follow him in, heat climbing my neck. The room's already tense when we enter.

Coach Cross sits at the head of the conference table. Beck Tate claims the seat to his right, arms crossed, expression unreadable. An analytics kid I don't know hunches over a tablet, tapping through data. Juliet sits at the far end with her legal pad and one foot tucked under her chair. Ivy exudes stress, tapping her pen against the table.

Assistant coaches Ryan and Pat scribble notes. No one seems happy.

Silas drops into a chair near the door, trying to look casual despite the awkward angle of his sling. I can't stop watching him from the corner of my eye. The way he shifts carefully, the micro-expressions of pain he's trying to hide. He's not fooling anybody.

"Good. You're both here." Cross looks between us. "How do you feel, Silas?"

Silas clears his throat. "Uh, fine."

"No, you're not fine." Juliet looks up. "You're staying with us. Somebody has to take care of you."

Silas sits up straighter. "No. I'm going back to my condo after I leave here."

"Like hell you are," Juliet says. "I heard you cursing while you were trying to get dressed this morning. Our walls are very thin."

Silas drums his fingers on the conference table. "Another reason I should leave."

"Everyone, shut up." Cross doesn't exactly shout, but his

voice rings with authority. "Let's start with Scout's program proposal. Then we'll circle back to Silas."

Juliet smiles and nods at me. My stomach does cartwheels.

"Scout here has a degree in sports medicine. And she's a certified yoga teacher. I've watched her take care of players with aches and pains before. I think we're crazy not to use her as a resource. Scout, do you want to explain the proposal?"

Beck narrows his eyes, drumming his fingers on the conference table. The room shifts. Their attention lands on me like a spotlight I didn't ask for. Heat prickles the back of my neck. My hands want to shake, but I force them to be still.

I start, voice steadier than I feel. "Right. I want to start Mobility Mondays. The scope would be twenty minutes post-practice, once a week. We'd focus on hips, thoracic spines, and shoulder capsules. I'd take notes to track key performance indicators. Things like subjective soreness ratings, missed practice minutes, measurable improvements in hip internal and external rotation, and shoulder range of motion from baseline to goal. Plus I'd ask a two-question mood check to track the players' mental state."

"I see. How does yoga figure into your plan?" Coach Cross asks.

I nod, getting into the swing of it now. Talking about one of my passions helps steady my nerves. "I see yoga as a corrective tool. You obviously can't fix an athlete's pain by having them do one position once. I'd assess what a player needs, teach them poses that help strengthen muscles, and track their pain. In addition, I'd assign homework. Hockey players already stretch at home. The more often they incorporate my suggestions into their home routines, the better the outcomes will be."

Assistant coach Pat snorts. "We're not a yoga studio. We need hits, not hamstring stretches."

The dismissal stings but I don't let it show. "You need both. Looser hips mean faster first steps off the line. Better thoracic spine rotation means cleaner exits under pressure. And fewer penalties born from fatigue and compensating movement patterns."

"My suggestion is that we have a trial for eight weeks," Juliet says decisively. "If the numbers don't move, we can reconvene."

Cross nods once. "Done. Mobility Mondays it is."

Relief floods through me for half a second before Cross's expression darkens.

"Now, the other issue." His eyes land on Silas. "We need to discuss your shoulder."

Silas stiffens in his chair. "It's fine."

"The MRI results say otherwise," Beck cuts in. "Grade two separation. Partial rotator cuff tear. You're looking at a minimum of eight weeks. And that's if you don't make it worse."

"I said it's fine." Silas glares at Beck.

"You can barely lift your arm," Ryan observes. "You need round-the-clock care for at least a few weeks. Basic tasks are going to be impossible. And your current situation, staying with Hunter and Juliet, isn't going to cut it."

"The sports medicine wing of the hospital has an excellent rehab facility," Cross says. "That would be the best decision. You'd have professional medical supervision."

The temperature in the room drops. Silas's face goes from stoic to thunderous in a heartbeat.

"Absolutely not." His voice is granite. "I'm not moving into a facility. That's a terrible suggestion."

"It's not really a suggestion. You don't have a choice," Ivy says gently. "You can't even button your own shirt right now."

I watch him, this prideful man trying so hard not to show weakness. His jaw works like he's grinding glass between his teeth. The sling holds his arm at an awkward angle. I can see the strain in his neck from compensating.

I could fix that. Or at the very least, manage his symptoms.

Coach Cross speaks up. "What if we had someone move into your home to help you, Silas?"

Silas's eyes narrow to slits. "What do you mean?"

"I'm talking about Scout." Cross tilts his head at me. "She has training in this area. Right?"

My face starts burning, but I nod. "Absolutely. I could help out." My voice comes out smaller now but committed. "I have sports medicine training. I understand hockey injuries."

"But would you be willing to do it full time?" Ivy asks, leaning forward. "Otherwise we should just put him in the facility. It's a significant commitment."

Silas goes rigid. "I am not being put anywhere!"

"Easy." Cross tries to take the anger down a notch. "It's either Scout moves in with you, or you stay at the rehab facility."

Ryan looks between Silas and me, then sighs. "Actually, that might work. If Scout's willing to move in temporarily, say a month or two, we could avoid the rehab facility situation. She's trained in sports medicine, as we just established. She'd know exactly what recovery protocols to follow."

"Absolutely not," Silas repeats, but there's less force behind it.

"Silas, be serious." Cross studies him. "Live at your house with Scout or at the hospital. I know what I'd choose."

Silas looks like he's swallowing broken glass. His eyes

find mine, angry as a thunderclap, searching for something I don't understand. The silence stretches until my chest feels tight.

"She'd be better than the hospital," he finally grinds out.

"Then it's settled," Juliet says, already making notes. "We'll work out the arrangements. Scout, you'll need to be compensated appropriately for this. It's way above and beyond your regular duties. We're talking a substantial bonus for the inconvenience of relocating temporarily. And for... you know, dealing with him."

"Uhh... sure?" I squeak. "Whatever you need."

Ivy nods. "I'll have HR draft up the paperwork. Hazard pay, essentially. You're giving up your personal life for the team." She turns to Silas. "And you. You'd better be nice to Scout. If I were you, I'd be thanking my lucky stars that you have someone so accommodating who's willing to stay at home with me while I recuperate."

Silas glares at the table, muttering something I think could be interpreted as *thanks*.

My mouth goes dry. I jumped without looking because I saw Silas suffering, hating the idea of strangers witnessing his vulnerability. Now reality's setting in. I just volunteered to move in with Silas Huxley.

The very same man who alternates between ignoring me and making me feel like my skin's too tight.

"We'll get you moved in today," Juliet continues, all business. "We'll get everything sorted. Keys, security codes, medical supplies."

I force myself to look at Silas. He's still staring at the table like he wants to set it on fire with his mind.

"Is that... okay with you?" I ask quietly.

He doesn't look up. "Does it matter?"

Juliet and Ivy keep talking, making arrangements,

discussing logistics and timelines. But all I can think about is what I've just agreed to. I'm going to be living with Silas, taking care of him when he can barely stand to be in the same room as me.

I wasn't thinking when I volunteered. I just couldn't bear the thought of anyone in pain.

Now I have to hope there's a soft place to land when I get to his condo.

Chapter Eight

Silas

When Scout arrives, I'm waiting in my living room. My arm's in a sling. Opening the door feels awkward.

Scout's standing there with her curly hair down, wearing yoga pants, a purple tank top, and a white cardigan. She has an oversized duffel over her shoulder, two yoga mats under her arm, and a suitcase trailing behind her.

That's all she needs?

"Am I early?" she asks.

I step back. "You're fine. It's not like I have anywhere to be."

Scout comes inside and sets down her stuff.

"You're supposed to be on complete bed rest." She looks me up and down, frowning when she sees my black jeans and black t-shirt. "You should be in sweats." She shoos me toward my bedroom.

"I'll go back to bed when I'm tired."

I lean down to pick up her duffel bag and she yanks it out of my hand, giving me a hostile glare. "I've got this. Bed, now."

I grit my teeth. "You're not the boss of me."

"I am, though. That's why I'm here, Silas." She starts to herd me into the hallway, toward my bedroom. All the condos are the same here in the Sinclair, so it doesn't shock me Scout knows her way around. But her attitude surprises me. I've never seen her scowl at anyone else.

"What the fuck?"

When she's about three inches away, moving toward me with her hands up like she's trying to prevent my escape, I step back.

"Yeah, what the fuck," she echoes. "That's what I'm wondering. Did I make a mistake in agreeing to this? The doctors and nurses at the rehab clinic wouldn't put up with you being an asshole. They'd sedate you if needed."

I snort. "Would not."

"That's enough out of you." She keeps walking, forcing me to move. She can tell I don't want her to touch me. That would be crossing some sort of invisible line I've drawn in my head.

"Wait, wait. What if I want to rest in the living room?"

Scout pauses. "Will you change into more comfortable clothes first?"

I glance down at myself. "I'm fine. What's wrong with jeans?"

"We both know you wouldn't be wearing jeans if I wasn't here."

"Yeah, well. If you weren't here, there's a good chance I'd be naked. So you can deal with jeans as a compromise."

"Silas." She crosses her arms and rolls her eyes. "The point I'm trying to make is that you should be in your softest sweatpants. You don't need to try to impress anyone, least of all me."

"I'm not," I grate out.

"Fine." She rolls her lips, drops her arms, and looks around. "Your condo's exactly what I expected. An absence of… almost everything."

She thought about what my living space would be like? That makes me tense. I look around, trying to see things from her perspective.

My place is concrete floors, steel appliances, and leather furniture in black and gray. No art on the walls. No rugs to soften the echo. The only color comes from the red light on the espresso machine and the green temperature display on the fridge.

She turns in a slow circle, taking it all in. Her mouth lifts into something between a smile and a wince. The fact that she doesn't seem to approve of my condo shouldn't mean anything to me, but it doesn't sit well. I don't have a lot of stuff, but everything's top of the line.

What could I possibly add that would make the space better? Nothing, I reason.

"Let's get this over with." I turn and head back toward my bedroom. "Guest room's down the hall. We'll have to share the bathroom."

She follows me, padding along in damp sneakers, looking at everything like she's cataloging evidence. We come to her temporary bedroom and I stop outside as she walks in. I feel suddenly conscious of how empty the room is. Just a bed with two white pillows and a lamp with a small LED bulb. The closet's empty. The nightstand drawer holds a spare phone charger and a Sudoku book.

That's it.

She lowers the duffel onto the bed and exhales like the shape of the room's pressing on her lungs. "Okay." Then softer, "I know you don't want anyone in your space, Silas. I promise to be as quiet and stay out of your way as much as possible."

"It's done now." I shrug, then wince. I shouldn't have tried to move my shoulder yet.

Scout's eyes cut to my right arm. "You're hurting."

"I'm fine."

"You're not." Her voice gentles. Not condescending. Not pitying. Just certain. She motions to the bed. "Sit. Let me make it hurt less."

"I said..."

Her eyes flash. "Silas, don't be so stubborn. Sit."

I should walk away. I don't. My legs carry me to the bed. I sit.

Scout's thumbs press into my shoulder blade. Heat shoots down my spine.

Everything goes rigid. Her fingers find the knot that's been bothering me all day. Small, strong, deliberate pressure through my shirt.

I haven't been touched like this in years. Not with care. My body doesn't know what to do with it. I sag forward slightly, my eyes closing without permission.

"This is just pressure," she says quietly. "Breathe in for four. Out for six."

"I'm not..." Her thumb finds the knot under my shoulder socket.

White fire explodes.

A sound tears out of me. Raw and loud in the quiet room. She's not even touching me sexually, but my body responds anyway. My cock stirs, awakened from his slumber. Fucking asshole.

My face burns. Scout doesn't stop. Another involuntary sound scrapes up my throat. I clamp my jaw.

"Breathe," she murmurs. Closer now. "That's it. In. Out."

I try. It comes out ragged. The knot gives a fraction. She works it steady and present.

My hands fist in the comforter. Another sound leaks out.

Scout shifts her touch and the world tilts. Heat races down my arm. My breath hitches before I strangle it.

Every point of contact burns. I'm starving for this. Touch without expectations? My whole body's screaming for her to never quit. But my brain is flashing bright red warning signals.

"Stop," I rasp. Not because it hurts. Because it feels good.

Scout's hands still immediately. "Okay." No argument. She steps back.

I get to my feet. The room tilts for half a second. My shoulder throbs.

"Okay."

She narrows her eyes on my face, but doesn't say anything. I don't look at her response too closely. If she's pitying me, I'll choke. If she's not, I'll choke anyway.

I mumble out an excuse that doesn't do much to cover up what just happened. "I have to... go... lie down."

I make it down the hall on legs that feel miswired. My bedroom door shuts with a sharp sound. I hit the lock and crumple on the big bed.

I close my eyes for several long seconds. When I open them again, my phone's already in my hand, though I don't remember taking it out.

The app stares up at me, alive. Her username at the top of the thread. **Yoga4Lyfe**. Ridiculous. Bright. She's not ten feet away in the guest bedroom and I'm pretending she's miles away. She's too close.

Now that I've retreated into my cave, I can say things in this room, in the dark, with a fake name, that I cannot make my mouth form. I can still feel the ghost of her touch against my shoulder. My dick is still hard.

My thumbs hover on the screen.

STATMAN12

You there?

It only takes a few moments for Scout to respond.

YOGA4LYFE

I am.

STATMAN12

I'm needy.

YOGA4LYFE

Oh? Tell me more.

STATMAN12

I want you spread out under me, sobbing into my hands while I ruin you.

I close my eyes. One beat, two, then my phone vibrates.

YOGA4LYFE

That's filthy.

I want you to tell me more.

A noise cracks out of me, less of a laugh than something shattered. I type before shame can overcome me.

STATMAN12

> I want my face buried between your legs until you can't remember your name. Your curls belong wrapped around my fist. You should beg me, because I want nothing more than to see you wrecked. I want it so bad I can taste you. I want to ruin your pussy.

Silence stretches long enough to make my pulse ring in my ears. Then her reply comes through.

YOGA4LYFE

> What would you do with your hands? I want you to tell me everything.

I swear softly under my breath. My hands, shaking when she pressed into that knot in my shoulder. Gripping the duvet because I didn't know what else to do with them.

I suck in a breath and move back on the bed, laying back amongst the pillows. My erection thickens. The urge to pull my dick out and rub one out's nearly overwhelming. But Scout's too close for me to do that without feeling like a fucking creep. So I just tell her what I'm thinking about instead.

StatMan12: One hand on your throat, just enough pressure to tell you where I want you. The other on your hip, keeping you exactly there while I lick you open. I suck your clit, shove two fingers into that hot pussy, and enjoy the sounds you make. I don't stop until you're shaking so hard you beg. I don't stop then, either.

My heart's a fist slamming against my ribs from the inside. The bedroom feels too small. The wall between us might as well be skin.

Her reply comes delayed and then not.

YOGA4LYFE

That's not what a nice man would say. Are you nice, StatMan?

STATMAN12

No. I'm not nice. I'm not soft. I'm not built for gentle. I'm built for ruining your pussy, stretching you out, making you mine.

Another buzz.

YOGA4LYFE

Oh, god...

I set the phone down and press my hands into my eyes.

I can smell her on my shirt. Lavender and eucalyptus.

She's Enzo's ex. Off limits. Forbidden. It's better if I remember that and don't start pining after her again.

Chapter Nine

Scout

Living with Silas means my job has evolved from *fetch coffee for everyone* to *babysit one extremely grumpy defenseman*. It's not exactly the career advancement I dreamed of, but at least I only have to deal with one giant man-child instead of thirty.

Small victories.

I'm at the arena gym, hovering near Silas while he rides an exercise bike and glowers at the wall like it personally insulted him. I'm supposed to be working on my Mobility Monday instructions, but it's hard to concentrate when Ice Man over there looks like he's plotting the bike's murder.

Silas is my responsibility now. Coach Cross made that crystal clear. Monitor him. Keep him from doing something stupid that sets back his recovery. Make sure he doesn't hulk out and destroy equipment.

I can do all of those things. If Silas would stop snarling at me every five minutes, anyway.

One of the newer trainers, a guy named Mike who looks about twelve years old, sidles up to me. "Hey, will you grab me an almond milk latte? I went out too late last night and I'm fading."

I smile. "I would normally say yes, but I'm not doing coffee runs today. I have to stay here."

Coach Ryan walks into the gym. He's tall, dark, and has that ex-pro-athlete thing going on. His blue eyes land on me and Mike.

Apparently oblivious to his boss watching, Mike frowns. "Listen, sweetheart. Your job is to get me coffee when I say so. That's your entire reason for existing. So run along."

He makes a shooing motion. My face heats. I smile even though what I really want is to kick him in the shins.

"That's not my job today—"

"Mike!" Coach Ryan growls. "Surely you have work to do."

"I was just telling her to grab me a coffee," Mike explains, completely missing the danger he's in.

"It's fine!" It comes out squeaky. "I can text Jessa. She's picking up slack while I work with Silas."

"Don't move." Coach points at Mike. "Is there a reason you think you're better than her?"

Mike goes pale. "Uh, no..."

"You're the lowest man here, Mike. From now on, you get your own coffee. You come in ready to work. And for fuck's sake, you don't tell my employees what their job is. Scout reports directly to me now. That makes her higher than you. Now get to work before I start rethinking your employment."

"Yes, Coach," Mike mutters, scurrying away like a scolded puppy.

Ryan rolls his eyes. "Amateur. I bet he washes out in a few months."

"Let's hope not." I clear my throat. "Thanks for the rescue."

"Coach Cross told me to look out for you." His lips curl. "Now go work on Mobility Mondays. Silas will be busy here for a couple hours."

I nod and pull a chair over by the doorway, settling in to multitask. Watch Silas. Work on my tablet. Try not to stare at Silas. Fail at not staring at Silas.

The gym has a few other injured players doing rehab, but most of the action's around my favorite grumpy patient. Two trainers hover over him, guiding him through resistance bands and balance drills. Silas looks miserable and rigid, jaw tight with frustration.

He also looks unfairly good. The black workout shirt clings to everything. Sweat slides down his neck. His hair's pulled back, showing off that sharp jaw and those blue-gray eyes that refuse to meet mine.

Even injured and furious, he's stupidly attractive. It's honestly offensive.

He always has been. Eight years ago I asked him out and he turned me down flat. End of mortifying story.

But watching him now, I can see through the Ice Man act. Everyone calls him cold, emotionless, a machine. I see the way his left hand flexes when he can't complete a movement with his right. The micro-grimace when pain flashes before he locks it down. How he counts reps under his breath like numbers are the only thing keeping him sane.

He's not emotionless. He's just terrified of showing emotion.

I shouldn't care. There are a dozen reasons to stop wishing Silas had said yes eight years ago. But here I am, finding excuses to check in. Bringing him water. Correcting his trainer when they suggest exercises that could hurt his shoulder.

Silas growls at me. His trainer thanks me.

Standard operating procedure.

You're supposed to be working, I scold myself. *Stop staring at the angry giant.*

Then I see him moving toward heavy dumbbells for lateral raises and I squeak, "What are you doing? Don't! That'll strain your stabilizers!"

Silas and his trainer both look up with matching *are you kidding me* expressions.

"I don't need a babysitter, Scout," Silas snaps. "Do me a favor and work somewhere else."

His tone stings. I plaster on a bright smile. "Sure thing. I'll just... go upstairs."

I walk off with as much dignity as I can muster. Which is not much.

Upstairs in the office, I throw myself into Mobility Mondays planning for a solid hour. Then I make a list of other suggestions and email them to Coach Ryan. Shifting travel meal schedules. Adjusting practice timing. Small things that might help players feel better.

Being useful is my superpower, after all.

When I drive Silas home, he's extremely short with me, growling every other word. He moves so slowly getting into the car I have to wonder if it's because he's really hurting. Or maybe he's just run ragged. When he closes his eyes and seems to fall asleep on the way home, I conclude it's more likely to be the latter.

The big caveman's just exhausted.

He disappears into his room when we get back, shutting the door and boxing me out. Getting down to business, I prepare a sensible dinner of sliced chicken breast, pasta with pesto, and a large serving of asparagus. I find myself hesitant to knock on his door. What if he's still asleep? Will he yell at me?

Because I'm not sure what kind of state he's in, I leave a plate of pasta in Silas's kitchen before I retreat to my room. I leave no note, no explanation. It's food for someone who can't take care of himself.

Surely I can't be chastised for that.

I hear him come out of his room later. Cracking my door, I listen to the sounds of a fork scraping against a plate. He eats in silence, not looking for me, not saying thank you. I pretend I don't care.

He's cold as ice, colder than I remember him being. What can I do to thaw him a little bit?

My phone buzzes on my nightstand. I glance at it and my stomach drops.

Enzo.

ENZO

You still haven't picked up your stuff. I'm starting to think you're using my storage unit as a free service. Come get all of your shit out of my house, Scout.

I flip the phone over, jaw tight. I don't respond. There's no point. Enzo only texts when he wants to pick at a scab. When he needs to remind me I'm not worth the space I take up.

Another buzz a minute later. I almost ignore it but the name on the screen makes me reach for it.

Sable. My lovely big sister, older than me by a year, also lives in the city. She travels a lot for her job as a sports therapist, seeing patients in Vancouver and Portland as well as here in Seattle.

My sister's voice note is warm and excited.

SABLE

Scout! I'm organizing a free clinic for
athletes dealing with burnout and mental
health stuff. I thought maybe you could help
with the physical side? Mobility work, injury
prevention? Let me know if you're
interested!

I smile despite everything. Sable knows exactly how to brighten my day.

ME

That's amazing. Count me in. When you're
back in the city, we should have lunch!

SABLE

I miss your face! Let me text you some
dates tomorrow.

Silas drifts through the hallway while I'm typing, shoulders massive in his t-shirt. He pauses just outside my door, long enough I know he can hear the audio playing. When I turn to acknowledge him, to maybe include him in the conversation, he mutters something under his breath and stalks away.

The door to his bedroom closes with a sharp click. I stare at the empty doorway, phone still in my hand, wondering what I did wrong this time.

Later, I unroll my yoga mat in the living room. There's no amount of scowling Silas can do that will make me not do yoga. My body slips into stretches on autopilot, long slow pulls that make tension leak out of my muscles. My wild curls fall forward when I fold. I breathe through each pose, trying to find the quiet center I usually access through practice.

I feel him before I see him.

Silas stands in the hallway, watching. His gaze is heavy, almost scorching on my skin. I arch my back in a deep back-bend, hands reaching for my feet. The stretch opens my chest, pulls tight through my hip flexors.

"Want to join?" I ask, my voice breathless.

His gaze lingers too long. His jaw goes tight. Then he turns on his heel and disappears down the hall without a word.

Heat blooms low in my stomach anyway. He's way more of a jerk than I remembered him being, but it's still hard to convince my body his being thorny means he isn't crazy hot.

When I'm done, I shower and crawl into bed with my phone. The apartment's quiet around me. Silas is locked away in his bedroom, probably counting Sudoku numbers or organizing his sock drawer by fiber content. I think about texting Jessa but I'm not ready to explain the weirdness of living with a man who alternates between ignoring me and watching me like I'm a problem he's trying to solve.

Instead, I open the dating app. There's already a message waiting.

STATMAN12

How was your day?

My chest warms. I type back quickly.

YOGA4LYFE

Complicated. How was yours?

STATMAN12

Frustrating. I'm not good at asking for help.

YOGA4LYFE

You don't seem like the type that would be.

STATMAN12

Oh yeah? What have you noticed?

I bite my lip, considering. There's so much I could say. That he seems guarded. That he might push people away. But I stick with easier truths.

YOGA4LYFE

You're careful. You don't let people in easily.

STATMAN12

Guilty. But I let you in.

My heart skips.

YOGA4LYFE

Why?

STATMAN12

Because you're different. You don't want anything from me except honesty.

YOGA4LYFE

That's all anyone should want.

STATMAN12

You'd be surprised how rare that is.

We talk for another hour. He tells me about the pressure of performing when everyone's watching. I tell him about trying to prove I'm more than useful. We dance around specifics, keeping our real identities hidden, but the emotional honesty cuts deeper than any confession.

There's something fun in texting this stranger about my life.

STATMAN12

So, what? You have a list of dirty things you want to try?

My cheeks flush. The Naughty Girl Scout List sits folded in my nightstand drawer. I haven't looked at it in days but I know every word by heart.

YOGA4LYFE

Yeah, but... the list is too embarrassing.

STATMAN12

Nothing you want is embarrassing. Tell me one thing.

I close my eyes and type before I can talk myself out of it.

YOGA4LYFE

1, let a man talk filthy to me without flinching and 2, sext until the phone dies.

The reply comes fast.

STATMAN12

Please say that you want to use me to fulfill your wish list.

My breath catches.

YOGA4LYFE

You don't even know what I look like.

STATMAN12

I've seen your profile. I've talked to you enough to know you're hot. Plus, I know I'm hard just thinking about you.

Heat floods through me, settling low in my belly. My thighs press together.

YOGA4LYFE

You can't say things like that.

STATMAN12

Then stop reading.

I don't stop. I can't.

YOGA4LYFE

What would you do to me if you were here?

STATMAN12

I'd make you come at least twice with my tongue.

YOGA4LYFE

Fuck.

STATMAN12

That's next.

I gasp and cover my mouth even though I'm alone. My phone buzzes again before I can formulate a response.

STATMAN12

Now tell me what you want most. Don't lie to me.

My pulse stutters. The lists flash through my mind. *Let someone go down on me until I cry. Get fucked on the kitchen counter. Ride his face just because I want to.*

My thumbs hover over the keyboard. Then I take a photo of the list, dropping it in the chat. I pause the moment before I hit send. What if StatMan crushes my feelings? After a half second more, I delete the photo.

YOGA4LYFE

I want to be wanted. Not for what I can do or how I can help. I just want to be needed so badly that someone just takes me. You know?

The reply is instant.

STATMAN12

I want to see that list, sweetheart. I want to know exactly what you're thinking about.

My whole body shakes. This is too much.

YOGA4LYFE

Maybe tomorrow.

STATMAN12

I'll hold you to that.

YOGA4LYFE

You're dangerous.

STATMAN12

You like dangerous.

He's not wrong. I do like it. I like feeling reckless, being wanted, acting brave enough to ask for things I've never asked for before.

STATMAN12

I'll make every single thing on your list come true. I promise you that.

My breath catches in my throat. I clutch the phone tighter,

pulse racing. I don't know if I believe him. Promises from a stranger behind a screen can't mean anything real.

Right now, in the dark of my room with the lists spread beside me on the bed, I let myself pretend they can.

YOGA4LYFE

That's a big promise.

STATMAN12

I don't make promises I can't keep.

YOGA4LYFE

How would you even start?

STATMAN12

By taking you apart piece by piece until you're begging me not to stop.

My thighs clench. Heat spreads through me like wildfire. I should put the phone down. Should stop this before it goes further.

Instead I type back.

YOGA4LYFE

Keep going.

STATMAN12

I'd start with my mouth. Everywhere. Your neck, your breasts, between your thighs until you're shaking. I'd make you come at least twice before I even thought about fucking you.

YOGA4LYFE

God.

STATMAN12

Then I'd take you against the nearest wall because I wouldn't be able to wait long enough to get you to a bed.

YOGA4LYFE

This is insane.

STATMAN12

You started it.

YOGA4LYFE

I should go to bed.

STATMAN12

Are you wet?

The bluntness of the question steals my breath. I should lie. Ending this conversation like a responsible adult is the only reasonable thing to do. I type my answer anyway.

YOGA4LYFE

Yes.

STATMAN12

Touch yourself. Tell me what it feels like.

My hand slides down my stomach before I can think about it. I'm already wet, have been since this conversation started. My fingers slip between my legs, exploring my slit, and I gasp.

YOGA4LYFE

It feels good.

STATMAN12

Tell me what you're thinking about.

YOGA4LYFE

Your hands. Your mouth. You taking control
and making me beg.

STATMAN12

I'd make you beg so prettily. I'd make you
say please until your voice broke.

My fingers move faster. I'm close already, wound too tight from a day of watching Silas move through the gym, from the tension crackling between us in this apartment, from weeks of wanting things I'm too scared to ask for.

YOGA4LYFE

I'm close.

STATMAN12

Come for me. Right now.

The command pushes me over the edge. Lightning strikes, shattering me into dust. I bite down on my fist to muffle the sound, body arching off the bed. It takes a full minute for my vision to clear, for my breathing to even out.

YOGA4LYFE

That was...

STATMAN12

That was just the beginning.

I lie there in the dark, phone still clutched in my hand, body still buzzing. I just had texting sex with a stranger. Someone I've never met. Someone who could be anyone.

Enzo's poison feels far away. The sting of Silas's rejection doesn't hurt quite as much.

Best of all, I feel alive in a way I haven't felt in years.

Chapter Ten

Silas

I don't like bars. Paying to yell over music while your friends get hammered isn't my idea of a good time. But when Scout came out of her room in a pink dress and said she was heading to the Secret History, I followed.

Someone needs to make sure the idiots downstairs don't harass her.

Now I'm sitting in the Havoc's private room, pretending to listen to my teammates while I watch Scout.

She's wearing that short pink dress. Heads turned when she walked in. Of course they did.

Scout sits with Juliet and Jessa, doing what she always does. Taking care of everyone. Sliding drinks closer before they can ask. Handing out napkins. Offering to run upstairs when Ivy forgets something.

Always making herself useful.

I scowl into my beer. Watching how she operates around everyone, not just me, makes me angry. I have no right to feel jealous. No claim on her. No reason to care who she talks to or helps or smiles at.

Especially after last night.

I think about her messages. The way she typed out her wants. The memory of her coming while I gave instructions through text.

My cock stirs.

It was hot. I needed a release, but it wasn't enough.

And now I'm jealous of my online persona. Why does Scout like StatMan? We don't even talk about real things. We just flirt and sext.

She'll stop eventually. Women always do. They get bored with the mystery. They want something *real*.

Then they're gone.

Hunter nudges my arm, playing with his wedding band. "Shoulder holding up okay?"

I shrug with my good side. "Fine."

"Liar," he says. He doesn't push it.

Thorne leans back across from me, grinning. "He's more worried about his babysitter. If Scout hates living with you, she can crash at my place. I wouldn't mind the company."

The words land like a punch. "Funny."

"It's not really a joke." Thorne drinks his beer. "She's hot. Sweet. Probably needs someone who doesn't growl at her constantly."

I growl low. "Real supportive."

I want to wipe that smirk off his face. Thorne's the team's golden boy. Power forward. Fan favorite. Flashy and smooth-talking. Probably Scout's type, too. Just look at Enzo.

Scout appears at our table. Her smile's aimed at Thorne. "Hey guys."

Thorne's eyes light up. "Hey, Scout. I heard you teach yoga."

Scout turns pink. "I do. How'd you hear that?"

He shrugs. "I have my sources. You ever teach outside the arena? I'd be interested."

"Oh! Really? You'd do yoga?"

"Sure. Especially if it's hands-on instruction. Maybe a private lesson?"

Scout beams. "Absolutely!"

Heat flares in my chest. "Thorne, quit being an asshole."

"What?" Scout's smile falls. "Were you joking?"

"He's fucking with me," I growl.

Scout tilts her head. "How so?"

"I was serious about yoga," Thorne assures her. "He's just grumpy because he doesn't want me flirting with you."

"Oh! I didn't, um..." Scout's eyes widen. She stares at anything but me. "I'm not sure how you came up with that, Thorne. Silas doesn't care who I talk to."

I'm not allowed to care. But I do.

"Is she right, buddy?" Thorne grins. "You don't mind if I try to take Scout home?"

"Call me buddy again." I lean forward. "I don't care that you're captain. I'll still wrap you around a telephone pole."

Thorne's grin widens. "See? He does care. So, Scout. How about we practice some down dog at my place?"

Juliet comes over just in time to hear that. Anger flashes across her face.

"You two are being inappropriate with Scout. She's a team employee." She gives Thorne a withering stare and grabs my hand. "You're already in trouble. I suggest you go home."

"Can no one take a joke?" Thorne mutters.

I point a finger at him. "You're making things worse."

"Or am I helping?" Thorne replies. "Only time will tell."

I grind my molars until my jaw aches. I can't tell Thorne to shut the hell up. And it's not like I'm allowed to tell Scout not to glow like that for anyone else.

What would I even say? She's not mine. She's living in

my condo temporarily because the coaches mandated it. That's all.

So I take the coward's way out.

"Enough socializing," I mutter, pushing my chair back. The legs scrape against the floor. "I'm going to bed."

I know what will happen. Scout will follow. She always does. It's built into her DNA or something, this need to take care of people who don't deserve it. I definitely don't deserve it, but I'm also technically under her care. If I have to, I will use that to my advantage.

Predictably, Scout follows.

"Silas, wait!" she calls out, gathering her jacket. "I'll come with you. You still need to be monitored."

Thorne sits back, looking pleased with himself. Hunter shoots me a look that says he knows exactly what I'm doing. He's right, but I don't fucking care. I ignore him and head for the exit.

The elevator ride up to my condo's quiet. Scout fidgets with her phone. I keep my eyes on the ground and try not to think about how good she smells even after hours at a bar. Lavender and eucalyptus cutting through stale beer.

I can't help but picture me sliding my hand into her dark blonde curls and leaning down, pressing my nose to her crown. Inhaling more of her scent.

Once we're back in the condo, she hovers like I'm made of glass. "Do you want food? I could make something. Or heat? Ice for your shoulder?"

As if on cue, my shoulder throbs. I rub it, but I can't reach the healing incision or the aching knots bunched up just below my right shoulder blade.

Scout stops in front of me, her lips puckering. "Silas, let me help you. Please? I can heat up a wrap, or massage your shoulder..."

"Massage," I bite out before I can stop myself.

She lights up. "Come sit on the couch."

She touches my left arm, guiding me into the living room, moving around behind me as I sit down. I stiffen when her hands land on my shoulders. God, her touch is too warm, her hands moving carefully against my skin. As though she thinks I might break if she presses too hard.

"You can do it harder than that."

"Okay," she says. Her fingers dig into the knot near my shoulder blade. "How's this pressure?"

I'm built like a nuclear fallout shelter. Obscenely tall, beefy, low body fat percentage. There's no room for pretty architecture on my frame. And what she's currently doing to my back makes me want to close my eyes and whimper. I can't have that happen, so I lie.

"Feels okay," I grunt.

Scout sighs, though her hands never leave my shoulders. "I'm over here wasting my time on a grumpy man who acts like I'm torturing him."

I wince as she hits an especially tender spot. "You might be."

"Oh, Silas. God forbid someone tries to help you," she mutters. Her thumbs press harder, finding the exact spot that makes white heat explode down my arm. "Ice cold one minute, needy the next. Make up your mind."

They call me Ice Man. The nickname stuck years ago when I didn't react to a dirty hit that should've started a line brawl. Everyone thinks I'm emotionless. Unaffected. A machine. But right now, with her hands on me, I'm anything but cold. I'm burning up from the inside out, desperate for more contact, more touch, more of her.

My jaw clenches so hard I think my teeth might crack. I

want to shove her off. Or maybe I should pull her closer. I find myself wanting things I have no business wanting.

"I'm not your project," I manage.

"No," she snaps, pressing deeper into the knot. "You're impossible."

Her curls brush the back of my neck when she leans in for better leverage. I swear under my breath. That shampoo she uses taunts me, lavender and eucalyptus folding into my lungs with every breath. It's like being in a field of flowers. I want to lie on my back, legs and arms spread wide, and be engulfed in that scent.

The sound rips out of me before I can stop it. A guttural moan, rough and low and completely involuntary. Shame floods through me hot and immediate. My cock stirs against my sweatpants, traitorous and obvious and humiliating.

Her hands pause. Just for a beat. Then they resume, polite and careful, like nothing happened.

I haven't been touched like this in so long. Years of keeping people at arm's length, of refusing physical therapy that required hands on my body, of jerking off alone in the dark because letting anyone close felt too dangerous. My skin's starving for this. Every nerve ending screams for her to press harder, touch more, never stop. The contact rewires something in my brain, short-circuits my carefully built defenses. I want to beg her to keep going. I want to grab her hands and put them everywhere.

Fuck me. What she's doing feels so good. Somehow, it makes everything worse.

"Stop," I grind out, shifting forward to hide the evidence of my body's betrayal. "That's enough."

Her hands still immediately. I can hear the worry in her voice when she says, "Did I hurt you?"

The shame swirls inside my chest, rising higher.

"You couldn't hurt me. I just hit my limit."

"Fine." She steps back. Her tone is clipped and professional. "I get it."

"You did… fine. Good." I'm fucking this up even more, somehow. "My shoulder just needs to rest."

Scout's eyebrows rise, but thank fuck she doesn't press the matter. "I'm going to my room. Let me know if you need anything."

She disappears down the hallway without another word. My head droops forward. I sit alone in the living room, shoulder still throbbing, cock still hard, shame coating everything like oil.

Fuck me. I'm letting my old crush on my pretty neighbor resurface, and it's only growing, getting worse. How am I supposed to keep Scout at a distance when she's in the next bedroom?

I spend the rest of the night reviewing film highlights of my upcoming opposing team. But when I'm done, I realize I might have just kicked back and zoned out. I can't remember a single stat or think of how best to defend against them.

Before bed, I head through my ironclad routine because routines are safe. Predictable. Shower, stretch, Sudoku. I step out of the steam with a towel slung low on my hips, my chin-length hair still dripping water down my shoulders.

Scout rounds the corner from the kitchen. She blinks when she sees me. Her eyes go wide for half a second before she catches herself.

"Wow," she says. There's something in her voice I can't identify. "You brought the steam with you."

Something hot flashes between us. The air goes thick and charged. Her eyes drop to my chest. I watch them track down the muscle, following water droplets. Then they snap back up to my face, cheeks flushing pink.

I should say something normal. Anything that defuses this moment before it gets more awkward.

Instead I snap too sharp. "Go to bed."

Her mouth shuts. The warmth in her eyes cools to something flat and distant. She turns and disappears down the hall without another word.

Fuck me. Opening my mouth guarantees that whatever comes out is rude and surly.

Getting into sweats and lying in my bed feels almost too good. My injury is beyond painful. I look at the bottle of pain pills I've been prescribed sitting on my bedside table. By grinning and bearing the pain, I've gone all day without needing any opiates. But now I think I might actually need one.

I shake a pill out and down it with the bottle of water I keep on my bedside table. Then I close my eyes. My shoulder aches, pain radiating from the epicenter out into my neck and down to my sternum.

I tell myself that the pain's good. *I don't need more than this.*

But I know I'm lying.

Chapter Eleven

Scout

"This is so fancy," I mutter while filling Silas's ridiculously expensive blender with ice, protein powder, almond milk, and frozen strawberries. Following the directions, I put the lid on, then lock the container inside a shield that promises to vacuum seal and blend simultaneously.

The blender is still loud, shrieking through the condo at six in the morning like the world's angriest alarm clock. I grin as I pour two tall glasses of bright pink smoothie. It smells amazing, which means Silas will probably hate it.

From the hallway comes a gravelly growl. "What the hell is that noise?"

"Breakfast," I chirp, setting a glass on the counter. "I noticed you only have coffee before the gym. That's not enough calories. It slows down your metabolism." I wait, looking over my shoulder with my brightest smile. "You're welcome!"

Silas appears in the doorway looking like murder in sweatpants. His dirty blond hair sticks up on one side, sleep-mussed and somehow endearing despite the scowl. Those blue-gray eyes are flat and cold. He's shirtless, all broad shoulders and defined abs on full display. Six foot eight of barely contained morning rage wrapped in gray sweatpants. The bandage on his shoulder's visible. Even freshly woken and radiating hostility, he's unfairly attractive.

Honestly, it's rude.

"It's six in the morning."

"Early bird gets the worm."

"What if I don't want the worm? I love silence."

A bit of his hair is sticking up on the side. I stare at it, willing myself not to think it's cute. He's Oscar the Grouch, not a puppy. Puppies don't have razor blade edges.

I cross my arms. "You are seriously grumpy in the morning."

"I'm always grumpy when someone wakes me up by blending something at maximum volume."

"It just so happens I got permission for you to return to the ice."

Silas's hand stops where it was scratching his beard. "You did?"

He sounds uncertain. I beam anyway.

"Yes, Bossy. I did. In practice, you'll wear a red 'No Contact' jersey, but you can do skating drills. Nothing that requires bending or contact. The Havoc have a game tonight. You'll be benched, but you'll be with the team."

Silas's face screws up. I'm not sure what he's going to say, but he surprises me with a grated-out, "Thanks."

"You're very welcome." My smile's so big it hurts. "You need to be ready to go soon. I've got a car picking you up at 7:30. Now come drink this smoothie."

He scowls and mutters something about rookies who get fined for being late but I get to run a juice bar in his kitchen. I ignore him and sip my smoothie, watching him over the rim.

He stands there glaring at the pink drink like it personally offended him.

Then he picks it up and chugs the whole thing in four long pulls.

Victory tastes like strawberries and vindication.

He sets the empty glass in the sink and stalks back down the hallway. His bedroom door closes with a loud thump.

I hide my smile in my smoothie. When I head to the shower later, I notice he's already left. In my head, I'd planned to help him carry his bag downstairs since he shouldn't risk his shoulder. But I guess I didn't mention that plan.

If I had, he probably would've accused me of smothering him.

At noon I climb out of an Uber in front of Enzo's house. My house, once upon a delusional time. The brick still gleams like money. The glossy red front door still sticks on the bottom hinge. I know it will smell like smoke and cologne before I even step inside. That scent used to make me feel safe. Now it just makes my stomach turn.

I'm here to pick up the last of my things. Clothes in the back of the closet. Books from what used to be my office before Enzo turned it into a home gym. The framed photo of my mom I couldn't look at during the final months of her life.

I should've texted first. Or better yet, coordinated a time when he'd be gone. Part of me wanted to walk in here and prove I could walk back out without falling apart.

The door swings open before I can knock.

Enzo stands there shirtless in gray sweatpants. His hair is artfully messy in that way that probably took twenty minutes to perfect. Behind him, three women drape across the leather couch like trophies. One of them is wearing what looks like Enzo's shirt and nothing else.

Classy.

His grin is knife-sharp. "Scout. Didn't know you were coming by. You should've texted. I would've told the girls to put pants on."

"Not on my account." My pulse spikes but I keep my face neutral. "I'm just here for my things."

"Things," he echoes, leaning against the doorframe. His eyes drag over me like I'm inventory. "Funny. I always thought you wanted me, not things."

"Don't flatter yourself." I push past him into the foyer.

He follows close enough that I can feel him at my back. His voice drips acid. "You really think you're going to find better? You'll just latch onto some other guy. Fix his meals. Wash his socks. Take notes on how he likes his shirts folded. You're not a girlfriend, Scout. You're staff."

I stop in the middle of the living room, hands clenched. The women on the couch watch us with bored interest, like we're a reality show they've seen twelve times. I hate this. I hate all of it.

The second I pushed back on Enzo's flirting, the moment I had a problem with his parade of side pieces, he lost interest in me. He started nitpicking everything I did. I should've seen it coming the first time I found someone else's lipstick on his collar.

"I'm dating Silas," I blurt out.

My eyes widen the second it leaves my mouth. Enzo makes me stupid. If I could snatch the words back and stuff them down my throat, I would.

His grin dies. Something ugly flashes in his eyes. "I knew it."

My stomach drops. He couldn't know. I just made it up. But the flash of fury on his face feels like victory anyway. Petty and small but victory nonetheless.

"Figures you have to entice him with pussy just to get his attention," he sneers, circling closer. "Big, broken bastard like him. You probably think he needs you just like I did. Newsflash, Scout. You didn't save me. You just made it easier to cheat."

My throat tightens. I force words through it. "You couldn't keep it in your pants if your life depended on it."

"Better than being boring." He moves closer, voice dropping to something soft and cruel. "How long are you going to keep riding my coattails? You still work the job I got you. You're still living off my connections. You're nothing without me."

Tears threaten but I blink them back. Fury cuts through the hurt, sharp and clean. "Throw the rest of my stuff out. I don't want it."

I grab the two boxes of stuff he's got ready for me and shove past him toward the door.

He calls after me, laughter sharp and mean. "You'll come crawling back when that machine of a man freezes you out. It's what you do. You're forgettable, Scout."

My chest seizes but I don't cry. Not here. Not for him. I spin on my heel at the door and spit the words at him.

"Go fuck yourself, Enzo."

I slam the door behind me. My hands shake so hard I can barely pull out my phone to call an Uber. I stand on the curb clutching the boxes while trying not to cry in front of Enzo's building.

The driver shows up seven minutes later and loads the boxes without asking questions.

You're okay. You're fine. You're strong. I repeat it to myself until I pull up outside the Rainier Bank Center. At the arena, I throw myself into work because work is safe.

Work is something I can control.

I can smile and make sure everyone has everything they need in order for the night to be a success. I track down a set of keys Ivy lost, help Juliet make press packets, and even film a TikTok with Mollie, the extremely shy social media liaison. She's the newest hire and barely old enough to drink, which makes her the right age for an influencer.

"Please do this dance with me?" Her words are sweet and shy. "No one else will do it."

I take pity on her. "Okay. Let me put this stuff down and then I'll try. No promises that I'll be any good at it."

After setting down a carrier tray of coffees and the stack of merch t-shirts I'm running down to the promotions crew, I watch Mollie do a quick dance. It only has a few steps, repeated three times. She looks amazing doing the simple dance. I feel stupid doing it, but I figure she needs help. Most of the players growl at her when they see her coming.

"Is this right?" I ask. I walk through the simple steps of the dance, then finish by looking straight at the camera and doing jazz hands. Mollie laughs and tucks her shiny red hair behind her ear. "You did it perfectly. Most of the other people here in the office won't do my dumb dances."

"They're not dumb if they help introduce more fans to hockey."

She beams at me. "That's what I've been saying! I've been telling Beck that."

"Beck as in Beck Tate? The captain?"

"Co-captain. He shares it with Alex Thorne. God, don't give him more credit than he deserves." Her cheeks turn bright pink. "He's also my big brother. It's kinda how I got this job."

I wave her off. "It seems like you know your stuff. Besides, I don't see anyone else filming dances while they talk about the team." I give her a wink. "Plus, if you're a nepo baby, I'm a double nepo. I got this because of my ex husband."

"It seems like you're working hard." She looks pointedly at the stack of stuff I abandoned. "One nepo to another. I notice the hard work you put in."

My face flames. "Thanks, Mollie. Same." Tilting my head at the t-shirts, I say, "Want to walk down to the tunnel with me? Maybe you can grab one of the players for an interview."

She frowns. "I'll go downstairs with you, but I don't think anybody wants to do an interview. Believe me, I've asked."

Giving her an empathetic glance, I grab my stuff and lead her down to the tunnel. The arena's packed to the gills with roiling, raging fans. I'll never understand how someone can get that excited for a game. People here take hockey so seriously. Mollie splits off, waving, and I head to hand off the coffees and the t-shirts to the very grateful promo team.

Then I walk into the tunnel, where I look for Silas.

Silas is back on the bench tonight. Not playing, just dressed in his suit, helmet sitting in his lap, shoulder heavily taped under his jacket. His dirty blond hair's pulled back in a low bun, emphasizing the sharp angles of his face. That tailored charcoal suit fits him perfectly, stretched across broad shoulders even with the bandaging underneath. He looks every inch the professional athlete. Polished, controlled, impossibly handsome. But I can see past the Ice Man facade everyone buys into. The stiffness when he shifts positions gives him away. The way he rolls his shoulder like it's bothering him makes me wince.

People call him Ice Man like it's who he is. Cold. Unfeeling. A machine built for defense. I watch the micro-expressions that flash across his face when he thinks no one's looking. The way his jaw tightens when a teammate takes a hard hit. How his left hand flexes against his thigh when he can't be on the ice helping. He's not cold at all. He's burning with the need to be out there, to protect his team, to do what he does best. The ice is just a defense.

I make a mental note to corner the team trainer later. Someone needs to know. Someone needs to make sure he's not making it worse by pretending he's fine.

Just as they're about to drop the puck, the arena signage system crashes. Sponsors are scrambled, logos in the wrong sections, names misspelled on the jumbotron. My phone lights up with angry messages from Juliet and the sponsorship coordinator. Corporate sponsors are threatening to pull money if they don't get the visibility they paid for.

I bolt across the concourse, heart pounding. This happened once, when I was first married to Enzo. Thankfully, I watched how they fixed the system carefully. So now, I can jump into action. First, I reroute display tables. Then I hustle the PA announcer to swap out copy. Finally, I physically climb onto a table to adjust a banner that's hanging crooked. By the time I'm done, gasping for breath, I've missed puck drop by fifteen minutes.

Everything's fixed. Everyone got what they needed. That's all that matters.

Juliet finds me in the tunnel and catches my arm. Her voice is low and warm. "Invoice for overtime. You earned it. That was a disaster."

My cheeks flush hot. "I'm just doing my job."

"You're doing more than your job." She squeezes once and walks away.

I stand there for a second, breathing hard, feeling something warm unfurl in my chest. Pride, maybe. Or just relief I didn't completely screw everything up.

Jessa appears at my elbow, smirking. "Your face always does that when someone compliments you."

I bat her away, cheeks flaming hotter. "Shut up. How's the apartment? I hope it's not too lonely."

"The apartment wants you back. So do I." She follows me back to the staff area, still grinning. "So when are you going to tell me about your mystery man on the dating app?"

I mentioned StatMan to Jessa over text yesterday, but I didn't give her any details. Hell, I don't know any details. I shrug.

"There's nothing to tell."

"Liar. I saw you texting him last week. You get this look on your face when your phone buzzes. All flushed and distracted. It's adorable."

I do my best imitation of a scowl. "It's not adorable. It's pathetic."

"It's progress," Jessa says firmly. "You're allowed to have fun, Scout. You're allowed to want things. That's what the Naughty List is all about."

I don't answer. How can I explain wanting things feels dangerous? Every time I let myself want something, it gets taken away or used against me. It's turned into proof I'm too much or not enough.

Luckily, the Havoc scores a goal. Jessa's eyes light up. "Ooooh, I have to catch the replay!"

She's out the door before I can even say anything. My heart wants nothing more than to follow her, make sure Silas is still sitting and looking like a grumpy cave troll in a hot as fuck suit. But I know he is.

What, is he going to jump over the boards and start defending the goal in that sleek Armani getup? No. Instead, I start worrying about other things.

My very first Mobility Monday is tomorrow. In order to be prepared, I've gone a little bit overboard. I print individualized mobility cards for Monday's launch. Each one has a QR code linking to short demonstration videos I filmed in Silas's living room last night while he was locked in his bedroom. Leading the players through the process, talking about the upsides of what I hope to add to their routines. Even some basic yoga poses.

I also add a stack of Mobility Mondays paperwork. Basically, it's a syllabus of what we're going to be doing and a simple survey to establish a baseline for each player. I get caught up in my work and don't even realize the game's over until Coach Cross and Coach Ryan come in, talking about what they could've done differently to win the game.

The team lost, then. I frown. Heading outside into the tunnel, I realize not only did I lose track of time, but I didn't talk to Silas about taking a rideshare home together. Damn.

He's gone by the time I track down my coat and purse. When I get in the door, his bedroom door's closed, the light off. It must've been a tiring game for him.

I curl up in my room with my phone and my lists spread out on the bed beside me. The Naughty List stares back at me, all those filthy things I told Jessa I wanted but have never been brave enough to actually do.

My thumbs fly across the screen before I can talk myself out of it.

YOGA4LYFE

I had a long day. My roommate's an ass.
The only bright spot is talking to you.

The reply comes fast.

STATMAN12

That sucks. You live with a guy or a girl?

YOGA4LYFE

A guy. And he's impossible. He's needy and cold at the same time. He always seems like he doesn't know what he wants.

STATMAN12

I know what I want. You.

My breath catches. Heat floods through me, settling low in my belly.

STATMAN12

Tell me what you want most. Don't lie to me.

I type before fear can stop me.

YOGA4LYFE

I want you to get me off. Talk me through it. Tell me exactly what to do.

The reply is instant.

STATMAN12

Lie back. Don't rush this. Drag your fingers slow over your clit until you're shaking.

YOGA4LYFE

You're insane. I can't just...

But my hand's already sliding under the waistband of my sleep shorts.

STATMAN12

Keep your legs spread. Use two fingers. Circle, don't press hard. Not yet.

YOGA4LYFE

Oh god. I'm already wet.

My breath hitches as I follow his instructions. My thighs tremble with the effort of going slow when everything in me wants to rush.

STATMAN12

Good girl. Now spit on your fingers. I want you wet and messy before you even slide inside.

YOGA4LYFE

Fuck. You're ruining me.

I do it anyway, cheeks burning hot, shocked at myself for following orders from a stranger. For trusting him to know what I need better than I know myself.

STATMAN12

Imagine it's my tongue. Every stroke, every circle. Pretend I'm there holding you down so you can't squirm away.

YOGA4LYFE

I can feel it. I can feel you.

My hips buck against my palm. I bite my lip hard enough to hurt while I try to stay quiet. If I make sounds, they might carry through the walls to where Silas is probably working or watching film or doing whatever he does in his dark bedroom.

STATMAN12

When you can't stand it anymore, push two fingers inside. Curl them up. Think about how I'd fill you.

YOGA4LYFE

Ohhhhhh. Fuck.

My body arches off the bed, needy and raw. I can't believe I'm typing through the shaking. Honestly, I can't believe I'm doing this at all.

STATMAN12

Don't come yet. Edge yourself. Hold it right there. I want you whimpering before you let go.

YOGA4LYFE

You're cruel. I can't... please.

Please?

My thighs are quivering. My stomach's tight with the ache of holding back. Everything in me wants to tip over the edge but I force myself to wait. I can obey this man.

I want to. I keep picturing StatMan as a big, bulky hockey player. One who happens to look a lot like my current roommate. Big body, blond hair, intense broody expression.

Oh yeah. That does it for me. I whimper.

STATMAN12

When I say so, rub harder. Faster. Grind into your palm. Say my name when you break.

YOGA4LYFE

Oh my god oh my god... please...

My moans spill into the quiet room. I grab a pillow and press it to my face, muffling the sounds.

STATMAN12

Now.

Permission crashes over me like a wave. My body seizes,

back arching, fingers working frantically as the orgasm rips through me. Unstoppable. Humiliating. Glorious.

I drop the phone, chest heaving. My whole body shakes with aftershocks.

Another buzz.

STATMAN12

After you come, don't close your legs. Stay open. Stay wet. Imagine me licking you clean.

I gasp into the dark, reaching for my phone with trembling hands.

YOGA4LYFE

That was... I can't even...

STATMAN12

You're perfect. I wish I could see you right now.

YOGA4LYFE

I'm a mess.

STATMAN12

The best kind of mess.

I lie there in the dark, phone clutched to my chest, trying to catch my breath. Trying to process what just happened. I'm not going to think about the fact Silas is right next door and I just came thinking about hands that might be his.

Off limits, I tell myself. *He's completely off limits.* All men are supposed to be off limits this year. That was the deal I made with myself. Focus on work. Focus on building something that's mine. No distractions.

My body doesn't care about deals or rules or the fact that getting involved with anyone right now would be a terrible idea.

I roll over and close my eyes. My body hums with the afterglow, warm and sated and impossibly alive.

Chapter Twelve

Silas

Practice is supposed to be routine. Light bag skate, zone exit drills, nothing that should light me up or make my shoulder scream. But Connor Li cuts too sharp on a crossover. I'm already committed to closing the gap.

We collide.

The impact isn't hard enough to make the boards sing, but my bad shoulder takes the full brunt. Pain rips down my arm like lightning. It's white-hot, immediate, and mean as hell.

"Oh, fuck." I bite it down, jaw locked tight, and finish the drill skating backwards like nothing happened.

Coach Ryan blows his whistle at me. He barks, "Silas! Get off the ice. You're in a No Contact red jersey. That means NO CONTACT!"

I skate toward the bench. My shoulder throbs and sends little ripples of pain through my body. I try to tune it out and pretend my body isn't falling apart. My trainer Mike gestures from the boards, face tight with concern. I wave him off. "I'm fine."

Mike gives me a skeptical look. "No contact. This is serious, Silas. If you can't do that, I'll pull you."

My muscles go rigid with defiance because weakness isn't an option. It never has been. Between clenched teeth, I manage, "I hear you."

By the time practice ends, the shoulder's screaming. I strip out of my gear in silence, ignoring the way my right arm won't lift without a visible hitch.

In the locker room, trainers Mike and Annie hover near my stall.

"You're stiff on that right side," Annie says.

I won't be on the injured reserve list for a second longer than I have to be, so I just reply with a stone-faced, "No."

Mike considers me for a long moment. "We literally watched you wince."

"Coincidence," I offer.

"Uh-huh," Annie says, rolling her eyes.

They don't push. They don't need to. Their eyes say everything. I hit the showers, relaxing when my aching shoulder's under the radioactively-hot spray. I release a tense breath. See, when I'm under the heat, my shoulder feels okay-ish. I just need more of that. A heat wrap, maybe.

Beck Tate corners me near the showers before I can escape. "You need to let them look at it."

I try to play it off. "I said I'm fine."

"You're compensating. We can all see it." His voice is flat, factual. It's worse than if he was shouting. "If you won't listen to the trainers, you'll sit out."

The threat lands like a body check to the chest. Sitting means losing ice time. Losing ice time means losing my spot. Losing my spot means I'm done. I'd be finished and washed up at twenty-six.

I can't be done yet. I've devoted my entire life to hockey.

My older brothers are still playing. I'm not ready to let this dream get ripped away.

"I'll... behave," I say.

"Scout will monitor your recovery. She'll report back to the coaches. You can continue with practice if you're cleared, but she tracks everything. She's got a mobility routine, and you're the perfect test run for it."

My throat goes tight. "I don't need a babysitter."

"Then don't act like you do. The team needs you, Silas." Beck walks away before I can form a response.

The team. Well, that's a hard response to combat.

The thought of Scout's hands on me again makes my chest feel too tight. My body remembers exactly how those small, strong hands felt pressing into the knot in my shoulder. The sounds I made. The way I got hard and had to flee the room before she noticed.

God, I'm so incredibly fucked.

"Huxley." I look up to find Coach Cross watching me, his concern evident in his gaze. "How are you dealing with being benched?"

I lick my top lip, unsure what answer he's looking for. "Fine."

Coach walks over to me, his expression unreadable. He offers me a business card on heavy linen stock. There, in an expensive-looking font, is a name.

Dr. Sable Sports Psychology & Performance Conditioning

Flipping it over, I find a list of ways to contact her on the back of the card. Looking up at Coach Cross, I arch a brow. "What's this for?"

"That's our sports psychologist." Coach puts his hands in his pockets, appearing relaxed. "I want you to make an appointment with her."

"What?" I'm startled. "Why?"

He studies me for a beat and then sits down on one of the trainers' rolling stools. "I'm going to shoot it to you straight. You're under a lot of pressure from trainers and the coaching staff and even fans to keep performing at the highest level, despite your body showing signs of wear and tear. Two years ago, you had an MCL sprain and a groin strain that showed up a few times. Then last year, it was a repeated wrist sprain and a concussion. Now it's your shoulder."

I rub at my right shoulder, his words landing on me like they're made of lead.

I snipe, "Are you saying I should stop being an aggressive D-man?"

"Silas." Coach's expression tightens and he heaves a sigh. "You've had an excellent career so far. Even on a team that's going through a period of rebuilding, you shine. It's clear to everyone you give 110% and leave everything on the ice. They call you Ice Man, and yeah, it's because you're willing to freeze yourself out. Ignore pain, push through injuries, sacrifice your body for the team. That's admirable. It's also unsustainable."

The Ice Man nickname. I've worn it like armor for years. Better to be called cold than to let anyone see the desperation underneath. Better to be a machine than to admit I'm terrified of being replaced, of losing the only thing I've ever been good at.

Coach sees through it anyway.

"You've had an excellent career so far," he continues. "But you have to come to grips with the fact your body can't take this kind of punishment forever."

An icy jolt hits me square in the sternum. "Are you saying I should retire? Or… are you going to trade me?"

"No! No." Coach grabs my forearm and gives it a

squeeze. He's not the most affectionate guy, so him touching me at all is startling. "You should be prepared, though. You need someone who knows the ins and outs of athletic careers to help you figure out whether you want to keep playing for the Havoc or not. When the right time will be to start easing up, letting younger defenders take the big hits. And eventually, how to leave the Havoc on your own terms." He eyes me. "Assuming you get the choice. Not every player does."

That troublesome ache that lives in my shoulder has landed right where my heart beats. "You think I'm on my way out?"

"I think it would be wise for you to talk to Dr. Sable. Figure out what your priorities are. Make a plan for your life after hockey. I'm not in any hurry to see you leave, Silas. There aren't many defenders like you in the world. I'd have a hundred of you if I could. The reality is I don't control what happens out there on the ice any more than you do. Your last game could be three years from now. Or if you don't start taking your PT more seriously, it could be next month."

That scenario steals my breath from my lungs. "I won't... I won't let my shoulder keep me down. I'll work on it, I promise."

"You need to talk to a professional." Coach points at the card I'm clutching. "Make an appointment with her. She doesn't work for the team, so you have zero fear of her leaking your conversations to the Havoc. Hopefully, seeing her will give you the kick in the ass to jump start your physical therapy."

"I'll make an appointment." My chest feels tight. "I won't let you down, Coach."

"You never have." Coach stands up. "Now go take care of yourself."

After spending the next hour hitting the ice bath, getting a massage, and having my shoulder taped, I'm still turning his words over in my head. The end of my career has never seriously been part of the discussion. I wander through the locker room, shell-shocked.

What is happening to my life?

When I round the corner toward the parking lot, that's when I nearly run straight into Enzo.

He's leaning against the wall like he owns it, suit perfectly pressed, smile slick as oil. Everything about him makes my teeth grind.

"Huxley." His voice is smooth. Too smooth. "I heard Scout's living with you now. Cozy arrangement."

I grunt and move to step past him. He shifts to block my path.

"Listen, man to man." His smile sharpens into something uglier. "You don't want to get tangled up with her. She's clingy. Hovering. Smothering. It's cute at first, sure, but then it drags you down like an anchor wrapped around your neck. Trust me, I lived with her for six years."

I can't put into words exactly how much I don't care about his shitty opinions. Heat flashes through my chest and my hands curl into fists. "Back off."

He claps me on my good shoulder. "I'm your agent. It's my job to look out for you."

"You're my agent for business. Not my life." I step closer, using every inch of my size. "Scout's your ex. That means she's none of your concern. And you sure as hell don't get to tell me what to do."

Enzo's jaw ticks. Something flashes in his eyes. Anger maybe, or satisfaction he got a reaction. "Fine. But when you need to retire early because you're too broken to play, don't say I didn't warn you. We could find you something more suitable than a has-been ex-wife who couldn't even keep her own marriage together."

"Are you offering to be a matchmaker for me now? Isn't that a little fucking none of your business?"

My fist curls tighter. I want to swing. My greatest desire is to break Enzo's perfect teeth and shatter that smug smile. My arm pulls back half an inch before I catch myself.

I can't hit. Not here. Not with security cameras everywhere and media still lingering in the building. Even if I did get into a fight with Enzo, he's a tall, broad dude. And I'm injured.

It seems unwise, all things considered.

"I'm done with you," I say. My voice comes out low and lethal. "After my contract renewal closes, we're done. Find yourself a new client."

Enzo laughs, throwing me off balance. "You can't fire me, Huxley. I've got deals in motion. Equipment sponsors. Energy drink companies. Appearance fees. Endorsements worth millions. You walk away now, you lose all of it."

"I don't deal with bullshit like this. So make your deals, Enzo," I grit out. "But come February, you're gone. And if you say one more word about Scout, I'll fire you today. I'd rather take the financial hit than let you think for one second you control her or me."

I shove past him, shoulder burning, fists shaking. It's an effort not to turn around and finish this the way my body wants to.

He calls after me, voice echoing down the concrete hallway. "Scout drags partners down, Huxley. It's what she does. Don't say I didn't warn you."

I keep walking. If I stop, I'll do something I can't take back. Something that will end up on every sports news site and probably get me suspended.

The cold air in the parking lot hits my face like a slap. I stand there for a minute, breathing hard, trying to calm the rage burning through my chest.

Enzo's never done well with being told he can't touch something. Scout's a prime example. He had her and threw her away and now he can't stand that someone else might want what he discarded.

That night's game is a disaster.

We play like we've never met each other before. Passes die on sticks. Coverage gaps open wide enough to drive a truck through. I watch, dying inside, as my teammates can't seem to get their shit together. And I'm stuck here riding the bench, impossibly angry.

We lose by three.

Scout's waiting by my truck when I get to the parking lot. She's wrapped her arms around herself against the cold, breath coming out in visible clouds. Her dark blonde curls are wild from the wind, falling loose around her shoulders. She's in those black leggings that drive me crazy and an oversized Havoc hoodie that swallows her frame. No makeup, cheeks pink from the cold, green eyes tracking me as I approach. Even freezing and windblown, she's beautiful. Too beautiful for someone like me to deserve.

She doesn't ask how I'm feeling or offer empty platitudes. She just opens the driver's door and climbs in.

The drive back to my condo is silent. Tense. My mind spins through the game on repeat, looking for angles I missed, plays I could've made differently. The thing is, I give this sport every piece of me. Discipline in the kitchen, punishment in the gym, film until my vision blurs. Perfect habits don't guarantee results. Sometimes it still fails me.

As we head upstairs, Scout touches my arm. Her voice is

the same as her touch, light and careful. "It's okay to have an off night."

Her soft voice saying exactly what I need to hear cracks something in my chest. I sigh, shoulders dropping an inch. "Today was tough."

"I know." She unlocks the door to the condo. "Tomorrow will be too. Especially with finding a new agent."

I freeze halfway through the doorway. "How'd you know about that?"

"Enzo can't keep his mouth shut. He's already been texting people. Word travels fast in this organization." She doesn't look at me, just moves into the kitchen to fill a glass with water. "You should fire him. Why don't you?"

I look at her. "It's complicated."

"He treats you like garbage. How is that complicated?"

"He gets results." The same excuse I've used for three years. "Knows people. Knows how to work the system."

"That's worth putting up with him?"

"I didn't say that."

She crosses her arms. "So fire him."

"It's not that simple."

"Why not?"

My mother. The threats. The fallout. I'd rather be miserable than deal with any of it. I shake my head without answering.

"He crossed a line."

She waits for more, but I don't elaborate. And she doesn't push. Instead she sets the glass down and says, "Go change. If you sit on the couch, I'll give you a massage."

"Scout..."

"Sit, Silas."

The command in her voice makes my cock twitch. I hate it. I go change into sweats and a t-shirt anyway because the alternative is standing here arguing with her. It's been a long day and I'm too tired for that.

When I sit down, she moves behind me without a word. Her hands land on my shoulders and I tense immediately. My whole body goes rigid because if I'm not on high alert, I'll do something stupid.

I haven't been touched with care in years. Not like this. Her hands carry intention and warmth and the kind of attention that makes my chest feel too tight. Her palms on my shoulders, fingers pressing into muscle. The accidental brush of her thighs against my back when she shifts for better leverage. My body's been starving for this and now that I have it, I don't know what to do with the need it creates in me.

My head drops forward.

It feels too damn good to make her stop. Her thumbs work into the knots with firm, sure pressure. She knows exactly where to press, exactly how hard. Every stroke makes something in me unwind against my will.

"Where'd you learn this?" My voice comes out rough.

"Enzo had a nagging groin injury a few years ago. I learned sports massage in school, but I took another class in it to help him through the worst of it." She says it matter-of-fact, no emotion coloring her tone.

Jealousy knifes through me sharp and sudden. The thought of her hands on him. Rubbing him down, caring for him while he probably took it for granted. He probably cheated on her at the same time as she doted on him.

Fucking Enzo.

I have no right to this possessive rage. But the image makes my teeth grind together so hard my jaw aches.

"Done," I say abruptly, standing before I embarrass myself. Before my body's reaction to her touch becomes too obvious to hide.

"Okay." She doesn't sound offended. Just steps back and moves toward the kitchen. "I'll prep your morning shakes for the week."

"Thanks." It comes out gruff, ungrateful. She's too good. Too kind. Certainly too good for a man like me who can't even say thank you without sounding angry about it.

"You're welcome." Her surprised smile makes me feel even deeper shame.

I retreat to my room and close the door. Leaning against it, I try to breathe. My shoulder throbs. My cock throbs worse.

I pull out my phone and open up the dating app. Her username glows at the top of my messages.

I shouldn't do this. I know it's bad. Every rational part of my brain's screaming at me to stop before this gets more complicated than it already is.

And I do it anyway.

STATMAN12

Tell me about your day.

She responds a few minutes later. I hear her door close softly down the hall. Now I'm picturing her shedding clothes, curling up in that guest bed surrounded by pillows. My hand wraps around my cock through my sweatpants before I can stop myself.

YOGA4LYFE

Long. Frustrating. My roommate's in a mood.

STATMAN12

Forget him. Focus on me.

Yoga4Lyfe

> Bossy tonight.

STATMAN12

You like it when I'm bossy.

> YOGA4LYFE
>
> Maybe.

STATMAN12

Not maybe. You do. You like when I tell you exactly what to do.

The conversation slides fast. One teasing comment turns into breathing hard over our phones.

STATMAN12

What are you doing right now?

> YOGA4LYFE
>
> Lying in bed. Trying not to think about your hands on me.

STATMAN12

Don't try. Think about it. Think about me coming in, pushing you back, pinning your wrists to the mattress.

> YOGA4LYFE
>
> You'd pin me?

STATMAN12

I would hold you still so you can't squirm away when I take my time with you.

> YOGA4LYFE
>
> You're... intense tonight.

STATMAN12

You seem to like intense. Maybe you crave
someone who won't hesitate with you.

A beat. Three dots pulse. My pulse hammers with them.

YOGA4LYFE

What would you do next?

STATMAN12

Spread you open. Lick your clit, put my
fingers in your pussy. Eat you like you're a
Sunday roast until you forget your own
name. Until you beg for it.

YOGA4LYFE

God.

I'm touching myself already.

Heat punches through my gut.

STATMAN12

Slow down. You only move when I tell
you to.

YOGA4LYFE

Bossy again.

STATMAN12

Always. Now tell me exactly what your hand
is doing.

Silence. Then she responds.

YOGA4LYFE

My fingers are just... resting on my clit.
Barely there. Waiting for you.

I grip myself harder, breath ragged.

STATMAN12

Good girl. Don't move them yet. I want you
desperate for it.

YOGA4LYFE

I already am.

STATMAN12

Say it.

YOGA4LYFE

I want you. I want your mouth. I want you
holding me still and dominating me.

I swear under my breath and stroke faster, imagining her just down the hall, flushed and needy and waiting for a command.

I fist my cock properly now, groaning quietly into the dark of my room. I picture her in the room down the hall doing the same thing. It's wrong. It's a lie. But it's also the only thing keeping me from losing my mind completely.

YOGA4LYFE

I'm close already. Just thinking about you.

STATMAN12

Don't come yet. Wait for me.

YOGA4LYFE

You're killing me.

STATMAN12

Good. I like you needy.

I work myself faster, biting back sounds that would carry through the walls. My shoulder burns but I don't care. Everything narrows to this. Her words on my screen and the image in my head of what she looks like right now.

> **YOGA4LYFE**
> Please. I need to come.

> **STATMAN12**
> Now. Come for me now.

I follow my own command, spilling into my hand with a bitten-off groan. My whole body shakes with it. It takes a full minute for my vision to clear.

> **YOGA4LYFE**
> That was intense.

> **STATMAN12**
> You okay?

> **YOGA4LYFE**
> More than okay. I wish you were here.

> **STATMAN12**
> Me too.

And I mean it. God, I mean it so much it physically hurts.

> **YOGA4LYFE**
> I want to meet you. IRL. Soon.

My hand freezes on my phone. Panic floods cold through my chest, washing away the afterglow in an instant.

> **STATMAN12**
> Maybe. I travel a lot for work. My schedule's unpredictable.

YOGA4LYFE

> Then when you're back in town. Please? I
> feel like we have something real here.

STATMAN12

I'll let you know.

It's a coward's answer. A dodge. I can't give her what she's asking for. If I were to reveal that her gruff, broken roommate who snaps at her in the kitchen is the same man she's sharing her deepest fantasies with... If she knew, she'd run. She'd be horrified. Disgusted. She'd move out and I'd never see her again except in passing at the arena where she'd look through me like I'm nothing.

That's the worst case outcome.

I set the phone down and stare at the ceiling, heart hammering, cock softening, chest still tight with want and shame in equal measure.

I can hear her moving around in her room. She opens the door and goes into the bathroom. I try not to think about how close she is. It would be so easy to just get up, walk down the hall, knock on her door.

I already know it's impossible.

I lie awake for hours before exhaustion finally drags me under.

Chapter Thirteen

Scout

"I'm so glad you moved back to Seattle," I say while video chatting with my sister. "Living in Vancouver is cool, but living where I can actually hug you whenever I want is way better."

Sable has her phone propped on her desk so I can see her whole face. She's dressed for work in a cream sweater and tweed pencil skirt because she's a sports psychologist who actually has her life together.

Unlike some of us.

My big sister laughs. "The two Nash girls, back at it. We should plan a night out soon. Paint the whole town vermillion."

"As long as we stick to wine. Last time there were a lot of tequila shots. If I remember correctly, you puked behind a dumpster."

She feigns shock. "Would you rather I puked in the Uber? I was being responsible."

"Yeah, sure." I grin. "The last two rounds were your idea, Miss Thing. You were so busy flirting with those guys at the next table that I had to drag you home. You were a mess."

Sable snorts. "I was gorgeous."

I can't argue with that. Of the two of us, Sable has always been the homecoming queen. She's insanely pretty. Where my curls frizz at the first sign of humidity, hers fall in perfect spirals. Her blue eyes are sharp and intense. Even when she's not trying, she looks like magazine cover material.

I'm sunshine. Sable is firelight. Controlled, smoldering, impossible to ignore.

She's just back from Venice with her latest *this is definitely the one* boyfriend. I've been through this about fifteen times in ten years, so I just nod while she describes the trip. The city, the canals, the food, the architecture.

I listen while pinning my curls back and debating earrings.

"How's Josh?" I ask, leaning closer to apply mascara without stabbing myself in the eye.

"Oh." Sable sighs dramatically. "He dumped me. Apparently I'm too intense." She waves it off. "His loss. I love love, you know? Someday I'll find my Prince Charming. There's actually this cute guy at my coffee shop I'm going to ask out next week."

I make sympathetic sounds while changing into a soft dress. Nothing fancy, but nicer than my usual yoga pants and staff polo. The fabric actually shows that I have a shape under all the errands and coffee runs.

Sable notices mid-sentence. Her eyes widen. "Wait. Are you dressed up? What's going on?"

Heat climbs my cheeks. "Community skating event. It's just for work."

Sable leans closer, practically vibrating. "Just work? Scout, you're blushing. Is there something happening with the hockey player you're living with?"

I shut it down fast. "No. God, no. It's complicated. We're just roommates. Temporarily."

Her shoulders drop. "Sorry. I get so excited about relationship prospects, even if they're not mine." She looks wistful, vulnerable in a way Sable rarely shows. "I just want someone to stick around, you know?"

The admission makes my chest ache. We're not so different. Both chasing something we can't name. Both terrified of ending up alone. Growing up watching our father shatter after Mom's death really did a number on us.

"I know, Sabe." I glance at the time and panic. "Oh, shit. I have to go. But let's hang out soon, okay? I miss you."

"Miss you too, Girl Scout." Sable blows a kiss and the screen goes dark.

I check myself in the mirror. The dress is simple and modest, but it makes me feel pretty. Like maybe I'm more than just the smoothie-making, data-tracking girl who disappears into the background.

I grab my coat and head downstairs.

Silas is waiting by his truck in the parking deck, scowling at his phone. He's in dark jeans and a Havoc quarter-zip that shows off every muscle. His dirty blond hair is loose tonight, falling to his shoulders. Those blue-gray eyes flick up and I legit forget how to breathe for a second. Even scowling, he's unfairly handsome.

When he sees me, his jaw ticks. His eyes drag over my legs. His throat works.

I stop, glancing down at myself. "Do you think this will be okay?"

"You look... nice." His voice comes out rough. "Are you ready to go?"

"Yeah." I climb into the truck, cheeks warm.

The drive is silent except for the engine and the turn

signal. His scent is stronger here. Sandalwood, cedar, woodsmoke. Whoever makes his cologne deserves a Nobel Prize. I pretend I don't notice his white knuckles on the steering wheel or the way my heart hammers just from sitting next to him.

I'm a mess around this man.

The rink is trying way too hard when we arrive. There are banners everywhere, sponsor logos on every surface, and folding tables loaded with hot cocoa. There are even crafts for kids who'd rather be making snowflakes than skating.

I smooth my dress, suddenly feeling overdressed compared to all the staff polos. I might've overthought this.

At the entrance, I spot Enzo lurking near the boards in his usual sharp suit and smug smile. My stomach drops. Without a word, Silas drapes an arm around my shoulders. His hand curls over my arm like he's claiming me. He shoots Enzo a territorial glare.

Thank god. Silas doesn't know I told Enzo we were together, so now I don't have to awkwardly engineer this moment.

Not the best feeling in the world, but I've known worse.

"Stick close to me." Silas watches Enzo like he's plotting murder. "Fuck your ex."

I raise my eyebrows. "Enzo's going to think we're together."

No need to fill in the part where Enzo thinks that because I told him so.

Silas shrugs, voice low and rough. "So what? Like I said, fuck him."

My heart kicks hard against my ribs, pulse stumbling over itself. Silas usually moves through the world like the darkest thundercloud, all tension and thunder building behind his eyes. Tonight, that same storm has stepped in front of me, bracing itself between me and the man who once made me feel small. Relief's so sharp it's almost dizzying.

Dismissing Enzo, Silas keeps his arm around me and walks me down to the benches where kids are already skating clumsy circles on the ice. I grab rental skates and lace them up quickly. Years of being married to a hockey player means I learned to skate well enough. Enzo dragged me to enough team events that I had to get comfortable on the ice.

When I step onto the rink, muscle memory takes over. I'm not doing any fancy footwork but I can glide smoothly enough to help wrangle the kids.

Silas watches me from the boards, something unreadable crossing his face. Surprise, maybe. Or appreciation. His eyes track my movements as I skate backward to demonstrate proper form for a group of giggling kids.

Jessa glides up next to me, cheeks pink from the cold. "Look at you go. I didn't know you could skate like that."

"Enzo made sure I learned." I shrug, helping a little boy in a blue helmet find his balance. "He hated showing up to events with a wife who couldn't stay upright on the ice."

"Of course he did." Jessa rolls her eyes. "Well, at least you got something useful out of that disaster of a marriage."

I laugh despite myself and we split up to help different groups of kids. I spend the next hour teaching basic stops and starts, catching wobbly beginners before they face-plant, and racing a few of the more confident kids around the rink. It's fun. Easy. One of the few things I can do without second-guessing myself.

When I circle back toward the boards, Silas is still there, arms crossed, watching. His expression's softer than usual. Almost... impressed?

"You're good at this," he says when I skate up to him.

"Thanks." I'm breathless, cheeks flushed from exertion and cold. "I had a lot of practice."

His jaw tightens at the mention of Enzo, but he doesn't say anything. Just keeps looking at me like he's seeing something new. Something he hadn't noticed before.

Hunter appears at Silas's elbow, grinning. "You gonna get out there and help, Ice Man? Or just stand around looking pretty?"

Silas growls something under his breath, but he grabs skates and laces them up. When he steps onto the ice, he's all power and grace. Completely different from the careful, measured way he moves off the ice with his injured shoulder. Out here, he's in his element.

Confident, commanding, and beautiful.

I try not to stare, but I fail miserably.

We work opposite sides of the rink for a while. Him with the older kids who want to learn slap shots, me with the younger ones still mastering forward momentum. Every so often, our eyes meet across the ice. Every time, my stomach does a little flip.

It's Jessa who eventually skates up with that knowing look on her face. "So," she says, drawing out the word. "Roommate, huh?"

My face burns hotter than the rink lights. "He's just... he's very nice."

"Nice." Jessa repeats the word flat and skeptical. "That's not exactly the word I'd use for Silas Huxley. More... hmm. Gruff and thorny?"

I try to defend him, breathless and fumbling. "He is nice, though. When you get past all the growling and scowling, he's actually really sweet."

"Oh!" Understanding dawns on her face. "Oh my god, you've got a crush on him."

"What? No." My face heats and I shake my head emphatically. "We're just friends. Not even that. Friendly, at times. It's really noth—"

A kid crashes into my legs and I stumble, catching myself on the boards. Jessa doesn't look swayed by my argument, but she rushes to check on the kid. When she gets him upright and skating again, she lets the subject drop.

Phew. I need her questioning me like I need a hole in the head.

I spend the rest of the event helping kids, occasionally glancing at Silas across the ice. He's good with them, patient in a way I didn't expect. Stoic, sure, but gentle when it counts.

By the end of the night, my legs ache in that good way that comes from real exercise. My cheeks hurt from smiling at kids and their parents. Despite spending two hours on my feet, I feel energized instead of drained.

Unfortunately, Enzo finds me near the exit while I'm unlacing my rental skates.

"Still slaving away for the Havoc, I see." His voice is slick and cutting, his face twisted in a sneer. "I'm sure you were mostly upset because you couldn't chase after the players and hover over them constantly. You know you drag people down with all that smothering, right? It's why I had to get out. You were suffocating me."

The old wound splits wide open. My throat tightens.

"Enzo, did you come to this event just to be mean to me?"

He looks amused. "No. I rep a lot of the players on the ice. You're the one who isn't supposed to be here."

Fixing him with a look, I sigh, "I don't understand why we keep having the same argument. We're divorced. I swear, I hear more complaints from you now than when we were married."

Enzo looks over my shoulder, sucking in a breath. That's

the only warning I have before Tropical Storm Silas rolls up, furious.

"Say one more word to her, loser. Do it. I'm begging you." Silas points a finger in Enzo's face. "I'll drag you somewhere private so I can put you out of your misery, you ugly sack of shit."

Enzo raises his hands in mock surrender, that smug smile still in place. He's flushed though, right around his hairline. That's Enzo's tell. He plays it cool, but I can see he's sweating.

He says, "Just a little friendly advice between exes, Huxley. No need to get territorial."

"Fuck off. I don't want to see you in the arena anymore, Morelli." Silas is spitting mad.

"For her?" Enzo snorts. "She's not worth it. But I guess you'll find that out for yourself."

Silas lunges toward Enzo, who stumbles back over a bleacher seat. When Silas bares his teeth, Enzo continues to back away.

"Are you okay?" Silas asks me.

Pressing my lips into a firm line, I nod. Silas doesn't wait around, choosing instead to follow Enzo out. Maybe he's making sure his agent really leaves.

The damage is done. I'm left trembling in the aftermath, my hands shaking as I finish taking off my skates. I don't know if Silas defended me because he actually cares, or if he just wanted to flex his power over Enzo. Either way, it leaves me unsure and confused.

An hour later, alone in my room at Silas's condo, I log the Mobility Monday data on my laptop. Two players mentioned their backs feeling better after the stretches I prescribed. Juliet cc'd me on a *nice work* email to the GM. Small victories that should make me feel proud.

Instead, I curl on my side with my phone clutched tight. The emptiness yawns wide in my chest.

Before bed, I unroll my yoga mat on the floor, trying to center myself. The stretches are familiar, grounding. I move through sun salutations, warrior poses, breathing deep. Yoga can't quite shake the feeling that I'm caught between two impossible things. Two men who want me in completely different ways, neither of which feels complete.

I roll up the mat and tuck it away, no calmer than when I started.

Silas only half-claimed me tonight. He put his arm around me to make a point to Enzo, but didn't actually say anything about liking me or even being able to tolerate me. He's willing to say something to his agent if Enzo's downright rude to me, but that's all.

Money and career and Enzo being Silas's agent still chain him. I feel alone even with the memory of his hands on my waist burned across my skin.

So I do what I do best. When faced with the awfulness of my daily life, I retreat into the world I've created and open the dating app.

I know it's bad, but I need validation.

YOGA4LYFE

Can I be the worst sexting buddy ever and just vent for a second?

After a few moments, I see the three dots appear. He's typing something.

STATMAN12

Hello to you too. Vent away.

The speed of his response warms the frozen, achy place

inside me. He may not really know me, but he's interested in what I have to say. At least, he pretends to be.

YOGA4LYFE

> Sometimes I feel like I don't matter. I'm always on the outside, my nose pressed against the window, trying to figure out how other people make connections.

Dots appear and disappear for a minute. Then:

STATMAN12

> You do matter. Every filthy thing you say to me, every confession, every want. You're perfect. If I had you in front of me right now, I'd show you exactly how much you matter. I'd worship every inch of you until you believed it.

I hide my face in the pillow, whispering, "Oh God". Heat rolls through me.

YOGA4LYFE

> I had a rough night. Someone said something that got under my skin.

STATMAN12

> Tell me who. I'll handle it.

The protective tone makes my chest squeeze tight. He can't actually handle it. He doesn't even know who I am or where I live or anything real about my life. The intent behind the words settles something in me anyway.

YOGA4LYFE

> My ex. He always knows exactly what to say to make me feel small.

STATMAN12

He's an idiot. You're not small. You're not
anything he said you are.

YOGA4LYFE

You've never met me.

STATMAN12

I know you're strong and kind and braver
than you give yourself credit for.

Tears sting my eyes. I blink them back, typing with shaking hands.

YOGA4LYFE

Thank you. I needed to hear that tonight.

STATMAN12

Anytime. I mean it. If you need reminding,
I'm here.

YOGA4LYFE

I wish I could meet you. For real.

StatMan12: Soon. I promise.

YOGA4LYFE

You keep saying that.

STATMAN12

I know. I'm sorry. It's complicated right now.

YOGA4LYFE

Is it? Or are you just scared?

The three dots appear and disappear several times. Like he's typing and deleting responses.

STATMAN12

Maybe both. I don't want to ruin this by making it real and having it not live up to what we have here.

YOGA4LYFE

Or maybe it would be even better.

STATMAN12

Maybe I'd just disappoint you.

The vulnerability in that admission cracks something open in my chest.

YOGA4LYFE

I don't think you could. I think you're probably amazing and don't even realize it.

He doesn't reply to that. I set my phone on the nightstand, not wanting to push too hard, and stare at the ceiling. Down the hall, I hear Silas moving around in his room. He's probably getting ready for bed. He's certainly not thinking about me at all.

My lips part and a small, sad sigh escapes.

Two men exist in my life right now. Silas, who touches me in the real world but won't give me the time of day otherwise. And StatMan, who claims my attention through my phone screen but won't meet me in person.

I don't know which one of the men I'm more let down by. All I know is I'm tired of feeling invisible. I'm useful, but I'm not wanted. I can shrink myself to fit into tiny spaces, but they were never meant for me in the first place.

I set my phone aside and stare at the ceiling. The conversation with StatMan should've made me feel better, but it only highlights what's missing. He wants me through a screen. Silas wants me at arm's length.

Neither one is enough.

Chapter Fourteen

Silas

The BeastMode+ Endurance Drink sponsorship gala is everything I hate. Bright lights. Fake smiles. Men in suits who measure your worth by your last stat line and whether you'll move product. I'm stuffed into a jacket that feels like a straitjacket, tie strangling me slowly, standing in a ballroom that smells like money and cologne that's trying too hard. I feel like a circus sideshow act that's being brought out and paraded around.

Look at the freak! Isn't he terrifying?

It doesn't help that I tower over everyone else, or that I'm built like a big, boxy refrigerator that knows how to skate. They call me Ice Man. I let everyone think that's all I am, because it's easier than admitting the truth.

I'm not cold. I'm just terrified of letting anyone close enough to see how badly I want things I can't have. So I play the part. Stone-faced. Unaffected. Frosty inside and out. Better to be the machine than to let them see me break.

"Silas!" Enzo spots me. It isn't hard, even in this crowd of giants from my team. I stand out no matter where I go. Enzo might be tall and look good in a designer suit, but he's easily almost half a foot shorter than me.

A vindictive little voice in the back of my head whispers, *Scout notices the height difference. She'd probably be excited that my dick is bigger than Enzo's, too.*

Keeping the smirk off my face is impossible.

"Enzo." I cut through the crowd easily, because people naturally move out of my way. It's the same here as it is on the ice. "I'd say it's nice to see you, but we both know that would be a lie."

Enzo gives me an oily smile. I size him up, wondering how sugar-sweet Scout ever fell for this idiot. He's going to tolerate whatever comes out of my mouth because I make him a fat paycheck.

"Circulate," he says. "The sponsors are looking for someone intelligent and personable. We're trying to sell you as that combo."

I nod, looking around. Mostly I'm thinking that I should just cut Enzo loose right now. Yeah, he is making deals for me. He's brought me a lot of success. But I can't even look at him without feeling guilty.

Scout is my temporary roommate and nothing more, but I still feel a lot of loyalty to her. Even though I have no real reason to, other than despising Enzo's treatment of Scout.

"Hey." Enzo snaps his fingers at me. "Go talk to the sponsors. Try not to be a fucking caveman. This is a six-inch tap-in, Huxley. Don't let it bounce off your damn stick."

Glaring at him, I shake my head and move toward a group of BeastMode execs. They're the shortest men in this room and have been cackling amongst themselves the entire time I've been here. I suck in a deep breath and put my game face on.

I can do this. One more obligation I have to grit my teeth through before I can finally cut him loose.

Working my way over to the group, I introduce myself. There are the usual joking comments about my height and frame. Questions about how I keep my fitness level so high, as if I don't work out four to eight hours per day, every day. Talk about the product and how I could fit it into my routine to maximize my workouts. Blah blah blah.

"I'm actually already a fan," I lie. "I'd... uh... be excited to represent a product I actually use."

I've never once tasted BeastMode+, but I'm sure it has the same sickly sweet fake cherry flavor as every other endurance drink I've ever had. One of the execs claps me on the arm because he's too short to reach my shoulder. He tells me the team's very interested in me and my story.

Great. Just great. Someone just shoot me now and put me out of my misery.

Out of the corner of my eye, I see Scout. She has a clipboard and a headset. She's wearing a black dress that hits just above her knees. It's modest and professional, though seeing her in a semi-dressy outfit does something to me.

But the way it fits her body isn't professional at all. Not to me. Her curls are pulled back, showing her neck. She's not trying to be noticed. Too bad that's not remotely possible. Has she even seen herself in the mirror lately? All curves and temptation.

I stare, willing my cock to calm down. I didn't know she'd be here tonight. If I had, I would've asked her to be my date. Not that she enjoys my company or anything. But at least I could hover close and put my hand on her lower back.

I'm pathetic. So desperate for affection I'm dreaming of stealing it in public where she can't make a scene.

I watch Scout adjust a banner that's crooked. A waiter

passes by her and she grabs him, pointing to a group that's looking around for service. She smiles at a sponsor's wife who looks lost and engages her for a few moments. The BeastMode execs mill around me, making jokes and suggesting promo ideas.

But my eyes are only for Scout. She's always working. She makes everyone else's life easier while she disappears into the background.

It makes me want to drag her front and center. Everyone should get to see what I see.

As I watch Scout, Theo Kozlov corners her near the refreshment table. Kozlov's a rookie defenseman with a cocky smile and hair gelled within an inch of its life. He leans in too close, hand gesturing at the room like he's offering her the world on a platter. My whole body tightens.

It's so loud in here. I can't hear what he's saying from across the ballroom, but I can read her body language. The way she takes a half step back, the tightness in her smile that doesn't reach her eyes, the polite shake of her head. Scout is willing and soft, but she doesn't want whatever he's selling.

Kozlov is young, overenthusiastic, and used to women who swoon whenever he swings his attention their way. So even though Scout's eyes dart around, looking for a way to escape, he keeps talking anyway. He gestures at himself, then at her, then at the crowd of photographers setting up near the entrance. My jaw locks when I realize what he's asking.

He wants her on his arm for photos like she's some kind of pricey accessory. Proof he's important enough to have a pretty girl next to him for the cameras. Scout sucks in a breath and looks unhappy. But in the next second, she bobs her head and starts toward the photographers. And because he's a fucking moron, Kozlov signs his own death warrant by touching the small of her back as he urges her onward.

I see her stiffen, her cheeks coloring. Oh, he's a fucking dead man walking.

Before I even decide to move, I'm crossing the ballroom in long strides, shoulders squared. The fire that's always present for me, smoldering, ignites like a wildfire that fills my veins with red-hot fury. Everything in me is coiled tight and ready to snap.

"...just think it would be good for both of us," Theo's saying when I get close enough to hear. All charm and zero awareness. "You'd look great in the photos. I could use someone who knows how to work a room. Win-win, right?"

"I'm not sure you want to pick me. I'm on the team's payroll," she says, her voice hushed. "It might look a little... fake?"

"Nahhh." He drapes his arm around her shoulders, which makes me see red. That arm might be better off dislocated and separated from his corpse.

"Get the fuck away from her," I growl. Lunging, I separate them. I'm not even sorry about using my size to make him take a step back. His eyes widen and he drops his arm, stuttering.

"Hey, man. I didn't see you coming. I—" He licks his lips and looks to her for help. Pathetic. "We were just going to take some photos."

"She's not a prop, Kozlov. Get your own damn dates."

Theo blinks, startled. His cocky smile falters. "Whoa, man, I was just..."

"You were just leaving." My voice drops lower, lethal. "And if I ever hear you talk to her like that again, I'll make sure you spend the rest of the season riding the bench. Or playing in the minors. Your choice."

His face goes red. He mutters something that might be an apology and bolts like his ass is on fire.

Scout's hand lands on my chest before I can chase after him. Warm and small. Her touch steadies me in a way that makes me want to cover it with my own.

I haven't been touched like this in so long. Not with care. Not even to calm me down. Her palm burns through my shirt. Every nerve ending screams for more contact. I want to grab her wrist and hold her there. I'm desperate to pull her closer, but I don't.

She looks up at me, those green eyes searching my face. "Silas. Calm down."

I look down at her. Her eyes are wide, worried but not afraid. She seems concerned for me, not about me. The realization knocks something loose in my chest.

I touch her shoulders, rubbing them slightly. "You all right?"

"Of course." She's still touching me. "He was just being a rookie. I would've done it."

"That doesn't make it okay."

Before she can answer, Enzo materializes with two Beast-Mode reps trailing behind him. Perfect timing, as always. His eyes land on Scout's hand on my chest, and something ugly flashes across his face.

I nod at the reps. Keep my mouth shut. It's easy enough to let Enzo do his job while I silently plan his firing in excruciating detail. My hand comes up to gently brush against Scout's back. It's hard to pretend interest in this fucking conversation when all I want is to drag Scout out of this room and somewhere quieter to resume our conversation.

I'm pretty sure it's going to lead to me kissing her senseless.

One of the suits gestures at Scout with his drink. "And who's this lovely young lady?"

Before I can answer or introduce her properly with the respect she deserves, Enzo laughs. He's putting on a show.

"Oh, that's Scout. She works as a gopher for the Havoc." He grins like he's sharing an inside joke. "We're here to talk about my man Silas, not to meet all the support staff."

The words land like a punch to the gut. Scout's cheeks turn bright pink but her expression stays neutral. It's clear to me she's been hit like this before and learned to hide the damage.

My fists curl at my sides. Everything in me goes cold and sharp and deadly focused.

"Actually," I find myself shouting more than starting. "Scout's with me. My, uh, girlfriend." I slide my arm around her waist and squeeze her close. "Isn't that right, baby?"

Scout stares up at me, her expression startled. "Uh... yes?"

Enzo stares at us, his expression strained. "Right. Girlfriend."

The exec seems blithely unaware of our tensions. "It's nice to meet the woman who tamed Silas Huxley. You know, they're calling him Defense Daddy over on TikTok. I'm assuming you get treated pretty nice, huh?"

"Oh." Scout's cheeks turn from pink to a mottled fuchsia. Her gaze falls to the ground before us and sticks there. "Uh, yep."

"I knew it." The guy has the fucking stones to elbow me and wink. "You guys make a cute couple."

Enzo snorts. Everyone looks at him and he seems to realize he's not getting paid if he doesn't make me look like a catch. "They're really something," is the best he can come up with.

"Thanks, Enzo." Ignoring him, I stare down at Scout, but she's busy picking at a loose thread on her dress. "Why don't you go sit down? Take a breather. I'll come find you when I'm ready to leave."

"Oh." Scout looks up at me, her eyes filled with questions. "Okay. Sounds good, Si."

Her pet name hits me hard. She's just playing the game, but hearing her chosen pet name makes my cock stir.

Enzo stares a hole in my chest as I finish up with the BeastMode+ execs, then excuse myself. I head to the open bar. I'm not normally a drinker, but this is an exception. My brother Jett appears at my elbow, nursing a whiskey that's mostly ice. His expression is dark.

I feel his heavy gaze on me. "What?"

"I saw what just went down."

I accept a beer from the bartender, my lips twisting. "Still eavesdropping, huh?"

"Enzo makes your girl uncomfortable and yet, he's still walking around." His voice is low and serious. "What the fuck is wrong with you?"

"She's not my girl." The words taste like ash in my mouth. "She's just crashing with me because the organization made her take care of me. It's a temporary arrangement."

"Yeah? Just in a casual relationship with the girl you've been in love with for years?"

The back of my neck heats. "I am not in love with Scout."

"That's not what I heard." He jerks his thumb over his shoulder. "You just called her your girlfriend. I don't think you've ever had a girlfriend."

"Dude." I roll my eyes. "I was just saying that to get Enzo's goat. He talks about her like she fucked him over in the divorce. But I think it was the exact opposite."

Jett straightens his tie while giving me a look. "So you're saying that not only do you not love her, but you aren't desperately trying to figure out how to wife her?"

Taking a long sip of beer gives me time to make my reply believable. "That's what I'm saying, Jett. Scout and I aren't even friendly."

He gives me a look that says he doesn't believe a single word of it. "Sure. And I'm the king of Spain. Keep telling yourself that, big guy."

I don't answer. I grab my beer and watch the door, waiting for Scout to come back so I can make sure she's okay. I need to see her face and know if I made things better or worse by antagonizing Enzo.

She doesn't reappear for twenty minutes. When she does, her smile's back in place. Professional. Helpful. She acts like nothing happened.

Something feels different, though. I can still feel her hand pressed against my chest. God help me, I fucking want that again.

The rest of the event blurs together. Handshakes with people whose names I forget immediately. Forced smiles for photographers. Promises I'll play better next season, sell more jerseys, be the kind of player sponsors want on their billboards. I do it all on autopilot, but my mind's stuck on the way Enzo's words landed. The way Scout's face went blank.

I should've hit him, but I didn't. Part of me wonders if I shouldn't just find him and wail on him for good measure. Sure, it would piss the sponsor off. But it would feel so *good*.

"Ready to go?" Scout asks. I blink and realize the room has mostly emptied. I grunt and follow her.

Thank god she's not still insisting on driving. Since I've gotten the all clear from the doctor to return to the ice, I've taken back this small measure of control. Driving back to the condo is a silent affair. Scout stares out the window, chewing on her bottom lip. I keep my eyes on the road and try to think of something to say that won't sound hollow or useless.

Nothing comes.

When we get inside, Scout takes off her heels. I stand in the foyer, feeling awkward and I study her. It's usually easy to tell what she's feeling from her expression, but she keeps her head down. Maybe hiding from me, I realize.

"Are you okay?"

Her lips turn up in the ghost of a smile, but she doesn't look at me. "Thanks for pretending to be my boyfriend."

Then without another word, she disappears into her room and closes the door with a soft click. I stand in the hallway for a full minute, staring at that closed door, wanting to knock and knowing I don't have the right.

I retreat to my bedroom with the door locked and the lights off. My phone glows in my hand, the app open, her username staring up at me like an accusation.

I know it's wrong, but if I text Scout, I know I can ask her about her feelings. And because StatMan is anonymous, there's a chance that she'll tell him all about it.

God, if she ever finds out I've been milking her for information, there will be hell to pay. I can already see her packing up and moving out. Too bad that doesn't stop me from texting her.

STATMAN12

Tell me about your day.

She doesn't answer right away. It's long enough that I start to panic. I imagine her deleting the app, blocking me, moving on to someone who isn't a coward hiding behind a screen.

Then her reply comes through.

YOGA4LYFE

Rough. My ex showed up at an event. He said some things that stuck.

My chest tightens. I know exactly what he said. I was standing right there. I heard every word.

STATMAN12

What did he say?

YOGA4LYFE

He just made me feel like shit.

Rage floods through me hot and immediate. I want to find Enzo right now and break his jaw.

STATMAN12

He's wrong. You're perfect.

YOGA4LYFE

You shouldn't say that. You don't know me in real life.

STATMAN12

If you were mine, I'd shut him up by going down on you until you couldn't say his name. You'd be so blissed out that all you could say was mine.

The reply comes faster this time.

YOGA4LYFE

I know I should want more from you. I should only spend time with men who're willing to be seen with me. But I think I'm addicted to getting off with you.

Shame floods through me, hot and sick and overwhelming. She needs more than what I can give her. She deserves someone who'll claim her in daylight, not just in the dark behind a screen. I'm lying about who I am in order to keep this sick game going.

It's going to burn me in the end, but I don't let that stop me. Pretty sure I'd walk across a pit of asps if it meant being closer to Scout.

STATMAN12

That isn't the reason why I can't meet you. I want to. God, I want to. I have to keep my face private because of my job, but never doubt that you're beautiful and perfect. It's because of work, sweetheart. Not because I don't want to be seen with you.

I wait. The three dots appear, then disappear. Then nothing.

She doesn't answer. I pick up my phone again and type before I can stop myself.

STATMAN12

You're not just beautiful. You're everything. And someday, when I can, I'll show you. I promise.

Send.

I don't expect a reply. Hell, after feeding her more lies wrapped up as promises I might never keep, I don't deserve one. My phone buzzes a minute later.

Yoga4Lyfe

We'll see.

I close my eyes and let the shame wash over me in waves. She'll wait and hope and believe my lies until she finally figures out the truth. And when she realizes I've been lying to her this whole time, playing with her through a screen while living in the same space, she'll leave.

I set my phone on the nightstand and scrub my hands over my face. The guilt sits heavy in my chest.

But it's not heavy enough to make me slow down.

Chapter Fifteen

Scout

The arena buzzes with post-practice energy. Today marks my first full mobility class, and excitement thrums through my veins as the players filter in. They're sweaty and tired, muscles warm and pliable. Perfect for mobility work. Mini-bands and lacrosse balls fill my arms as I move through the training room, helping where I can.

Connor hunches on the bench, wincing every time he tries to roll his neck. The pattern screams levator scapulae, tight from looking down at his phone too much.

"Hey." Setting my supplies down next to him, I offer a smile. "Mind if I help?"

Surprise flashes across his face, but he nods fast. "Please. It's killing me."

I guide him through a doorway stretch that takes seconds. Then I hand him a lacrosse ball to use against the wall for trigger point release. His relief comes, immediate and vocal.

"Holy shit, Scout." A grin splits his face, genuine gratitude lighting up his features. "How'd you know exactly where it hurt?"

"Kinesiology degree." Warmth creeps into my cheeks as I

smile back. "And lots of practice. Keep doing that twice a day. And maybe look up from your phone more often."

Laughter bursts from him, and he gives me a two-fingered salute. "Yes, ma'am."

Two more players drift over, asking for help with tight hips and sore shoulders. Working with them comes naturally, patient and thorough, explaining each stretch and why it matters for their game. "This opens your hip flexors, gives you a longer stride off the line. This one improves your thoracic spine rotation, helps with your shot mechanics and passing accuracy."

They listen, actually *listen*. Then they thank me. Delight floods through me as they ask follow-up questions like I'm someone worth learning from.

For the first time in months, my brain gets used for something that matters. No more fetching coffee or running copies or making myself useful in ways anyone could do. This work feels specific and valuable, something only I can offer.

I feel eyes on me from across the room that make my skin prickle. Glancing up, I catch Silas watching. His face stays blank, unreadable, arms crossed over his chest in that way he does when he's judging something. No words come, just that intense stare.

People call him Ice Man. And right now, the nickname fits perfectly. He looks cold. Distant. It seems like he might be evaluating me from behind a wall of ice I'll never crack.

But the wall comes down sometimes. The way he defended me from Enzo proved that. Those flashes of heat in his eyes when he thinks I'm not looking tell the real story. He's not actually cold. Everyone just thinks he is because that's what he lets them believe.

"You know, your grumpy face is bumming everyone out," I call over to him.

His jaw ticks. For a second, ignoring me completely seems like the likely outcome. Then he moves across the training room and plunks himself down on the bench beside the rookies.

"Okay," he mutters. "Help me stretch."

My pulse jumps. My shaking hands betray me slightly as I position his leg for a hip flexor stretch. He's massive up close, all muscle and heat radiating through his practice gear. Touching him feels dangerous, electric in a way that makes my skin prickle.

Guiding him through the hip opener requires my hands on his knee and thigh. I try to remind myself that I'm a professional. Except my body refuses to cooperate. His skin burns through the thin fabric of his shorts. His muscles coil tight under my palms, resisting the stretch.

God, he's handsome. Even scowling. Especially scowling, if I'm being honest with myself. His dirty blond hair's damp with sweat, pushed back from his forehead, making those blue-gray eyes more intense. A tower of pure muscle, all hard lines and sharp angles.

The athletic shorts ride low on his hips, showing the cut of his obliques. His thighs are massive beneath my hands, corded with muscle from years of explosive skating. The black compression shirt clings to his chest, outlining every ridge of his abs, the breadth of his shoulders. Even his forearms are distracting. They're veiny and strong, the kind of forearms that make you think about being pinned down. His jaw stays tight, that familiar scowl making him look severe, but there's a flush high on his cheekbones that gives him away.

This is affecting him too.

The sharp line of his jaw catches my attention. The way

his dirty blond hair falls over his forehead. The intensity in those blue-gray eyes when they lock on mine.

My crush on Silas is proving itself to be very much alive. I look at the curve of his shoulders, the strength in his thighs, and the way his breathing changes when I press deeper into the stretch.

God, I need to get laid, and *soon*. Hopefully my sexting buddy will agree to meet up in person because this crush on Silas has gotten completely out of hand. Something, anything, needs to redirect this energy before I do something monumentally stupid.

Ripping Silas's shirt off, licking his abs, and begging for him to fuck me comes to mind.

"You're good at this," he mutters.

Startled, I blink. It's the closest thing to a compliment he's given me. "Thanks."

Beaming at him probably looks insane, but stopping myself proves impossible. My whole chest warms with the praise. Pathetic, really, how much I crave his approval. This tiny scrap of acknowledgment means everything to me.

Okay. An official crush on Silas Huxley has definitely developed. Well, less developed and more awakened again, after years of dormancy. Whatever existed before I moved into his condo has morphed and grown, doubling itself in size like fresh dough in a proving drawer.

That's all fine... as long as it stays buried. Acting on my feelings, letting them show, or doing anything to make this living situation more awkward than it already is… that can't happen.

So what if he occasionally stands up for me in front of Enzo and lets me pretend he's my boyfriend? He has the emotional depth of a frozen puddle. And that doesn't exactly scream *relationship material*. Better to keep my distance from him and focus on work.

Finishing the stretch, I step back, putting space between us. "You should do that twice a day. Morning and night. It'll help with your stride and take pressure off your shoulder."

He nods, then stands and walks away, leaving me standing there with my hands still tingling from touching him. *Damn it.*

Later, the staff lounge becomes my workspace as I review Mobility Monday metrics. Juliet breezes in with Mollie in tow. Mollie looks frazzled, clutching a tablet like it's a life raft in stormy seas.

"Scout, perfect timing." Juliet's smile is sharp and efficient. "Mollie's shadowing me on the promo shoot next week. She'll be wrangling Thorne for the social media content."

Mollie groans, her face going pink. "I'd rather die."

Tilting my head, amusement bubbles up at her reaction. "That bad?"

"He's impossible," Mollie mutters, not meeting my eyes. "All charm and zero substance. I can't stand him."

"So you know each other?"

Though it didn't seem possible for Mollie to blush any harder, she manages it. "Unfortunately. He and my brother go way, way back. To them, I'll always be a nuisance in pigtails."

"I bet you look amazing in pigtails."

"Yeah, well." Mollie sighs and looks at Juliet. "Juliet's been helping me get ready. If we can get the players on board to help, we can really boost the team's TikTok account."

"You're doing such a good job, Mollie. I'm sure this will turn out well." Juliet turns to me, tablet out and open to a document. "Also, I added your name to the Recovery Protocol documentation. I gave you co-author credit. It's going to the coaches and GM today."

My stomach drops. "Juliet, you don't have to do that. It was your idea to implement the program. I just helped with the details."

"Are you kidding? You designed it. You built the metrics and tracking system. You're running it and getting results." Her voice is firm, brooking no argument. "You get credit for your work. Don't argue with me about this."

"Thanks." A wobbly smile manages its way onto my face. "I promise to make you look good."

After she leaves with Mollie, I look down at the document. Juliet sharing credit with me feels too big. What if the coaches think I'm overstepping? What if they decide I don't have the credentials to be listed as a co-author?

But erasing my name without telling Juliet seems sneaky. Causing her to lose trust is the last thing I want to happen, so I leave it for now.

By late afternoon, Hunter shows up to collect Juliet. Leaning against the doorframe, all brooding intensity and barely-contained energy radiates from him. His eyes lock on his wife like she's the only person in the room. Everyone else fades to background noise.

Part of me thinks she's lucky. Part of me is worried that Hunter will kill her and wear her like a skin suit. She doesn't seem the least bit concerned, though, so I mind my own business.

When Juliet walks over to him, he murmurs something in her ear that makes her blush and swat at his chest. She's smiling though. It's a private smile that says whatever he said was filthy and perfect and exactly what she wanted to hear.

Keeping his hand on the small of her back as they leave shows his possession, but also his gentleness. Claiming her without making her small.

Back at the condo, I put my leggings on and unroll my

yoga mat in the living room. Centering myself, shaking off the weight of the day feels necessary. Moving through sun salutations, breathing deep, letting the familiar poses ground me helps. Warrior one. Warrior two. Triangle pose.

My body knows these movements like a language, flowing from one to the next without thought. It doesn't bring any sense of calmness or peace, though. My body is restless.

That night, I lie down and open up Twinge, needing to feel some connection. And, I guess, I want to feel some positive affirmation. So sue me. I pull up the conversation with StatMan, the only guy I've even talked to, and fish for compliments.

YOGA4LYFE

What drew you to talk to me?

STATMAN12

What do you mean?

YOGA4LYFE

My profile? My photos??

STATMAN12

If I'm honest, the pic of you teaching a yoga class grabbed my interest. But then we started talking, and I realized how pure and good you are.

YOGA4LYFE

I'm not that pure and good.

STATMAN12

You are. You're sweet and clean as sunshine.

YOGA4LYFE

What if I want to be dirty?

STATMAN12

Are you a little horny?

YOGA4LYFE

Exceedingly horny.

STATMAN12

Then close your eyes. Imagine my hands on you. Rough and desperate because I've been holding back for too long. I'd grab your hips, pull you hard against me, make you feel exactly how much you affect me. I'd fist your curls, tilt your head back, and mark your throat so everyone knows you're mine.

My thighs clench. Heat pools low in my belly, spreading through me like fire.

YOGA4LYFE

Keep going.

STATMAN12

I'd strip you slow. Kiss every inch of skin I uncover. Tell you how perfect you are with every touch. How much I've wanted this. I've been thinking about your taste, your sounds, the way you'd feel wrapped around me.

YOGA4LYFE

God. You've got me so worked up. What else would you do to me?

STATMAN12

I'm going to tell you just what to do, Yoga Girl.

Touch yourself for me. Slow at first. Pretend it's my hands. My mouth. My cock buried deep inside you. And when you come, I want you to say my name even though you don't know it yet. Imagine what it would sound like falling from your lips.

My hand slides under the waistband of my sleep shorts. My breathing comes faster, ragged and desperate. Following his instructions, I rub my clit myself while imagining his hands instead of mine. I hear his voice in my ear, feel his body covering mine.

I come hard, muffling my cry in the pillow so Silas won't hear through the walls. My whole body shakes with the force of it. My muscles tremble, skin flushes and grows sensitive.

When my breathing returns to normal, when my heart stops trying to punch through my ribcage, I type one shaky message.

YOGA4LYFE

I want to meet you. Please. I need to know you're real.

The reply takes longer this time. He's typing and deleting responses. Shit, he's deciding how to let me down easy.

STATMAN12

Soon. I promise. When the timing's right.

Frustrating. It's exactly what he said before.

YOGA4LYFE

When will the timing be right?

STATMAN12

I'm dealing with some complicated work stuff right now. I don't want to meet you when I'm distracted or stressed. I want to give you my full attention. You deserve that.

Reasonable. Thoughtful even. So why does it feel like an excuse?

YOGA4LYFE

Okay. I can wait. But not forever.

STATMAN12

I won't make you wait forever. I want this too. More than you know.

I want to believe him. But I've been promised things before, things that could never be true. I don't want to believe that StatMan would lie to me, so I choose to believe that he just happens to have a complicated work situation, even though that's bullshit.

YOGA4LYFE

Goodnight. Dream about me.

STATMAN12

I always do, baby.

Setting the phone down on my nightstand, my body still hums with aftershocks. My skin is still sensitive, but my mind won't settle. As much as texting StatMan is enjoyable, I'm starting to feel like he's just using me. A fun fantasy every night before he goes to sleep.

I'd like it to be more, but he obviously doesn't want that.

My mind wanders, picturing who he could be. Traveling for work makes sense. Obviously he does something physical, because abs like he has in his photo don't come from spending time on the couch.

What else do I know about him? He could be a personal trainer. Maybe he works for a moving company or fells trees for a living.

Or maybe... he's an athlete. A hockey player.

A burst of giggles escapes from my throat. Yeah, right. He's one of Silas's teammates and he picked me because he liked my downward dog photo. The chances of a pro athlete picking a soft-bodied girl whose only true love is pizza are so unbelievably low, it's laughable. Hockey god meets shy yoga nerd.

Besides, I'm *done* with hockey players. Leaning back into my pillows, a smile forms on my lips and my eyes drift closed. The very silly notion that StatMan could be a ripped hottie instead of a photo stolen from Facebook follows me into my dreams.

Chapter Sixteen

Silas

Her text pings before warmups.

Attached is a photo. She's curled on the couch back at my condo, blanket bunched at her thighs, tank top dipping low enough to show the curve of her breasts. Dark blonde curls tumble loose and wild over one shoulder. Those green eyes look straight at the camera, warm and sleepy, like she just woke up. No makeup, just her natural beauty on full display.

Casual. Comfortable. Sexy as hell. She's smiling, just a little, like she knows exactly what this picture will do to me.

Convincing myself not to stare at the photo proves useless. I stare anyway, zooming in like a creep, imagining what she's wearing under that blanket. Probably those sleep shorts that ride up when she moves. Maybe nothing at all.

Scout doesn't usually text me. Especially not selfies. I'm not sure how to respond, but I don't want to discourage her from sending me more photos. So I snap a selfie of myself in my gear giving a gloved thumbs up. I feel like a huge chump sending it, but I do anyway. This communication from her was unexpected, but very welcome.

"Silas!"

I look up to see Thorne staring at me. He's the last player to leave the locker room and is waiting for me to get my ass up. "Yeah. Coming."

I shake off thoughts of Scout and focus on following my teammates. Game day. My head needs to stay on the ice. We need the win. The Havoc have cleaved a path right down the middle, winning just as many games as we lost.

The game is a complete disaster.

Toronto owns us from puck drop. I play like a machine. Every shift clean, every gap closed, every passing lane covered. It doesn't matter. We're hemorrhaging goals from mistakes I can't fix alone.

Hunter does his best as right wing, aggressively going after the puck, checking the opposition into the boards, taking every shot he has. Between him and Thorne, at least they score two goals.

Jett, on the other hand, has a really bad game. Standing in front of the net, masked and padded, looking every bit the intimidating goalie doesn't help when soft goals keep slipping in glove-side that should get saved in his sleep. Hunter takes a stupid retaliatory penalty after a clean hit and chirps his way into a double minor. Tate coughs up the puck at our own blue line and suddenly it's a breakaway. Thorne misreads coverage and leaves Jett hung out to dry.

I'm left chasing the puck around the ice, desperately trying to knock it back on their side and keep it from getting near the goal. Time and time again, the puck gets through. It's a massacre.

Four to two by the end of the second period.

I throw my weight into every hit. Block shots until my ribs scream and my shoulder feels like it's tearing apart from the inside. Grind through shifts until my lungs burn and my legs turn to lead. And nothing fucking works. We still lose.

Six to two. Humiliating.

Reporters circle like vultures in the tunnel afterward. One sneers, "Are you washed up yet, Huxley?" Another shoves a microphone in my face. "Should the Havoc be looking for younger talent to replace you?"

I mutter something about team effort and learning from losses. Juliet's voice echoes in my head, telling me not to bite, not to give them ammunition.

If I said what I really think to the journalists who've never laced up skates but love to tell players how to do their jobs, looking for new work tomorrow would follow immediately.

The worst moment, though, comes later.

Coach Cross: Did you make that appointment?

No, of course not. Dr. Sable's card got dumped in the bowl by my front door that holds my keys. I crack my neck and sigh.

Me: Not yet. I plan to.

Coach Cross: Get it done, Silas.

Right. Doing a piss-poor job of delaying my own execution seems to be my specialty.

When we reach the hotel, every member of the Havoc looks like they've taken a beating. We bumble into a line at the buffet set up for the players, eating like condemned men. Steam trays line one wall. Overcooked chicken. Bland pasta. Rice that tastes like cardboard. But we pile our plates high anyway because a loss like that needs fuel for anger as much as for strength.

Beck stacks protein high on his plate. Double chicken breasts and three hard-boiled eggs. "We'll review tape tomorrow. Reset and move forward," he says to the whole team. His voice stays even but tight with tension.

Hunter stabs at his food like it personally insulted him. "Refs were blind out there. They could've been offsetting penalties on half those calls." His scowl could turn men to stone.

"Or maybe," Thorne cuts in with a pensive expression. "The truth is that we just sucked tonight. Except Silas. He was a fucking wall out there."

The compliment scrapes like sandpaper. It doesn't fix the loss or change the fact that we got embarrassed on national television. I just chew my bland chicken and swallow.

Jett drops into the seat beside me, cracking open a bottle of water. "You look like shit, man."

"Fuck off," I mutter, but there's no real bite in it. "I did my best with what I had to work with."

Hunter leans against the wall across from us, arms crossed, eyes sharp as knives. "How's your roommate situation working out?"

My fork stops halfway to my mouth. "Fine..."

"Fine," Hunter echoes with a snort. "That's what you say when your kitchen's on fire but you don't want to admit it."

"Pretty sure his kitchen is on fire," Thorne drawls from down the table. "Scout moves in and suddenly Mr. Iceberg looks human. I can't say I blame you, man. She's hot as hell. Don't know how you're not all over her."

"Shut it," I snap, sharper than intended. My fork scrapes loud against the plate.

Jett finally huffs a laugh. "Jesus. Touchy subject."

"Maybe he's just tense," Hunter mutters, lip curling into something that might be amusement. "If she were my roommate, I'd get her to give me a massage."

I slam my water glass down hard enough that liquid sloshes over my hand and onto the table. "She's not yours."

Mr. Iceberg. Ice Man. The nicknames stings more than they should. They think I'm cold, unaffected, a machine. No idea exists about what's burning underneath. Right now, the ice is cracking. One mention of her and I'm ready to throw punches at my own teammates.

Beck lifts one eyebrow but doesn't comment. Thorne just smirks wider, like he's got me completely figured out.

"Fuck you guys," I grumble. "Stay out of it."

I shovel the rest of my food down as fast as I can. The bland pasta could be ash for all I taste it. All I can think about is that picture Scout sent before puck drop. Her curled on my couch, curls tumbling loose over her shoulders. Warm and soft and completely off limits.

I hate that the only thing keeping me awake tonight won't be replaying our defensive breakdowns.

Back in my hotel room, the silence irritates me. I stretch my shoulder until it twinges with warning pain. Ice it for twenty minutes. Scroll through my phone because I can't settle.

A text from Scout lights up my screen.

SCOUT

How's the shoulder?

Fuck my traitorous heart for beating faster at the slightest interest from her. She's just checking on me because I'm her project. Remembering that would serve me best. I type a response, delete it, type again.

SILAS

Tight. Can yoga help?

SCOUT

Depends on the stretch. Want me to send you one?

SILAS

Maybe. How's home?

SCOUT

Boring without you here. How's your hotel room?

Impulse wins over common sense. I peel off my shirt, adjust the ice pack strapped to my shoulder, and snap a photo. Shirtless in the hotel bed, abs on display, just enough to make my point. I hit send before I can overthink it.

SCOUT

You're ridiculous. But at least you're icing like I told you to.

I almost type something about missing her. My thumb hovers over the letters. Then I delete it and set the phone face down on the nightstand.

But the silence doesn't stick. My phone vibrates again. This time, a notification from the dating app scrolls across my home screen, demanding attention it shouldn't get.

A new message waits.

YOGA4LYFE

Want to get a drink tonight?

Staring at the message, my jaw works. Meeting her sounds incredible. It also sounds terrifying. It's impossible, because explaining why I can't show up in person would require confessing that I'm Silas, her roommate, the guy who created a fake profile just to stalk her.

Telling her the truth would be the smart move. The right move. It's the only move that makes any kind of reasonable sense.

But I'm an idiot, so I don't do any of that.

STATMAN12

Right now, all I want is to pin a woman down, fist her curls in my hands, and bury my face between her thighs until she's sobbing my name.

The three dots appear almost immediately. Her reply hits fast.

YOGA4LYFE

Fuck. Keep going.

STATMAN12

I'd start slow. Drag my tongue over your clit until you're begging me to go faster. Make you spread wider for me. Hold you there when you try to squirm away because it's too much.

YOGA4LYFE

God. I'm already wet just reading that.

I groan out loud, shifting against the hotel pillows. My cock strains hard against my sweatpants. The room suddenly feels too hot, too small.

STATMAN12

Good. Don't touch yourself yet. Just picture it. My mouth on you, my hands keeping you open. I want you desperate before I let you come.

YOGA4LYFE

You're killing me.

STATMAN12

You don't even know how good you'd taste
on my tongue. How perfect you'd look
falling apart for me.

Her next reply lands like a punch straight to my chest.

YOGA4LYFE

I want it so bad. I wish it was you here
instead of my hand.

A noise cracks out of me. Something between a groan and a laugh, raw and broken. I shove my sweatpants down and wrap my hand around my cock. The tip's already leaking a fat drop of precum, making desperation flood through me.

STATMAN12

Touch yourself. Rub in slow circles. Make
yourself messy for me.

I barely finish typing before my orgasm slams into me. Hot and harsh, tearing through me with a force that makes me groan. My free hand smacks the headboard. The ice pack slides to the floor with a dull thud.

My phone buzzes in my grip.

YOGA4LYFE

I can't stop thinking about your mouth. I
dream about what it would feel like.

I squeeze my eyes shut, breathing ragged and uneven. My chest heaves. I type one line with a shaking thumb.

STATMAN12

You won't have to think about it much
longer.

Then I drop the phone on the bed beside me and press the heels of my hands into my eyes until sparks dance behind my eyelids.

What the hell am I doing? Why did saying that seem like a good idea? She can't know who I am. This anonymous thing is all I can give her, but it doesn't feel like nearly enough anymore.

The shame should stop me. I should make me delete the app and confess everything before this gets any worse.

It doesn't. I pick up the phone one more time.

STATMAN12

When I get back to town, I want to hear
every detail of what you did tonight. Every
touch. Every sound you made. Don't leave
anything out.

Her reply comes almost instantly.

YOGA4LYFE

Promise. When do you get back?

STATMAN12

Soon. A few days.

YOGA4LYFE

I'll be waiting.

I set the phone down for real this time and stare at the ceiling. The textured white surface blurs in and out of focus. Our loss replays in my head on a loop. The reporters' cutting questions. My teammates' expressions when I snapped about Scout at dinner.

Being so very fucked is an understatement. But every single chance to pull back gets met with me rushing toward her instead. Fucking stupid. This will end in nothing but misery.

Down the hall, deep male voices echo. Thorne and Jett, probably. Heading to their rooms, or maybe going out despite the loss. Living their lives without this crushing weight of deception pressing down on them.

Instead of continuing my self-flagellation, I reach for my phone and pull up her actual text thread. The one where we're just roommates. Here, I'm just Silas and she's just Scout. Nothing's complicated by anonymous confessions and filthy promises.

The photo she sent before the game is still there. Her on my couch in my condo, looking comfortable and beautiful and completely at home in my space.

I save it to my phone before I can stop myself, making it my wallpaper. Something nice to look at whenever I need a boost. Of course, I hate myself for doing it.

Did I mention that I'm fucked?

Soon I'm falling asleep thinking about going home to her.

I wake up at five a.m. feeling worse than when I went to bed. My phone shows three new texts from Scout. Good morning messages and questions about when my flight lands and whether I want her to pick up groceries.

She's taking care of me even when I don't deserve it. My whole body's slow-moving as I get out of bed, knowing all the while I'm actively deceiving her.

I text back that I'll be home by late afternoon and add that she doesn't need to get groceries but thank you for offering.

Then I make my situation worse by texting that I'll see her soon.

What I don't tell her is that I can't wait. Coming home to her is the only good thing about this trip. If I start spouting off about my so-called feelings to Scout, it might reveal how deep this goes.

And no way can that ever happen. She'd shut me down immediately, that's for sure.

I just pack my bag and head down to the lobby to meet the team bus. Hunter gives me a look when I climb on. Jett smirks. Thorne says something I don't catch.

I ignore all of them and take a window seat in the back, pulling up my hood and closing my eyes.

A few hours from now, I'll walk through my door and Scout will be there. Probably cooking something. Maybe wearing those sleep shorts and a tank top. She'll probably smile at me like I'm not the worst kind of person.

And I'll smile back. I'll eat what she made. Groan while I let her touch my shoulder and work out the knots.

Being touched with care hasn't happened in so long. Every time Scout puts her hands on me for PT, every professional press of her fingers into tight muscle, I have to fight not to grab her wrist and hold her there. It's hard not to pull her closer and beg for more.

Her touch is clinical, therapeutic, but my body doesn't know the difference. It just knows it's been starving for years and she's offering crumbs. I want to devour every second of contact, hoard it like a dragon sitting on a pile of gold. The worst part is knowing she's just doing her job while I'm cataloging every brush of her fingers, every accidental touch, storing them away to replay later when I'm alone.

I want to fuck her. Buy her things. Take her places.

What is this weird feeling in my chest? It's a malformed monster, lurching forward with the possessive need to claim.

"Hey, Silas." Juliet comes down the aisle of the plane, stopping at my seat. She looks perfectly coiffed in a knee-length white dress, five inch heels, and perfectly-applied red lipstick. "I need you to do a charity event on Vashon Island. They run a clothing drive out of their rec center every year. I'd like you to attend."

I make a face. "Sounds boring."

"But not torturous," she's quick to point out. "I have Thorne and Tate judging a local talent show this weekend. Count yourself lucky you're just helping with a clothing drive. You can show up with a couple of boxes of Havoc shirts and track pants like a damn hero."

Something possesses me to ask, "And... would I have to be alone?"

"Well, no..." Juliet's eyebrows rise. "Most of the players have their own local charity events this weekend, though. Do you have someone in mind?"

Just my roommate who I'm obsessed with. No biggie.

I shrug. "Maybe. I'll let you know."

"O...kay." Juliet touches my shoulder ever so gently. "Let me know if you need any help. I'll send you the details and have someone drop the merch off at your house."

"Sure. Uh... Thanks, Juliet."

She moves on to the row behind mine, talking to Connor Li about his charity assignment. An idea worms itself into my brain. I grab my phone and shoot Scout a text.

Me: How do you feel about ferries?

Chapter Seventeen

Scout

The ferry cuts through dark gray water, steady as a heartbeat under my boots. Seattle fades into haze behind us while wind needles across the car deck, keeping my cheeks cold and my thoughts anything but clear. I stand with my gloves tucked under my arms and pretend I'm not cataloging every detail of Silas Huxley's body.

Juliet dispatched Silas to Vashon Island, about an hour from downtown Seattle, to help with a charity drive event the island puts on every winter. Because I live with Silas and need to make sure he takes it easy and doesn't strain his shoulder, of course I volunteered to keep him company. It just makes sense for me to accompany him rather than Juliet in her role as public relations manager.

Not at all because I want to see what Silas will be like outside of the rink and without the pressure the Havoc brings.

That would be crazy.

Silas leans against the bulkhead a few feet away, hood pulled up over his Havoc cap, hands loose in his pockets. Even dressed down in jeans and a hoodie, everything about him screams athlete. The hoodie's charcoal gray, stretched tight across his chest and shoulders, the fabric pulling at the seams when he shifts. His dirty blond hair falls in those messy waves beneath the cap's brim, catching the weak sunlight filtering through clouds. Those blue-gray eyes scan the horizon with that focused intensity he brings to everything.

Pure controlled power, even at rest. Coiled and ready despite the injured shoulder. The width of his shoulders blocks wind from reaching me. His thighs strain against dark denim when he shifts his weight, muscle evident even through heavy fabric. The scruff along his jaw is a few days old, making him look rugged instead of polished. He's beautiful in a way that has nothing to do with being pretty and everything to do with his masculine presence.

I force myself to look at the water instead.

A deckhand swings past with a coil of line, does a double take, then grins. "You're Huxley, right? Number twenty-three?"

Silas draws a quiet breath, and I watch his chest expand with it. "That's my brother Hunter. I'm number twelve."

"Right, right, sorry. Big fan." The guy fumbles for his phone, cheeks reddening. "Can I...?"

That muscle in Silas's jaw flexes, the one that makes me want to trace it with my fingertip. He nods once. They angle toward better light near the stairwell. For three seconds, he gives the camera a neutral half-smile that doesn't reach his eyes. When the deckhand disappears down the ladder well, Silas's gaze finds mine immediately, like he's been aware of exactly where I was standing the entire time.

"Got your boss hat?" His voice is lower than necessary, rough from the cold or something else. "Since I fully expect you to boss everyone around."

"You know what? I've got my medical clearance clipboard." I keep my tone light even though my pulse kicks up when he steps closer. "And a mean glare if you try to lift something you shouldn't."

"You could try." He's close enough now that I can smell him over the salt air. Cedar and something clean, masculine.

I raise my chin defiantly. "I could succeed."

His eyes drop to my mouth for a fraction of a second before returning to the horizon. The wake spreads behind us in a foamy V while a gull hangs weightless over the stern. I tuck a strand of hair behind my ear, aware of how his gaze tracks the movement.

Yeah, I need to change the subject, stat.

"Juliet says the rec center's been organizing the Winter Warm-Up Drive for twenty years. Coat and blanket donations, kids' boot fittings, and a mini market for fundraising."

He watches the shoreline pull closer, but I catch him looking at me in his peripheral vision. "You say that like I'm going to enjoy it."

"You might. It's a lot of people. Not all of them bite."

"They're missing out." The way he says it, low and almost predatory, sends heat straight through me. My eyebrows rise.

"Was that a joke?"

Silas rubs his hand over his mouth. "Maybe."

"I didn't know you made jokes. You know, I wondered if you were going to be weird away from the ice. But I never thought you'd be funny."

"I'm an enigma," he says, looking off over the water. I catch the smirk on his lips, though.

Oh, this is a side of him I've never seen before. And it might be more deadly than his usual growly, alpha assholeness. Be still my freaking heart.

The captain announces our approach over the loudspeaker. As we file toward the gangway with other foot passengers, Silas stays close behind me, close enough I feel his body heat. His hand hovers near my lower back when someone jostles past, not quite touching but there, protective. The gesture shouldn't affect me but it does.

Come on, self. Pull it together, I think. *Not everything he does can be swoon-worthy.*

The town spreads before us like a postcard once we dock. Two blocks of storefronts with cedar shingles, dark firs pressing in at the edges. The rec center sits at the end of the street, a brick building with paper snowflakes taped to the windows and a banner reading KEEP WARM, STAY KIND.

Inside, the gym smells like wet wool and coffee. Volunteers bustle around sorting donations while children's voices echo off the walls. Silas shoulders through the vestibule and freezes when three elementary schoolers stare at him with open mouths.

"Is that a Seattle Havoc player?" one whispers loudly. "He's on my poster!"

I step between them and Silas, accidentally brushing against his chest. He goes rigid at the contact, but now's not the moment for Silas and me to size each other up. The kids are still whispering amongst themselves.

"Don't crowd," I tell the group gently. "Mr. Huxley will be around. He's here to help."

The kids gawp at me as if I just confirmed that Santa was real and would be making an appearance. I glance at Silas over my shoulder. The look he gives me is pure heat disguised as irritation. It feels like a physical touch and I have to look away before I do something stupid like lean back into him.

The coordinator, a brisk woman with bright eyes, hands us clipboards. "You're here! Thank god. We weren't sure the Havoc assignments would show."

"What?" Silas scowls at her. "Of course we're here."

"What he means is," I say, smiling pointedly at Silas. "We're here to help. Put us to work, coach. Just no heavy lifting for him, please."

She nods. "Boot stations on the tables over there, coats over by the far wall, blankets on the tables in between. Media arrives in an hour. Try not to vanish before then."

"I'll tie him to a chair if I have to," I say. Immediately regretting the image that puts in my head. Silas, squirming, at my mercy. God help me.

"Good girl," she beams before rushing off.

"She seems friendly," Silas grunts. He watches her go with a suspicious expression.

I wave his comment off. "She's a busy lady. Come on, let's help her get these boxes sorted before people start arriving."

Silas follows me to the coat tables, shrugging out of his jacket in one fluid movement that makes his shirt ride up, revealing a strip of skin above his jeans. I look away quickly but not before he catches me looking. He smirks as he lifts a box.

"Light stuff," I warn. My voice comes out breathier than intended.

He snorts, then immediately proves me right when the box tilts sideways and mittens cascade everywhere. A five-year-old in a purple jacket gasps at the tragedy. Silas freezes halfway between embarrassment and cursing.

"Emergency," I gasp, being dramatic. "Mittens down!"

Purple Jacket scrambles to help while I crouch next to Silas to gather the spillage. Our hands brush as we both reach for the same mitten. The contact jolts through me like static electricity. His fingers linger against mine for a heartbeat before pulling away.

Silas surrenders the mittens to a volunteer for careful sorting. When he stands, I'm still crouched, which puts me at eye level with his hips. I stand too quickly, stumbling slightly. His hand shoots out to steady me, gripping my elbow. Even through my sweater, his touch burns.

The corner of his mouth tilts up. I have the insane urge to kiss him right there in front of children and volunteers and God himself. Big problem. Huge problem. I step away, my fingers tingling. Silas coughs and moves on.

I'm making this weird. I really need to get my shit together.

An hour blurs past in a rush of activities. Matching kids with boots in their size. Helping an elderly woman select a warm coat. Organizing blanket bundles for distribution. Through it all, Silas stays close. Not hovering, but present.

When a father thanks him for the autograph, Silas signs without the usual grimace. When kids cluster around asking about hockey, he actually answers their questions. Patience replaces his normal gruffness.

I watch him crouch to a child's eye level, explaining how to hold a hockey stick properly using a broom handle. Something warm and soft blooms in my chest. This version of Silas, patient and kind, feels more dangerous than the Ice Man persona he wears at the arena.

The media arrives, cameras flashing, and Silas handles the questions with practiced ease. I stand slightly behind him, watching how he deflects praise to the community, mentions the rec center's twenty-year legacy, and thanks the volunteers.

Professional and polished. Nothing like the growly man who barely speaks to me even though I live in the same condo.

When the last reporter packs up, the coordinator thanks us

profusely. "You two are wonderful together. Such a lovely couple."

"Oh, we're not..." I start.

"We work together," Silas finishes, but his hand finds the small of my back again.

Outside, the sky has darkened to pewter. Snow begins falling, fat flakes drifting down in lazy spirals.

"Ferry's probably still running," I say, pulling out my phone to check the schedule, but I frown when I get no signal. "Or not. I can't get reception."

Silas tries his phone. "Same. The storm's moving in faster than predicted."

"Mr. Huxley?" A woman rushes out from the rec center. "I'm so sorry. The ferries stopped ten minutes ago. A storm warning just came through on the radio. You're stuck until the morning at least."

My stomach drops. "There's got to be somewhere we can stay."

"There's a bed-and-breakfast two streets over." She points. "Mrs. Zhao usually has rooms. Want me to call?"

"Please," Silas says.

She disappears inside. Returns a few minutes later. "You're in luck. The last room is available. She'll hold it for you."

We thank her and head into the now-heavy snowfall. The walk takes ten minutes, long enough for snow to accumulate on our shoulders and hair. Silas walks close, using his larger frame to block the worst of the wind. His jacket stays open, angled to shield me from gusts of fresh snow.

I pull out my phone to check for messages but there's still no signal. Everything important got left in the car we took from the ferry dock anyway, except the small backpack I brought for the day.

The bed-and-breakfast appears through the storm like something from a painting. Yellow light spills from windows onto a wraparound porch. We make a mad dash from the street to the front door, with Silas taking the brunt of what has now become a full-fledged snowstorm. Inside the inn, I shake off my jacket, laughing.

"I can't believe we were just caught in that," I say. Silas runs a hand over his hair, sending a pile of snow onto the floor.

A woman in an oatmeal-colored sweater greets us with practiced warmth that widens slightly when she recognizes Silas. "You must be our stranded guests. I'm afraid you'll have to make do with the Honeymoon Suite. It's the only room that isn't occupied at the moment."

"Sounds fine," Silas says, shaking off some residual slush from his jacket. "We'll take anything."

"Sounds perfect." She hands over a brass key. "Breakfast at eight, unless the power goes out. Then it's coffee if the generator cooperates."

We climb narrow stairs to the top floor. The room waits behind a white door with a ceramic plaque. Inside, a fireplace flickers in a tiled hearth. The bed dominates the space, built for newlyweds who can't keep their hands off each other. Quilts in red and cream, mismatched nightstands, a window seat overlooking dark water.

And outside, the beautiful backyard scene is quickly overtaken by piles and drifts of fast-accumulating snow. Silas sets my backpack, which he insisted on carrying, down carefully. "I'll take the floor."

"What? Are you crazy?" I cut my eyes at him. "You aren't sleeping on the floor, Silas."

"I've slept on worse."

"That risks your shoulder." I peel off my gloves, trying to

sound professional instead of breathless. My fingers tingle as I flex them. "I'm not signing off on that."

He has the nerve to say, "You're not my boss."

He peels off his coat and tousles his chin-length blond hair, which is somewhere between damp and soaking. His white Henley clings to his muscular chest, wet from melted snow. With his blue-gray eyes, chiseled cheekbones, and broad shoulders, he looks like he just stepped off a runway in Milan.

I tell myself not to gape even as I can't help but look my fill. Silas seems to sense my heavy gaze. He looks up, flushing slightly.

"I think I get a say about things that could affect your shoulder." I stretch, thinking the room's too small for the two of us. "I can sleep on the floor."

His jaw tightens. "You're not sleeping on the floor while I take the bed. You don't need to do that here, Scout."

"Do what?" I put my hand on my hip.

"Take care of everybody. I know what you're doing. I'm not about to let you sacrifice your own comfort just to make sure I don't have a crummy night's sleep."

My cheeks heat and I drop my gaze. He's got me there. "Can we share the bed, then?"

He works his jaw, eyes dark in the firelight. The tension between us thickens until I can barely breathe through it. He looks at the bed, then at me, then away. "That's fine."

"Fine," I echo. "That's what we'll do."

Silas stares at me for a second. At his tight swallow, I realize he's watching a drop of water as it glides down my neck to my collarbone. Does he somehow find me attractive right now? I'm drenched, the snow melting and wetting gaps at the front of my shirt and the back of my coat. My hair's likely frightful. And yet, the way Silas looks right now, hungry and longing, makes a bright bloom of want pool low in my belly.

He clears his throat. "I'm going to try to hunt down some dinner." He escapes before I can respond, leaving wet footprints on the floor.

Left alone, I hang our coats to dry, prop boots by the fire, and arrange gloves on the grate. The room warms slowly while a nasty gust of wind rattles the windows. I'm too aware of the bed. I can't stop thinking of how Silas looked at me when he realized we'd be stuck here together.

My body's humming with nervous energy, so I drop to the floor between the bed and the fireplace. I move through a few gentle stretches, nothing intense, just warrior pose and triangle pose to ground myself. Deep breaths, centering my thoughts. But even yoga can't quiet my racing pulse.

He returns with a tray balanced in his good hand. Two bowls of soup, crusty bread. "Mrs. Zhao's apologizing with food. I told her you accept."

"That was thoughtful." I'm surprised by how normal my voice sounds. "I have a few sets of Havoc-branded sweatpants in my backpack."

"Oh, that's amazing. I thought I was going to have to sleep in my jeans."

"You could've just worn your skivvies."

He arches a brow. "Assuming that I'm wearing any."

"What? Oh!" I get tongue-tied when I picture him going commando.

"Kidding." He sets the tray on the trunk at the bed's foot, then settles on the mattress edge like he's testing its stability. We eat quietly, but it's not awkward. It's the silence of two people hyperaware of each other, measuring every movement.

Okay, it's a little awkward. But it's still progress.

"How's the shoulder?" I ask.

He rolls it carefully. "Better than this morning. Worse than I want."

"Oh, Si. You should rest it tonight."

He stiffens. "What'd you call me?"

"Si?" My brain sputters and my cheeks heat. "Sorry, it's been such a long day. I'm only working with two brain cells and right now, they're in overdrive."

"I don't... mind." His voice is low and rough.

The fire shifts, sending shadows dancing across his face. He's watching me with an intensity that makes my skin flush.

"You don't?"

"Scout." It's a sigh as much as it is him calling my name. He's looking past me into the storm, gathering words. "You did good today."

I shrug a shoulder. "That's my job."

"I know. Still."

Praise from him is rare enough to treasure. "You were good with the kids. You warmed right up to them."

"Don't spread it around." His mouth almost smiles. "I have a reputation."

"It'll survive."

He stands, giving the bed a look like it personally offends him. "Mrs. Zhao says the storm might turn to freezing rain. We could lose power."

"So a normal Tuesday."

He makes a noise that could be interpreted as a laugh. I look at the bed because someone has to address it. "We'll keep to our sides. You won't hurt your shoulder, I won't kick. We'll manage."

He studies me like I've suggested something dangerous. "You get the window side. If something happens, I'm closer to the door."

"Always thinking in contingencies."

"You don't?"

"Not really. I think about what would make people happy." I slide him a shy smile. "Coming to Vashon was a good idea, by the way. Even though we're stuck."

He jerks his head in what might be taken for agreement. I clear my throat and dig out a set of sweats for him, then take mine into the small bathroom and quickly change clothes. When I get out, he's stripped off his Henley, leaving him in a white t-shirt and a pair of too-tight gray sweatpants.

I swallow and jerk my gaze away. He's not interested in having me stare.

"Lights off in ten?" I ask.

"Make it five. I'm beat."

I check locks and screens, then slide under my half of the quilt. The mattress dips when he joins me. We're careful not to touch, but I'm aware of every inch between us. His body heat radiates across the small space. His breathing sounds far too loud in the quiet.

The fire settles with a soft snap and a buffet of wind braces the windows. He shifts. I feel the mattress move, feel him testing the space between us without crossing it.

"Good work today," I whisper into the darkness.

A soft grunt leaves him. "You too, sunshine."

I close my eyes and try not to think about how easy it'd be to roll toward him, to close this careful distance between us. I clench my eyes and try not to think about his massive hands, the brooding curve of his mouth, and the way he looked at me in the firelight.

Chapter Eighteen

Silas

I stand at the window, looking out onto the unfamiliar snowy landscape of the Puget Sound coast. On the shore, the snow has stopped falling, leaving a crisp strip of darkness where the water meets the sand.

My hair's still damp from the hot shower I took at five. I woke and it immediately became clear that lying beside Scout would be impossible. Listening to her quiet, almost innocent breaths instantly stiffened my cock.

It's better to be jerking off silently in the shower than to do what I really wanted, which was to turn her sleeping body over and explore her with my touch. She looks so damn soft. I think I made the right call.

"Morning," she says. Her voice is soft and slow with sleep.

I look over my shoulder. She's sitting up with messy hair and a loose shirt that slips down one arm. Her dark blonde curls are wild from sleep, spilling across her shoulders in waves. Her t-shirt hangs off her shoulder, revealing smooth skin and the curve of her collarbone. Her green eyes are still hazy with sleep, unfocused and soft. No makeup, lips slightly parted, cheeks flushed from the warmth of the bed. She's rumpled and beautiful and completely unaware of what she does to me.

Arousal hits me fast, so I turn away before my body reacts and embarrasses me again. "The ferry's still down. They're saying maybe it'll be working tomorrow."

We're going to spend another night here. Restraint's usually my superpower. I've lived for years working out all day, eating a low carb high protein diet, abstaining from liquor and women. All in the name of being the best defender I can be.

But I suppress a groan at the idea of spending another night here without touching Scout. My stupid brain won't shut up about how she smells like lavender and sunshine. I think I've gone way past want at this point; I need to find out if she tastes as good as she smells.

I bet she does.

Scout stretches, unaware of my perpetual state of horniness. Her shirt inches up, revealing a tantalizing strip of midriff. I jerk my eyes away, angry at myself.

"We'll make the best of it," she says.

"I went downstairs and grabbed a tray." I hand her a mug of coffee and our fingers brush. The jolt from contact is immediate. I pull back too fast and grip my own mug until my knuckles go pale. She swallows. I think she feels the spark too. Her breath hitches, but she doesn't comment and neither do I.

Instead, I blurt out, "Do you want cream? For your coffee?"

Her lips curl up in a smile and she shakes her head, taking a sip of the dark brew. She hums appreciatively. "This is really good."

Breakfast waits on the dresser. Muffins, fruit, cream for the coffee. I take the armchair near the window while Scout settles on the bed. She bites a piece of fruit and licks the juice from her fingers. I keep looking away because every movement makes me want her.

And then I wish I could flog myself. The last thing Scout needs is her horny roommate leering at her.

After we finish eating, Scout showers and emerges from the bathroom in the same clothes. An oversized Seattle Havoc sweatshirt and a pair of soft dark gray Havoc joggers.

"I was thinking we should go for a run. I need to get out of here and move my body."

I study her face for a moment. She's flushed from the warmth of the shower, and she won't quite meet my eyes. She needs space from whatever's building between us. I understand the feeling too well. "You want to run in this weather?"

"Walk. Maybe jog. I'm antsy."

Movement might take the edge off the restless pool of energy simmering under my skin. I grab my boots without arguing. "I don't have running shoes, but I'm fine with a trek outside."

Cold air hits hard when we step out the inn's front door. It wakes me up and cuts through the leftover heat from being too close to her in that room. Snow covers the island, softening everything. There are no more hard lines. Just a blanket of soft-looking snow flowing as far as the eye can see. Scout walks beside me, struggling to keep up with my brisk pace. I find myself slowing my steps to match hers. The path we take heads straight down toward the beach, our boots crunching over frozen ground.

"It's strange seeing you quiet," she says. "You usually mutter threats under your breath when you walk."

I give her a look. "I don't do that."

She smirks at me. "You do. It's comforting in a weird way."

The idea that she watches me that closely settles somewhere I don't want to touch. "Didn't realize my charm had layers."

"Somebody's got jokes." Her smile is dazzling. "You have layers. People just don't look long enough to find them."

She says it with an easy certainty that shakes me more than it should. I look away before she sees the effect.

The beach opens in front of us. Dark rocks piled high with snow dot the sand. Slow waves bang sluggishly against the shore. Scout moves toward the rocks, drawn to the view. "The air smells incredible. It's so fresh."

"Watch your footing." I point out a particularly jagged rock. "It's slick."

"You're so bossy. It just so happens I grew up on the beach, so I know how to..."

Her foot hits algae. She slides, ankle rolling, pain flashing across her face. I reach her before she fully hits the ground, wrapping an arm around her waist, and tug her upright.

I breathe, "Scout."

"It's okay." Her voice is thin from pain. She flattens her palms against my chest, bracing and trying to regain her equilibrium. "I just need a second."

She tries to put weight on her foot. Her knee buckles and she sags against me. A surge of fear hits hard and fast. I growl, "For fuck's sake, Scout. Don't move."

Her eyes flash as she looks up at me. "It's probably just twisted..."

"Don't," I cut in. The idea of her being injured hits a place I don't want to name. "You're not going to like this."

I lift her without waiting for her to protest. One arm under her knees, the other around her back. She gasps and grabs my neck, her face close to mine. Her body's warm against my chest. My heart kicks hard enough that she must feel it.

I haven't carried anyone like this in my entire life. The intimacy of it should make me want to put her down immediately. But instead, I'm cataloging every detail. The way she fits perfectly in my arms, how her breath hitches when I adjust my grip, the softness of her body pressed against mine. Her fingers curl into my shoulder. She's trusting me completely with her weight. She smells like lavender and something uniquely her.

I want to bury my face in her hair and breathe her in until I'm drunk on it. If I could, I would carry her like this forever. I would feel her warmth seeping into me, filling all the cold empty spaces I've lived with for years. It's terrifying how right this feels.

"You don't have to carry me," she whispers, but her arms tighten.

"Yeah, I do. There's no way you're getting back to the room with that busted ankle."

Her lips twist. There's no room for argument, though. She knows I'm right.

"Okay." She sounds resigned.

The walk back feels longer than it should. Every shift of her weight, every breath against my neck, pushes my control a little thinner. When she shivers and moves closer for warmth, I almost lose my footing. By the time we reach the bed and breakfast, I'm wound so tight I can barely think.

I carry her into the room and lower her onto the bed with more care than I should. My hands stay on her waist, though I should let her go. Stepping back feels wrong.

"Stay there," I say, heading for the door.

"I'm not going anywhere."

I trudge down the stairs and talk to the innkeeper about some ice for Scout's ankle. She returns with a bag of frozen blueberries and a thin tea towel. After thanking her, I take the steps up two at a time. It's like I'm eager to get back to the same room where I felt trapped only an hour ago.

When I walk back in, Scout's exactly where I left her, watching me with those green eyes that see too much. I kneel beside the bed and lift her foot carefully, wrapping the ice pack around her ankle with the towel. She winces but doesn't pull away.

"How bad is it?" My voice comes out rougher than intended.

"It'll be fine. Just a twist." She's lying. The swelling's already starting, purple blooming across her skin.

"You need to rest it. Elevation, ice, compression."

"Yes, Dr. Huxley." Her teasing tone should lighten the mood, but it doesn't. Not when I'm this close, still able to feel the phantom press of her body against my chest.

I force myself to stand and put distance between us. "I'll see if they have anything for the pain."

"Silas." She catches my wrist. The contact sends electricity through me. "Thank you."

I swallow hard, nod once, and pull away before I do something stupid like lean down and kiss her.

The innkeeper provides ibuprofen and offers to bring lunch to our room. Hours blur together. Scout props herself on pillows, ankle elevated, while I pretend to read on my phone. The tension between us thickens with every passing minute. Every time she shifts, I look up. Every time our eyes meet, the air crackles.

"Want to watch something?" she asks finally, breaking the silence.

"Sure." Anything to stop sitting here drowning in want.

She finds a movie on her phone and props it on the nightstand. The only way to see properly means sitting on the bed beside her. Dangerous territory, but refusing would be obvious. I settle next to her, careful to keep distance, but it proves impossible. The bed's too small. Our shoulders touch. Her warmth spreads and seeps into me.

The movie plays, but I can't focus. All my awareness centers on the woman beside me. The way she absently plays with her hair. She makes these soft sounds of amusement as she watches the movie. After she flicks her long hair over her shoulders, my eyes keep finding the graceful curve of her neck. It would be so easy to turn my head and press my lips at the tender juncture where her neck meets her shoulder.

Fuck me. I'm painfully hard and grateful for the blanket. I try to think about anything except how easy it'd be to tilt her face up and kiss her. Her mouth's right there, pink and plump, her lips looking like they'd be warm and soft.

When the movie ends, she shifts and winces. I notice immediately and gesture to her.

"Your ankle's swelling more. Let me see."

"It's fine."

I snort. "Don't lie to me."

She scoots forward on the bed. I make a split-second decision and pull her legs onto my lap. Talk about intimate. Now I've undoubtedly upped the ante. I hear her sudden intake of breath as my hands slide down her calf to her ankle, checking the swelling and testing the range of motion. She's tense under my touch. Her breathing isn't steady.

"You're tensing," I murmur. My mouth's too close to her ear.

"I wonder why." Her voice is breathless.

"Relax. I won't hurt you."

I work my thumbs into the muscles around her ankle, careful but firm. Every sound she makes goes straight through me. Small gasps. Quiet sighs. The way she leans back toward me without thinking. My control hangs by a thread.

I find myself wondering, *What would happen if we hooked up? Just this one time, to get it out of our systems?*

"You're surprisingly good at this," she says.

"I'm a professional hockey player." My voice sounds rough. "Sore ankles are my thing."

After a minute, she turns her head slightly and looks at me over her shoulder. "Your shoulder must be killing you after carrying me. Let me work on it."

Every alarm in my head goes off. "No. I'm okay."

She purses her lips. "Silas."

"It's fine."

"You're lying. You've been favoring your left side all day."

She's right. We both know it. My right shoulder throbs constantly, and it was made worse when I carried her. "I don't need help."

"Turn around," she says gently. "Let me, please."

The refusal sticks in my throat. Slowly, like I'm walking toward something I won't be able to undo, I turn my back to her.

The first touch of her hands makes me jolt. She starts at the base of my neck with steady pressure. A sound escapes me before I can stop it. Relief and desire twist together, too close for comfort.

"You're carrying so much tension," she murmurs. She works deeper.

Her hands feel too good. Every touch sends heat through my body. I grip my thighs, trying to anchor myself, but she finds a tight knot and presses her thumbs into it. I groan before I can stop myself. My body responds instantly. Heat builds low and fast. My cock hardens with every pass of her hands.

They call me Ice Man. The guy who doesn't feel anything. But right now, with Scout's hands on me, the ice is shattering. Every touch cracks the facade I've built over years.

I'm not cold. I'm *burning*. Desperate. Starving for contact I've denied myself for so long I forgot what it felt like to want someone this badly. Her professional touch shouldn't affect me like this, but it does. Because it's Scout. I've wanted her for years, even when I tried to pretend I didn't. Now every touch is one more I'll remember when this is over and she's gone.

"Scout." Her name comes out as a warning.

"It's okay," she whispers. Her breath hits the back of my neck.

It's not okay. I'm sitting here getting hard from her innocent touch. I'm imagining her hands moving lower. I'm imagining turning around and pressing her into this mattress. My hips rock forward slightly without permission, searching for friction that isn't there. Another groan escapes, and this time I know she hears the want in it.

Scout puts a hand to my chest, as though trying to settle me. Our eyes meet, her green gaze questioning. We're stuck, trapped in a moment together. I don't dare to move because I don't want this spell to break.

Then Scout dips her head and brushes her petal-soft lips against mine. A groan rips its way from my throat. I thrust my hand in her thick curls and tug her head back, licking the seam of her lips until she parts for me, lets me in. A mistake, surely, but I take full advantage of the weakness. I tangle my tongue with hers, plunging inside her mouth.

She tastes as sweet as candy bursting across my tastebuds. My instinct is to lean in, move her back into the pillows behind her. I'm crazed enough that I just want to be inside of her body any way that I can.

Just as I moan again and move closer, I feel her hesitant palm against my chest. She breaks away, whispering against my lips. "Si, wait."

Fuck. I scramble back and swipe at my lips. My eyes fasten on her face, her flushed expression, the hard breaths she's taking. Fuck me.

"Silas..." she starts, reaching for me.

Yeah, that's not gonna happen. I've already crossed so many lines. I bound to my feet, moving so fast I nearly knock her over. "I need a shower."

The look of perfect surprise on her face nearly does me in.

I'm in the bathroom before she can respond. I lock the door and turn the water on full blast. My hands shake as I strip off my clothes. I'm so hard it hurts. My cock strains as I climb in the shower. Precum beads at the tip. I grip myself with my good hand and jerk my cock, a man on a mission. I'm not gentle. I'm not patient. Before I do something truly stupid, I need this handled.

The first stroke makes me hiss. I lean against the shower wall and let the water run over my back, giving in to what I've been fighting all day. I think about Scout's hands on me and imagine them moving lower. I think about her mouth, how she tasted when I kissed her, and how she'd taste everywhere else. I imagine the moment she parts her thighs and begs me to fuck her.

My hand moves faster and rougher.

"Scout," I groan. I don't care if she hears through the thin door. I'm too far gone to care about anything except the picture in my head. I imagine her on her knees, looking up at me with those eyes, taking me in her mouth. Or lying on the bed, begging me to touch her.

That's it. The image pushes me over the edge. I come hard with her name on my lips, my whole body shuddering with the force of it. Good, some release. But not the same as touching her.

Reality comes back fast. Shame and want and frustration twist together. I stay under the water until it cools and I can think again. When I finally step out and wrap a towel around my waist, I can't look at her. She's sitting on the bed with her phone. Her cheeks are flushed, her hands shaking.

She heard. She knows. She clears her throat.

"The ferry's running again," she says. Her voice sounds raw. "The owner came up and let us know."

"Oh." I must sound disappointed. "That's good."

She purses her lips. "Silas..."

"Just..." I pull my shirt over my head. It's still damp but I can't bring myself to care. "Let's forget this happened."

Scout stares at me for a long beat. "Do you want to forget it?"

"Yeah." The lie hits hard, but it's necessary. This thing between us can't happen. I won't let it happen. I grab my bag and head for the door. I need distance before I lose whatever control I have left. "We'll leave in five minutes."

She doesn't argue. She only nods with a hurt look in her eyes.

We pack in silence. I steel myself as I scoop her up, then carry her to the car. It's silent as we drive to the ferry. I did this. I fucked it up.

She lays her seat back and closes her eyes. I get out, pacing over to the ferry's bow. Looking out, I tell myself this is for the best. We can go back to normal, to professional distance and careful boundaries.

But I can still feel her against my chest. I can still hear her breathing shift when I touched her. I can still taste her.

The storm isn't over. It's getting worse, building inside me with nowhere to go except toward sure disaster.

Chapter Nineteen

Silas

While we were on Vashon Island, Coach texted me a third time, demanding a date for my appointment with the sports therapist. A therapist is just going to dig into my past and drag up a bunch of memories that are better off forgotten. I already know that my childhood was screwed up. My mom was all the Huxley boys' agents for years, stole a bunch of money from all of us, then disappeared. If it weren't for Mom blackmailing Hunter to get more money, I doubt that I'd have ever heard from her again.

So yeah, I have some issues. And while I'm perfectly content to hold my feelings in until the end of time and die repressed, Coach Cross is going to lose his shit if he has to ask me again when my appointment is.

I finally text Dr. Sable's number late at night, explaining who I am and that I need to schedule an appointment. Scheduling sounds better than actually seeing a shrink, somehow. I've never been so glad to put my phone on silent and head to bed.

Hell, maybe Dr. Sable doesn't even get texts on that number. A guy can hope, right?

Unfortunately, when I wake up, there is a text waiting for me.

DR. SABLE

Silas, I have a last-minute cancellation this morning. Any chance you can make it?

Fuuuuuuck. I can't say no. I text the doctor that I'll be there in an hour, then hurry through showering and getting dressed. Scout isn't up yet as I stealthily sneak out of the condo.

Good. I don't want her realizing what a basketcase I am.

Soon enough, I'm sitting on the couch in Dr. Sable's office, my palms sweating. The office is too warm. There are two low bookshelves full of books dedicated to sports. *The Complete Athlete: Mind and Body. 1042 Races: How I Conquered the Sport of Running. Psychoanalysis and the Professional Athlete. Life After Sports.*

They should make me feel some sort of confidence, like Dr. Sable knows what I'm going through. Instead the titles batter me, making me feel raw and brittle. I feel perspiration begin to dot my forehead.

"I'm so glad that you were able to make it here on such short notice." Dr. Sable sits down across from me and crosses her legs, notepad balanced in her lap. She's professional and calm in her stylish white button up and black pencil skirt. On the tall side for a woman, she has a heart-shaped face, green eyes, and long blonde hair.

She looks sort of familiar, though I have no idea why. Maybe it's because she's hot, in a buttoned up, corporate suit kind of way. Shit, if I wasn't so averse to therapy, I might actually think about asking her out.

Well, I'm also obsessed with my roommate. So there's that. I have enough on my plate.

"Uh, yeah." That's all I can manage to say. Dr. Sable is going to see right through me, pin me like a butterfly in a case.

"Thanks for coming in, Silas." Dr. Sable's voice is warm without being patronizing. "I know this isn't easy."

I grunt and shift on the couch. The leather squeaks under my weight.

She uncaps a pen and smiles at me. "Why don't we start simple. What brought you here today?"

"Coach Cross gave me your card. He said I needed to talk to someone." I cross my arms over my chest. "I've been hurt a few times over the past seasons, bad enough that it's looking like I'll have maybe three more seasons if I get super lucky. So Coach sent me here to talk about my career and figure out a plan for... whatever comes next."

"And how do you feel about having your coach ask you to see me?"

I break eye contact. "Shit makes me angry. He should know that I'm fine."

"You mention your temper." She writes something down. "Tell me about that."

Silence reigns for a moment as I struggle to decide how to phrase it. "I take bad penalties. Sometimes I get baited into scrums. I can't seem to stop myself even when I know better. It... costs my team games."

"And that frustrates you."

"Yeah. And like… hurts me. Physically, I mean."

She nods slowly and waits. The silence stretches between us, heavy and expectant. I hate silence in rooms like this. It feels like a trap designed to make me fill it with things I shouldn't say.

I supply, "Mostly, Coach Cross sent me here to figure out an exit strategy from hockey."

Dr. Sable nods and scribbles another note. "Can you tell me more?"

"Not really." I rub the back of my neck. "Like I said, I've had a lot of injuries. I play defense on a hockey team, so the hits just keep stacking up. A couple of weeks ago, I tore my labrum and had to have surgery on it."

"That's a tough injury. How is it feeling? How's the PT?"

"Rough." I lean my head back against the couch, looking at the ceiling. "I've tried so hard to do everything right. My sleep schedule is on point. My diet is mind-numbing, but I hit every macro I set. I fucking live in the gym." I pause. "Sorry, can I curse?"

Dr. Sable waves a hand. "Of course."

"Thanks. Yeah, I basically eat, sleep, and play hockey. For years, I have been so focused on that. I don't have hobbies. Music? Movies? I haven't seen or heard anything. All I know is hockey. It's the only thing I'm good at."

"It sounds like you've really put all your eggs in one basket, huh?"

I snort. "Yeah. And now Coach is telling me to like... prepare myself for leaving the Havoc. What the fuck? What am I supposed to do?"

The doctor writes a note and then looks up at me, her expression thoughtful. She taps her pen against the notepad once, twice, then sets it down completely.

"Silas, I want you to try something with me. A thought experiment." She leans forward slightly. "If you weren't a hockey player for a year, who would you be?"

The question hits like a slap shot straight to the sternum. I stare at her for several seconds, mouth opening and closing like a fish out of water. "I don't... that's not... I *am* a hockey player."

"I understand that. But imagine, just for a moment, that you couldn't play. Maybe you're injured. Maybe you're taking a sabbatical. For one full year, no hockey. Who are you then?"

My hands clench into fists on my thighs. The leather couch creaks as I shift forward, then back, unable to find a comfortable position. "Nobody. I'd be nobody."

She writes that down, her face neutral. "Nobody?"

"Look, hockey isn't just what I do. It's who I am. Without it..." My voice trails off because finishing that sentence feels like admitting something I can't take back. "My dad played. My brothers play. It's the family business. Take that away and I'm just some guy with no skills, no purpose, no fucking point."

"What about a team outside the NHL? Have you considered that?"

Another gut punch disguised as a question. My shoulder throbs as if responding to the thought. "That would mean I'm done. Washed up. It feels like all those years of sacrifice were for nothing."

"Sacrifice," she repeats, latching onto the word. "Tell me about those sacrifices."

"College relationships that never went anywhere because hockey came first." My neck heats, because of course I'm talking about Scout. "Really one relationship in particular that could've been a thing. But I was worried that if I didn't focus on hockey a hundred percent, I'd lose my shot."

Dr. Sable's pen stills against her notepad. Something flickers across her face, too quick for me to read, before her professional mask slides back into place.

"One relationship in particular," she repeats carefully. "That sounds like it still weighs on you."

"Sometimes." The admission burns coming out. "It was eight years ago. I should be over it by now."

"Should is an interesting word choice." She sets her pen down entirely, giving me her full attention. "There's no time-line for processing regret, Silas. Especially when it represents a pattern that might still be active in your life."

"What do you mean?"

"You chose hockey over this relationship because you were afraid of losing your shot. Are you still making that same choice? Still sacrificing connections for the game?"

My jaw tightens. "Hockey demands everything. That's just how it is."

"Is it? Or is that the story you tell yourself to avoid taking risks?" She leans back slightly, studying me. "What if that person, that particular relationship, could have existed along-side hockey? What if it wasn't actually an either-or situation?"

Bitterness fills my tone. "You don't understand. I had to be completely focused. Any distraction could have cost me everything."

"And did that total focus get you everything you wanted?"

The question sits heavy between us.

"I'm in the NHL," I say finally.

"That's not what I asked." Her voice stays gentle but doesn't let me off the hook. "You're in the NHL, yes. But are you happy? Fulfilled? It doesn't sound like you are."

Scrubbing my neck, I can't help but picture Scout again. Her scent, her warmth, the way she touches me and makes me feel like I'm not some broken robot.

"I don't know." I peek up at the doctor. "Can I skip that for now?"

"Of course. This is only our first session. I'm just trying to find your baseline." Dr. Sable shifts in her chair, recrossing her legs. "You mentioned anger earlier. That it's been an issue on the ice. What happens if you let yourself feel anything besides anger?"

The question catches me off guard. I've been ready to talk about fighting, about penalties, about the rage that sometimes takes over when an opponent goes after one of my teammates. This is different.

"I don't understand the question."

"Anger is often what we call a secondary emotion. It usually covers something else. Fear, hurt, disappointment. What happens when you let those other feelings surface?"

My throat goes tight. People call me Ice Man. The nickname's supposed to be about my icy feelings in the face of chirping. But the truth is darker than that.

I'm not icy because I'm calm. I'm icy because I've frozen everything else out. Anger is the only emotion I let myself feel because it's useful. It gets me through games, through pain, through the empty hours when I'm alone with my thoughts. Everything else—the fear, the loneliness, the bone-deep exhaustion—I've locked behind walls of ice so thick I sometimes forget they're there.

But they are. And Scout is melting them, crack by crack, whether I want her to or not. I shake my head. "Nothing good happens."

"Can you give me an example?"

"No." The word comes out too sharp, too fast. She doesn't flinch, just waits patiently. After what feels like an hour but is probably thirty seconds, I cave. "If I let myself feel scared about my career ending, I can't function. I can't get up for PT. I don't know if I will push through the pain. So I get angry instead. Anger works. It gets me on the ice."

"I see." Her pen scratches for a moment. "Okay. You've mentioned being injured. How much pain are you in on a typical day?"

The shift in topic gives me whiplash, but maybe that's the point. "Scale of one to ten?"

"However you want to quantify it."

"Six. Sometimes seven. On bad days, eight." The admission comes easier than expected, maybe because it's just numbers. "It's been that way for two years, maybe three. You get used to it."

"Do you think that's sustainable?"

I consider that for a long beat. "It has to be."

"Okay." She makes another note, then looks back up at me. "What do you think your teammates expect of you?"

This one's easier. I've thought about it enough. "I'm supposed to be the enforcer. The guy who takes the hits so they don't have to. I fight when someone goes after our skilled players. I'm reliable, consistent, and tough."

My voice gets quieter on the last word.

Dr. Sable nods. "And what do you expect of yourself?"

"More." The word escapes before I can stop it. "Always more. Tougher, stronger, faster. Play through more pain. Take more hits. Score when it matters. Be better than I was yesterday, even when yesterday was already everything I had."

Dr. Sable sets her pen down entirely and looks at me with something that might be concern. "That sounds exhausting."

"It's hockey."

"Is it? Or is it something else?" She doesn't wait for an answer. "Do you have support at home?"

Scout's face flashes through my mind. I push out my cheek with my tongue. "Define support."

"Someone you can talk to. Someone who sees you as more than just a hockey player."

"There's..." I stop, then start again. "My roommate. She's helping with the injury. Making sure I eat and do my PT exercises. That kind of thing."

"She?"

Heat creeps up my neck. "Just one of the physical therapists that works for the team. It's temporary, just until my shoulder heals."

"I see." Dr. Sable's eyebrows rise slightly but she doesn't comment on that. "Who do you talk to when things get hard?"

"I don't."

"Never?"

"What's the point? Talking doesn't change anything. It doesn't heal injuries faster or make the team need me more. It can't make me younger or less broken."

"Broken." She absorbs that, then leans back in her chair. "You used an interesting word there. Need. You want the team to need you." She pauses, watching my face carefully. "You want to be indispensable. What happens if you're not?"

The words land like body blows, one after another. My chest goes tight, breath coming shorter. The room feels smaller suddenly, walls pressing in. "Then I'm replaceable. Expendable. Just another guy who used to play."

"And that terrifies you."

It's not a question but I answer anyway. "Well, yeah."

"What do you do when you're overwhelmed? When everything feels like too much?"

"I hit things." The honesty surprises me. "Usually I have a go with the heavy bag at the gym. Sometimes I drive to the rink at two in the morning and shoot pucks until my arms shake. Other times I just... shut down. I lock myself in my room and stare at game tape until my eyes burn."

"Does that help?"

I shake my head. "No, but it passes the time."

"Thank you for confiding in me, Silas." She smiles a little. That weird feeling of having met her somewhere before passes over me again. Almost a sense of *déjà vu*. Dr. Sable glances at the clock on the wall, then back at me.

"We're almost out of time for today, but I want to leave you with something to think about." She uncrosses her legs and leans forward, elbows on her knees. "You've built your entire identity around being useful to other people. But what if your value isn't tied to what you can do for others? What if you matter just because you exist?"

The words feel like a foreign language. I stare at her, unable to formulate a response that doesn't sound like complete rejection of the concept.

"I'd like to see you again in the next couple of weeks," she continues, standing up. "I'll reach out to you for scheduling."

"Sure." I stand too, grateful for the excuse to move. "Coach says I have to, so I'll be here."

"Silas." Her voice stops me at the door. "This is hard work. What you're doing, coming here, being honest. That takes courage. Real courage, not the kind that throws punches on the ice."

Something in my chest cracks. I scrub at the back of my neck as I mutter, "See you around, Dr. Sable."

The hallway feels too bright after the warm dimness of her office. The elevator ride down stretches forever. By the time I push through the building's front door, my hands are shaking. Seattle's gray morning air hits my face, cool and damp, and I gulp it like I've been underwater.

My truck sits where I left it. I climb in and just sit there, hands gripping the steering wheel hard enough to leave marks. The session replays in fragments.

Nobody. Replaceable. What if you matter just because you exist?

Those are heavy questions.

My phone buzzes. As if he knew I was already in a tail-spin, there's a text from Enzo.

Enzo: Got your contract numbers from the Havoc. Call me.

I dial before I can think better of it, already bracing for whatever manipulation he's about to try.

"Huxley!" His voice is too bright, too cheerful. He sounds as though he's won something. "I've got some news about your contract negotiations."

I need to rush him off the phone. "Let's hear it."

"The Havoc's offering two years, but the numbers are lower than we initially projected." He rattles off a figure that's nearly forty percent less than what I'm worth. I know what players with my stats and experience typically get.

My jaw locks. "That's insulting."

"I know, I know. But the market's tight right now. Your age, your injury history, the questions about your shoulder..." He trails off, letting the implications hang there like a noose. "I can push back hard, but I'm not sure how much wiggle room we have here."

"You're my agent. That's your job. Push back."

"I will, I will. Just managing expectations, you know?" He sounds too pleased about all this. I'm pretty sure he's enjoying delivering bad news.

Something clicks in my brain, a pattern I should have seen before.

My voice goes frosty. "Why do you sound happy about this?"

"What? I'm not happy. I'm just being realistic about market conditions..."

"You want me to take less money. Why?"

"Silas, that's ridiculous. I make more when you make more..."

"Do you?" I grip the steering wheel hard enough that my knuckles go white. "Or is there another reason you want my contract value lower? Something you're not telling me?"

Silence. It stretches on, too long and heavy.

"I'll call you back when I have more information." He hangs up before I can respond.

I sit there in my truck with my pulse pounding in my ears, pieces falling into place like a puzzle I should have solved months ago. Enzo's been sabotaging me. Feeding the organization doubts about my age, my injuries, my value as a player. Driving my price down deliberately.

But why? What does he gain from lowering my contract value when his commission goes down too?

I don't know yet. But I will. I'll figure it out and then I'll burn him for it.

When I finally drive home, Scout's in the kitchen when I walk in. She's wearing black yoga pants and an oversized gray Havoc sweatshirt, hair piled on top of her head in a messy bun, face scrubbed clean of makeup. Those dark blonde curls escape in soft tendrils around her face, making her look younger somehow. Her green eyes are soft, unguarded in the quiet of the morning.

The gray sweatshirt hangs off one shoulder, revealing smooth skin and that delicate collarbone I want to trace with my fingers. Her lips are bare, pink and full without any gloss. She's beautiful in a way that makes my chest ache. Comfortable and real and completely unaware of what seeing her like this does to me.

She looks comfortable, like she belongs here in my space. Glancing up when I walk in, she smiles. "Hey. How was your day?"

"Fine." The lie tastes bitter on my tongue.

Her smile fades. Those green eyes see too much. "You don't look fine."

"I'm handling it."

She sets her mug down carefully on the counter. That look she gets when she's trying to figure out an injury crosses her face. "Silas. Talk to me."

I shrug a shoulder. "There's nothing to talk about."

"That's bullshit. You've been wound tight since we came back from Vashon. Something's wrong and you won't tell me what it is."

I should walk away. Work through it myself until I have a solution or at least a plan. But I'm tired. So fucking tired of carrying everything by myself.

"Enzo's screwing me on my contract." The words come out rougher than I intend. "Deliberately driving my value down with the organization. I don't know why yet, but he is."

Scout's face hardens. "That bastard."

"Yeah."

"What are you going to do?"

"Fire him. As soon as I can afford to." I lean against the counter, suddenly exhausted. "But he's got his hooks into me deep. Deals in motion, endorsements that'll fall through if I walk away. He built a cage around me. I hate that I didn't even notice until I was already locked inside."

She moves close enough that I can smell her shampoo, that lavender and eucalyptus that's become familiar. "You'll figure it out. You're smarter than he is."

"Am I?" The question comes out sounding bitter and self-loathing. "Right now it feels like I'm drowning and he's the one holding my head under water."

Her hand finds mine on the counter. She twines her

fingers with mine. Hers are small and warm and steady in a way that makes my chest ache.

The contact hits me like a physical blow. I haven't let anyone hold my hand since I was a kid. It's too intimate, too vulnerable. It feels like admitting I need something.

But Scout's fingers lace through mine like it's the most natural thing in the world and suddenly I can't remember why I've been avoiding this. Her palm is warm against mine, her grip firm but gentle. Every point where our skin connects sends heat radiating up my arm. I want to pull her closer, wrap her entire body against mine, feel her everywhere.

Fuck, I want to hold her hand like this all the time. Walking down the street, sitting on the couch, falling asleep at night. The simple touch grounds me in a way I didn't know I needed. It makes me feel less alone for the first time in years.

Something in my chest eases. Not much, just enough to let me breathe a little deeper.

"My mom did the same thing," I hear myself say. The words just fall out, bypassing every filter I usually keep in place. "Built a cage. She stole from me and Hunter for years. We didn't even know until it was too late."

Scout's fingers tighten around mine. "Silas..."

"She was our agent. Our mother. The person who was supposed to protect us and look out for our interests." I stare at our joined hands because I can't look at her face while saying this. "And she robbed us blind. Embezzled millions from our accounts over the years, forged signatures, created fake investment accounts. The whole nine yards."

"I'm so sorry."

"Don't be. She made her choices." I force myself to meet her eyes. "She's in federal prison now. Fraud, embezzlement, tax evasion. They threw the book at her. Hunter lost millions before we caught it. I lost less, but only because I didn't trust her as much as he did. Even then, she got away with plenty before we figured it out."

Understanding flashes across Scout's face. "That's why you keep everyone at a distance. I wondered why you didn't let people in."

"It's one of the reasons." My voice comes out raw. "She taught me something valuable. People you trust can hurt you worse than anyone else. Because you let them get close. You give them access to the vulnerable parts and they use it to take everything you have."

She steps even closer. I can feel her warmth radiating through the space between us. "I'm not your mother. And I'm sure as hell not Enzo. I'm not here to take anything from you."

"I know that."

Scout pulls a face. Is that why you put up with Enzo?"

The question catches me off guard. "What?"

"He knows. About your mom, I mean. Does he use it against you?"

Fuck. She's too smart. Of course she figured it out. I nod my head, expelling a breath.

"If it gets out, the endorsements start asking questions. They'll wonder about my judgment when my own mother stole from me." I shake my head. "Star player gets robbed by his own mother. Great headline."

"You're a victim. She's a criminal."

"Yeah, well. The media won't see it that way."

"I see it that way." Her voice turns fierce. "You can't let him hold that over you forever. You deserve better."

"I know. Shit." I rub a hand over my face.

Scout's free hand comes up, cups my jaw with a gentleness that undoes me. "Let me in. Just a little bit? See what happens."

I should pull away. I've worked so hard to keep the walls up where they've always been and keep her at a safe distance where she can't reach the parts of me that are too damaged to fix.

But her eyes are so warm and steady. And I'm so goddamn tired of being alone with everything.

"I'm not good at this," I whisper.

"At what?"

"Letting people in. Trusting anyone with anything that matters."

"I know." She smiles but it's small and sad. "You've said as much. Listen, I'm not great at it either."

"Why not? You're good with everyone. You make it look easy."

She takes a breath that shakes on the exhale. "Because Enzo spent five years systematically destroying my self-worth. He made me feel like I was too much and not enough at the same time. Clingy, but not interesting enough to keep his attention. Helpful, but not accomplished enough to be proud of. Present, but not pretty enough to stay faithful to." Her voice shakes. "I gave him everything I had. And he *still* cheated. He *still* left me. He made me feel like I was funda-mentally broken."

Rage floods through me, hot and immediate and focused. "You're not broken. He's a fucking idiot who couldn't see what he had."

"Maybe." She shrugs one shoulder. "Or maybe I'm just not what men want."

I growl, "That's complete bullshit."

"Is it? Because I've been living here for weeks and you still won't even look at me half the time. You push me away every time we get close. I keep thinking that you feel the pull that I feel too, but I'm always wrong. So maybe Enzo was right about me all along."

The accusation lands like a fist to my chest. Because she's right. I have been avoiding her, keeping her at arm's length, pretending I don't want her when I think about her constantly. Scout's the first thing I think about in the morning and the last thing on my mind before I fall asleep.

My voice is gone to gravel as I say, "I look at you."

"Not like you mean it."

"Scout..." I run out of words. So I kiss her instead, brushing her lips with mine, bringing her close. Under my hands, she's all woman. Flared hips, ripe tits, and the sweetest taste imaginable.

This kiss is slow, more deliberate than the one we shared on Vashon Island. A promise, instead of just a claim. She melts into me immediately, hands fisting in my shirt, making a small sound against my mouth that goes straight to my chest and lodges there. Her taste is so heady that my hands tremble with the urge to crush her against me and plunder her mouth.

When I pull back, she's breathless and flushed and absolutely perfect.

"I look at you," I say again. My words are quieter this time and a hell of a lot more honest. "All the fucking time. I look at you and I want things I have no right to want."

Scout's lips are glossy, pink, and parted. She looks up at me like I'm someone worth talking to. "What kind of things?"

"You. This. A future where I'm not so damaged that I destroy everything good that gets close to me."

Her eyes shine with tears she's trying not to let fall. "You're not damaged, Si."

"I am." I rest my forehead against hers, breathing her in.

"But maybe you're a little broken too. Maybe two broken people can figure out how to be less broken together."

She chuckles. "Two broken people trying to figure their shit out. Sounds like a complete disaster."

"Probably."

"Definitely."

My heart pounds. "How about we don't think about any of that right now?"

She pulls back just enough to look at me properly. "Okay, big man. We can do that."

God, when she calls me big man, I can't refuse her anything. So I kiss her again. Softer this time, sweeter. It feels fucking great.

And for the first time in years, maybe ever, I let myself believe that maybe this could work. It's entirely possible that I can have her and hockey, too. Maybe I can let her in without destroying everything. I can be the man she deserves instead of the broken thing I've always been.

Maybe.

Chapter Twenty

Scout

I stand outside the locker room double-checking my supplies for the third time. Laminated instruction cards sit on top of the cart. Mini resistance bands in three different tensions fill one box. Lacrosse balls for trigger point release fill another. Foam rollers lean against the side. Everything's arranged on the equipment cart in a way that looks organized and professional.

My hands shake. I smooth them down my jeans and take a breath.

Twenty minutes. I can do anything for twenty minutes. This is the third class I've put together, so at least I have some idea of what's to come.

The door swings open and players start filtering in, loud and restless with pre-game energy. A couple of rookies glance curiously at my setup. But no one says anything. I don't hear any mutters or see any players rolling their eyes. That's good, at least.

Beck Tate shoots me a look sharp enough to slice through steel. Coach Cross nods once, giving me permission to start.

My voice comes out steadier than I feel. "All right, everyone. Twenty minutes of mobility work. We're hitting hips, shoulders, and thoracic spine. Two minutes each side. You can pretend you like me later."

A few scattered laughs come from the back. Jett grins. "What's next, downward dog in the crease?"

More laughter ripples through the room but they're already moving into position, copying the hip opener I'm demonstrating. The rookies are eager, mimicking my movements with the kind of focus that makes my chest warm.

The veterans are more skeptical. Moose does the bare minimum until Thorne elbows him. Hunter participates, but I can tell he's humoring me.

Silas is trying gamely to balance, but he's pretty wobbly.

"Silas," I say, keeping my tone light. "Bring your left shoulder down and balance the pose."

"I feel stupid," he mutters, but he drops into the shoulder opener against the wall.

I fight a smile and watch him hold the position longer than anyone else, face going tight with the stretch. His shoulder must be killing him but he doesn't quit until I tell him to switch sides.

"Good," I say quietly as I walk past. Just that one word. Something flickers in his eyes before he looks away. My cheeks feel warm as I remember our kiss last night.

We went to bed in our own rooms after kissing for a while. We didn't talk about what it meant. I don't want to, honestly. But now all the restless energy flows under my skin, puddling at the base of my spine. I can't wait until I'm alone with him again.

Twenty minutes later I pack up my cart and head to my spot in the tunnel to watch warmups. My heart pounds in my chest. I can't believe they actually participated instead of blowing me off.

Players hit the ice and I notice the difference immediately. Rookies look lighter on their feet, quicker through their strides. Even the veterans move with more fluidity through their warm-up drills.

The game starts and I hold my breath.

It's not pretty. The other team is Santa Fe, not one of the teams they face regularly, and the Vultures have an extremely aggressive offensive line. By the time the third period rolls around, the score is tied two to two. An opposing forward gets in Silas's face after a clean hit, chirping and shoving, trying to draw a retaliation penalty.

Everything happens in slow motion. Silas's jaw goes tight. His fists start to curl. Every line of his body says he's about to snap and take the bait.

He pauses instead and takes a visible breath. He rolls his shoulders back exactly the way I showed them in the locker room. Then he skates away clean.

My heart is pounding out of my chest. I beam at him from the tunnel. Silas can't see me, but I'm so proud of him.

The ref doesn't call anything because there's nothing to call and Silas stays on the ice instead of sitting in the penalty box. Two shifts later he assists on the game-winning goal.

We win four to two. We're messy, but it's effective. Those twenty minutes of mobility work made a difference. I *feel* it in my bones.

Players stream past in the tunnel after the final buzzer. Juliet brushes by me with a proud smile and a squeeze to my shoulder. Beck mutters something to Coach Cross that I can't quite hear but Cross nods and says, "Keep it on the schedule."

Keep it.

Staying on the schedule means my program's permanent.

Silas comes through last, hair damp from his helmet, eyes unreadable in that way he has. He slows as he passes me. He doesn't quite stop, but his words ring out. "Your thing worked."

Not praise exactly. It's certainly not warm or effusive. And the corners of his mouth curl up just a hint. He's smiling. He's fucking smiling! I feel like all my veins are suddenly filled with pop rocks, fizzing and snapping.

Coming from Silas Huxley, it might as well be a standing ovation.

My pulse pounds in my throat. I grin as I watch him disappear toward the locker room.

Standing there alone in the tunnel, I feel lighter than I have in weeks. Maybe months. Tonight my work mattered. It made a tangible difference that showed up on the ice.

For once, I wasn't just useful. I was actually good at something that counts. After the game, I crash hard, barely making it into my bed before I fall asleep. Too many late nights, staying up and texting StatMan. So it's not too surprising that I sleep a little late.

The next morning, I wake up buzzing with residual adrenaline. Silas is on my mind, big time. What I want to do most of all is go into his room and crawl into bed with him. When we stayed on the island, he spooned me for a while in the morning, gloriously warm and sleepy. I really want more of that. And then we could... explore... when he woke up.

But creeping into my roommate's bed and feeling him up would be massively weird, so I think about what I would like to do second most. And then I smile.

I find Silas in the kitchen with his protein shake, watching him scroll through his phone with that permanent scowl etched on his face.

"Come to hot yoga with me," I blurt out.

He looks at me like I just suggested we jump out of a plane without parachutes. "No."

"Yes." I'm grinning, half teasing but completely serious. "You owe me. One hour. That's it."

"I don't do yoga."

"You did mobility work yesterday and it helped. This is the same thing but sweatier."

His jaw ticks. "Scout..."

"One hour, Silas. Come on. Be reckless with me."

Something shifts in his expression. Maybe it's the challenge. Or maybe it's the way I'm looking at him. He sets down his shake with a resigned exhale and gives in.

"Fine. One hour. But I'm not wearing those tight pants."

I beam at him. "Deal."

When we arrive at the yoga studio, the airy room is already filling up with bodies. We squeeze into two slots in the middle of the class and unroll our mats. Silas looks like a glacier someone dropped into a sauna. He unfolds his massive frame onto the too-small mat. His knees practically reach his ears.

Other women in the class steal glances at him. Pride pricks at me because I'm the one who brought him here. This mountain of a man actually listened when I asked him to do something completely outside his comfort zone.

The instructor starts and Silas struggles immediately. His too-tight shoulders resist the poses. His hips are beyond stiff. Rugged as rebar, he tries to bend into shapes his body actively fights.

"This is torture," he grits out during a particularly deep lunge.

I kneel beside him and adjust his front knee, guiding his arm into better alignment. Hot skin slick with sweat burns under my hand. "Breathe. In through your nose, out through your mouth. *Slowly.*"

He follows my instruction, actually listening to me for once instead of fighting everything.

Something shifts in his body. Not ease exactly, but surrender. He lets it wash over him like a wave and stops struggling against it.

Most people never see this Silas. Vulnerable and unguarded, willing to look foolish if it means he might feel better. His massive frame folds into shapes it wasn't designed for, sweat dripping down his temple, jaw finally unclenched. They call him Ice Man but he's melting right here.

Right now in this humid room surrounded by strangers, he's just Silas. Not the enforcer. Not the damaged veteran fighting to stay relevant. He's just a man trying something new because I asked him to.

Silas watches me. Heavy and focused, his gaze tracks my movements like I'm something worth studying. Maybe he's seeing parts of me he didn't notice before. I like that idea.

When we move into the next pose, Silas immediately tries to muscle his way through it. His jaw sets. His shoulders lock. He treats the stretch like an opponent instead of a conversation, forcing his body into place with sheer will.

I lower my voice and call to him. "You don't have to meet every sensation with force."

He stills. Looks at me, confused, like that idea has never once crossed his mind.

"Try it again," I say gently. "But don't fight it. Just… stay."

He exhales and resets. He wobbles immediately, irritation flickering across his face. For a second, I think he's going to bail. Instead, he loosens his grip on the pose and stops pushing. Then lets his weight settle where it wants to go.

And his balance finds him.

Silas holds it this time. Not rigid or strained. Merely

present. His breathing evens out, and something in his posture softens, like his body finally believes it doesn't have to be on guard.

"That's it," I tell him quietly. "See how much better that is?"

He nods once, his eyes focusing on a far-off point on the wall. "It feels better."

My heart warms. During the final pose, savasana, everyone sprawls on their mats. Silas stretches out with his chest still heaving, eyes closed, looking more at ease than I've ever seen him.

For just a moment, he looks almost peaceful.

I sneak a glance from my own mat and he catches me, cracking one eye open. The corners of his mouth curl up ever so slightly.

"This isn't terrible," he admits, voice low.

My heart does a stupid flip in my chest. "I'm glad."

After class I insist on smoothies from the juice bar next door. I'm ready to plead with him to get the smoothie teasingly named the Toxic Sludge. But Silas orders one after looking at the menu for approximately two seconds. He sees my raised eyebrows.

"What? My diet is 90% kale and Greek yogurt. When I see it on the menu, I always go for the kale."

"Interesting." I give him a once-over. Even after the intense yoga class, he might as well be a supermodel. His tousled hair is tied back, his cheekbones sharp enough to cut, and he wears his sweatpants and soft-looking sweatshirt like they were made for him.

We sit at a small table by the window.

"I feel like I got hit by a truck." His voice has less edge than usual, almost relaxed.

"Yeah?" I hide my grin behind my smoothie. "You look like you just smoked pot for the first time."

He shoots me a sly look. "That *would* be a first."

"Wait, you haven't smoked pot? Not even in college?"

"Nope." He smiles into his smoothie. "I've always had drug tests hanging over my head. It's not worth stressing myself out."

"Wowww. You know, I've known you for years. But I'm still learning all kinds of things about you, Silas."

"Stick around. Next I'll juggle a pile of flaming chainsaws."

"Look who has jokes all of the sudden." I bite my lip, leaning in and smiling. "You need to do yoga more often."

We're quiet for a minute, comfortable in the silence. People flow past the window outside while morning light streams through the glass, warm on my face. I glance at him.

"Tell me something."

"Like what?" He takes the final sip of his smoothie and then nudges his cup away. "Something funny? Or something serious?"

Playing with my straw, I shrug. "Whichever one you feel like."

He stares off into the distance for a moment. "I had a dream about my mom."

That's not what I expected him to say at all. "Yeah?"

His head bobs. "You know about the whole extortion thing?"

Silas is referring to the fact that his mom went to jail last year over continued attempts to extort money from his brother Hunter. From what I read, Silas's mom managed all the brothers' money at one point and likely stole from all of them. I nod slowly. "A little."

Silas purses his lips.

"My mom liked to draw. Sketches mostly. Landscapes, buildings, people's faces." He stares at his smoothie cup like it might hold answers. "After she left, after everything came out about the embezzlement and the extortion, I threw all her drawings away. I thought it would hurt less if I erased her completely."

My throat goes tight. I set down my cup carefully, giving him space to continue or stop.

"It didn't help. I still thought about her. I missed her even though I was so fucking angry. Am, actually. I *am* so angry at her. It really pisses me off that I had a nice dream about her. She doesn't deserve that."

"You're allowed to miss her and be angry at the same time," I say softly. "Those things can exist together."

He nods once with this tiny gesture of vulnerability.

"I regret throwing the drawings away," he admits. "They were good. She was talented. That part of her was real even if everything else was a lie."

I reach across the table and stop just short of touching his hand. The choice is his whether he wants the contact. He doesn't pull away, just stares at where our hands almost meet.

"Thank you for telling me," I say.

"Yeah." He clears his throat and pulls back, pointing at his smoothie. "This is still disgusting, by the way. Kale or no kale, I wish I had gotten something fruity."

I laugh and the tension breaks. "Noted. Next time I'll get you something better."

He glances at me. "So there's going to be a next time?"

"Absolutely. I'm dragging you to hot yoga every week now. It's happening."

He groans but there's something in his eyes that looks almost like affection. "You're the worst."

"You like it."

"I really don't."

His mouth curves slightly. I'll take it.

Chapter Twenty-One

Silas

The Seattle Havoc are supposed to be blowing off steam. Juliet arranged for us to rent out this retro bowling alley with sticky lanes, neon lights flickering overhead, and pitchers of cheap beer making the rounds. The women have claimed lanes on one end. The guys roughhouse and trash talk on the other. I sit with my arms crossed, nursing one warm beer, counting down the minutes until I can leave without looking antisocial.

I can't wait to be out of here.

Scout's at the far end with Juliet, Jessa, Wren, and Mollie. Her dark blonde curls are pulled up in two pigtails that make her look younger than she is. The custom bowling shirt fits her perfectly, black fabric hugging her curves, silver lettering catching the neon lights. Those green eyes sparkle with genuine happiness as Jessa pulls out the shirts. Pink yoga pants hug her legs, showing off her shape in a way that makes my mouth go dry. Watching her clutch the shirt to her chest, I can see the emotion flooding her face.

Beautiful doesn't begin to cover it.

Jessa just pulled out custom bowling shirts for what she

keeps calling the Coven, apparently their name for the women that work for The Havoc. But my eyes follow only one person. As I watch, Scout gets visibly emotional over her bowling shirt. She clutches the black shirt with silver lettering to her chest like it's something precious.

"I'm so grateful. You ladies have been so welcoming." Her voice carries across the lanes. "I was so lonely after the divorce. But you have made me feel like I'm a part of a team."

Her words tug at my heart. Hearing her say that she was lonely feels like pouring acid on an open wound.

"Oh, girl." Juliet pulls her into a hug. Jessa beams like a proud mother hen. Mollie looks on, smiling at Scout's reaction.

Something twists in my chest watching her. She's so desperate to be included. So grateful for basic kindness. It makes me want to find Enzo and break his jaw for making her feel like she had to earn acceptance.

She's amazing and beautiful. And Enzo is fucking scum.

Their game finishes around the same time ours does, so we meet in the middle of the alley, taking up several tables. Hunter sits down and pulls Juliet onto his lap. She turns to him and whispers something in his ear. He obviously likes whatever secret she has, because his pleased murmur rumbles from his chest as he rubs a circle in her back.

A part of me wonders if I'll ever be lucky enough to have a relationship like theirs. Sure, it started out a lie. Two people fake engaged, pretending that they were in love. But soon enough, it became apparent that their feelings weren't fake.

My eyes travel over to Scout. She's wearing her custom bowling shirt with a pair of pink yoga pants. My breath hitches when I see her lean over to pick up a pile of napkins from the floor. The thin material of her yoga pants stretches, becoming ever so slightly see-through. And I'm not the only one who notices. My brother Jett looks on, sipping his beer. And Thorne bites his lip as he gazes at her, his expression a little dreamy.

Like fuck I'd let Thorne hook up with Scout. He's a huge playboy, different girl every night of the week. Definitely not down for any kind of commitment. If he acted on his obvious desire to take Scout home, he'd leave her crushed.

Luckily, after a few seconds, he blinks and looks away, responding with a laugh to something Tate said. Note to self: tell Thorne to keep his dick in his goddamn pants for once.

I watch Scout slip into caretaker mode without even realizing she's doing it. Making sure everyone's beers stay topped up. Ordering more nachos when plates run low. Juliet jumps up and fusses with the lane settings for the next game. When she makes a frustrated noise, Scout steps in and smoothly corrects it for her. They beam at each other.

Scout's a helper at heart. A sunshine-filled goddess.

A few minutes later, I empty my cup. Scout appears at my elbow, offering me a cold bottle of the non-alcoholic beer I prefer. She remembered. Of course she did. Scout remembers everything about everyone.

I don't even think they have this beer at the bowling alley.

"Thanks," I say. "You always know just what I need."

"You're welcome, Si." Scout's cheeks flare with pink, her blonde curls arranged in pigtails.

Ugh, that nickname does things to me. It's a sign of closeness, one I shouldn't allow. But it warms my chest to hear it.

"Hey." Juliet leans close to Scout during a lull, voice pitched low. I catch her words anyway, because I'm a fucking creep who's attuned to everything Scout. Juliet touches Scout's arm. "Don't burn yourself out taking care of everyone. You're allowed to just exist here, you know. Without being useful."

My jaw tightens. Scout burning herself out? Of course she is. She's always smiling, always fetching, always fixing things for other people. Making herself indispensable so people won't leave her. I sip my beer, washing down the bitterness in my throat with the brew.

The next hour, I refuse Scout's help three separate times.

She tries to grab me a fresh beer. "I'm good."

She offers to get me food from the counter. "Sit down, Scout."

She starts to adjust my lane settings. "I can handle it myself."

Each time she looks confused. A little hurt. But she listens, settling back in her seat by the women instead of hovering over me.

I tell myself I'm helping her. She doesn't have to work for acceptance and I need her to see that. But really I just feel like an asshole, because watching her take care of everyone makes me want things I can't have.

I shouldn't want Scout Nash. I shouldn't feel this bone-deep longing for her smiles and her adorable blushes. She's my agent's ex and my roommate. Oh, and she works for the Havoc. Like I could forget that little nugget of information.

I should know better than to dip my pen in the company ink. But I can't stop staring at Scout, who is all rainbows and sunshine on the cloudiest day.

Though I know better than this, I move closer, finding a seat that allows me better access to the girls' conversation.

Mollie bowls a gutter ball and laughs at herself. But my eyes are stuck on the curve of Scout's hips. The way she moves is so graceful. Now that I've done yoga with her, I see where she gets it from. Scout moves quickly toward the lane, carrying her bowling ball, and knocks down seven pins. She spins, beaming with pride like she won a whole tournament.

My pulse jumps before I can stop it. Fuck, she's hot. The thought, unbidden, comes to the surface: the feeling of her beneath me as I kissed her, the way she tasted. Before I can stop that line of thinking, my cock stirs.

Yeah, not helpful. We're in a bowling alley.

People call me Ice Man because I try not to react. I don't let my emotions show. Everything is kept locked down tight where no one can see it.

Right now though, watching Scout laugh at something one of the women said, seeing her lean over to help Mollie with something, the ice is melting, big pieces shearing off, dripping away into nothing.

Then Theo Kozlov appears.

Tall, dishwater blond hair, stupidly handsome in a seedy way that women probably love. He's young, too young for her, but that doesn't seem to stop him. He slides into the seat next to Scout with an easy smile that makes my teeth grind.

Jealousy burns bright, the flame growing hot in my chest. I feel possessiveness claw at my throat. Apparently he's forgotten my threat in light of Scout's pretty smile.

Every instinct screams at me to walk over there and claim her in front of everyone. Mark her as mine so they all know she's off limits. The control I've built over years is splintering, fracturing, falling apart piece by piece.

"Hey, Scout. Didn't know you bowled."

"I don't. Not well, anyway." She laughs brightly. Something in my chest goes volcanic.

Kozlov leans closer, all charm and confidence. "You look great tonight. Love the shirt."

She actually blushes. Pink rises in her cheeks. "Thanks. The Coven made them. It was Jessa's idea."

"Well, she has excellent taste." His grin gets wider. "Listen, I was thinking that after this, we could go grab a drink?"

My fist curls around the beer bottle so hard I hear it creak. The urge to throw it at his head is overwhelming.

Scout hesitates, smile faltering. "Oh, Kozlov, that's really nice of you to ask, but..."

"Think about it," he says, standing before she can finish declining. "No pressure at all. Just let me know before you leave."

He walks away with that easy swagger, leaving Scout sitting there staring at her hands with that flush still staining her cheeks. I'm moving before I consciously decide to move. Crossing the lanes, shoulders squared, everything in me coils, tight and ready to snap. I grab her elbow, tugging her away from the Coven.

"Let's go home," I grate out.

"Home?" She looks up, startled. "What? Why?"

"Because I want to." I grit my teeth. "Now, Scout."

She puts a hand to my chest, peering up into my face. "Silas, what's wrong?"

"Just come with me." It comes out as more of a plea than I mean it to. I don't wait for her to argue. Instead, I lift her, grabbing her purse and coat. "Here."

"Silas! Wait, I need my shoes."

Gritting my teeth, I walk her up to the counter and impatiently wait as the teenager who works the shoe exchange gets to us. I'm on edge as we both shove our feet into our shoes. She slides me a look while she's knotting her laces.

"Are you going to tell me what's going on?"

"Outside." I drag my coat on as I wait for her. When she's finished, I tow her out the doors. Thorne is watching us, his eyes narrowed, but he doesn't call attention to us.

I'll deal with him later. Right now, I wrap an arm around Scout's waist as I pull her toward my truck.

She runs out of her admittedly saintlike patience. "What the hell was that? You just dragged me out of there in front of everyone."

I point at the door. "Get in the truck."

"No." She plants her feet. "Not until you tell me what's going on."

It's hard for me to be so out of control. I round on her, hissing. "Kozlov asked you out again."

"So?"

"So?" My voice rises. "Were you going to say yes?"

"I wasn't! I tried to let him down gently. Then you got all caveman and demanded that I leave with you." She crosses her arms. "And even if I was planning to say yes, why would you care? We've barely even kissed."

The words hit like fists to my ribs. Using my own bullshit against me. "Scout..."

"No. You don't get to be jealous." Her eyes flash. "You don't get to act like you own me when you treat me like kryptonite most of the time. You kiss me and then you stare at me. Like… what? The math ain't mathin'."

She isn't getting it. "I'm trying to protect you."

"From what?"

"From me!" The words tear out of my chest. "From the fact that I'm broken and angry and I don't know how to be what you need."

"Si." She pauses for a long beat. "I need you to stop pushing me away every time we get close."

The space between us crackles with electricity. It's charged and dangerous, ready to ignite.

"You deserve better than me."

"You don't get to decide what I deserve." She steps closer,

chin lifting in defiance. "That's my choice to make. Not yours."

"Scout..."

"Do you want me or not?" Her eyes are the exact shade of green of a juniper tree. "Just be honest. For once in your life, just be honest with me."

The truth claws up my throat. "I want you so much I can't fucking breathe around it. I think about you constantly. I dream about you. Fuck, I wake up hard and aching and hating myself because you're ten feet down the hall and I can't have you."

Her breath catches audibly. "Then why..."

"There's a line I shouldn't cross. And damn it, I keep crossing it anyway. I'm terrified that if I let myself actually have you, I'll ruin you the way I ruin everything good that comes near me. Not to mention, you're my agent's ex wife."

She stares at me for a long moment. Then she lets out a bitter bark of laughter. "Enzo. You're worried about Enzo?"

"He's still my agent. It's complicated."

"He's nothing. He's in the past, a mistake I'm never making again. And if you can't see the difference between him and you, then you're an idiot."

She turns to walk away. I catch her wrist and spin her back around to face me.

I growl, "Don't walk away from me."

She sucks in a breath. "Then give me a reason to stay."

I kiss her, hard and desperate. Claiming her mouth like I've every right to, when I know I don't. She gasps against my lips and I swallow the sound, backing her against the truck. My hands are everywhere at once. Her hips. Her waist. Fisting in her curls the way I've been dying to.

"Silas," she gasps when I break the kiss to breathe. "Someone could see..."

"I don't care." I drag my mouth down her throat, sucking hard enough to leave a visible mark. "Let them see. Let everyone know you're mine."

"Am I?" Her voice is breathless but challenging. "Because half a minute ago you were telling me I deserve better."

"You do." I bite down on her pulse point and she moans. "But I'm too selfish to let you fall in love with anyone else."

She gasps, "Then don't let me go."

I look around the parking lot. Mostly empty now, growing dark. The bowling alley's back entrance is twenty feet away, nestled in shadows between dumpsters and a locked delivery door that no one uses.

I grab her hand. "Come with me."

"Where..."

"Just trust me."

I pull her into the shadows, pinning her against the brick wall. The space is narrow, barely wide enough for both of us. Anyone walking to their car could see us if they looked. If we're not careful, we'll be heard.

The danger makes everything sharper.

"Silas, we can't..." Her protest dies when my hand slides under her shirt. I cup her breast through her bra. She hisses.

"We can." I thumb her nipple through the fabric and she arches into my touch. "And we will. But you have to stay quiet."

"Someone could..."

"Then you better not scream." I drop to my knees. My hands shake as I yank her yoga pants down her legs.

"Oh my God." Her hands fist in my hair as I push her right thigh up, zeroing in on the wet spot spreading across her lacy white thong. "Si!"

I look up at her. Her eyes are wide, pupils blown dark, lips parted in shock and arousal. She's perfect. Terrified and turned on and trusting me completely even though this is reckless and stupid.

"Hold on to me," I growl. "And don't make a sound."

Pushing the damp fabric on her panties aside, I bury my face between her thighs and lick her slit.

She bites her fist to keep from crying out. Her other hand grips my shoulder, nails digging in through my shirt hard enough to bruise. I devour her with no finesse, no patience. Fastening my mouth over her clit, I kiss her just the way I would her mouth. It's just raw need and possession and the driving urge to mark her as mine in every way I can.

I want her to come on my beard, soak my face with her juices.

Voices drift from the parking lot. People are leaving the bowling alley. Scout's whole body goes rigid with panic.

I don't stop. If anything, I go harder. Tongue circling her clit, two fingers pumping inside her, crooking them to hit a spot that makes her shake.

"Oh god." She clutches at my shoulders for dear life. "Fuck, Si. You're so good at that."

Her thighs tremble. She's close, so close I can feel it in how her muscles tighten. I pull back just enough to whisper against her wet skin. "Come for me, Pretty Girl. But stay quiet. Don't let them hear what I'm doing to you."

That's it. She breaks, silently. Her mouth opens in a soundless scream, body convulsing, flooding my tongue and covering my chin. I lick her through it, groaning against her, cock so hard it's painful.

When she can stand again, I rise and spin her to face the wall. She presses her palms against the cool brick and shivers. "Silas..."

"Be a good girl." I free my straining cock from my jeans with shaking hands. Pressing against her from behind, I marvel at the flushed skin of her bare ass. I can only imagine how it's going to feel when I sink deep inside her, filling her to the hilt with my huge cock. "You said you wanted this. You said you wanted me to claim you."

"Yes," she gasps. "God, yes."

It takes me a minute to grab a condom out of my wallet and sheathe my cock. While I'm doing that, I lean over and growl in her ear. "Make it easy for me. Step back and spread your legs, baby."

She responds in an instant, rocking her hips so that I can see her perfect pink slit.

"Fuck yeah." I line my pulsing cock up, notching the thick head at her entrance, then pushing inside her heat in one hard thrust. My eyes roll up in my head. Just as I imagined, her pussy is so tight and wet, so fucking warm. She bites her own arm to muffle the sound. I don't give her time to adjust.

I fuck her hard and fast and desperate, one hand clamped over her mouth, the other gripping her hip hard enough to leave bruises.

"Mine," I growl against her ear. "Say it."

She nods frantically, making muffled sounds against my palm that might be agreement.

"You're mine. Not Kozlov's. Not anyone else's. Mine."

I reach down between us with my free hand, find her clit, rub in tight circles. Her whole body goes taut. She comes again, clenching around me like a vice. I wish I could hold out for longer, make her come again, but I'm weak. I groan into her shoulder, biting down to muffle my own sounds, pulsing and spilling inside her.

We stay frozen like that for a moment. Both panting, shaking, pressed against the wall like we're holding each other up. I drop languid kisses against her shoulders, as though I'm in no hurry. She chuckles, breathless.

I pull out carefully. Scout moves to straighten her clothes with trembling hands and I help as much as I can while I tuck my cock back in. I don't know what to do with the condom so I put it in my pocket. I'll probably have to wash these pants a thousand times. But I'm distracted as Scout turns to face me, putting her arms around my neck.

"Silas..." Her voice is completely wrecked.

God, she's too good. I cup her face between my palms and kiss her softly. "I'm sorry."

"For what?"

"For being jealous. For dragging you out here. For..." I gesture helplessly at the wall. "This."

She laughs, breathless and bright and disbelieving. "I'm not sorry."

"You should be. It was completely reckless."

"Maybe I like being reckless." She looks up at me through her lashes. "When it's with you."

My chest goes tight. "Scout..."

"You can't take it back now." Her smile is gentle. "You claimed me. In *public*. Anyone could have seen. That means something."

She's right. It does mean something. It means I've crossed a line I can't uncross. I just staked a claim I've no right to make and marked her as mine when I'm still lying to her every single night.

It means I'm in too deep to back out now.

"Yeah," I say finally. "It means something, baby."

I kiss her then, tipping her head back, lazily tongue fucking her again. When I pull away, she stares at me, her green eyes glazed. She shivers and I curse.

"Fuck. It's cold out. Let's go get you warm."

After tucking her in the passenger seat, I drive home with her hand in mine, thumb stroking over her knuckles. Holding her hand shouldn't feel this monumental. It's just fingers laced together, palm pressed to palm, simple contact that people do without thinking. But I can't remember the last time I held someone's hand like this.

Her hand's small and warm in mine, fitting perfectly like it was made to be there. Every point where our skin connects sends heat up my arm, anchoring me in a way I didn't know I needed. This is more intimate than what we just did against that wall.

More vulnerable. More real. Because this is the part that means something beyond physical need. This is me choosing to keep touching her even when the desperate urgency has passed. Choosing connection over the isolation I've wrapped myself in for years.

It feels unbelievably good.

Chapter Twenty-Two

Scout

It actually happened. After Silas fucked my brains out in a parking lot, I climbed into his bed and fell asleep in his arms. And then when I woke?

He was still there, though half-awake. A thousand questions flared to life. What did last night mean? Are we a thing? Should we be exclusive?

Silas didn't say a single word, which is rather infuriatingly *him*. None of my questions are answered. But he leans over and kisses me, ignoring my morning breath to light up all my neurons. It's so good that I swear, I can still feel it when I press my fingertips to my lips.

After a long shower and dragging myself through the processes of getting dressed and making breakfast, I find Si gone. Pushing out a disappointed breath, I sigh. That was bound to happen, I guess.

My phone buzzes while I'm neck-deep in spreadsheets, tracking recovery metrics that all blur together after the third hour. A text from Silas lights up my screen.

SILAS

Street hockey tonight. You're coming.

Not a question. A statement. My stomach does a little flip.

ME

Where?

SILAS

West Seattle lot. 6pm. Bring water.

Me

Is this a date?

SILAS

It's family.

The word family sits heavy in my chest. I stare at it for a long moment, trying to process what that means. He wants me there for something he does with his brothers, I guess? Choosing to see that as him bringing me into his inner circle could happen.

SCOUT

Okay. I'll be there.

Trying to focus on my spreadsheets after that proves difficult. Data flows in endless streams in front of me, but I can't focus. On the best day, I struggle with data analysis. Now my mind keeps drifting back to that one word.

Family.

By six, I'm standing in a cracked asphalt lot in West Seattle that looks like it's seen significantly better days. Battered hockey nets sit at either end, held together with duct tape and determination. The surface is more pothole than pavement but being the first one to gripe about it won't happen.

The Huxley brothers are already there when I arrive. Hunter strips down to a faded t-shirt, hockey stick in hand like an extension of his arm. Jett winds tape around his blade with the focused precision of someone who's done this ritual a thousand times. They all put on blacked-out rollerblades. The corners of my mouth tip up at how seriously they seem to take their street hockey.

To my surprise, Juliet perches on the hood of Hunter's truck looking elegant in jeans and a cream sweater. She spots me first and waves. "Hey girl!"

"Look who actually showed," Jett calls out, eyes narrowing on me with curiosity. "Ice Man brought company?"

I wave awkwardly, suddenly feeling like I'm intruding on something sacred. "Hi. I'm, uh... here."

"Yes you are," Juliet supplies warmly, sliding off the hood to hug me like we're old friends. "I'm really glad you came."

Silas appears at my elbow before I can respond. His hand finds the small of my back, warm and possessive through my shirt. He doesn't say anything, just guides me back to the truck's tailgate. I look up at him, my breath visible in the night air.

"Hi."

One corner of his mouth turns up. "Hi. This looks good on you."

He tugs my hoodie, which is actually his. It's black and grey, Seattle Havoc colors, and enormous on me. The sleeves are pushed up and the hem hits my thighs. I bite my lip, unable to suppress a smile. "Thanks."

"Will you watch?" His gaze anchors me.

"Of course." My smile is meant to be soothing.

Jett whistles low, gaze flicking between us with knowing amusement. "Didn't know you were bringing a plus-one, Ice Man."

"She's wearing my hoodie," Silas says, loud enough for everyone to hear. "That should tell you everything you need to know."

Hunter groans from where he's stretching. "Christ. Here we go."

Juliet's smile is absolutely knowing. She pats the bench beside her. "Come sit with me. Let them posture and be ridiculous."

I sink down gratefully on the truck's gate. Silas and his brothers take to the cracked asphalt lot like it's Madison Square Garden. It seems like they have a loose game with no particular positions. The only goal they seem to have is to be the one to score and they're utterly ruthless with each other, competitive in ways that should probably concern me. When Hunter drives his elbow into Jett's side and leaves him doubled over while he swoops away, chasing the puck, I cringe.

"Don't worry." Juliet leans toward me. "They play hard but they know better than to do any lasting damage."

"Thanks." I bite my lip. "They're all grown ups, I guess."

"Ehh. Sometimes you wouldn't know it." She winks at me.

For his part, Silas looks lethal out there.He's controlled aggression skating across cracked pavement like it's smooth ice. His shirt's already damp with sweat, clinging to his broad shoulders and defined chest. Dirty blond hair under a backwards black baseball cap that should honestly be illegal. It shows off the sharp angles of his very-kissable jaw. Those blue-gray eyes are focused and intense as he tracks the puck. Massive thighs power him across the asphalt with explosive speed.

Every line of his body radiates controlled violence barely leashed. Watching him check Hunter hard enough to rattle teeth, I see the raw power in his frame. The way his muscles coil and release with killer precision. He glances over at the truck occasionally, making sure I'm still there and watching.

My heart does this stupid flip-and-squeeze thing every single time.

"So," Juliet says quietly beside me. "It finally happened?"

I'm blushing too hard to meet her eyes, so I just keep watching the boys. "What happened?"

"You two got together." Juliet's eyes are kind when she looks at me. "I've known the Huxleys for a while now. And Silas? He doesn't let people in. He keeps everyone at arm's length. People call him Ice Man for a reason. Cold and unapproachable, locked down tight. But he let you in somehow. He thawed for you."

My lips curve into a soft smile. "I don't know if I'd say that."

"I'd say it." Juliet squeezes my hand. "And I'm glad he found you. He needs someone like you in his life."

I don't know what to say to that. How do I explain that being terrified of being too much for him consumes me? Enzo spent five years telling me I smother people. Now I keep waiting for the moment when Silas realizes I'm not worth the effort because that feels inevitable.

I just paste on a smile and watch as Silas bodies Jett against the low wall, clean and brutal, then looks back at me immediately after. He's making sure I saw, that I'm paying attention.

I did see. God, I saw everything. I shouldn't find the way he's throwing his weight around and trouncing both his brothers so attractive, but I definitely do. Something about a sweaty alpha male dominating the field just makes me hot and tingly.

They play for another half hour. By the time they finish, all three brothers are drenched in sweat and grinning like idiots. Hunter scores the final goal and Jett throws his stick down in mock outrage.

"Rematch next week," Jett demands. "I can't let Silas win."

"You'll lose again," Hunter says cheerfully. "He's the best at hockey and we all know it."

"Fuck off."

Silas skates over to where I'm sitting, breathing hard. "You cold?"

"A little."

He immediately strips off his outer shirt, leaving him in just a damp undershirt. He wraps the other one around my shoulders even though it's sweaty. "Better?"

I tip my face up to him, trying to suppress a grin. "You're disgusting."

"You like it."

He's not wrong. I do like it. The smell of him, being wrapped in another piece of clothing that's unmistakably his. I like the casual way he takes care of me without making it a big deal.

After they clean up, we pile into the corner booth of a greasy spoon diner I've never been to called Ria's Bluebird Café. The place has cracked vinyl seats, a U-shaped counter with worn barstools, and laminated menus sticky with decades of use. A waitress with gray hair and tired eyes calls everyone *hon* without discrimination. She shoos us toward a huge round booth at the back.

Hunter drapes an arm around Juliet's shoulders, as easy as breathing. She leans into him automatically, fitting against his side like she was designed for that exact space. Jett keeps ordering chocolate milkshakes just to irritate the waitress. She keeps shooting him dirty looks every time he asks for another.

Silas slides into the booth and I follow. He immediately presses against me, thigh to thigh, massive and warm and silent.

"So," Jett says, lifting his coffee mug. "You're really living with this grump? On purpose?"

"Temporarily," I say, then feel Silas tense beside me. "I think?"

"Temporarily?" Silas echoes. But his hand finds mine under the table and squeezes it. "Or maybe not."

My pulse jumps hard.

"Be nice to her," Hunter mutters around a mouthful of fries. "She's brave for putting up with you."

"Or completely insane," Jett adds, a teasing smirk on his lips. "There's really no in-between."

"Seriously, shut up." Juliet reaches across the table to swat Jett's arm. "Stop terrorizing her. They're sweet together."

"Sweet," Jett repeats like he's never heard the word before. He shakes his head in wonder. "Silas Huxley. Sweet. I never thought I'd live to see the day."

Silas glares at him with zero real heat. Jett just grins wider, completely unfazed.

The banter flows easy after that, comfortable in the way that only comes from years of knowing. They tease each other mercilessly and share stories I only half understand because I wasn't there for the context. Silas interrupts several times to explain inside jokes when I look confused.

And I realize, sitting there squished between Silas and Jett, that this is his circle. His brothers and the few people he chooses to let in. People who actually matter to him beyond hockey and obligations.

And he brought me into it without hesitation.

The weight of that sits heavy in my chest. It feels terrifying and wonderful in equal measure.

"You're quiet," Silas murmurs near my ear while Jett and Hunter argue about whose goal was more impressive.

"I'm just processing."

"Processing what?"

I look up at him. "This. All of this. It's a lot."

His jaw ticks. "Too much?"

"No. It just feels... significant."

Understanding flashes in his eyes. His head dips. "Mhm."

He slides his hand around my shoulders and leaves it there, like planting a possessive flag that dares other men to even look my way. It sends a shiver down my spine. Silas glances at me, assuming that I'm cold, and tucks me closer against his warm body. He smells sweaty and masculine.

Am I crazy for wanting to roll around in his scent?

Later, after we've eaten too many fries and Jett has finally been cut off from milkshakes, we walk back to Silas's truck. The Seattle evening is growing chilly. The stars are barely visible through the city's light pollution.

Silas catches my hand and laces our fingers together like it's the most natural thing in the world. This is boyfriend shit. I stare at our hands, swallowing.

One part of me wants Silas to sweep me off of my feet and carry me into the sunset. The other part, the scared little girl inside my head, worries that this is exactly how I fell into a relationship with Enzo. He never asked me to be his girl-friend. He never really even asked me to be his wife.

I woke up to Enzo sliding a ring on my finger and was so breathless that somebody chose me, I didn't bother asking the right questions. Namely, *do you hate me?* So much grief could've been avoided if Enzo answered that one.

Si touches my arm and I practically jump out of my skin. "Huh?"

"You okay?" His voice is rough.

My cheeks heat. "Yeah. Just thinking."

"About?"

I stop walking and turn to face him fully under the glow of the streetlight. "You brought me to street hockey. Your family thing with your brothers and Juliet. That means some-thing big."

His jaw ticks. "Yeah. It does."

Not really what I was looking for. "Silas..."

"I want you in my life, Scout." He cups my face with his free hand. "We slept together, but I've wanted more for a long time. Since we were in college, before you asked me out. I fucked it up because I'm a giant chicken." He pauses and blows out a breath. "Now I'm getting a second chance and I don't want to blow it. I need you to be a part of my life." He hesitates again, his eyes boring into mine. "Is that okay with you?"

Tears sting my eyes without warning. "Yeah. It's more than okay."

God. I had no idea that Silas had feelings for me for so long. Because he turned me down, I just automatically assumed that I'd made up the chemistry that I felt between us. Turns out I was right all along.

A pang of sadness hits me. If Silas had said yes when I asked him out, I might not have met Enzo. Certainly I wouldn't have been swept off my feet by him. What kind of idiot would I be to let a guy like Silas go for a pushy creep like Enzo?

Then again, there was a lot I didn't know before I said yes to Enzo's proposal.

"Good deal." He kisses my forehead gently. "Because you're stuck with me now. I live by the law of no take-backs."

I laugh. The sound comes out wet and shaky. "Lucky me."

"Lucky me," he corrects firmly. Then he kisses me properly, slow and sweet and claiming in the middle of the sidewalk where anyone could see.

My breath catches. "Can I ask you something?"

Silas tilts his head. "Shoot."

"Are we like…" I feel so dumb having to ask this. "Dating?"

His eyebrows rise and he slowly repeats my question. "Are we *dating?*"

"Yeah, you know. Are we exclusive? Am I… your, um…"

His lips twitch. "My girlfriend?"

"Yeah." I wrinkle my nose. "I guess."

"Scout." He leans down, brushing his lips over mine in a way that sets loose a riot of butterflies in my stomach. "You're mine."

My heart pounds. Against his lips, I ask, "And does that mean we're exclusive?"

"Yes, Pretty Girl. There's no one else. Just you."

I press up on my tiptoes, cupping the back of his neck and pulling him down to me. Our mouths meet, slow and passionate, the kiss less insistent but no less intense. Damn, Silas knows how to kiss.

When we part, I realize that I have more than a crush on him. It's not love yet, but it will be. It's obviously heading there. My feelings are so sharp right now, I have the sensation of walking over shards of glass… but in a good way? I can't explain it better than that.

When we get back to the condo, I'm buzzing with emotion I don't quite know how to process. Overwhelmed in the best possible way, happy in a way that feels almost dangerous. Because what if it gets taken away? The things that feel best never stay.

I change into silky sleep shorts, keep Si's hoodie, brush my teeth, then climb into his bed without asking if it's okay or second-guessing myself. Because this is where I belong now, apparently.

He follows a few minutes later, fresh from his own shower. "Mm."

He pulls me against his chest and buries his nose in my hair like he missed me in the half hour I was showering. I exhale slowly, trying not to pinch myself.

"Today was good," I whisper into the dark.

"Yeah. It was."

"Hunter and Jett are great. Juliet's amazing."

"They liked you. In your new position as my plus-one, I mean."

"Yeah? How can you tell?"

"Because Jett didn't roast you too hard. That's his version of approval." His hand strokes through my curls, gentle and repetitive. "And Hunter only warns people off when he cares about them. So when he cornered me after and told me not to screw this up, that was basically his blessing."

When he pets me like this, he turns off my brain. I smile against his chest. "Your family is weird."

"Yeah. But they're mine."

"And I'm yours?" The question comes out smaller than I intend. More vulnerable.

"Yeah, Pretty Girl. You're mine. Is that what you want?"

"More than anything."

He sounds relieved. "Good."

The words should scare me. And they do feel like too much too fast. But they also feel like coming home after being lost for years.

Sleep pulls at me, wrapped in his arms, listening to his heartbeat. Maybe I've finally found where I belong.

Chapter Twenty-Three

Scout

I wake up to my phone buzzing on the nightstand. The screen shows February 14th. Valentine's Day.

I stare at the ceiling, chest tight. Does Silas even know what day it is? Does he care about things like that? Is that what girlfriends and boyfriends do?

Actually, I never got a clear yes or no from him about the am-I-your-girlfriend matter. I don't want to press the issue because I'm busy being light, breezy, and not making things complicated. After Enzo, there are a lot of patterns I'm not looking to replicate.

Rolling over to ask him, his side of the bed is already cold and empty. Faintly, I can hear him in the kitchen through the closed door. His protein shake bottle clinks and there's a rustle of meal prep containers as he opens and closes them. Dragging myself out of bed, I find him standing at the counter with his back to me. A tower of tense muscle barely contained in gray sweatpants and a black t-shirt stretched across his broad shoulders.

His dirty blond hair's messy from sleep, sticking up in ways that make him look softer than usual. But his shoulders are coiled tight like wire. When he glances over, those blue-gray eyes are unreadable, jaw set in that way that says he's locked down tight. Beautiful even when he's brooding.

"Morning," I say, voice still rough with sleep.

He grunts. "Morning."

He doesn't quite look at me, just goes back to measuring out his supplements with mechanical precision. Silas isn't the warmest, most friendly guy at the best of times. But right now he's like stepping into a blizzard.

Then he surprises me with a soft, "Sorry. I haven't had coffee yet."

Giving him a soft smile, I walk over to the coffee pot and flick it on. He has one of those fancy machines that grinds the beans fresh, so it emits a loud, grating whine as it starts. A few minutes later, the smell of fresh coffee makes my mouth water. Si sits at the kitchen island and sips his protein shake. I pour two mugs, fixing his cup up how I've seen him do before, and slide one in front of him.

His eyes widen with childlike surprise, even though he just heard me brewing the coffee. "Thanks, Scout."

"No problem. It seems like you could use a little."

He ducks his head. "Yeah."

I take the stool next to his and sip my coffee. Si glances at me, smile tugging at his lips, and drinks his coffee in silence. There are a million things that we could talk about. The holiday, our plans for the day, how we're planning to handle things post-hookup. But we both keep quiet, enjoying the moment.

He wolfs down a prepared meal, finishes half of his protein shake, and then pushes up from the counter. As he's doing his dishes, he casts an eye over the broad expanse of windows in the living room. Overhead, the sky is a dark gray, a solid wall of brooding clouds.

"The weather is supposed to be shitty today."

I glance behind me, sighing. "I should stay home and hang out on the couch, but I need to drive to the coast."

He looks up. "What? Why?"

"I need to go to Port Townsend to see my dad. My sister went last week and texted that he's not doing well. I need to check on him. The weather is terrible, but I'll just rent an SUV instead of a car."

"You're planning to rent a car?" He says it like the idea is foreign to him.

I wave off his concern. "Yeah. It's fine. I'll be back tonight."

"No." His voice is flat.

Oh brother. I repress an eye roll. "Silas, I can handle..."

He cuts me off. "The roads up there are bad. They're narrow and windy. You don't drive enough to be safe on them." He sets his shake bottle down with a thunk. "I'm taking you."

"You don't have to do that..."

"Yes I do." He meets my eyes fully for the first time this morning. "It's going to be easier for you to just say yes than to argue with me. I can't let you drive in this weather. Especially not on Valentine's Day."

My mouth goes dry. So he does know about it. I should tell him that being perfectly capable of driving myself is true. But the truth is, relief at his insistence floods me. The roads to Port Townsend twist along cliff edges and wind through dense forest. Every time I make the trip, I white-knuckle the steering wheel the entire way.

"Okay," I say quietly. My shoulders slump. "Thank you."

His jaw ticks like he wants to say something else. But he doesn't. He just drains his shake and goes to get dressed.

"We'll leave in 20," he calls over his shoulder before he disappears into his room.

The drive north is tense from the start. We sit in silence except for rain hammering the windshield hard enough to test the wipers. I turn on some jazz really low, but as soon as we get outside Seattle proper and on the ferry, there's so much static that I turn it off again. For his part, Silas is wound impossibly tight. His hands clench the wheel. And his jaw is clamped shut so hard that I worry about his teeth.

He's furious about something, but I can't begin to guess what. People call him Ice Man. Cold and controlled, never letting anyone see what he's feeling. Right now he looks like that nickname personified. Frozen solid, locked behind walls I can't climb. Does he regret letting his walls down and having sex with me? Maybe he woke up with some clarity about how I'm going to smother him to death.

It's impossible to know with him.

I stare out the passenger window, watching evergreens blur past. As we drive, anxiety builds with every mile that brings me closer to that house. When the road climbs steadily upward, I start to see snow flurries. Not a great sign, but not unusual around here. My dad lives on the coast of Washington, the house nestled snugly on top of a ridge overlooking Port Townsend Bay. When we get through the heavy forest of Chimacum, the sea will be close enough to drive the snow away.

But then I will have to face my father. It's my turn to take care of him. Sable and I trade off, and she visited Port Townsend last.

Forget my current situation with Silas. I haven't seen my dad in almost two months. The idea of facing the memories that saturate every room of that house fills me with dread. Unless something is radically different since being there last, the weight of my mother's absence still hangs in the air like smoke.

Silas clears his throat. "I, uh. I got you something."

"You... got me something," I repeat. I feel like one of those Lucky Cat statues, wide-eyed and nodding.

"We didn't talk about doing anything for Valentine's Day. I know that it's sort of a couple's holiday. But I thought just to be safe, I'd get you a treat and some flowers." He rubs his hand over the back of his neck. "Don't want to be accused of being a terrible Valentine."

His speech takes me by surprise and I burst out laughing. "Silas, you didn't have to do anything. We're obviously not doing the normal V-Day stuff." My cheeks heat. "Driving to see my dad isn't exactly what most people would consider romantic."

He stares straight ahead, but his lips lift at the corners. "Let me decide what's romantic."

He directs me to the backseat, where I find a bouquet of winter flowers tied with a pretty bow and a metal tin full of pear-flavored jelly beans. "These are my favorites!"

"It's almost like I know you," he teases. "In college, you'd always keep a huge jar of these to study with. You even brought it into the library a few times."

"That's true! I forgot about that." I dig in immediately, scooping out a pile of the light green candies and popping them in my mouth. "These are amazing. Thank you for knowing just what would make my day brighter."

"You're welcome, Pretty Girl." Silas slides me a satisfied look. "That should top up your supply for a week or so."

I eat another palmful of the candies, smirking at him. He thinks he knows so much. And maybe, in this one circumstance, he's right.

As we start to get closer, driveways leading to small

houses dot the windy country road. By the time we pull up in the driveway and bump down the road to the house, my stomach is in knots.

The two story house of rotting wood and its lopsided porch stand in relief against the heather-gray cliffside and the dark water of the sea. The yard is overgrown, with weeds choking the flower beds my mother used to tend so carefully. The gutters sag under accumulated debris. Paint peels around the window frames and hangs in sad curls.

A stifling weight presses on my chest as I look at the house. Once beloved, the place has now been left to molder. Nothing happy can grow here. I rub my hand absently over my heart, willing the ache to disappear.

"Scout." Silas's voice startles. "You okay?"

"Yeah. Fine." I force a smile that feels brittle. "I should prepare you. My dad isn't... he's not doing great. Since my mom died five years ago, he's just kind of... given up."

His jaw tightens. "I understand."

"No, you don't." My voice cracks. "He doesn't clean. Doesn't cook. Barely leaves his bed most days. I come up here to take care of him because if I don't, he'll just waste away."

"Scout..."

"I know what you're thinking. Why doesn't he take better care of himself? Why do I have to do it?" Tears sting my eyes. "Because he's my dad and someone has to. My sister can't handle it on her own. So we split it."

Silas reaches across the console and takes my hand. "I wasn't thinking that. I was thinking that you shouldn't have to carry this alone."

My throat goes tight. "Well. Here we are."

We get out of the truck and I lead him up the sagging porch steps. The door sticks when I push it, swollen from rain and neglect. Inside smells like must and unwashed dishes and the particular stale sadness that comes from a house where no one really lives anymore.

"Dad?" I call out. "It's Scout. I brought someone with me."

Shuffling comes from the living room. My dad appears in the doorway looking exactly like I expected. Gaunt, unshaven, wearing the same flannel shirt he's probably worn for days. His eyes are hollow and distant, barely registering that we're here.

"Scout," he says. Flat. No warmth. His eyes go to Silas, narrowing suspiciously.

"Hi, Dad. This is Silas. He's... he's my boyfriend." The word feels strange coming out. I probably should have asked Silas about labels.

Then again, he did get me a Valentine's Day present.

My dad gives Silas a distrustful once-over. "Nice to meet you."

"You too, sir," Silas says, his voice gentle.

Dad shuffles back to his recliner in front of the TV. It's already on, some daytime show flickering with canned laughter. He sinks into the chair with a sigh.

I look around the house and my stomach drops. It's undeniably worse than last time. Dishes piled in the sink, probably growing things. Laundry scattered across every surface. I'm sure there's a fine coat of dust on everything.

"I'm just going to..." I gesture vaguely at the mess. "Clean up a bit."

Handing the remote to my dad, I flash Silas another apologetic look. "We'll be out of here before you know it."

"Please." Si's gaze hardens. "Just tell me what to do."

"Honestly, just sit."

Silas gives me a hard look. "Put me to work, sweetheart."

I give up, looking around. "It'd be nice if you dusted in here. I can start doing the dishes. Then I can try to fix dinner."

"Scout..." Dad grunts, leaning back and scratching his beard. "I don't want you going to any trouble on my account."

"It's no trouble, Dad. Honestly." Except for the fact that I've dragged Silas into this mess. I shouldn't have agreed for him to drive me. It wouldn't be the first trip I've made up here in poor driving conditions.

"Can I get some dusting supplies?" Si asks. Because he's the best guy in the world and he's rolling with this, even though it's way outside his role as maybe-boyfriend.

"Right." I hustle into the kitchen and grab a feather duster, some paper towels, and some Windex for dusting. Silas meets me in the doorway and grabs them.

"Thanks," I whisper. "We'll be out of here in no time. I promise."

He smiles at me, his ash-blond hair falling in soft swoops around his face. Reaching out, he brushes a stray curl back from my face with gentle fingers. He's so tall and broad and just all together hot.

"Don't rush. I'm here as long as you need me."

I almost swoon. This hot guy is here for me? He's smiling at me and helping me clean my dad's house? Enzo certainly never did any of those things the entire time he was my husband. He never set foot in this house.

"Thanks, baby." I give Si a quick kiss, not trusting myself to stop getting all mushy. Crying isn't going to help this house get clean.

With stars in my eyes, I move to the kitchen on autopilot and start washing dishes. Scrubbing counters and sweeping floors is next. The familiar rhythm settles something in me. Knowing how to do this, cleaning and taking care of somebody else, makes sense when nothing else does.

We work in silence for the next two hours. Kitchen first, then living room. Vacuuming, dusting, throwing out the trash that's collected around the room.

Silas helps me when he's done dusting and vacuuming. Not a word passes between us, but I can see Silas looking at my dad now and then. The entire time, my dad watches TV. He doesn't say a word or even thank Silas.

It's fine when it's just me my dad is ignoring. But it burns me up inside that Dad would pretend this stranger cleaning his house is normal. I swallow the bitterness like every other complaint I've ever had.

But I'm embarrassed by it nonetheless.

By the time I finish, my hands are raw and red. My back aches from bending over. To my relief, though, the house looks better. Almost livable.

Next, I make dinner. There isn't much in the fridge, but I keep the pantry well stocked and the freezer full of veggies. I pull out the ingredients for chicken broccoli fettuccini. It's the kind of simple, hearty meal my mother used to make on a weeknight. Soon, the smell of pasta fills the house. And for one brief moment, it feels like before my mom died. Any moment now, she might walk in from the other room, smiling and asking if I need help.

I stir the fettuccini noodles and wipe my eyes. Mom would always stand right here, humming and making dinner. Smiling, talking to me as I helped, washing the potatoes and dicing the carrots. God, how I miss her right now. If only my mom hadn't gotten sick...

But it's not the time to get emotional. My dad can't handle anyone else around him being sad. He has enough grief to fill any space he's in. He doesn't need to deal with my tears on top of that.

When I turn the pasta out into bowls, I call my dad and Silas. "Dinner's ready."

Dad finally turns off the TV and shuffles in the kitchen, sitting at the small dining table. He sits in the same chair he's occupied for thirty years.

I serve him with shaking hands, waiting for some kind of response. Silas watches me with a carefully neutral expression. God, what kind of pieces is he fitting into place in the puzzle of my life? He accepts a bowl of pasta and sits, his frame dwarfing the small kitchen chair. In his hands, the fork looks ridiculous.

Dad takes a bite and chews slowly, then swallows. Then something in his weathered face softens just slightly.

"This is good. Real good, Scout. Just like your mom used to make."

My eyes sting with tears that I refuse to let fall. "Thanks, Dad."

"The house looks nice too." He glances around like he's actually seeing it for the first time today. "You're just like her, you know. Always doing things for me. Taking care of everything. Making sure I'm fed and the place is clean."

His words land like punches. Suddenly, I can't breathe.

"I should grab... something." I rush to the other side of the kitchen, pressing my palms flat against the counter, fighting the tears that want to come. Behind me, I hear Silas's chair scrape. *Please. Please don't come over here right now. I'm barely holding it together.*

I slink out of the room, just out of sight. Sitting at an angle where I can see Silas and part of my dad's back, but they can't see me, helps me to calm down. I blow out a slow stream of breath.

Si clears his throat. "Thank you for having me."

My dad takes a second to answer. "I think I should probably be thanking you, son."

Silas waves his fork. "I'd do anything for your daughter, sir."

"You can call me Tom." My dad sizes Silas up. "So I'm guessing that you're a hockey player?"

Silas pauses then says, "Yeah."

A few moments pass before my dad says, "Scout just divorced a hockey player."

"Yeah. Enzo." Silas's voice goes hard as steel. "I'm not him. We're nothing alike."

"Didn't say that you were." Dad's laugh is thin as paper. "Scout's wonderful, you know. She's always been so helpful. It's how she shows she cares, I guess. Must have learned it from her mother."

"She is helpful," Silas says. His voice is quiet but absolutely fierce. "I try not to take advantage too much. Scout's always looking out for everybody. She needs someone who'll take care of her."

"And that's you?"

Silence stretches. "I'd like it to be."

"I see. Well, I don't care how big and brawny you are, son. If you hurt my little girl, I'll kick your ass."

Si's head dips. "Yes sir."

God, Silas is pushing all of my buttons. Wiping my eyes hastily, I force myself to go back out, even though I want to hide. My dad is standing now, looking uncomfortable in a way I've never seen. Silas has barely touched his food.

"I should go lie down," my dad mutters. "Thanks for dinner, Scout. And for cleaning. Both of you."

He gives me a half-hearted hug and kiss on the cheek, then totters off toward the staircase. It hurts my heart to see him walk. He's out of shape and sort of shuffle-hobbles up the stairs.

Silas looks toward the window. "The weather is getting worse. Visibility's going to be terrible on those mountain roads. We should probably hunker down here for the night."

"Oh god." I rush to the window and see flurries falling from the sky. My stomach drops. "We can't stay here. There's a motel a few miles down the road toward town that I usually stay at."

"Why not stay here? The house has room."

"It's just... wouldn't be good. Dad doesn't like the house disturbed by overnight guests."

Silas looks pointedly at the cluttered living room I just cleaned. The pile of junk mail. The years of accumulated neglect. "The house was already disturbed."

"Silas. Please." My voice cracks. "We'd have to clean out a room, okay? Trust me when I say that it's a whole can of worms. Let's just go."

I say goodbye to my dad through his bedroom door. He gives me what might be a 'drive safe' without opening the door. That's all I get.

Silas helps me into my coat and hustles me out the door. Luckily the snow flurries are mixed with rain, so it's sleeting more than anything. Still not great driving weather, but way better than being trapped in this American Gothic rerun.

He drives slowly, taking every turn with care in the growing darkness. When we get to the motel, it's small and run down, but clean enough. Bev, the woman at the front desk, recognizes me and gives me a sad smile.

"Back again, honey?" she asks.

"Yeah. Just for tonight. We don't want to risk driving back to Seattle."

"Very sensible." Bev eyes Silas and winks at me. "I

wouldn't mind staying the night with a big hunk of a man, either."

As she rings up the room, Silas's jaw tightens. He leans down to whisper in my ear. "You stay here often?"

"Sometimes. When I visit Dad." I sign the register with numb fingers. "Like I said, he doesn't like overnight guests disturbing his routine."

He arches an eyebrow. "His house was a complete disaster when we got there."

"Can we please just leave it alone?" My voice cracks dangerously.

"That'll be $125, please." Bev taps a sign taped to the glass. "Charge only."

Silas growls at me when I try to pay. I put my wallet away as Bev grins.

"You two are cute. You're in room twelve."

Taking the room key, Silas guides me outside with a hand on my lower back.

Our room is extremely basic. One bed, thin walls, questionable carpet. The works. But it's warm and dry and blessedly far from my dad's house.

I stand in the middle of the room dripping rain, shaking. Not so much from cold as from everything. Today was a lot. Silas locks the door and puts on the deadbolt, then strips off his jacket and tosses it on the single, spindly chair.

"Strip," he says.

My fingers are partway through my insane nest of curls and I pause, looking at him. "What?"

"You're soaked through. Strip down and get under the covers." His voice is gentle but commanding. "Now, Scout."

"Bossy," I admonish. But even as I teasingly complain, I start to strip. I peel off my wet clothes with fingers that barely work and climb into bed in just my damp bra and underwear.

Silas strips too. As I watch, he pulls off his t-shirt, revealing those swoon-worthy biceps and miles of yummy-looking abs. Then he kicks off his shoes, shucks his pants, and slides in beside me. He pulls me against his chest with arms that feel like safety and makes this deeply comforting groan, like he's been waiting very patiently for me for years and he's just now getting his wish.

I've never felt that wanted, that special, to anyone before. It's not a desire for how useful I can be or how I can practically fade into the background. He genuinely wants to be close to me.

The answer isn't dry-humping his leg, I'm pretty sure.

"You take care of everyone," Si murmurs into my hair, nuzzling. "Every single person around you. Now it's my turn to take care of you."

I try to protest, I swear. Just say that I'm fine and don't need anything. But... the words won't come. Instead, a sob breaks free from somewhere deep. I'm consumed, frazzled, turned on, and a million other conflicting, confusing things. Another sob works its way out of my throat. Then suddenly I'm crying so hard I can't catch my breath.

He holds me through it. One hand stroking my back in steady circles, the other tangled in my hair. He's solid and steady and safe as he helps me ride out the storm.

"It's like my dad doesn't even see me," I choke out between sobs. "I clean his house. I make his food. I try so hard to matter. And he doesn't even look at me."

Silas sounds pained. "I know, sweetheart. I know."

"My whole life has been like this. If I'm useful, if I'm helping, maybe he'll love me. Maybe he'll actually see me as his daughter instead of just another person doing tasks." The words pour out now, unstoppable. "But he never does. He never has."

He makes quiet soothing sounds, but doesn't try to shush me or stop my tears.

I hiccup uncontrollably. "Now I do it with everyone. I can't stop myself. I smother people until they leave. They can't s-stand me anymore. They have to get a-a-away." Shaking so hard my teeth chatter happens. "Enzo was right about me. I'm too much. I drive people away by h-hovering."

"That isn't true." Silas's voice is fierce. He tilts my chin up with gentle fingers and forces me to look at him through my tears. "Enzo was a fucking idiot. Your dad is depressed and broken and trapped in his own grief. He can't see past his own pain. But that's not on you. None of that's your fault."

"But..."

He shakes his head, putting a finger to my lips. "You're not too much. You're not smothering anyone. You're caring and generous and you love people by taking care of them. That's not a character flaw. That's a gift most people would kill to have."

Fresh tears slip down my cheeks. "Then why does it always feel like I'm drowning people with it? I'm always too m-much for anyone to handle."

"You've been giving yourself to people who don't deserve you, sweetheart. People who take and take and never give anything back." He wipes my tears away with his thumbs. "But I see you, Scout. I see what you're doing and why you do it. And I'm not going anywhere. I promise you that."

I sniff, willing myself to get it together. "You say that now..."

"I mean it." His eyes are intense and unwavering. "You can take care of me. You can hover and pester and do all the things that make you feel loved and secure. And I won't leave. I won't push you away. I'll just hold you tighter. I'll care for you, Scout. I know I'm rough around the edges, but I swear to god I'm trying."

I break completely and sob into his chest while he holds me like I'm something precious. He lets me take the weight I've been carrying alone since I was a little girl trying to earn her father's attention.

"You're not your father's savior," he whispers against my hair. "You're his daughter. And you've done more than enough for him. More than anyone should have to do."

My words are halting. "I don't-- I don't know h-how to stop trying."

"It's okay. Just let it all out. I've got you, Pretty Girl."

I cling to him, breathing in cedar soap and rain and the scent that's uniquely his. He's an anchor when everything else feels like it's spinning out of control. For the first time in my entire life, someone is taking care of me without me having to ask. Being good enough or useful enough doesn't matter.

And for once, I let him.

"Happy Valentine's Day, Pretty Girl," he whispers in my ear.

Falling asleep in his arms, exhausted and wrung out but somehow lighter happens. Silas holds me through the night, steady and solid and exactly what I need even when not knowing how to ask for it was the problem.

Chapter Twenty-Four

Scout

I wake up wrapped in Silas. The motel room is dim, rain still pattering against the window in a steady rhythm. My eyes feel swollen from crying and my throat is still raw and scratchy. But his arms are solid around me.

For the first time in a long time, I can actually breathe.

"Morning," Si murmurs into my hair.

"Is it?" My voice comes out wrecked. "It feels like the middle of the night."

"It's almost nine. We should probably eat something." Ever the practical athlete. It's so Silas, it makes me like him more.

I don't want to move. Leaving this cocoon of warmth and safety where nothing can touch me sounds terrible. "Can we just stay here forever?"

"Don't worry, Pretty Girl. You just stay put. I think there's a diner across the street."

I smile, remembering the Original Hotcake House. "There is."

"All right." He climbs out of bed and starts pulling on clothes. "Anything special?"

I shake my head. "Just come back as quickly as you can."

Silas surprises me by donning his jacket and then leaning over me, snagging a kiss. The action is so out-of-left-field for him that he leaves me with my mouth open in a gentle O.

I get up and putter around in the bathroom, rinsing my mouth with mouthwash and splashing cold water on my face. By the time I'm finished making the bed, Silas returns with a brown paper bag of hot pancakes, scrambled eggs, hashbrowns, bacon, and steaming cups of coffee.

"You are my hero," I say, gladly accepting one of the cups of coffee. The first sip is bitter and burned, but I slurp it up. Coffee really is the nectar of the gods. Taking it in any format works for me.

We eat in bed with the styrofoam plates balanced on our laps, not talking much. Every bite of our breakfast is slathered in melted butter, making for a tasty but heavy meal. Silas plows through his entire plate of carb-lover's delight. When I push my plate away half-finished, he points to it.

"You gonna eat that?"

I grin. "All yours, big guy."

As I watch, he destroys the rest of the food, folding the bacon inside the pancakes, pouring syrup on the hashbrowns and using the pancake to shovel it all into his mouth. When he uses his fingers to get the last drips of syrup off the plate, he makes eye contact with me and cringes.

"Sorry. I've been hungry since we went to sleep last night. Shoulda eaten more at your dad's."

"I like watching you eat. My dumb lizard brain thinks it's sexy."

He chuckles. "Wait till you see me during the off season. Hunter and Jett and I have a fourth of July party that's just an excuse for inhaling hot dogs and hamburgers. We eat until one of us taps out or pukes."

"Gross!" I wrinkle my nose playfully. "I'd say I don't believe you, but I've seen you on the ice. You three are insanely competitive."

"Puking is a badge of honor," he assures me. "Besides, I'm the tallest, broadest Huxley brother. I dominate."

"I'll believe it when I see it." Realizing that we're making plans for months from now, which is decidedly relationship territory, happens. Sticking to safer topics seems better. I clear my throat. "So what now?"

"It's icy outside. I think we should wait a couple of hours for the sun to warm up the roads."

I look at him, nibbling on my lower lip. "And what do you suggest we do to pass the time?"

Fishing for an invitation to get Silas naked becomes my strategy. But he turns stiff, uncertain what to do.

"We can, uh... just... hang out?"

Right. The thing about Silas is that he's excessively polite, to the point of stringent self-denial. I turn to him, my cheeks heating.

"What if I said I wanted you to fuck my brains out?"

His gaze snaps to my face, turning heated. "Scout... I don't want to take advantage of you. You were just sobbing in my arms last night."

"Please?" I press my lips to his before he can say more, desperate to taste him. "Please, Si? I want you."

He kisses me back, slowly. It feels as though he's testing to make sure this is really what I want. When I whimper and press closer to him, he deepens the kiss with a groan. He digs his hand into my curls, taking control, and gives me exactly what I'm asking for.

His hands are everywhere at once. Stripping my clothes off. Sliding down my body with purpose. I arch into his touch, gasping, already so wound up that every nerve ending feels exposed and raw. I yank at his clothes, frustrated, needing to feel his naked skin against mine.

Silas stands for a minute, shucking his clothes. He's a hockey god made of pure muscle and he towers over me. His broad shoulders ripple as he moves, those defined pecs and cut abs catching the dim motel light. Dirty blond hair falls in messy waves around his face. Blue eyes gone dark with want, pupils blown wide.

His thighs are massive, all corded muscle and raw power. But mostly, my eyes are focused on his cock. Like the rest of Si's body, it's fucking enormous, thick and long, veiny and flushed. Just looking at it makes my clit ache. Needy, I whine and writhe every second he's not touching me. When he crawls back over me, I feel this enormous sense of relief.

"The walls are thin," he murmurs, pressing kisses against my throat. He shapes my breasts. In his giant hands, they almost seem dainty, even though I'm a G-cup.

"I don't care," I breathe.

"I can't have anyone else knowing what you sound like when I make you come." He bites down on my pulse point and I moan despite myself. "So you're going to have to be quiet. Can you do that for me?"

I nod frantically.

"Good girl." He slips his huge hand down between my legs and slowly slides two fingers inside me. My eyes roll up in my head. I have to bite my fist to keep from crying out. He whispers, "Jesus, Scout. You're so wet for me already. You need this, don't you? Need me to make it better?"

"Yes," I gasp, my hips bucking. At this point, I'm pretty sure he's the only man that can make it better. "God, yes. Please."

Silas alternates between slowly finger fucking me and swirling two fingers around my clit. It's good, but not enough.

He works me with his fingers, slowly and deliberately, building me up until I'm shaking with need. I run my hands through his shaggy hair and scrape my nails down his back. My hips roll of their own volition and beads of sweat break out across my brow.

Aggravatingly, Si growls whenever my hands wander down his body, heading for his cock. "Be patient, Pretty Girl. Let me take my time with you first. My cock is big enough that it'll hurt unless you're ready to take it. I have to warm your pussy up, get you needy and to the point of begging for my cock."

I both love that and hate it. He keeps up his finger-fucking and clit-swirling, driving me crazy. The need to come is riding me so hard that I'm about to come out of my skin. When he gets me close, right on the edge of breaking, he pulls back. "Uh uh. Not yet."

I whine and writhe. "Silas, please..."

"I want you to remember this." His voice is rough, possessive in a way that makes me clench around nothing. "After we fuck, you'll feel me for days. Every time you sit down, every time you move, you'll remember exactly who you belong to."

The words should scare me. They're controlling and possessive, growled in my ear. But they only make me wetter. There is something wrong with me, I'm sure of it. But there's something wrong with Silas, too. We're matched in that way, like two halves of a shattered stone. Dark edges and razor-sharp crags when apart made perfectly smooth when pressed together.

Silas pauses to tear open a condom, but I stop him with a hand.

"Can you-- will you go bare? I'm on birth control."

He pauses for a second. "Are you sure? I'm clean."

"I trust you, Silas. I need to feel you."

"Fuck, sweetheart." He pins my wrists above my head with one hand. The other slides down my spine, over the curve of my ass, between my thighs where I'm already dripping.

"Yes," I hiss. "Fuck me, Si. Don't hold back."

"Stay quiet," he growls. "Or I'll stop. Understand?"

Nodding, I bury my face in a pillow as he lines up the fat head of his cock and pushes inside me. If being honest, Si's cock is too big. He's a lot of man and his throbbing dick doesn't just slip in with ease. Even though he's got me so turned on that I thought I'll die if he doesn't fuck me, he has to work his hips, stretching me, filling me. As he struggles to fit his cock in my pussy, tears prick my eyes and my breath leaves my lungs.

"Okay?" he asks, biting his lip as he tries to hold himself in check.

That's not what I want. I want all of him, right now. I wrap my arms around his neck and push my hips up, encouraging. "I want more, Si. Don't be gentle."

"You sure?"

"Yes. Please."

He drives in the rest of the way in one hard thrust. Pain and pleasure blur together, overwhelming every sense. Feeling so full, so stretched, so completely his takes over. He stills for a moment, letting me adjust, forehead pressed against my shoulder as he breathes hard.

"Fuck, Scout. You feel incredible. So tight. So perfect."

Then he starts to move. Slow at first, careful, letting me get used to his size. But I don't want him to be careful. I rock my hips, urging him faster, harder. He groans and gives me what I need, pounding into me with long, deep strokes that make stars burst behind my eyelids.

"That's it, sweetheart. Take my cock. You're doing so good for me."

His dirty talk undoes me. Combined with the relentless pace he sets, I'm hurtling toward the edge embarrassingly fast. He reaches between us, finds my clit, circles it with rough fingers.

"Come for me, Pretty Girl. Let me feel your pretty pussy choking my big cock."

Silently screaming into the pillow, clenching around him, pleasure ripping through me in devastating waves, I come undone. He follows seconds later, teeth sinking into my shoulder to muffle his own sounds, spilling hot lashes of cum inside me.

We collapse together on the cheap motel bed. Both panting, both shaking. His weight pins me to the mattress and I've never felt safer in my entire life.

"Fuck," he breathes. "Baby, you okay?"

I flutter my eyelashes open. "More than okay."

He pulls out carefully, mindful of how battered my body must be. My whole vagina does feel a bit used and abused, but I don't mind in the least. I asked him to fuck me into the mattress and he absolutely did just that. A contented, groggy smile snags on my lips.

Sliding a hand between my legs, he explores my pussy with gentle fingers. When I realize that he's touching the white dribble of his cum where it seeps out of my pussy, I try to close my legs.

"Silas!" It comes out half-strangled. "What are you doing?"

He pushes my legs apart again, seeming transfixed. His look is intense as he starts pushing all his cum back inside my body, stuffing it in my pussy with two fingers. "I've never been with a woman bare before."

"Are you crazy?" I ask.

When his gaze snaps to mine, sizzling hot, he grunts. "Don't think so." He licks the tip of his index finger and moans. "We taste so good together. Try it."

He puts his fingers to my lips, as if this is perfectly normal. Being with only one other guy means maybe it is normal, but it seems weird. I grip Si's hand tentatively, my tongue darting out to taste the glistening liquid. It's earthy and sharp and salty, pungent on my taste buds.

He's right. We do taste good together. Making eye contact with Silas, I pull his fingers into my mouth again and suck. Desire flares bright in his eyes.

"You are the perfect woman, aren't you?"

My cheeks flush and I drop his gaze. Si lets it go, rolling us so I'm tucked against his chest. His hand finds the mark on my shoulder where he bit down and traces it with gentle fingers.

"Did I hurt you?"

"No." I turn my head to look at it in the mirror across from the bed. The bite mark is deep. Dark red. I'll definitely bruise. "I like it."

"Yeah?"

"Yeah, Si." I kiss his jaw. "I want everyone to know I'm yours."

Something in his expression goes soft and vulnerable in a way I've never seen. "You mean that?"

"Every word."

He kisses me then. Sweet this time, tender instead of claiming. "You're perfect. You know that?"

"I'm really not."

"You are to me."

An hour later, we finally manage to get out of bed and into the small shower. The shower is so small that there's no way we can both fit, so I let him go first. When it's my turn, I quickly wash, then climb out, wrapping myself in not one, not two, but three itty-bitty hotel towels. Wiping off the foggy mirror, I see Si's bite mark on my shoulder. Doing a quick check finds a matching set of dark bruises blooming on my hips.

Evidence. Proof that I'm wanted. Claimed. *His.*

I trace the bite mark with my fingertips, smiling at my reflection.

Silas appears in the doorway. Still naked, hair damp from the shower. His eyes go dark as they track over my marked body.

"See something you like?" I tease.

"Always." He steps closer and drops a kiss to my bare shoulder. "How are you feeling about yesterday? You know, your dad and... all of it."

The question makes my chest go tight. "I don't know. Sad, I guess. Angry. I can't save him from himself and it kills me." I lean into his touch. "And that you were there. You saw where I come from. And you haven't run away..."

"Never." He turns me around, lifting my chin and forcing me to meet his stormy blue-gray gaze. "I'll never run. Now that I've let you in, the trick is going to be getting me out."

I huff a breathy laugh. "Even when I actually am too much? When I hover and pester and smother people?"

"Especially then." He kisses my forehead. "Because that's not smothering, Scout. That's how you show love. And anyone who can't see the difference doesn't deserve you in their life."

Tears sting my eyes. "How are you so good at saying exactly what I need to hear?"

"Honestly? I don't know. It's so hard for me to..." He pauses, waving a hand. "Talk to people. Everyone thinks I'm frozen like a block of ice, but really, I just don't know what to say."

"You're not made of ice. I have several hickeys that prove it." I smile up at him. "Want to see who can get dressed the fastest?"

We drive home late in the afternoon. The rain has finally stopped, leaving everything clean and bright. I watch the scenery pass through the passenger window, feeling lighter than I have in weeks despite the emotional devastation of yesterday.

"Thank you," I say quietly. "For coming with me. For staying. I really needed everything you did."

Si shrugs a shoulder. "You don't have to thank me for that, Scout."

"I do, though. You didn't have to drive all the way up here. You didn't have to stay in that terrible motel. But you did anyway, and it meant everything to me."

His hand finds mine across the center console and laces our fingers together. "You matter to me, Scout. If something is important to you, then I'll do my best to help."

He's so sweet. How could anybody think that Silas is anything but an overgrown teddy bear?

I joke, "Even my broken, depressed dad who can't see past his own grief enough to actually parent?"

"He's your dad." He glances at me. "But we should figure out a better situation than what he's got now. He can't stay in that house. You cleaned the living room and made a dent in the beer cans and newspapers accumulating there. But what about the upstairs? I hate to imagine it, Scout."

I push out a frustrated breath.

"I know. My sister and I have been talking about it for months. We just don't know how to make him leave. He won't listen to us."

"Then we make it impossible for him to stay."

"What do you mean?"

"Find him a place closer to Seattle. Somewhere with built-in support. People around him who can check in. And we move him whether he likes it or not."

I stare at him. "You'd help with that? That's a huge undertaking."

"Yeah. Of course I'd help. I'd do the whole move by myself if I needed to."

"Silas, that's a lot to take on. You don't have to..."

"I want to." His voice is firm and final.

"So bossy," I murmur. I flush and look away, trying to repress a shudder. When he uses that tone on me, it reminds me of him being dominant, telling me to be quiet, commanding me to lick his cum off his fingers.

By the time we get back to the condo, I can't wait to be out of the car. Being exhausted down to my bones, wrung out emotionally and physically consumes me. But in a good way somehow? I feel as though I've gone through something hard and come out the other side.

Silas pulls me against his chest.

"My bed," he says. "Right now."

"It's only two o'clock."

"I don't care. You need rest."

I don't argue. He takes my hand and leads me to his bed, where I just let him tuck me in like I'm something precious. When he joins me under the covers, I curl into his side.

"Silas?"

"Hmm?"

"Thank you. For today. For all of it. For being exactly what I needed."

His arms tighten around me. "Anytime. I mean that."

I want to say more, but instead I just hold him tighter,

breathing in cedar soap and clean skin. This is so warm and nice. I'm intoxicated just by hanging out with him.

Drifting off in his arms, I push away the small voice whispering Enzo's poison.

Not now. Not when things feel this good.

Chapter Twenty-Five

Silas

Coach Ryan's whistle cuts through the scrimmage for the third time in ten minutes. I skate to a stop, breathing hard, trying to figure out what I did wrong this time.

"Huxley!" Ryan's voice echoes across the ice. "You trying to put your own teammates in the hospital?"

The rest of the team circles back, looking between me and Ryan. Thorne rolls his eyes. Jett shakes his head like he saw this coming.

"Just playing my position," I call back.

"Your position isn't human wrecking ball." Ryan skates closer, his expression tight with frustration. "That's the third clean hit you've thrown in a scrimmage. Against your own guys. You keep playing like that and you're going to wind up hurt. Or worse, you're going to hurt someone who matters."

Heat crawls up my neck. "I'm an enforcer. That's what I do."

"No. What you do is protect your team. You're demolishing them in practice." Ryan jerks his thumb toward the bench. "Take five. Cool off."

Skating to the bench feels like a punishment I don't deserve. My job is to be physical. Hit hard. Make the other team think twice about touching my guys. That's what enforcers do. That's what I've always done.

Ryan's right about one thing though. My hits are getting sloppier. More desperate, as if I'm trying to prove something with every single play.

My phone buzzes during cooldown. *Enzo.* I let it go to voicemail.

He'll want to know why I missed the endorsement meeting, why I'm not returning calls. The truth is that I don't care about another protein powder deal.

He calls again. I decline. Then a text pops up.

Enzo: We need to talk about your attitude problem.

I stare at the screen.

Enzo: Unless you want Page Six to hear about some interesting family financial issues?

The threat sits there in black and white. He's been doing this for years without ever saying it outright. My mother's crimes hang over my head while he keeps me in line.

The big endorsements would probably survive. Nike, Gatorade. The smaller deals would vanish, and he knows it.

Scout's voice echoes in my head. *You can't let him hold that over you forever.*

She's right. But knowing it and doing something about it are two different things.

I delete the message. One problem at a time.

Practice continues without me. Watching from the bench, I see what Ryan means. The scrimmage flows better when I'm not in it. Plays develop naturally instead of getting interrupted by my constant physicality. My teammates move with more confidence, not bracing for impact every time I'm near.

Watching them play without me pisses me off. It makes me feel useless.

When the final whistle blows, Ryan catches my eye and jerks his head toward his office. A one-on-one talk. Just what I fucking need.

His office is small and cluttered with game footage, play-books, and empty coffee cups. Ryan drops into his chair and gestures for me to sit. I stay standing.

"You want to tell me what's going on?" Ryan leans back, studying me with that coach look that sees through bullshit.

"Nothing's going on. I'm playing my position."

"You're playing scared."

The words hit like a punch to the gut. "I'm not scared of anything."

"Not scared of getting hit. Scared of being irrelevant." Ryan picks up a pen, tapping it against his desk. "You think if you're not throwing your body around every single play, you don't have value. That's not how this works, Huxley."

My jaw clenches. "I'm an enforcer. If I'm not being physical, what's the point of me being on the ice?"

"To be smart. To be strategic. You protect your team when they actually need it, not every five seconds." Ryan sets the pen down. "You know what enforcers really do? They punish players. They send a message. But that message only works if you're selective about when you deliver it."

"So what, I'm supposed to just skate around and do nothing?"

"You're supposed to read the game. See when your guys need backup. Then you handle it." Ryan stands up, moving to the whiteboard covered in play diagrams. "Right now, you're using your body in every single play. That's not enforcing. That's just being reckless."

The word stings because it's true. Scout said something similar last week. Different context, but the same idea.

"Scout told me something." The words come out before I can stop them. "She said I don't have to meet every sensation with force."

Ryan's eyebrows rise. "Scout said that?"

"Yeah. We were talking about something else, but..." I shrug, feeling exposed. "Maybe it applies to hockey too."

"Smart woman." Ryan nods slowly. "She's right. You don't have to hit everything that moves. Save it for when it counts."

"What if I can't?" The admission wrenches out of my chest. "What if being physical is the only thing I know how to do?"

"Then you learn something new. Or you trust that the physical part works better when you're not exhausting yourself with constant contact." Ryan crosses his arms. "I want you to try something tomorrow night. Go into the game with one rule: you don't hit unless your team needs you to. Watch, wait, be patient. Can you do that?"

Everything in me wants to say no. I want to argue that my value comes from being the biggest, meanest presence on the ice. But Ryan's looking at me so sternly that I can't say no without feeling like a disobedient schoolboy.

"One game," I say finally. "I'll try it for one game."

"That's all I'm asking." Ryan claps me on the shoulder. "Now get out of here. You look like hell."

The drive home feels longer than usual. My head's full of static, thoughts tangling over each other. Ryan could be wrong. What if holding back makes me useless? What if the team realizes they don't actually need me?

Scout's at the kitchen counter when I walk in, chopping vegetables for dinner. She's wearing one of my Havoc t-shirts that hangs to her thighs, her dark blonde curls piled on top of her head in a messy knot. Bare legs, bare feet, humming along to some song playing from her phone.

She's always so damn beautiful.

"Hey." She looks up, smiling. Then her smile fades. "Rough practice?"

"Something like that." I drop my bag by the door, moving to wash my hands at the sink. "Sorry. My head's a mess right now."

"Want to talk about it?" She slides closer, those green eyes soft with concern.

"Not really." I dry my hands, pulling her against me just to feel her solid and real. "I just need to watch some film tonight. There's some shit I have to figure out."

"Okay." She doesn't push, just wraps her arms around my waist and holds on. "I'll make dinner. You do what you need to do."

That's the thing about Scout. Counter to what she believes about herself, she doesn't try to fix everything. She just lets me be whatever I need to be while making sure I'm not alone in it.

Dinner is some kind of stir-fry she throws together with chicken and vegetables. We eat in relative silence, her trying to make light conversation while I give one-word answers. Not because I don't want to talk to her, but because my brain won't stop replaying every hit from practice, analyzing what Ryan said, trying to figure out how to be useful without being physical.

"I'm going to watch film," I say after helping her clean up. "It might be a while."

"That's fine." Scout kisses my cheek. "I'll read or something. Don't stay up too late."

I set up in bed with my laptop, pulling up footage from

our last three games. Mainly, I'm looking for patterns. Times when I hit and it mattered. More times when I hit and it didn't change anything.

The more I watch, the more Ryan's words make sense. Half my hits are unnecessary. The other half are effective but poorly timed. I'm constantly moving, constantly engaging, never giving myself time to read the play and respond strategically.

I can't believe I never saw this before. It's like looking at the sky through a telescope for the first time. Everything is suddenly brilliantly illuminated.

Scout appears in the doorway about an hour later, changed into one of my oversized t-shirts. Seeing her dressed in my clothes, wearing what she thinks is comfortable, makes my mouth go dry despite my distraction. She's holding a physical therapy magazine, the kind with dense articles and diagrams of muscle groups.

"Mind if I join you?" She gestures to the empty side of the bed.

"It's your bed too."

She snorts and climbs in beside me, propping pillows against the headboard, settling in with her magazine. The rustle of pages becomes background noise as I continue watching film. Every so often I glance over at her. The way she chews her bottom lip when she's concentrating. The little furrow between her eyebrows when she reads something interesting.

Her bare legs are tucked under her, toes painted some bright color I can't name. Her dark blonde curls are loose now, falling around her shoulders in waves. Those green eyes track across the page, completely absorbed in whatever article she's reading about rotator cuff injuries.

Scout's fucking adorable and doesn't even realize it. Cute doesn't begin to cover it.

An hour passes. Then another. The laptop screen casts a blue glow across the darkened room. Scout's magazine slips from her fingers, her breathing evening out into sleep. She's curled on her side facing me, one hand tucked under her cheek, head tilted at an odd angle.

She doesn't stir as I gently move her onto a pillow. She just keeps breathing slowly, peacefully. Apparently she trusts me enough to fall asleep beside me while I'm wound tight with anxiety about tomorrow's game.

Looking at her now, something settles in my chest. A feeling that's been building for weeks but I've been too stubborn or scared to acknowledge.

I swear, I tried to lie to myself, to resist her. I told myself she was only a temporary roommate. Pretended that keeping her at arm's length and not letting her matter could work.

Scout's essential, though. Not just helpful or convenient or good company. She's essential. Like breathing. Like hockey. Like… the ice beneath my skates.

Closing my laptop, I slide down in bed and pull her against my chest. She mumbles something sleepy and incoherent, burrowing closer. Her body fits against mine perfectly, like we were designed to fit together exactly this way.

Sleep doesn't come easy. My brain's still churning through film, through Ryan's words, through the fear that being enough won't happen if constant physicality doesn't occur. But having Scout here helps. It grounds me.

Eventually exhaustion wins. I drift off with her curled in my arms, trying to believe that tomorrow will be okay.

The arena buzzes with pre-game energy. I'm consumed by lacing my skates in the locker room and trying to quiet the voice in my head that says this new approach is going to fail spectacularly.

"You good?" Thorne drops onto the bench beside me, already in full gear.

"Yeah. Just trying something different tonight."

"Different how?"

"Less aggressive. More… strategic." The words feel foreign in my mouth.

Thorne's eyebrows rise. "You? Less aggressive? Did Coach threaten to bench you?"

"Something like that." I finish with my skates and stand, rolling my shoulders. "We'll see how it goes."

Taking the ice for warmups, I repeat Scout's words in my head like a mantra. *You don't have to meet every sensation with force. You don't have to meet every sensation with force.*

Scanning the crowd during warmups, I spot her immediately. Section 112, three rows up. Scout's wearing my jersey with the number 12 stretched across her back, her dark blonde curls spilling over the dark gray fabric. She's leaning forward in her seat, elbows on her knees, watching me with those green eyes that see everything. When she catches me looking, she grins and waves.

Something in my chest tightens. She came. She's here wearing my number, cheering me on while I try something that terrifies me.

The first period starts and gameplay is choppy and quick-moving. The opposing team comes out swinging, all aggression and speed. Within the first two minutes, there's an opportunity. Their winger gets too close to Jett, stick up high, and I'm already moving to intercept.

Then I stop. Blowing out a breath, I pull back and watch.

Jett handles it himself. He shrugs off the contact and maintains possession, scooping it up with his stick and shooting it to Thorne. Thorne takes it and skates like his ass is on fire. Less than a minute later, Thorne shoots the puck past the other team's goalie and the horn sounds.

Glancing toward section 112, I see Scout on her feet, cheering. The jersey swamps her frame, hanging to her thighs. She looks ridiculous and perfect and... *mine.*

As I clamber back onto the bench, Hunter claps me on the shoulder. And all I can think is that the new approach works. Holy shit, it actually works.

More opportunities to try it out come. Small moments where normally throwing a hit just to send a message would happen. Instead, I hang back, wait, try to see if I'm needed. For the most part, my teammates handle themselves. They don't need me constantly intervening like some overprotective enforcer who doesn't trust his team.

Halfway through the second period, everything changes. Their defenseman slashes Thorne hard across the wrist, deliberate and vicious. The refs miss it completely. Thorne drops his stick, shaking out his hand, and skates toward the bench, unable to grip properly.

My blood boils. That's the kind of cheap shot that deserves an answer.

I look toward the bench. Coach Ryan catches my eye and jerks his head toward the opposing defenseman. The signal I've been waiting for. Now I have permission to handle it.

As soon as play resumes, I line up my target and wait for the perfect moment. When the defenseman chases the puck into the corner, I'm right there. I barrel into him, crushing him into the boards with enough force to knock the wind out of his lungs. His head snaps back and his stick clatters to the ice.

The refs blow the whistle immediately. "Two minutes for roughing!"

I'm not even pissed off. The hit was worth every second in the penalty box.

The opposing defenseman struggles to his feet, wobbly and disoriented. His teammates help him off the ice. He doesn't come back.

Skating to the penalty box, I catch Ryan's nod of approval. This is what enforcing actually looks like. It's not *constant* violence, it's *strategic* violence.

The two minutes in the sin bin pass slowly. Watching my team play without me, defending successfully, moving the puck with confidence, something clicks into place.

They don't need a big bad enforcer every single second of ice time. They just need me when it counts.

Glancing up at section 112, I see Scout still on her feet. She's watching me in the penalty box, hands pressed together like she's praying or just nervous. When I catch her eye, she mouths something I can't quite read. I point at her and she blushes.

My chest goes tight again. I'd do more than that, maybe make a heart with my fingers, but I don't know if Scout's ready for the kind of heat and questions that gesture would bring her.

When my time's up, I hit the bench and my teammates swarm me. I get pats on the back and fist bumps. Thorne especially, flexing his wrist with a grim smile.

"Thanks, man. That was perfect."

"No problem. He had it coming."

We win 3-1. Not my most physical game by a long shot. But, I think proudly, maybe my smartest one.

In the locker room afterward, Ryan catches my eye across

the melee of celebrating players. He just gives me a single nod that says everything.

I shower quickly and change, eager to find Scout. She's waiting outside the locker room, still wearing my jersey, bouncing on her toes with excitement.

"You were amazing!" She throws herself at me and I catch her easily, lifting her off her feet. "I mean it, Si. You were so smart out there. You were strategic, until you needed to pay that dude back for Thorne. That hit was perfect."

"You noticed all that?" I set her down but keep my hands on her waist.

"Of course I noticed. I was watching you the whole time." She grins up at me. "You didn't have to meet every sensation with force. You were patient. You waited for the right moment."

"Ryan was right." The admission comes easier than I expected. "Turns out there's more than one way to be useful."

"I'm so proud of you." She reaches up, cupping my face with both hands. "This was a big deal. You tried something new and it worked."

"You came to watch." I'm stating the obvious, but I can't stop staring at her. "You're wearing my jersey."

"Of course I came. And of course I'm wearing your jersey." She looks down at the oversized fabric, smoothing it over her hips. "I wanted everyone to know whose girl I am."

The words hit harder than any check I've ever taken. *Whose girl I am.*

"You look good in my number," I manage.

"Yeah?" She grins, doing a little spin that makes the jersey flare. "Think I should wear it more often?"

"Every day. Never, ever take it off."

She laughs, bright and happy, and links her arm through

mine as we head toward the parking lot. Scout keeps chattering about the game, pointing out plays I made, asking questions about strategy. She's engaged and interested and wearing my number. I don't fucking deserve a girl like her.

Ryan was right. Scout was right. What do you know?

Chapter Twenty-Six

Scout

It's official. This has been the longest week ever and it's only Monday. As I open the front door, I get a text from Jessa. Silas isn't home yet, so I have a little me time. I fling myself onto my bed and check my messages.

JESSA

So how's living with the Ice Man? Have you two stopped fighting?

I smile at the text from my roommate. She's always pushing buttons and giggling as they raise a reaction.

ME

We've found a rhythm. Turns out, Silas isn't frosty at all.

JESSA

•• Are you guys hooking up? Tell me that he's helping you tick off boxes on the Naughty Girl Scout list.

ME

I'll tell you over drinks.

JESSA

Ooooh girrrrrl! I'm out of town right now, but when I get back, I need hot deets STAT.

ME

Deal.

I hear the front door slam, followed by the blender whirring. No doubt Silas is having another protein shake after an intense practice. Considering that for a moment, I slide the top drawer of my dresser open and fish out my Naughty Girl Scout list.

The Naughty Girl Scout List

- Wear red lipstick every day for a week
- Dance on a table
- Download a dating app and actually swipe
- Have morning sex before coffee
- Try a toy with someone watching
- Fall asleep still sweaty and tangled up with him
- Confess my fantasies to a complete stranger
- Sleep naked and not feel weird about it
- Figure out what my body actually likes in bed
- Send a nude without apologizing for it
- Sext until the phone dies
- Let someone go down on me until I cry
- Give a blowjob and take control until he begs
- Ride someone's face just because I want to
- Have sex against a wall, messy and desperate
- Let someone tie my wrists and take whatever they want
- Watch myself in a mirror while he's inside me
- Let a man talk filthy to me without flinching
- Get fucked on the kitchen counter

- A finger up the butt (on either person)

Wow. I've done more of these things than I thought. A small burst of pride emanates from my chest. Suck on that, Enzo.

No one but Jessa has ever seen this list, but sitting here looking down at the list, the urge to make Silas the first guy to ever see it is strong. I'm almost certain he'll be into a few of these.

When he raps on my open doorway, I start. I smile at him, trying to still my racing heart.

Silas's lips curl at the corners. He's so damn handsome, his hair still damp from a recent shower, his tight black t-shirt stretched across his chest. "Hey."

I tilt my head, flushing. God, even that one word has me achy, my nipples tightening like I'm one of Pavlov's fricking dogs. "Hey. How was practice?"

"Good." His blue-gray eyes sweep over me. "Thought I'd see you there."

"I was stuck compiling stats for Mobility Mondays. I have to present my data to Coach Cross soon."

He takes a long sip of his protein shake. "It'll go well. I'm seeing big gains. I'm sure the other players are too."

"Yeah. That's what the data says. But convincing the team that my program is worthwhile is..." I search for the words. "I feel like I'm trying to sell myself and I'm seriously lacking in confidence."

He sits down and abandons his shake on my bedside table.

"You should see some of the junk that the coaches have spent money on. Light therapy booths, wearable stats bands, neurofeedback helmets. Absolute garbage that could reason-ably give the players an advantage. Mobility Mondays have a data-backed track record. Trust me when I say that they'll probably jump at the chance."

"Yeah?" I roll my shoulders, letting his words sink in. "Thanks, Si."

"Don't thank me. You've done a ton of work. Be proud of yourself." He picks up my hand, tracing a little pattern into my palm. "What's on the paper?"

"Oh." My cheeks heat again. "It's a list of things I want to try... um, in bed."

His eyes darken instantly and his spine snaps straight. "Show me."

I pass him the sheet of notebook paper and watch his face change as he reads each item. His jaw ticks, grip tightening on the paper until the edges crumple slightly. When those eyes finally lift to mine, they're absolutely molten.

"You wrote this?"

"With help. Jessa helped with several of them."

He clarifies, pointing to the list. "But you want to do all of these things?"

"Someday? Yeah."

Si pokes out his cheek with his tongue. "How about this week instead?"

My breath catches. "What?"

"This week." He stands up and moves closer, towering over where I'm sitting on the edge of the bed. I feel the heat rolling off him when he sets the list aside and tilts my jaw up to look at his eyes. "My suggestion is that we work through this list. Every single item. You think you can handle that?"

Heat floods through me, fast and overwhelming. "Y-yes, I can."

"Good." His palms cup my face. "Then let's start right now."

The kiss is hard, claiming, then he's walking me backward out of the bedroom, down the hall, into the kitchen still kissing me.

"First item," he growls against my mouth. "Get fucked on the kitchen counter."

My back hits the counter. "Silas..."

"Tell me no if you don't want this."

He's so damn bossy. I'm a mess of need, and I can't say no when he gets like this. "I want everything, Si."

One smooth motion lifts me onto the counter. He starts undressing me, my Havoc shirt flying into the living room, my underwear disappearing somewhere behind him. I scrabble with his t-shirt, pulling it off, and his sweatpants hit the floor seconds later.

"Hold on to me," he commands. "This is going to be rough."

"I like it rough," I pant. "Fuck me, Si."

"I fucking love it when you call me that."

He kisses me impossibly hard, parting my thighs, and brushes his fingers along the dripping-wet seam of my pussy. We both groan.

He pushes inside without warning, drawing a cry from me, nails digging into his shoulders hard enough to leave marks. Silas's cock is huge, nearly splitting me in two. And yet, I want more. He doesn't give me time to adjust to the angle or the stretch, just fucks hard and fast like a machine. One hand fisted in my hair, the other gripping my ass to hold me exactly where he wants me. I tilt my head back and let out a sultry moan.

"Eyes on me, Pretty Girl," he grits out. "I've been thinking about doing this since the day you moved in. I wanted to bend you over this counter where we eat breakfast and make you scream my name."

The angle hits perfectly, finding that spot that makes stars explode behind my eyelids. "Oh god, Si... Right there. Don't stop!"

I'm already close, wound impossibly tight from anticipation and the sheer wrongness of being taken on the kitchen counter.

"I can tell you're almost there. Come for me. Let me feel it, baby."

My release crashes through me. I come with his name on my lips, clenching around him as pleasure rips through in waves. He follows seconds later, groaning into my neck, teeth scraping my sensitive skin. Both panting, both shaking, we stay frozen for a long moment before he pulls out carefully and helps me down on unsteady legs.

"That was..." I lean against his chest, needing contact. "Really amazing."

"One down." His grin does wicked things to me. "What's next on the list?"

Laughter bubbles up, breathless and wild. "You're completely insane."

"You love it."

I nod. God help me, I absolutely do.

Tuesday brings him home from practice to find me waiting on the couch, wearing nothing but his Havoc hoodie with bare legs underneath, want written clearly across my face.

"Hi," I say. I'm shy now that we're in the same room.

Si comes around the couch, his expression dark with want.

"Why are you over there and not sitting on my face?" His eyes go feral. "Get over here. Right now."

He sits down on the floor, resting his neck on the seat of the couch. I look at him, licking my lips, uncertain how to position myself. Si taps the couch on either side of his head.

"Kneel right here and grab the back of the couch," he instructs. "I'm hungry, Pretty Girl."

The nickname sends a shiver down my spine. My face glowing like the tip of a cigarette, I kneel and put my hands on the back of the couch to brace myself. Si yanks me forward without hesitation until I'm hovering over his face.

"Lower," he commands.

I bite my lip. "I don't want to hurt you."

"You're not. If you haven't already figured this out, I'm a giant. And even if you were smothering me, I wouldn't care. Sit on my face and let me eat your pussy, honey."

Chewing on my lip, I gaze down at Si. His chin-length golden hair is tousled, his piercing blue eyes and dark brows startlingly handsome. He's dead serious as he starts kissing my inner thighs, urging me toward his mouth. I lower myself slowly, carefully, until his mouth brushes against the seam of my pussy. The first touch of tongue draws a moan from my lips.

"Oh fuck," I whisper. "Your mouth feels so good."

Si squeezes my ass cheeks and slurps, the sound obscene and pleasing at once. He's usually filthy-mouthed, but he seems to be entranced with nuzzling my pussy and giving me tender nips to my inner thighs and lips. I want to close my eyes and literally ride his mouth, but I can't look away from his face. He hums against my flesh, fucking my pussy with his tongue before sucking on my clit. The angle gives him total access to everything, tongue working relentlessly, hands gripping thighs hard, holding me in place when he focuses on my clit.

Looking down reveals his massive frame beneath, eyes locked on mine, watching every reaction. The sight makes my pussy clench.

"God, you look huge from up here," I murmur. I reach down and stroke his hair. "I bet your cock looks even bigger."

His groan vibrates against sensitive flesh, making me shake, rocking against his mouth without meaning to, chasing the pleasure building fast. This is too fucking good. Intimate, vulnerable, and erotic. Silas Huxley, the Havoc's star defender and frosty bully, is looking up at me with the fiercest look ever. It's just too much.

When I come, it's with his name falling from my lips and one hand fisted desperately in his hair. He doesn't stop, just keeps going until oversensitivity makes me squirm.

"Silas, please! I can't take it anymore..."

He finally whispers, "One more. Give me one more."

So I do. I close my eyes and roll my hips, groans and curses falling from my lips. Another wave crashes through. I come louder this time, thighs shaking on either side of his head, my pussy pulsing. When I finally shakily move to the side, his face is wet and eyes wild with satisfaction. He pulls me to the floor, kissing me, and I giggle as I pull at his waistband.

Wednesday night, the bedroom becomes our stage. The full-length mirror against the wall frames us perfectly when Silas positions me in front of it.

"Watch," he commands from behind, still fully clothed. "I want you to see what I see."

His hands slide under my shirt slowly, cupping breasts through the bra, and the mirror reflects everything. How he toys with my nipples through fabric, how my body arches into his touch automatically. My pussy is wet and hot and achy for him already.

"Look at you, so responsive, so perfect for me."

He strips each piece of my clothing off slowly, deliberately, until my naked skin contrasts with his fully dressed form behind me in the reflection.

"Spread your legs." His hands urge my knees to part.

The mirror shows everything as his hand slides between my thighs, touching my glistening lips. I've never seen myself like this. A wanton woman being fucked by a gorgeous man. His fingers circle with practiced precision, finding my clit. My hips buck forward against his touch.

I suck in a breath. "Si, you're killing me."

It's not really a complaint. He's teasing me, going slow, taking his time.

"I know, baby. Don't look away. Watch yourself take my fingers. See how wet you are for me? You're fucking desperate for me. Do you know how hot that is?"

My cheeks burn, but I stare at my reflection, watching her getting fucked. He hikes my leg up and as I watch, he pushes two fat fingers inside my pussy, stretching me, filling me. I cry out, rocking my hips, pleasure building low and insistent.

"Fuck," I breathe. "It feels so good."

He's in my ear, murmuring, "You're so beautiful like this, taking what I give you, trusting me completely, letting me see all of you. You're such a good girl. Such a Pretty Girl."

Those words hit as hard as physical pleasure. My throat tightens. No one has ever said those words to me, let alone meant them. My pussy clamps down on his fingers. He swirls his thumb around my clit and I'm primed like a rocket, ready to blow.

Silas looks on with hooded eyes.

"Keep watching. I want you to see exactly what I see when you fall apart for me."

The mirror reflects everything as release crashes through me, my body convulsing, my eyes locked on our reflection. I watch myself shatter in his arms, feeling the most vulnerable yet somehow the safest I've ever been.

Thursday brings blindfolds and ice cubes trailing down heated skin. His mouth follows the cold path, warming each spot until shivers become trembles. Feathers trace patterns that make my muscles jump. His fingers find places that make breathing impossible, his cock reaches that place deep inside me that no one else can touch. Every sensation builds on the last until I'm begging incomprehensibly. But he makes me wait, makes me sob with need before finally, finally giving what my body screams for.

In other words, he blows my freaking mind.

Friday transforms the entire apartment into something else entirely. Candles flicker on every surface when he comes home to find me in his jersey with nothing underneath.

"Fuck." He drops his bag, stalking toward the bed. He admires the jersey, lifting it up with two fingers. When he realizes that I'm bare underneath, his eyes snap to mine. "You wearing this for me?"

I nod, a smirk on my face. "Yes, baby. It's your reward."

"Keep this on," he breathes. "You're such a bombshell."

"Bossy." I climb out of bed and drop to my knees, looking up at him as I reach for the zipper of his jeans. "Show me how you taste, Si."

"You're the perfect woman, Scout." He looks at me like I'm the hottest thing he's ever seen. Plowing his hand into my hair, he says, "Now stick out your tongue and let me take control."

Saturday morning sunlight streams through windows, painting golden stripes across tangled sheets. Soreness marks every muscle in the best way, exhaustion mixing with deep satisfaction.

"How many items did we get through?" The question gets muffled against his chest.

The crumpled list appears from the nightstand. "Seven."

Smiling, I draw figure eights into the bare skin of his abs. Apparently, Silas isn't ticklish. "Not bad for one week."

"We have plenty of time for the rest. No rush." When I glance up, he's smirking. "It's not exactly hard having you here, Scout."

Breathing in his scent, courage builds in my chest again. "This week wasn't just about checking off the list, was it?"

Quiet stretches between us for a beat. "No, it wasn't."

"Then what was it really about?"

"Trust. You trusted me enough to show me that list. You let me see what you want without hiding it. That's a big fucking deal."

"Can I tell you something?" I catch my lower lip between my teeth. "You might not want to hear it. It's awfully relation-ship-y."

Si considers me. "You can always tell me what's going on in that head of yours."

I suck a breath, gathering all my courage. If I don't say this now, I might never say it. And I hate the idea of Si not knowing how I feel.

"I'm falling for you," I confess. My heart is beating fast.

His breath catches audibly. "Yeah?"

"Yeah." I prop up on one elbow and bring his face into focus. "Is that okay?"

He looks so serious that I'm surprised when he says, "More than okay, because I'm falling too. I have been for a while now. How could anyone not love you?"

My eyes well up. If he only knew how easy it was for some people. I sigh, "Oh, Si..."

The kiss he presses to my lips tastes different, soft and sweet, nothing like the desperate hunger of the past week. This feels deeper, scarier and thrilling in equal measure.

When we finally get so sleepy that neither of us moves or talks, I realize that I can't remember the last time I checked the Twinge app. Two weeks? Three?

I reach for my phone, and Silas glances over at me. His voice is raspy when he asks, "Everything okay?"

"Yeah. I just need to send something quick."

I open the app and navigate to my messages with Stat-Man12. The last conversation was weeks ago. It's funny. Around the time that Silas and I got together, StatMan went dark. Life is weird like that sometimes, like a convergence in the space time continuum.

Scrolling through our last few conversations, I don't feel guilty about the silence. I don't wonder what he's doing or if he's thinking about me.

I just feel... done.

I type quickly, not overthinking it.

YOGA4LYFE

Hey. I'm seeing someone now. It's going really well. I wanted to let you know I'm not interested in continuing our friendship, if you can call it that. Thanks for the conversations. Take care of yourself.

I hit send, then immediately put down my phone without waiting for a response. I don't need one. In a few days, I'll probably delete the app. Whatever I was looking for when I downloaded Twinge, I've found something way better.

"All good?" Silas asks.

I toss my phone back on the bedside table and snuggle closer into his side. "All good."

Lying in the dark next to Silas, I take a moment to feel lucky that I'm dating someone who seems to genuinely like me, is willing to be seen in public with me, and generally doesn't lie or hide behind a sexy profile pic.

A girl could get used to this.

Chapter Twenty-Seven

Silas

Everything about the training room is stressful. The air smells faintly like antiseptic and Windex. Fluorescent lights hum overhead. While head trainer Sam prods at my shoulder with all the warmth of a mechanic inspecting a broken machine, I sit on the vinyl seat and try not to spiral.

When I woke up this morning, I felt a familiar pins and needles sensation in the front, top, and back of my shoulder. The Havoc has played hard this week, going to Miami, Atlanta, D.C., and Charlotte. After a week of bliss with my girl, I felt good enough to push myself through the five days away.

Then I played too aggressively. We won two games, lost the third, and I had to watch the fourth from the bench as my whole shoulder throbbed. I got out over my wings, as they say.

"I need to conduct a range of motion test," Sam says, not bothering to look at my face.

He lifts my arm, tweaking it this way and that. He's moving it slowly but pain still rips down to my fingertips like someone dragging a serrated blade through muscle and tendon. My teeth grind together hard enough to make my jaw ache, but Sam just keeps moving my arm until I can't take any more.

"Stop," I grate out. I pull my arm from his grip and rub the top of my shoulder, my thumb digging into the sore spot along the deltoid. "It hurts."

"Sorry, Silas." His pen scratches across the clipboard as he makes notes. "It seems like you took too many hits to your already-injured shoulder. You're compensating. Guessing that you have scapular dyskinesis, rotator cuff strain, and capsular restriction seems accurate. If you keep playing with an injury like this, you'll need surgery."

Surgery would mean the end of the season, maybe more. His words land like a body check to the ribs.

"Say I had to have surgery. How long would I be out?" The voice that comes out sounds flat and emotionless, a machine asking for repair estimates. Ice Man is asking, not me.

"Depends. If you rest it and let us mobilize the tissue properly? Maybe four weeks. If you keep grinding through..." He shrugs like he's discussing the weather. "It could be career-ending."

Four weeks means a month of sitting useless while the team fights without me. It would prove that I'm expendable. And if the worst happens, my hockey playing days could be over, just like that. His words fill my veins with ice.

"That's not acceptable. What are the alternatives?"

"There are a few. Most of them require intense physical therapy and a lot of luck. We'll tape you up for now." Sam reaches for the roll of athletic tape, but doesn't stop writing. "I'll talk to Coach Cross about your case. I think the safest way to proceed would be benching you for the next few games."

The word benched sits heavy as stone in my chest. Suddenly I'm reduced to some farm-team kid who can't handle the physicality. Every instinct screams to rip the tape from his hands, scream in his face, and storm back onto the ice. But as usual, brooding silence wins.

I'm not about to have an emotional breakdown in front of Sam.

The door to the training room swings open without warning. Scout appears with her arms full of fresh tape and compression wraps, a headset hanging around her neck. Her dark blonde curls are pulled back in a messy ponytail, a few strands escaping to frame her face. She's wearing her Havoc staff polo tucked into black athletic pants that hug her legs. Those green eyes find mine immediately, and I watch her expression shift in half a second. Concern flickers across her features as she reads the tension in my body. She's too open, too readable. Beautiful even when she's worried.

"What's going on?" she asks.

Sam doesn't look up from his clipboard. "I was just about to tape Huxley's shoulder."

"I've got this," she tells Sam. "I know just how he likes to be taped. Right, Si?"

I nod. "Yeah."

Sam hesitates, glancing between us, then hands over the tape and heads out of the training room. The door clicks shut behind him, silence pressing heavier than it should. Scout sets everything on the counter with careful precision, moving closer but stopping just short of touching. She's waiting for permission.

"Are you all right? I meant to come check on you when I didn't see you in practice, but this morning has been crazy."

Sweeping my gaze over her, I say, "I'm fine."

"You're not." A gentle firmness carries in her voice. She knows I'm full of shit. It's obvious I'm not fine since I woke up in so much pain that I came straight here instead of heading out onto the ice with everyone else. She picks up the tape, starts prepping strips with practiced efficiency. "Let me help, big guy."

Big guy. The pet name sends a shiver sluicing down my spine. How can I say no to Scout when she calls me sweet names?

It's on the tip of my tongue to tell her that she doesn't need to hover and that I'm not a charity case. But when her warm, steady, competent hands settle on my shoulder, something cracks open slightly. Her touch hurts and feels good in equal measures, instantly.

She works in silence at first, her fingers pressing along the joint, testing for tenderness. Every touch is careful, precise, and professional. I lean my head to the side and sigh deeply.

Her hands feel like they're healing me.

"Someone filmed you at practice," Scout says.

I look up from my shake. "What?"

She shows me her phone. It's a TikTok video of me scowling at a rookie who dropped his stick, picking it up, handing it back without a word.

Ice Man has a HEART??

She gives me a mischievous look. "Three million views. You're a meme."

"Delete it."

"I can't delete it. I didn't post it." She's grinning. "But I saved it."

"Scout."

"It's cute. You're being nice and you look so angry about it."

I try to grab her phone. She dances away, laughing.

"I hate this."

"You love it."

"I absolutely do not."

Watching her this happy over something this stupid, though. I could get used to that.

"You know, mobility training would have prevented this." Her breath fans my neck as she drags her thumb along the tight band of muscle between my neck and shoulder. "If you'd let me work with you properly instead of fighting it every step..."

"Don't." I love being touched. I keep the pleased shudder out of my voice when I grind out, "Don't turn this into another lecture about yoga."

Her hands hesitate where they rest against my neck. "It's not a lecture. I'm not trying to trick you, Si. Yoga is a really powerful tool."

"You think you can fix me, like I'm another project to manage and improve with the right stretches and breathing exercises."

She pulls back, hurt flashing in her eyes before she can hide it. "That's not fair."

"None of this is fair." The gesture encompasses the shoulder, the medical wing, the whole goddamn situation. "But I don't need lectures about what should have been done differently. I know, okay? I know I fucked up."

"Your inner critic is an asshole, Silas." Scout's chiding is gentle. "Listen to me. You didn't fuck up. You just played too hard. Sometimes it's impossible to know how your body is going to feel about something until afterward."

My icy heart thaws a tiny bit more. "You're too sweet for this world, Pretty Girl."

"Si!" She smiles, blushing, and ducks her head. "Not at work, okay?"

"Yeah, I know." I shrug, rolling my eyes. "It's hard to keep you a secret."

"Flirt." Scout smiles and finishes taping my shoulder without another word. "Okay. You should be all set. Go home and ice this. If I come home and you aren't already sitting on the couch with an ice pack, I'm going to be pissed."

"Pissed, huh? That's something I haven't seen from you before."

Scout rolls her eyes. "Go on, big guy. Get out of here. I have to go back to practice."

She leaves the room, her hips swaying, her curls bobbing. She's bewitching. If I'm not careful, I'll be caught in her spell forever. It doesn't even sound that bad, though I should be focusing on my hockey career instead of earning another smile from pretty yoga girls.

My phone buzzes with a calendar reminder: therapy appointment in thirty minutes.

Today has been terrible outside of seeing Scout, and therapy isn't exactly what I need to round out this stellar day. But I already made the appointment. And I'm not looking forward to the look on Coach Cross's face if he finds out I skipped another therapy session.

Gray Seattle rain blurs past the window during the drive to Dr. Sable's office, mixing with darker thoughts. The closer I get to the clinic, the more my brain drags up things I don't want to think about.

I know former hockey players. Coach Cross and Coach Ryan, for instance. But I don't have much patience, so coaching is out for me.

And then of course there's Enzo. My agent. Scout's ex. Former Havoc center with hands like silk and a smile fans used to swoon over. Everyone said Enzo was born for hockey. Then a bad hit took him out for the rest of the season. The next thing I knew, the team was moving on without him.

Enzo isn't a man I'd consider wise, but he has been in my shoes. I hate that he knows how fast things can fall apart. Mostly, I hate the idea of becoming him. I'd become someone the Havoc talk about in the past tense. A used-up has-been. The coaches might only mention my name when they want to make a point about how fragile a career can be.

That makes me grip the steering wheel so hard that the leather creaks.

Pulling into Dr. Sable's lot, I park and sit there with the engine running for a moment, staring at the rain hitting the windshield.

Former player. Former asset. Former everything. It runs through my head on repeat. The word former feels like a fist around my throat. It's bad if just approaching the psychologist's office is bringing all these fears to the surface, isn't it?

I force myself out of the truck and take the elevator to the third floor.

"Come in," a calm voice calls.

Dr. Sable's office is warm, decorated in soft blues and grays, but it still feels like a room where bad news happens. Bookshelves line the wall. Diplomas glint under the lights. A silver framed photograph sits on her desk. In it, two women with their arms around each other, laughing. I glance at it without really seeing it.

I try to swallow away the feeling of dread.

"Silas," Dr. Sable greets me. "Thanks for coming back. Have a seat."

I sit. The couch squeaks under me. My palms are already sweating.

"How are you?" She looks at me, her expression pleasant, pen poised to take notes. "How is your injury?"

"Fine," I mumble. "I'm sitting out for a few games while my shoulder heals up."

"I see." She makes a note. "Other than that, how are you feeling?"

"Before we talk about your specific situation," she says, "I want to give you some context. A lot of players reach a crossroads like this. Some lean into coaching or scouting. Some move into player development. Some open gyms or sports clinics. Some step back from the sport entirely. It's a transition, not a failure. Part of my job is helping you understand what your options might look like."

Her calm tone hits every wrong nerve. My jaw locks. I don't want options. I want to stay on the ice. I want to contribute. I want to matter. I don't want to hear one more person, including Scout's ex boyfriend turned agent, tell me I need a backup plan.

She continues. "Today, I'm not trying to fix anything. I only want to understand what you've been carrying. Let's start with your support network. Do you have a partner or someone you talk to when things get difficult?"

Scout comes to mind instantly. My neck heats. "There's this woman. Scout. She works for the Havoc and she's living with me. Temporarily."

Dr. Sable's pen stills. Her eyes lift to mine. She seems tongue tied for a long moment. Her eyes drift to the photo on her desk.

"Silas, before we continue, I need to let you know I have a personal connection to someone you've mentioned. Because of that, I may not be the best therapist for you. I'm happy to refer you to a colleague."

I stare at the photo that I barely saw when I walked in. Two women in the woods. The blonde with sharp features and controlled posture. The other with curls and a softer smile.

Scout. That's why Sable looked so familiar. She's obviously related, somehow.

The world tilts sideways. My therapist knows the woman who's sharing my home, my bed. The same woman I have feelings for, who makes sure I eat and ice my shoulder and stretch even when I fight her about it.

The woman who looks at me like I'm still worth something even though I feel myself slide toward former player territory every day. God, if Dr. Sable told Scout a tenth of what I've said in this office, she'd probably never speak to me again.

Everything in my chest tightens. Sweat breaks across my back. The office feels too small and too bright.

"Silas?" Sable's voice cuts through the noise. "Are you all right?"

"I've got to go." I stand too fast and the chair scrapes across the floor.

"We still have forty minutes left in the session."

"I can't do this." My hand closes around my jacket. "I shouldn't have come."

"Silas, wait. If you're uncomfortable, we can talk about that. You should let me refer you to one of my colleagues. Please don't leave..."

But all I can think about is all the shit I've said here in this room. Scout shouldn't know any of it. She might know how close to broken I am. And now Scout's sister is sitting three feet from me, ready to hear every weakness I've spent years shoving down.

I push into the hallway. My pulse hammers in my ears. The elevator takes too long, so I take the stairs, shoulder screaming on every step. I don't stop.

By the time I reach the parking deck, my hands are shaking. I sit in my truck without starting it, staring at the rain through the windshield.

Scout's sister. Her sister now knows I showed up here. Her sister knows that I'm unraveling. If Sable talks to Enzo or management or anyone in the Havoc front office, it'll go straight into my file. Another note about instability. Like they need another reason to see me as a liability instead of a defenseman worth keeping.

And that's ignoring the fact that Sable will probably go straight to her sister and tell her to ditch me before I snap.

The thought makes me sick. I drop my forehead to the steering wheel and try to breathe. I'm not ready to be a former anything. And I'm definitely not ready for Scout to find out how close that future feels.

Chapter Twenty-Eight

Scout

The call I've been afraid of for years comes at two in the morning. I fumble for my phone, heart already racing before I'm even fully awake. The screen glows harsh in the darkness showing an unknown number with a Port Townsend area code.

My stomach drops immediately. This can't be good.

"Hello?" My voice comes out rough with sleep and rising panic.

"Is this Scout Nash?" A woman's voice sounds professional but tired.

My breath catches. "Yes, this is she."

"I'm calling from Jefferson Healthcare. Your father was brought in about an hour ago with a possible concussion and some broken ribs. He's stable, but he's confused. You're listed as next of kin."

Me? I know I'm the daughter he tends to lean on in times of need, but my older sister Sable is a psychologist. She's not a medical doctor, but she would be my first choice in this scenario. Not that I have a lot of options when it comes to next of kin. It's just her, my dad, and a distant aunt who lives in Canada.

The nurse is still talking, saying something about a neighbor finding Dad, his shed collapsing, a possible broken arm, and bruised ribs. All I hear is the roar of blood in my ears and the rushing sound of my world tilting sideways.

"Tell Dad I'm on my way." I rush her off the line. "I'll be there as soon as I can."

Beside me, Silas sits up, shirtless with sleep-mussed hair, rubbing at his eyes. "What's wrong?"

"My dad is in the hospital. I have to get to Port Townsend."

Climbing out of bed, I scurry out of Silas's bedroom, flipping the light on in mine. I'm too worried to pick out clothes, so I grab the first things I find, yanking on jeans and a t-shirt. My hands tremble so badly I can barely tie my shoes.

In my head, I'm spiraling. The shed has been my nightmare for three years. The same goddamn shed I've been telling him to fix since the last big windstorm. It's been leaning dangerously, but Dad kept saying he'd get to eventually.

I should've known better. It was impossible for Dad to fix by himself. I should've insisted on hiring help.

"Ready?" Silas appears in jeans and a black Seattle Havoc hoodie, keys in his hand. "I'm driving."

"Silas, you don't have to do that. It's two hours away. You need sleep and your shoulder needs rest..."

"We're not arguing about this right now." He's already moving, grabbing his wallet from the bowl by the door. Then he stops, looking at me. "You're not dressed warmly enough."

"Oh. I should go get a sweater."

Si is already unzipping and peeling off his hoodie, wrapping it around my shoulders and forcing my arms through the sleeves. I feel like a doll he's playing dress-up with. It's odd to be taken care of like this, but I don't try to fight it. Not when the hoodie smells so strongly of his vetiver and cedar scent. It's still warm from being on his body.

I give him a wobbly smile, pulling him close, pushing up to kiss his lips. He zips up the front of the hoodie as he kisses me back. "This looks good on you. You should always wear my clothes, Pretty Girl."

"Talk to me again in that gruff voice and I'll think about it." I bite my lip.

His eyes flare with interest. "As much as I want to take you up on that right now, I need to grab another jacket. Give me a sec and then we can go."

"So bossy," I chide him. Si doesn't respond because he's jogging down the hallway to grab another hoodie. He reappears, jerking his head to the door. "You ready, baby?"

God, the way he calls me baby makes my insides turn to mush.

"Ready," I whisper. "Thank you."

He pulls me against his chest, hugging me tightly for a few seconds. "Of course, Scout. You're my girl."

Closing my eyes, I want nothing more than to bury my head against his chest and hide from the world. When he pulls away and takes my hand, I have to swipe at my eyes with my sleeve. It's nice to be supported, for however much longer this lasts.

The drive blurs past in dark highways and scattered streetlights. Silas doesn't try to fill the silence with platitudes or ask questions I can't answer. He just drives with one hand steady on the wheel. When I start picking at my thumbnail hard enough to draw blood, his free hand finds mine and he laces our fingers together.

I stare out the window, watching Seattle give way to

smaller towns, then trees, then darkness broken only by occasional house lights. We have to go an unusual route around the land because the ferry isn't working at this time of night.

More time for me to be lost in nightmarish thoughts. My mind spins with worst-case scenarios about the shed that's been leaning for years. Every time I visit, I mention it and offer to hire someone to fix it. Dad always waves me off, says he'll get to it and he doesn't like me fussing about it.

Nothing is ever fine in that house. Since Mom died, everything has been exactly the same, but fine isn't a word that remotely describes the situation.

Getting out of the truck is amazing and nerve-wracking. The hospital smell hits me the second we walk in, like antiseptic and bad coffee. It's a smell I became intimately acquainted with when Mom was sick. A nurse with kind eyes directs us to the ER, down a hallway that feels too bright and too quiet at the same time. She points to a curtained area.

I take a breath, trying to prepare myself for what I'll find.

Tom Nash sits propped up in bed with his arm in a sling and his face mottled with bruises that look worse under the fluorescent lights. He looks smaller than I remember, older and more fragile, like a strong wind could knock him over.

"Hey, Scout," he wheezes, like I just dropped by for a casual visit instead of finding him after he was trapped under a collapsed shed for God knows how long. "I wondered when you'd arrive. I-- I didn't mean to scare you."

I can't speak at first. All the words I practiced in the car, the concern and relief and carefully modulated worry, dissolve on my tongue. What comes up instead is something sharper, something I've been swallowing for years.

"I'm okay." He scrubs his hand down the hospital smock, looking embarrassed. "I went out to the shed to grab a stepladder. Damn thing fell down when I opened the door. One of the new neighbors heard the crash and called 911. It's just some bumps and bruises. Nothing serious."

"Just some bumps and bruises?" My voice comes out strangled. "Dad, you were trapped under a shed. How long were you out there before someone found you?"

He shrugs his good shoulder, wincing slightly at the movement. "Couple hours, maybe. Hard to say. I lost track of time."

"A couple hours?" Something in my chest cracks wide open. It's like all the pressure I've been holding back for years has found a fault line. "You could have died, Dad."

"But I didn't." He sounds almost irritated by my reaction, like I'm making a fuss over nothing. "It was a scare, nothing more. I won't have you making a scene, Scout." He purses his lips. "Maybe I should've put Sable down as my emergency contact."

The casual dismissal is gasoline on a fire that's been banking since Mom got sick. I was sixteen and suddenly responsible for keeping our family functioning while she deteriorated. And Dad? He checked out emotionally.

I spent my college years driving home every weekend to clean and cook and make sure he was eating. I've been making this drive every other month for the past eight years, bringing groceries and paying bills and pretending everything is fine when nothing is fine.

"No need to make a fuss?" My voice comes out louder than I intend. The curtain does nothing to contain the sound, but I don't care anymore. The pressure building in my chest hits critical mass and I raise my voice, beyond angry. "Mom's hospital bed is still in the living room, Dad. Her shoes are still by the door. Her medications are still in the bathroom cabinet. You won't change anything, won't fix anything, won't let anyone help you. And now you're lying in a hospital bed because that goddamn shed finally collapsed like I've been warning you it would for three years!"

Dad's eyes widen in shock. Silas shifts behind me, becoming a solid presence at my back, close enough that I can feel his warmth. He doesn't interject or tell me to calm down, which is amazing given that every single person on this floor can hear just what I'm so upset about.

"Sable and I have been driving out there every month," I continue, voice rising with every word. "We bring groceries you barely eat. We pay bills you forget about. I clean that house while you sit and watch TV like nothing matters. You're just waiting to die so you can be with her. And I've been letting it go on, because I thought that if I just took care of you enough, if I just did enough, you'd want to live again."

My dad's face crumples. "Scout, honey, I..."

"No." Tears stream down my face now, hot and furious and cleansing. "I'm done. I'm so angry, Dad. You have given up and I've been enabling it. Tiptoeing around, not saying anything. I'm pissed that it took you almost dying for me to say any of this."

The silence that follows is deafening. Dad stares at his hands while his jaw works like he's chewing words he can't spit out. A monitor beeps steadily in the background. Somewhere down the hall, someone coughs.

Dad whispers, "I want to be different, Scout. You know I do. It's just hard."

"That house is killing you," I say. "I won't watch you drown anymore. You're moving to Seattle, somewhere close enough that I can help without destroying myself trying to keep you alive. Sable can check on you, too. You'll get a therapist. You need to start actually living instead of just existing. If I have to drag you kicking and screaming, you're going to let us help you move forward."

My dad looks down, his expression miserable.

When he doesn't respond, I take a breath and force myself to say the rest. "If you refuse to let me help you, if you stay in that house and rot away with Mom's ghost, then I'm done. I won't come back." Wiping away tears, I shake my head. "I can't do it anymore. I won't sacrifice myself the way she did."

I wait for the explosion. Surely this is the part where he tells me I'm overreacting or being dramatic or not understanding what it's like to lose someone. That's what he's done every other time I've worked up the courage to push back on the few times I've tried to broach this subject.

Instead, Dad's shoulders slump in defeat. When he looks up, his eyes are wet with tears tracking down through the bruises. "You're right."

I blink in surprise. "What?"

"You're right." His voice sounds rough, broken, scraped raw. "I've been hiding in that house, in the memories, in the past. Your mom would be furious if she saw what I've become." He swipes at his face with his good hand, smearing the tears. "I don't know how to start over. I'm lost, baby. I forgot how to be anything but the man who lost your mom."

Something loosens in my chest, painful and necessary, like pulling out a splinter that's become infected. "You don't have to figure it out alone. But you do have to try. You have to want to try."

Dad nods slowly, mechanically. "Okay. If you and Sable will help me, I'll try. I promise I'll try."

My eyes well up. "That would mean so much to me."

Silas's hand settles on my shoulder, warm and grounding. I lean back into him without thinking, needing his steadiness to keep me upright.

"We'll find you something," I say, wiping my face with

the back of my hand. "A fresh start. But you have to meet us halfway, Dad. We can't do this for you."

Dad's eyes drift to Silas, then back to me, and something shifts in his expression. "He's a good one."

My cheeks heat despite everything. "Dad, this isn't the time..."

"Don't let this one go." His voice is firmer now, more like the father I remember from before. "A man who drives you two hours in the middle of the night doesn't do that unless you matter to him."

I can't look at Silas, can't see his reaction to my father's words. But his hand tightens on my shoulder with fingers pressing in just slightly. He's still here, and that's answer enough for now.

We leave after Dad falls asleep, with the nurse promising to call if anything changes. They want to keep him overnight for observation to make sure there's no internal bleeding or complications. I'm wrung out and exhausted with emotions scraped so raw I feel like I'm walking without skin.

In the truck, Silas doesn't start the engine right away. He sits there with his hands on the wheel, staring straight ahead at the dark parking lot.

"You were right," he says finally. "Your dad probably won't tell you, but you made the right call. He should be living in Seattle where he's close by so that you can reach him without such a long commute. Living out here is only making him isolated."

I let out a deep sigh. "I shouldn't have yelled at him in a hospital bed."

"He needed to hear it." Silas turns to face me, his expression intense in the dim light from the parking lot lamps. "You've been carrying him for years. That's not sustainable, Scout. That's not healthy. And it's not fair to you."

I know he's right the same way I know my mother gave everything until there was nothing left, until the MS took what remained. But the guilt sits heavy anyway, a familiar weight I don't know how to put down.

"What if he doesn't follow through?" My voice comes out small and uncertain. "What if he agrees now but changes his mind once we get him settled? What if I just made everything worse?"

"Then that's on him, not you." Silas reaches over and cups my face in his big, warm hand. "My mom was a terrible person, but she did teach me one thing. You can't save people who don't want to be saved. You can only save yourself."

The words hit something deep, something I've been trying to ignore. I think about Enzo and all the years I spent trying to be enough, trying to make him love me the way I needed. Trying to fix his moods, manage his temper, smooth over his rough edges until I was nothing but a tool for his comfort. I think about my mother, pouring herself out for Dad and for us until the disease took what little was left. I've been repeating this pattern without realizing it, living inside this wound.

"I don't want to be like my mom," I whisper. "She disappeared into taking care of him and taking care of us. And then she got sick and before I knew it she was just gone. It was as though she never existed as her own person, only as what she could do for everyone else. I feel like I'm failing my dad by not being as giving as my mom was."

"You're not your mom." Silas's thumb brushes my cheek, gentle and certain. "You have other things going on. You're kind and wonderful, but you're also focused on Mobility Mondays and teaching yoga."

I close my eyes and let myself lean into his touch. When I open them again, he's watching me with an expression I can't quite read. There's something intense there, something hungry and tender at the same time that makes my breath catch in my throat.

"Thank you," I say. "For being here. And for driving me." I pause. "I guess thank you for everything, really."

He cuts me off with a kiss that's gentle and fierce all at once. His mouth tastes like coffee and something uniquely him. I melt into it without thinking. When he pulls back, his forehead rests against mine with our breath mingling in the small space between us.

"You don't have to thank me," he murmurs. "There's nowhere else I'd rather be."

The words settle in my chest, warm and sure. We drive home as the sun rises, painting the sky in shades of pink and gold that feel too beautiful for how exhausted I am. I pull his hoodie tighter around myself, the one he gave me weeks ago that I never gave back. It smells like him, with notes of cedar and clean soap and something indefinable that's just Silas. Wearing it feels like being held.

My phone buzzes with a text from Sable.

SABLE

Just heard about Dad. Is he okay? Are you okay?

I stare at the message, then type with shaking fingers.

ME

He's going to be fine. I may have yelled at him.

The response is immediate.

SABLE

Holy shit. Are you serious?

ME

Yeah. I couldn't watch him kill himself slowly anymore. Long story very short, he's moving to Seattle.

Three dots appear and disappear and appear again.

Sable: Can I call you when you're home? If we're looking at housing, Dad has a lot of money left from Mom's life insurance policy. Anything extra I can pick up.

ME

Okay. We can talk about that when I'm home.

Back at the condo, I collapse on the couch while Silas makes coffee in the kitchen. The familiar sounds of cabinets opening and the coffee maker gurgling are soothing and normal and grounding. When my phone rings, I answer immediately.

"Scout." Sable's voice sounds tight and wound up. "I'm so glad Dad's okay. And I'm proud of you for saying what needed to be said."

"I yelled at him in a hospital bed while he was bruised and broken. I'm an awful daughter."

"You're not awful. You told him the truth." I hear her breathing, careful and measured. "I should have done it years ago. I should have backed you up instead of making excuses about being too busy with work or too far away to help."

"Sable, you couldn't have known that this would happen. You're a very busy professional. It's not your fault your job is demanding. I could have taken a page from your book and learned to set healthy boundaries with Dad."

"You listen to me, Scout." Her voice cracks and breaks open. "You think I have it together? You think I'm this perfect, successful person who knows what she's doing? I cry in my car between sessions, Scout. Half the time I don't believe my own advice. I'm drowning too, just with better hair and a fancier degree."

The admission knocks the air from my lungs. I've spent so many years comparing myself to Sable, beautiful and successful and confident Sable. She always seems to glide through life while I stumble and fall and scrape my knees bloody.

"I didn't know," I whisper.

"I know you didn't because I didn't want you to. I can't have anyone see that I'm just as much of a mess as everyone else." Sable sniffles. "But seeing you finally set boundaries with Dad makes me realize how heavy this has been for both of us. We've been carrying so much without asking for help because we thought we had to."

Tears stream down my face again, but these feel different and cleaner somehow. "I thought I was the only one struggling."

"You never were. I just got really good at pretending." Her voice steadies and strengthens. "We'll help Dad together, okay? We'll find him a place, get him settled, make sure he follows through with therapy. But we'll do it as a team, okay? And we won't lose ourselves in the process."

"Okay," I manage. "We'll do it together."

After we hang up, I sit in the quiet of the living room wearing Silas's hoodie that swallows my frame while coffee cools in my hands. I feel raw and exposed, like I've shed a skin I didn't know I was wearing. I've been walking around with this weighted vest for so long that I forgot what it felt like to breathe normally.

Silas appears from the kitchen and sits beside me on the couch without a word. He doesn't ask if I'm okay or try to fix anything. He just pulls me against his chest and lets me cry into his shirt while his hand strokes my hair in slow, soothing motions.

"I like this hoodie on you," he murmurs eventually.

I huff a watery laugh against his chest. "It's basically a dress."

"I still like it." His arms tighten around me, solid and sure. "I love knowing you're wrapped up in something of mine."

The possessiveness in his voice should annoy me. It should trigger all my independence alarms and all my warnings about losing myself in someone else. Instead it makes me feel safe and claimed in a way that doesn't require me to disappear or demand I sacrifice who I am.

"We should figure out what to eat," I say. Neither of us moves, though.

"In a minute." He presses his lips to the top of my head, the gesture so tender it makes my chest ache. "Just let me hold you first."

God, I think I'm in love with him.

I let myself be held and cared for. I rest against the solid wall of his chest while the morning light streams through the windows. His heartbeat stays steady under my ear, a rhythm I could get used to.

For the first time in as long as I can remember, I stop carrying the weight of everyone else's world. I stop trying to fix what's broken in other people. I stop sacrificing myself on the altar of being needed.

I just let myself exist here in this moment, wrapped in Silas's hoodie and his arms. Being exactly who I am with all my messiness and anger and fear and hope tangled together becomes acceptable.

Chapter Twenty-Nine

Scout

Trudging down the hallway, I pull out the keys to the front door and let myself in. The spicy smell of hot sauce hits me first and I pause in the doorway, sneezing several times. Silas pops his head around the corner from the kitchen.

"Sorry about the smell."

I close the door and cover my nose with my hand. My eyes are already watering as I walk into the kitchen.

"What is it?" I ask, surprised to see what appears to be some kind of noodle-laden soup. Si is pouring it into a bowl. Sitting beside it is a bottle of generic hot sauce and a sleeve of saltines.

"Hot crack." He smiles and shakes his head at himself. "Jett used to make it for us. It's ramen, a bunch of hot sauce, and some crumbled up crackers. Get it? Hot crack."

I squint. That name sounds familiar to me, but I can't think why. The knowledge sticks with me for a long moment, like an itch on the roof of your mouth. "I think you've mentioned it before."

"Have I?" He purses his lips as he shreds the saltine wrapper and crumbles the crackers over the soup. "I didn't think you were coming home. Do you want a bowl? I can make another one for myself."

I try not to wince. "Uh, no. I'm okay. I'll eat... later. When the house smells less like Satan's asshole."

"Sorry." Si grimaces. "You're missing out, though."

Just then, I go into a series of several sneezes, each one more painful than the last. I need to get away from this horrible smell. "I'm going to go into my room."

He raises his eyebrows. "Should I open some windows?"

I sneeze again, then nod. "That'd be nice."

As I'm bolting to my bedroom, he calls, "Sorry, baby!"

I close myself into my bedroom and stuff a towel under the door for good measure. Silas is usually a respectful roommate, so he can get away with this one terrible roommate faux pas. At least he's not microwaving spicy fish.

I flop across my bed with a sigh. My laptop is plugged in by the couch, but no way in hell am I going to venture out into that acrid smell to get it. I grab my phone and check my work emails, finding it hard to focus on anything but the spice-laden air.

Hot crack, Si called it. It continues to tickle me, feeling like a hair from my head that's on my shirt and ever so gently driving me insane. I close my email app with a sigh and scroll through my phone to get to my notes app. I keep a running list of things I need to do. Maybe my list will inspire some spark of productivity.

But I stop scrolling when my eye lands on Twinge, the dating app I deleted weeks ago.

That same strange tickle in the back of my brain gets stronger. Something about Hot Crack...

I redownload the app, my heart beating faster. My conversation with StatMan should still be in the archived messages even though I deleted my account. The app takes forever to load, and when it finally does, I navigate to the message history.

There. **StatMan12**. I scroll through our old conversations, past the goodbye message I sent him weeks ago. I keep scrolling back, back, until I find what I'm looking for.

A conversation about his childhood comfort foods. He was away on business and staying in a hotel room, eating...

Hot Crack. Ramen, crumbled crackers, and a ton of hot sauce. Even then, I thought it was gross.

My heart speeds up. Is Hot Crack a local delicacy that I just don't know about? It seems impossible.

A quick Google search shows me a ton of results, mostly news articles about drug busts and releases promoting a band with the same name. But nothing about ramen, crackers, or hot sauce.

Hot Crack ramen

Hot Crack food

Hot Crack seattle

All the same results. I put my phone down, sneezing, and curse Si for making his concoction. It's ruining my ability to think.

What are the chances that StatMan and Silas both had the same juvenile joke about an unusual dish? It's possible. But... I pull up Silas's past travel schedule, comparing it with StatMan's comments about traveling and hating being on the road. Every single time that StatMan was traveling?

Silas was on the road, flying for the Havoc.

I screw my face up and make a frustrated noise.

Is... is Silas StatMan? The idea is so crazy that I feel

insane just having it. But they kind of talk alike. Especially when they talk dirty.

Oh god. Yoga Girl, Pretty Girl... Am I going crazy?

I toss my phone aside and make a face. The most mature thing to do would be to confront him about it.

I'd feel so embarrassed if they were actually one and the same. Vulnerable, violated. But mostly I'd need to know why. Why would Silas hide behind a screen? He proved that he was perfectly capable of seducing me in real life. So why would he need to pretend that he didn't know me?

I stand up and fling my door open. Somehow in the confusion, I forgot that Silas had filled the apartment with the stench of stewing hot sauce. Blargh. I pinch my shirt and put it over my nose, venturing out to the living room. Silas is on the couch, watching game tape on the tv and slurping his awful-smelling concoction.

I come around the couch and fold my arms as I level him with a stare. He's sprawled on the couch in gray sweatpants and a faded Havoc t-shirt, bare feet propped on the coffee table. Six foot eight of casual comfort, his dirty blond hair messy like he's been running his hands through it. Those blue-gray eyes flick up to mine, and I watch his expression shift from relaxed to wary in a heartbeat.

He raises the tv remote and pauses the game.

"Are you coming to ask me to make you some ramen?" he jokes.

My heart speeds up as I shake my head, pulling my shirt off my face. "I have a weird question to ask. You didn't pose as someone else and talk to me on Twinge, did you?"

Silas stills, a flush rising in his cheeks. "Err. Maybe?"

My jaw drops. "Yes or no?"

He bobs his head, a guilty expression on his face. "I did."

I can't believe him. "And you were just... never going to

mention that to me? You didn't think I'd want to know that you're StatMan?"

He rubs his hand over the back of his neck. "I was kind of hoping it would never come up."

My eyes bug out. "Silas! Do you know what StatMan was to me?"

Silas shakes his head once, careful, like he already knows he's not going to like the answer. "No."

"It wasn't just sex," I say. "It wasn't even mostly sex."

He opens his mouth, then closes it, giving me a small nod to continue.

"Our conversation was an escape. It was the one place I didn't think ahead," I say. "I didn't run scenarios or calculate outcomes. I didn't ask myself what it would cost me to want something." My chest tightens, but my voice stays steady. "And you turned it into a lie."

"It's not a lie. I want you," he says immediately. "I always have."

"That's not the same thing," I reply.

He frowns and twists up his face. "How?"

"Because wanting me privately doesn't carry consequences," I say. "Wanting me in real life does."

He shifts closer, then stops himself, like he's afraid of making the wrong move. "I never wanted to put you at risk."

"I know, but that doesn't make it better. What if someone from the team found out?"

"You know I'd protect you," he says.

"You don't get to be my shield and the reason I need one."

His jaw tightens. "I was scared. You were living in my house. I didn't want to cross a line and lose you."

"So you crossed a different one instead."

Silence stretches. He looks down, then back up.

"You're a hockey player," I press. "You have money, leverage, and an entire system designed to protect you."

"I'm aware."

"I'm barely a temp trainer," I say. "No contract. No guarantees. If things went badly for us and we accidentally started a scandal, you'd get a warning or a fine. Maybe a lecture. I'd get fired."

His face tightens, guilt flashing across it. "I wouldn't let that happen."

"News flash!" I shake my head. "You don't control everything, Si."

He nods slowly, absorbing it. "I'm sorry. Really, Scout."

"I won't be someone's secret," I say. "I won't be the place you hide because it's easier than standing in the open."

"Scout, that's not what this is. I wanted you and... I thought I couldn't have you."

A blow out a long breath. "I won't be in a relationship where I carry all the risk and you carry none. I did that with Enzo already. Whatever is between us, Silas, I need it to be different."

"It is different!" He scowls. "I'm nothing like him, Scout."

"I need space tonight," I say. "And you have some serious thinking to do."

"Scout." He stands and catches my wrist, gently tugging.

"I'm serious, Silas." I pull away and head to my bedroom. I grab my overnight bag from the closet and start throwing things in. A change of clothes. A toothbrush, my charger.

Silas appears in my doorway, his face stricken. "Where are you going?"

"Juliet's. I'm just going for the night. I need to think, and I can't do it here."

"Scout, please. Can we just talk about this?"

"We just did." I zip the bag. "I'm not breaking up with

you, Silas. I'm just... I need space to process this. I'll see you tomorrow at work."

I brush past him. He doesn't try to stop me, just stands there looking lost.

The weight hits once I'm in my car. Not heartbreak exactly, but something close to grief. Grief for the version of myself who thought there was one place in her life where wanting didn't come with a cost.

I text the Coven as I drive.

ME

I know this is last minute, but is anyone able to meet up? I'm having a crisis.

JULIET

What? Come over to my house! I'm hanging out with Wren while Coach Ryan and Hunter watch the game in the other room.

WREN

Yes! Please, come join us.

IVY

I'm out of town, but please catch me up ASAP!

JESSA

I'm putting on my coat and grabbing my keys. I'll meet y'all at Juliet's!

I show up with a bottle of wine and no plan. Jessa opens the door, takes one look at my face, and steps aside without asking a single question. I end up on the couch, elbows on my knees, staring at the floor.

Juliet sits on the floor in front of me, back against the couch, close enough that her knee presses lightly into mine. Wren takes the armchair, curling her feet under her. No one rushes me. No one fills the silence with meaningless comfort.

I start with, "Silas and I had a fight. A big one."

"What did he do?" Juliet's assumption that he did something puts a weak smile on my face.

"He set up a fake profile on a dating site, targeted me, and got me talking. And, um. I said a lot of things to him that I probably wouldn't have said if I knew who he was."

"What kind of things?" Wren lowers her voice to a whisper. "Sexy things?"

I nod. "Sexy things. But also like... a lot of really personal confessions? Like he asked me about what I want out of life and I told him... everything. God, I'm so embarrassed."

I hide my face behind my hands.

Jessa swears under her breath. When I peek out between my fingers, Juliet is frowning and Wren's mouth falls open.

"Oh my god," Jessa says. "That's... wow."

Juliet lets out a breath that sounds like a laugh, but it dies fast when she looks at me. "Okay," she says instead. "Okay."

"I can't believe Silas did that." Wren shakes her head slowly. "I didn't have that on my bingo card."

Jessa kneels on the floor, looking concerned. "You're allowed to be mad," she says. "And sad. And confused. Possibly all at once."

No one tells me to forgive him. No one tells me to run.

"What do you want?" Wren asks quietly.

The question lands differently than I expect. Not like pressure, but like permission.

"I don't know yet," I admit. "I mean, I think I love him. But I don't like being lied to."

"Girl, I get it." Juliet nods. "It's fine to be mad at him for doing that. It's a violation of your trust."

"I just feel like an idiot. Silas was in the room next to

mine, texting me all that stuff. And I was clueless." I shake my head. "I ended things with StatMan weeks ago because I was falling for Silas. I had no idea they were the same person."

"Maybe he thought it was safer to talk to you that way first," Juliet offers.

"I still fell in love with him, though. I'm so easy. It makes me look pathetic."

"Hey! Don't talk about my friend Scout like that." Jessa hugs me. "You're not stupid for wanting him."

"Silas is hot," Wren says. "Scary, but hot. I'm pretty sure that wanting connection with means you're human."

I sigh. "Maybe. But what am I supposed to do now? I told him I needed space tonight."

Juliet smiles softly. "Then take the space. Stay here tonight. Sleep on it. You'll know what you want to do tomorrow."

"Just remember that we've got your back no matter what," Wren says.

"I think I have to forgive him eventually." My cheeks grow warm. "I love him. Even if right now, I'm so mad I could spit."

"Well, your bed is still made at the apartment," Jessa points out. "And you're welcome to crash at Juliet's guest room tonight."

"I feel so left out." Wren wrinkles her nose. "Just because my husband is one of the coaches doesn't mean that you can't stay with us."

I can't help but smile. "Thanks, ladies. I really needed some girl time."

Jessa picks up the wine I brought. "I'm going to pour us each a glass."

"Oh! None for me." Wren blushes and bites her lip. "Ryan and I decided to try to start our family."

"Wren!" I look at her, grinning. "That's amazing!"

"Thanks. It's very exciting. Plus, it's..." Wren turns as red as a tomato. "Fun? To try?"

"We need to toast." Juliet pops up from the couch. "I have some sparkling cider. Let me get some glasses."

I look around the room and feel grateful that these are my friends.

Chapter Thirty

Silas

The film room feels too small even though I'm the only one in it. My hands won't stop moving, rewinding the same play over and over like studying tape will somehow fix what happened with Scout only hours ago.

Twelve hours since she walked out with an overnight bag.

Twelve hours since I watched her drive away.

I switch to a different game, pretending to analyze the opposing team's power play formation. But Scout's face keeps replacing the players on screen. The way she held herself so still when she said she needed space.

Not breaking up. Just… she needed space. Space means she's still considering us, right? She's not done with me yet? God I hope not.

My fingers drum against the desk, then move to the remote, then back to the desk. The urge to break something hums under my skin, not from anger but from fear that's eating me alive from the inside out.

Scout didn't give me anything to fight. She just asked for space and left.

"You look like shit." Hunter's voice cuts through the silence. I didn't hear him come in, but suddenly he's there, leaning against the doorframe with his arms crossed.

"Fuck off," I mutter, but there's no heat behind it.

He walks in anyway, because Hunter's never met a boundary he respects when it comes to family. Jett follows him, then Beck, and finally Thorne. They don't hover or corner me, just spread out around the room like they're claiming territory.

"Early morning film session?" Jett asks, sprawling in a chair.

I don't answer. My jaw works like I'm grinding glass between my teeth.

Beck snorts. "Right. Because you're definitely watching that tape and not just sitting here spiraling."

"Leave it alone," I warn.

"What'd you do?" Thorne kicks his feet up on the desk. "Hunter said Scout stayed in his spare room last night."

Her name hits me like a check into the boards. My whole body goes rigid, and something must show on my face because Hunter straightens up.

"What happened?" he asks. "She wasn't exactly talkative."

The words stick in my throat. I can't tell them about StatMan or the app or the months of lying. But the truth forces its way out anyway, stripped down to the simplest version.

"I fucked up. I wasn't completely honest about something and Scout found out. She said… she needed space."

Hunter snorts. Jett actually laughs. Beck rolls his eyes so hard I'm surprised they don't fall out of his head.

"That's it?" Hunter asks. "You had a fight?"

My hands clench into fists. "It wasn't just a fight."

"So you had a big fight," Thorne says, like that changes nothing. "Welcome to relationships, buddy."

I'm too confused by their reactions to care about the condescension. They're not looking at me with pity or disappointment. Hunter actually seems amused.

"Like you would know about relationships," Hunter says, looking at Thorne. "In all the time that I've been on the team, you haven't hooked up with the same girl twice."

"Fuck off," Thorne replies, giving Hunter a lazy grin. "That doesn't mean I don't have common sense."

"You all think I'm being dramatic?" I ask.

"I think you're being an idiot," Hunter corrects. His voice is warm, comfortable, the way you talk to someone you love who's catastrophizing. "Juliet and I fight all the time. Sometimes she storms out and stays at her sister's. Then we talk it through and move forward."

Thorne's voice goes quieter than usual. "Fighting doesn't mean it's over."

"Scout left," I say. "She chose to walk away rather than deal with my shit."

"Good for her," Jett says. I whip my head around to glare at him. He holds up his hands. "I'm serious. She's got boundaries. That's healthy. It doesn't mean your relationship is over."

"Couples fight," Hunter says simply. "People get hurt and work through it. If every argument ended a relationship, none of us would still be standing."

"To be fair, most of us are bachelors for life," Beck grunts.

"Hockey's really hard on any relationship. We're on the road so much and when we aren't, we're either at practice or resting. There's not a lot of room for girlfriends."

"My point is that until Scout breaks up with you, I don't think you should be preparing yourself for the worst."

My chest feels too tight. Growing up, mistakes meant punishment or silence. In hockey, they cost games, contracts, trust. The only way I learned to survive was to lock everything down, take the hit alone, and never let anyone see me break.

Yet sitting here, these guys are telling me something completely different.

"I lied to her," I admit, the words scraping my throat raw. "I mean, a lie of omission. But still."

"Then you apologize and do better," Beck says. As if it's that simple.

"What if she doesn't forgive me?"

Hunter shrugs. "Cross that bridge if you come to it. You're sitting here assuming the worst when nothing's actually ended."

The realization hits me slowly, like sunrise through blackout curtains. Scout walked away, but she didn't say we were done. She said she needed space. Time to think. Those aren't the same thing as goodbye.

"But I don't know how to fix it," I say.

Thorne sucks his teeth. "You show up and be honest. And you let her decide if she wants to try again."

My breathing starts to even out. The panic that's been clawing at my chest since Scout left loosens its grip slightly. I'm still scared, still uncertain, but the urge to self-destruct fades.

"I keep thinking I shouldn't have wanted her in the first place," I admit.

Jett makes a disgusted noise. "That's the dumbest thing you've ever said, and you once tried to fight three guys in a 7-11 parking lot."

I shake my head. "That was different."

"No, it wasn't. You were scared then too." Hunter moves closer, his expression serious now. "Listen. Wanting Scout doesn't make you weak. But being scared of wanting her does."

Beck stands, stretching. "We can sit here all night talking about feelings, or you can accept that you fucked up, she needs time, and that doesn't mean your world is ending."

"Thanks, man."

They start to filter out, but Hunter hangs back. He waits until the others are gone before speaking again.

"She'll come home tomorrow," he says quietly. "And when she does, you need to be ready to have a real conversation. I don't mean just you eating shit. You need to actually talk about why you did what you did."

"I know."

"Good." He claps me on the shoulder. "Come hit the weight room when you're ready."

I sit in the empty film room for another hour. The game tape runs on silent now, players moving across the screen in patterns I'm not really seeing.

I think about Scout's face when she left. Not angry, not vindictive, just tired. Tired of carrying my fears along with her own. Tired of being the only one taking risks.

My phone sits heavy in my pocket. I pull it out and stare at our last text exchange from this morning. She sent me a reminder about my PT appointment. I sent back a thumbs up.

I don't text her. Not yet. She asked for space and I'm going to give it to her. But I don't delete our conversation or block her number or any of the other self-destructive things I would've done before.

Hunter's right about one thing. Nothing has actually ended yet.

The thought is terrifying.

It's also the first hope I've felt in two hours.

I close the laptop and stand, my body stiff from sitting in the same position too long.

My whole life I've treated every mistake like a death sentence. Every argument was like the end of the world. But the guys are right. Couples fight and survive. People hurt each other and heal.

For now, I head to the locker room to change into my workout gear and haul myself into the gym.

Chapter Thirty-One

Scout

Proud Mary is packed with the Sunday brunch crowd. Sable managed to snag us a corner table anyway because she knows the owner. She's wearing perfectly tailored black pants and a silk blouse that probably costs more than my rent. I'm in yesterday's leggings and one of her cashmere sweaters that she lent me.

A server drops off our drinks. Sable ordered a matcha latte with oat milk. I got the creamiest coffee on the menu and asked them to make it a double. This place is somewhere at the juncture between snooty and hipster. Fine by me as they make a mean bananas foster latte.

"So," Sable says, stirring her matcha with precision. "Silas Huxley is StatMan."

"Yep."

"And you didn't know for months."

"Nope."

She takes a delicate sip of her drink. "That's really fucked up, Scout."

"I know." I take a long drink of coffee. "I'm so angry at him. But I also miss him, which makes me feel pathetic."

"You're not pathetic." Sable examines the menu even though she always orders the same thing here. "You're in love. Those are different things."

"Love shouldn't make me this stupid."

"Love makes everyone stupid. That's kind of the whole deal." She signals the server and orders the avocado toast with poached eggs and microgreens. I get the breakfast burrito because I need actual sustenance. "Have you figured out what you want to do?"

"Not really." I wrap my hands around the warm coffee mug. "I keep going back and forth. One minute I want to forgive him. The next minute I want to throw all his protein powder in the trash and move to Canada."

Sable laughs. "Both are valid options."

"The thing is, I keep thinking about all those conversations. How open I was with StatMan. I was *vulnerable*. And the whole time it was Silas." I set my mug down. "Did he ever say anything about being StatMan?"

"I can't answer that. You know I can't. HIPAA and shit."

"I know. You're a good doctor." Our food arrives and I take a bite of the burrito. It's loaded with eggs and cheese and perfectly spiced. "I just want to know why he did it. He was just more open as StatMan. He told me a lot of things that I have trouble imagining he'd say to my face."

Sable pauses, her fork poised in the air. "And what does that tell you?"

I consider the question. "That the problem isn't that he was a different person. It's that he felt like he needed to hide behind a screen to be himself with me."

"That sounds right." Sable reaches across and squeezes my hand. "The question is whether you can live with that. Do you need him to be capable of vulnerability without the distance?"

"I do need that. I can't be in a relationship where he only opens up through a screen."

"Then you need to tell him that." Her voice is gentle but firm. "When you're ready, I mean. You tell him exactly what you need from him if you two are going to work."

"What if he can't give me that?"

"Then you'll know. And you'll make a decision based on reality, not fear." She pauses, thinking carefully. "I'm going to try to avoid landmines here. I'm just talking about Silas in general, as a person. But for what it's worth, I think he'll give you everything he's capable of giving. Maybe more than that. But he's going to need help."

"He mentioned calling you. He said he was going to therapy."

Sable nods, taking another precise bite of her toast. "He did. I have to refer him to someone else, obviously. Conflict of interest. But I gave him Dr. Max Liehrstahl's information. Max is excellent with athletes who struggle with emotional vulnerability. 90% of them do."

"You think he's serious about getting help?"

"I can't really say that." She stands and refills both our coffee cups. "But I can tell you things that I notice about you. Your patterns, your fears, the things you bring into relationships." She sets her fork down and looks at me directly. "You want to hear them?"

"You know I always want to hear your advice. Hit me."

"You have a tendency to accommodate. You make yourself smaller so other people are more comfortable. You learned it from Mom, watching her disappear into taking care of Dad." Sable's voice is matter-of-fact, clinical. "And with Enzo, you did the same thing. You became what he needed instead of asking for what you needed."

The words land like boulders thrown from the Empire State building. "I know."

"The question isn't just whether Silas can be vulnerable. The real question is whether you can hold your ground. Can you demand honesty and openness without folding the first time it gets uncomfortable?"

"I left, didn't I? That's not folding."

"Leaving was good. The hard part is returning." She meets my eyes. "Scout, you love him. That's obvious. But love isn't enough if you're going to sacrifice yourself to keep it."

I heave a sigh. "I know that too."

"Good." She smiles. "Then you're already ahead of where you were with Enzo. Who, by the way, is a worthless piece of garbage."

"So you've said. You haven't had a nice thing to say about him since I told you I was leaving him."

Her eyes flash with amusement. "I thought he was a sack of shit before you got married, but I didn't feel like it was my place to judge."

"Well, you have my permission to tell me if you think that I'm crazy, rushing into the arms of another hockey player."

She smiles and slowly shakes her head. "Even if I thought you were being a teensy bit impetuous, I would never stand between you two. You've wanted him since college. Now, you finally get him. I just hope he treats you better than he has."

I screw my face up. "Silas is wonderful, except... this whole thing."

Sable nods. "There's usually something."

We finish brunch talking about lighter things. Her upcoming work trip. Dad's adjustment to his new retirement community. The latest Coven drama involving Mollie and Thorne's increasingly obvious tension.

By the time Sable pays the check (she insists as she always does), the sun is beginning to set. She hugs me on the sidewalk outside Proud Mary, tight and fierce.

"You're tougher than you think," she whispers. "Don't let him make you forget that."

"I won't."

"And Scout? Make him work for it. He hurt you. He needs to understand that actions have consequences."

"I will. Thanks, Sable."

The drive back to the condo takes twenty minutes. My stomach churns the entire way. I'm not sure what I'm going to say, how I'm going to feel when I see him.

When I unlock the door and step inside, I hear water running. The shower. Silas must have just gotten home from practice.

I drop my bag by the door and wait.

Five minutes later, he emerges from the bathroom with a towel around his waist. His hair is wet and messy. Water droplets cling to his chest and shoulders. I swallow, fighting the urge to peel off his towel and see where those water droplets trail down to.

I'm here to talk, not fuck him senseless. It's important that I remember that. When he sees me, Silas stops dead.

"Scout."

I feel shy, tucking a springy curl behind my ear. "Hi."

"I didn't know if you were coming back."

"I live here." I shove my hands in my pockets. "We need to talk."

He gulps. "Yeah. Of course. Let me just get dressed."

"No!" The word comes out squeakier than I intended and

I clear my throat. "Actually, stay like that. It's distracting. I need you distracted so you'll be honest with me."

His eyebrows rise but he doesn't argue. He moves to the couch and sits. I sit on the opposite end, as far from him as possible.

"Okay," I say. "I'm going to ask you questions. You're going to answer them honestly. No deflecting, minimizing, or trying to protect me from the truth."

"Okay." His throat bobs.

"Why didn't you just tell me that you were… *you?*"

"Because I was scared." His jaw tightens. "It was easy to joke and flirt as strangers. You were opening up to StatMan in ways you wouldn't with me. You were letting him see your real self. And I got addicted to it."

"But you were lying."

"I know." His voice cracks. "I know that now. At the time, I told myself it wasn't hurting anyone. It was just talking."

"It wasn't just talking. I told you things I've never told anyone. You were the first person I've been vulnerable with since I left Enzo." My throat gets tight. "You took advantage of that."

"I did. And I'm sorry. I'm so fucking sorry, Scout. I knew it was wrong, but I just couldn't help myself."

"Sorry isn't enough." I pull my knees up to my chest. "I need to understand why you felt like you needed to hide behind a screen. Why couldn't you just be honest with me?"

He's quiet for a long moment. Then he says, "I've never been good at being vulnerable. Hockey beats it out of you. My childhood beat it out of me before that. Being open meant making myself a target. So I learned to shut it all down."

"But StatMan was vulnerable."

"StatMan had distance. Safety. If you rejected him, it wouldn't destroy me because it wasn't really me." He looks at me now, eyes dark with pain. "But you? The real you, face-to-face? The girl that I've been obsessed with for years? Being rejected would have broken something unfixable."

The honesty in his voice cracks something open in my chest. "StatMan was real. Those conversations were real."

"They were. That's what I'm trying to say." He leans forward, elbows on his knees. "StatMan wasn't a lie about who I am. He was just the only version of myself I felt safe showing you."

"But I need you to be able to show me that version face-to-face," I tell him. "Without the distance or pretending to be someone else."

"I'm shitty at it." His voice is raw. "And I'm scared. But I want to try. I called Dr. Sable. Er, I guess you just call her Sable. She gave me a referral to another therapist because of the conflict of interest, so I have an appointment next week. I'm going to do the work."

"Therapy is a start. But I need more than that." I take a deep breath. "I need you to talk to me. Tell me when you're scared or upset or struggling. I don't want you to just bottle it up until you explode or hide behind a screen."

"I swear I'll do my best."

I take his hand, linking our fingers. "And no more secrets. No more lies. Not even little ones to protect my feelings or avoid conflict."

"No more secrets," he agrees. "That's my normal motto."

"And we need to figure out how to protect my job. If people find out about us, I'm the one who gets fired. You get a slap on the wrist. That power imbalance terrifies me."

"We'll talk to Juliet tomorrow and figure out how to disclose this properly so you're protected." His voice gets fierce. "If we can't make it work without putting your job at risk, I'll leave the team. Not you."

My eyes burn. "You'd do that?"

"Scout, I'd do anything for you. I just didn't know how to show you without being terrified of losing you." He shifts closer, hesitant. "I'm still terrified. But I'm more scared of losing you than I am of being vulnerable."

I study his face. There's honesty there, with fear and hope warring in his eyes.

"All right, Si." I suck in a long breath. Saying the words feels like jumping off a cliff. "If you're willing to be honest with me without hiding, I'm definitely willing to put in the effort. You're worth it."

"I am." He reaches for my hand. "I'll spend every day proving it to you if you let me."

I let him pull me closer. His skin is still warm from the shower. He smells like soap and that cedar scent that's just him.

"Thank you," he whispers against my hair. "For not leaving. And for giving me a chance."

"I'm tougher than you think," I tell him. "Try to trust that I'm not going to run the first time things get hard."

He groans. "I hope there won't be a next time."

I pull back and look at him. "There absolutely will be. We're going to fight. We're going to have moments where we screw up and hurt each other. That's what relationships are."

"That sounds terrible."

"It's also normal. And it's okay." I cup his face in my hands. "The question is whether we can fight and come back to each other. Can we be honest even when it's scary? Trust each other to stay?"

"I want to trust that. I want to believe you won't leave."

"Then practice." I kiss him softly. "Start small. Tell me one thing right now that scares you."

"I'm scared you'll wake up one day and realize I'm not worth the effort."

I slip my hand around the back of his neck, staring into that bright blue-gray gaze."I'm scared you'll decide being vulnerable is too hard and shut me out again."

Si's lips twitch and he sighs heavily. "I'm scared I'll fuck this up so badly you'll hate me."

I whisper, "I'm scared I'll lose myself trying to fix you."

I lay my head against his chest and he cradles me, rocking in a soundless rhythm.

Eventually I stand and pull him up with me. "I'm going to make us dinner. Something easy. And you're going to help me without trying to take over the whole kitchen."

"I can do that."

We cook together, moving around each other carefully. Pasta and marinara, nothing fancy. He chops vegetables while I boil water. We don't talk about the heavy stuff anymore. We keep it light and easy. His practice. My conversation with Sable. What movie we should watch later.

It's ordinary and domestic and exactly what we need.

After dinner, we do dishes side by side. He washes, I dry. The domesticity is soothing and familiar. I never had this with Enzo.

"Can I sleep in your bed tonight?" I ask as I'm putting away the last plate.

His eyes widen slightly. "You want to?"

"Not for sex. Just… to be close. I've been cold sleeping alone the last two nights."

Si blurts out, "Yeah. Of course. Whatever you need."

I have to smile at that. At the core of his being, Si just wants to make me happy. I absolutely believe that. An echo of the past overwhelms me, reminds me that though we've grown up, we're just two eighteen years olds, making eyes at each other and blushing.

I need to hold onto this feeling.

We lie in his bed in the dark. He's on his back, I'm curled against his side. His heartbeat is steady under my ear.

"I meant what I said," he murmurs. "I'll do whatever it takes to earn your trust back."

"I know." I press a kiss to his chest. "That's why I think we're going to make it."

"You really think so?"

"I really think so." I am sure, more sure than I've been about anything in a long time. Silas loves me enough to try. And I'm trying to love myself enough to demand honesty.

We're both willing to do the hard work.

"I love you," he whispers into the darkness.

"I love you too. Even when I'm mad at you."

"Especially when you're mad at me?" Although it's dark, I can hear his smile.

I grin against his chest. "Don't push it."

He laughs softly and tightens his arms around me.

We fall asleep tangled together, our first night rebuilding a fragile trust that's sturdier than we thought.

Chapter Thirty-Two

Silas

My phone buzzes while I'm icing my shoulder on the couch. Scout's at work, the condo is quiet, and I'm supposed to be resting before tonight's game. Instead I've been staring at the ceiling for the past hour, thinking about therapy and Dr. Sable and how badly I fucked up that last session.

The text is from a number I don't recognize.

UNKNOWN

Hi Silas, this is Sable Nash. Do you have a few minutes to talk?

My stomach drops. Scout's sister. The therapist I bolted from like a complete psycho three weeks ago.

ME

Yeah.

Three dots appear, disappear, reappear. My phone rings.

"Hello?" I answer, probably sounding as uncomfortable as I feel.

"Hi Silas." Her voice is warm, professional, the same tone

she used in our sessions. "Thanks for picking up. I wanted to talk to you about something important."

"Look, I'm sorry about leaving like that. It was unprofessional and I shouldn't have..."

"That's actually what I wanted to discuss." She cuts me off gently. "I've been thinking about our last session, and I need to be honest with you. I can't be your therapist."

The words land differently than I expect. Relief mixed with something that might be disappointment. "Because of Scout."

"Because of Scout," she confirms. "It's a conflict of interest. You're dating my sister, and that makes it impossible for me to maintain the professional boundaries necessary for effective therapy. I should have referred you to someone else the moment you mentioned her name."

"So that's it? I'm just supposed to find someone else?"

"Actually, I already have someone in mind." Papers rustle in the background. "His name is Dr. Max Liehrstahl. He's a sports psychologist who specializes in working with professional athletes. I've referred several clients to him over the years and the feedback has been excellent."

I shift the ice pack on my shoulder. "You think he'll take me?"

"I already spoke with him. He has an opening tomorrow afternoon if you're interested." Her voice softens slightly. "Silas, I know switching therapists isn't ideal. You were starting to open up in our sessions, and that's hard work. But Dr. Max is really good at what he does. I think you'll click with him."

"What did you tell him about me?"

"Just the basics. That you're a professional hockey player dealing with career transition anxiety and some intimacy issues. Nothing specific about our sessions. That stays confidential."

The tightness in my chest eases slightly. "Does Scout know you're calling me?"

"No. This is between us. Patient confidentiality applies even after termination." She pauses. "For what it's worth, I think you're doing good work. Don't let this setback stop you from continuing therapy. You deserve support, Silas."

The kindness in her voice makes my throat tight. "Thanks. I'll call Dr. Max."

"Good. I'll text you his contact information." Another pause. "And Silas? Take care of my sister. She's been through enough."

"I will. I am."

"I know." I can hear the smile in her voice. "That's why I'm rooting for you both."

After we hang up, I stare at my phone for a long minute. Sable could have written me off as a lost cause. Could have told Scout I'm too fucked up to be worth the effort. Instead she's handing me off to another therapist and wishing me well.

I don't deserve the Nash sisters, but I'm going to try like hell to be worthy of them anyway.

The text comes through with Dr. Max's information. I dial before I can talk myself out of it.

"Dr. Liehrstahl's office, this is Max speaking."

The voice is deep, casual, not at all what I expected from a therapist. "Uh, hi. This is Silas Huxley. Dr. Nash referred me?"

"Silas! Yeah, Sable mentioned you might call. Got time to talk now or you want to schedule something?"

"I can talk now."

"Perfect. Give me two seconds." I hear a door close, footsteps, then the creak of a chair. "Okay, I'm settled. So Sable told me you're a defenseman for the Havoc, dealing with some transition stuff. Want to fill me in on what's going on?"

The casual approach throws me off balance. Dr. Sable was professional, careful, measured. This guy sounds like he's talking to a friend over beers.

"I'm worried about my career ending," I say bluntly. "My shoulder's fucked and I don't know who I am without hockey."

"That's heavy shit." No judgment in his voice, just acknowledgment. "How long you been playing?"

"Since I was four."

"So hockey's not just your job, it's your identity."

"Yeah. Exactly that."

"Makes sense you'd be freaking out." Papers shuffle. "Sable said you've got some relationship stuff going on too. Want to talk about that?"

I think about Scout, about how badly I want to marry her and how terrified I am that she'll realize I'm not worth it. "I'm with someone. Someone really good. And I keep waiting for her to figure out I'm a mess and leave."

"You tell her you're a mess?"

"Some of it. I'm trying to be more honest."

"That's a start." His chair creaks again. "Here's the thing, Silas. Most of us are a mess in one way or another. The question isn't whether you're fucked up. It's whether you're willing to do the work to be less fucked up. You game for that?"

Something about his bluntness makes me relax. "Yeah. I'm game."

"Good. Let's get you scheduled for a real session. You free tomorrow at three?"

"I can be."

"Done. I'm texting you the address now. Fair warning, my

office isn't fancy. It's above a gym in Fremont. You're gonna smell chalk and sweat the whole time."

"That sounds perfect, actually."

"Thought you might say that." I can hear the grin in his voice. "Bring a notebook tomorrow. We're gonna start mapping out who Silas Huxley is when he's not on the ice. It's homework, so don't skip it."

"I won't."

"See you tomorrow, man."

He hangs up before I can say anything else. I sit there with the phone in my hand, the ice pack now lukewarm against my shoulder, and realize I'm smiling.

Maybe this will actually work.

The next afternoon, I find Dr. Max's office exactly where he said it would be. Above a CrossFit gym in Fremont, up a narrow staircase that smells like rubber mats and protein powder. The door has his name printed on frosted glass in simple black letters.

I knock.

"Come in!"

The office is small and cluttered in a way that feels lived-in rather than messy. Bookshelves line one wall, crammed with psychology texts and sports biographies. A worn leather couch faces two chairs. No desk, no diplomas on display, just a space that feels more like a living room than a doctor's office.

Dr. Max stands to greet me. He's shorter than I expected, maybe five-ten, with graying hair pulled back in a small ponytail and the build of someone who used to be an athlete. Faded tattoos cover both forearms.

"Silas. Good to meet you in person." His handshake is firm. "Have a seat wherever. Couch, chair, floor if that's your thing. I don't care."

I choose one of the chairs. It's comfortable, broken in, the kind of chair that doesn't make you worry about sitting wrong.

"So." He settles into the other chair with a notebook that's seen better days. "Sable gave me the basics but I want to hear it from you. What brings you here?"

"My last therapist was my girlfriend's sister. That got complicated."

"Bet it did." He grins. "But that's not what I meant. What's the real reason you're sitting in my office instead of pretending you've got your shit together like most athletes do?"

The directness catches me off guard. Again. "My coach made me start therapy. Said I needed to figure out my priorities before my career decisions got made for me."

"Smart coach. You pissed about that?"

"At first. Not anymore."

"What changed?"

I think about Scout, about almost losing her because I couldn't be honest. About the guys talking me down from my spiral. About realizing that being strong doesn't mean doing everything alone.

"I figured out I can't keep pretending I'm fine when I'm not," I say. "It's cost me too much already."

Dr. Max nods, scribbling something. "Tell me about your shoulder."

The next hour passes faster than I expect. He asks questions that cut straight to the bone, doesn't let me hide behind vague answers or deflections. When I try to minimize my fear about retirement, he calls me on it. When I start spiraling about Scout leaving, he makes me actually articulate why I believe that instead of just accepting the anxiety as fact.

"Here's your homework," he says as the session winds down. "I want you to write down five things you're good at that have nothing to do with hockey. Can be anything. Cooking, making people laugh, parallel parking, I don't give a shit. Just five things."

"That's it?"

"That's it. Sounds easy, right?" His smile is knowing. "Most athletes can't do it. They've tied their entire identity to their sport for so long they can't see anything else. Prove me wrong."

"I will."

"Good." He stands, walks me to the door. "Same time next week?"

"Yeah. Same time."

"And Silas?" He claps me on the shoulder. "You're doing the right thing. Therapy's not weakness. It's maintenance. You wouldn't skip PT for your shoulder, right? This is PT for your brain."

The comparison makes sense in a way nothing else has. "Thanks, Dr. Max."

"Just Max is fine. See you next week."

I leave the office feeling lighter than I have in weeks. No breakthrough, no magical cure, just the beginning of actual work. Work I should have started years ago.

My phone buzzes as I'm walking to my truck.

SCOUT

How did it go?

She knows I had the appointment. I told her last night, nervous she'd be weird about me switching therapists. Instead she just kissed me and said she was proud of me for going back.

ME

Good. Really good actually. New therapist is solid.

SCOUT

I'm so glad, baby. Dinner tonight to celebrate?

ME

Yeah. I'll cook.

SCOUT

You're perfect. I love you.

ME

Love you too.

I get in the truck and pull out the notebook Max gave me. Five things I'm good at that aren't hockey. The blank page stares back, challenging me to see myself as something more than a defenseman.

I tap the pen against the paper, thinking.

1. I'm good at taking care of Scout. Making her feel safe and wanted and seen.

I pause, then keep writing.

2. I'm good at parallel parking. (Max said it counted.)
3. I'm good at making Scout laugh, even when she's trying to stay mad at me.
4. I'm good with numbers. Stats, analytics, patterns.

5. I'm good at showing up. Even when it's hard or
   when I want to run.

I stare at the list. It's not much. But it's a start.

Pulling out of the parking lot, I head home to Scout. To dinner and therapy homework and the life I'm building that exists beyond the ice.

Hockey won't last forever. But I'm starting to think beyond hockey, into next steps. And I'm not scared as shitless as I was six months ago.

That's progress, right?

Chapter Thirty-Three

Scout

I stare at the invitation on the kitchen counter, my stomach twisting into familiar knots. The Seattle Havoc Annual Sponsorship Gala. Black tie. Plus-ones encouraged.

Enzo Moretti Sports Management is listed right there among the platinum sponsors.

"You've been staring at that for ten minutes." Silas appears behind me, hands settling warm on my hips. "What's wrong?"

I lean back into his chest, drawing strength from his solid presence. "Enzo's going to be there tonight."

His entire body goes rigid. "Then we're not going."

"We have to go. It's your job." I turn in his arms, meeting those blue-gray eyes. "Besides, some days his voice still gets in my head. I hear him telling me I'm too much, that I'm hovering, that everything I do is wrong. I hate that he still has that power. I want… I want to show him he doesn't faze me."

Silas's jaw tightens, but he stays quiet. His eyes are flashing, though.

"I don't want to see him," I admit. "But I'll be with you. So we're going."

He cups my face, thumbs stroking my cheekbones. "If he says one word to you..."

"Then I'll handle it." My voice comes out stronger than I feel. "I need to face him, Si. I need to prove to myself that I'm not afraid anymore."

Hours later, I'm smoothing down the deep green silk dress that makes Silas's eyes go dark with want. The fabric hugs my slender frame, falling to just above my knees. My honey blonde hair is styled in loose waves that cascade over my shoulders. I feel pretty.

In the car, Silas keeps glancing at me like he's waiting for me to change my mind. He looks incredible in his black suit, his dirty blond hair pulled back in a low bun, jaw sharp and clean-shaven. Those blue-gray eyes keep finding mine, protective and concerned. His hand finds mine, fingers lacing together.

"We can leave anytime," he says. "You say the word and we're gone."

"I know." That knowledge settles something in my chest. "That's why I can do this."

The gala is everything I expected. Crystal chandeliers throwing rainbow light across marble floors, champagne flutes catching gold reflections, people in expensive clothes pretending net worth determines human value. Silas keeps me close, his hand never leaving the small of my back as we navigate through clusters of sponsors and players.

I see Enzo before he sees us.

He's holding court near the bar, surrounded by younger players who don't know any better yet. Same sharp suit, same practiced charm, same smile that never quite reaches his eyes. My stomach clenches with old muscle memory, the instinct to make myself smaller, to smooth things over before conflict can start.

But I'm not that person anymore.

"There," I murmur to Silas, nodding toward the bar.

Silas follows my gaze. His hand tightens on my waist, protective but not controlling. "Say the word."

"Not yet."

We make it almost an hour without talking to him. I'm talking with Juliet about the overwhelming success of Mobility Mondays when I see him approaching. That old familiar dread, the way my body learned to sense his moods before he even opened his mouth.

"Silas." Enzo's voice is smooth oil, all practiced charm. "And Scout. How domestic."

I turn slowly, deliberately and meet his eyes without flinching, even though my heart is hammering. "Enzo."

Silas goes rigid beside me, but he stays silent. He's letting me take the lead.

"Walk away," I say. My voice shakes slightly, but it's steady enough.

"I can't do that. Business, you understand." Enzo slides a leather folder onto the nearest cocktail table, tapping it with one manicured finger. "I've got something Silas is going to want to see."

"He's not interested."

"He will be." Enzo's smile sharpens into something preda-tory. "New contracts. International sponsors. Endorsement deals that would set him up for life. Triple what he's making now, maybe more." His eyes flick to me, dismissive. "All he has to do is sign with me again. Drop the distractions. Let me handle his career the way it should be handled."

The word distractions hits like a slap. All those years of Enzo telling me I was too much, too emotional, too clingy. I was holding him back, making everything harder, ruining his focus.

Something snaps inside me.

"You need to leave," I say, but the shakiness is gone now. "You're a terrible human being and probably a shitty agent too. Players should avoid you like the IR list."

"This doesn't concern you, honey." Enzo's tone is patronizing, like he's explaining something obvious to a child. "This is business. Men's business. Why don't you go get us some drinks while Silas and I have a real conversation?"

The dismissal in his voice unlocks something I've been holding back for years. Silas growls and moves toward him, but I cling to his hand, holding him back.

"You were a horrible husband," I tell Enzo. The words come out clear and sharp, cutting through the ambient noise of the gala. People nearby start to turn their heads and listen. "You cheated on me multiple times. You made me feel crazy for accusing you. Then when I finally found proof, you acted like I was being dramatic!"

Enzo's face pales. "Scout, this isn't the place..."

"You're nothing but a snake oil salesman, Enzo. And you made me feel small." My voice gets louder, stronger. "I worked so hard to build you up and to support your career. I tried to be everything you said you needed. I organized your schedule, managed your clients, handled every detail of your life so you could focus on work. Then you turned around and called me clingy."

Enzo's eyes flash. "You're being emotional, Scout."

"The truth is that you never deserved me." The truth of it rings through my chest, settling into my bones. "If I hadn't been so young when we met, I probably would have seen right through your love bombing bullshit. But I was 20 and you were 32, and you knew exactly how to make me think I was lucky you chose me."

Enzo's jaw tightens, fury flashing across his features. "You have no idea what you're talking about."

"I know exactly what I'm talking about." My hands are shaking but I don't care. "You wanted someone who would worship you, who would make your life easier. Someone who would never challenge you or ask for too much. Then the second I needed anything from you, I stopped being useful. And off you went, looking for someone new to suck down to the marrow."

"Scout." Enzo licks his lips, noticing that everyone is listening. "That's not how it happened. Marriage isn't for everyone."

"You're a liar and a manipulator, Enzo. I wasted three years of my life trying to be small enough for you to love. But the problem was never me. It was always you."

Silas hasn't said a word, but I can feel the tension radiating off him in waves. His hand stays on my waist, solid and grounding, letting me have this moment.

Enzo's face twists into something ugly. "You ungrateful little..."

"Watch your mouth." Silas's voice cuts through the air like a blade, deadly quiet.

"Come on." Enzo's tone shifts, trying for camaraderie. "We both know she's baggage. Nice girl, sure, but she's going to drag you down eventually. Just like Juliet almost ruined Hunter's career. Don't make the same mistake your brother did. You're smarter than that."

The red haze that crosses Silas's face would be terrifying if it wasn't directed at Enzo.

"What did you just call her?" Silas's voice is low and dangerous.

"I'm just being realistic. She's a distraction you can't afford. Drop her, sign with me, and I'll have you set for life."

I don't even notice him moving at first. Silas's fist connects with Enzo's jaw before I can blink.

The sound is sickening. Bone on bone, the sharp crack echoing through the suddenly silent ballroom. Enzo staggers backward, hand flying to his face, blood already blooming on his lip.

Gasps ripple through the crowd. Phones come up, flashes popping. But I can't look away from Silas, from the fury radiating off him like heat.

Enzo roars, lunges forward with all the grace of someone who's never actually been in a real fight. His fist catches Silas in the ribs, sloppy and wild. Silas barely flinches, just grabs Enzo by the lapels and slams him back against the cocktail table. Champagne glasses topple, liquid spraying across white linen and expensive shoes.

"She isn't baggage." Silas's voice is a growl, low and feral. "She's the best thing that's ever happened to me. And you..." He draws his fist back again.

"Enough!" Hunter's voice cuts through the chaos like a blade. His hand clamps on Silas's shoulder, iron grip, hauling him back. Beck appears on Enzo's other side, captain authority radiating off him in waves.

"Off him," Hunter orders. "Now."

Silas releases Enzo, chest heaving. Every muscle in his body is coiled tight, ready to spring again.

Enzo straightens, trying to salvage his dignity while blood drips from his split lip. "You can't just assault me in front of witnesses, you idiot."

"You're fired." Hunter's voice is cold as January ice. "As of right now, you don't represent anyone on this team."

"You can't fire me. I've got signed contracts."

"Watch me." Hunter pulls out his phone, already typing. "Connor Li just dropped you. Shane Villarreal too. Check your phone in 15 minutes."

Silas steps closer, voice pitched low enough that only Enzo and I can hear. "The only useful thing you ever did was fuck up your marriage. Because you set Scout free. Now she's mine. And I'm not dumb enough to let her go. I'm not weak enough to throw her away the way you did."

The words land like body checks. I watch Enzo flinch, watch fury and humiliation twist his features into something ugly.

"Get out," Beck says flatly. "Trust me when I say that it would be a pleasure to have you removed."

Enzo's eyes dart to me one last time. I see the exact moment he realizes I'm not afraid of him anymore. I give him a small smile.

"You'll regret this, Huxley," he says, but his voice shakes.

"The only thing I regret is not punching you sooner," Silas replies. "I should have kicked your ass when I fired you."

"You'll see. You'll all see." Enzo chuckles, wiping blood from his nose, and disappears into the night. The room stays silent for one long, suspended beat.

Then Juliet starts a slow clap from across the ballroom and gradually others join in. My hand finds Silas's, his knuckles already bruising and swelling.

"Oh, baby. You didn't have to do that."

"Yeah, I did." He turns to face me fully, not caring about the audience or the cameras still recording. "Nobody talks to you like that. Not him. Not anyone."

Tears prick at my eyes, but they're not sad tears. "You punched him for me."

"I'd happily kill him if you asked me to." He cups my

face, thumbs stroking my cheekbones. "You make the world go 'round."

I pull him down for a kiss that earns whistles and cheers from the remaining crowd. When we break apart, I'm crying and laughing at the same time.

Because this is what Enzo never understood. This is the difference between a man who uses you and a man who chooses you. Between someone who makes you carry all the weight and someone who stands beside you, ready to fight.

"Now that?" Hunter approaches, grinning like a fool. "That was the most reckless thing I've ever seen you do. I'm so fucking proud."

"Really impressive work, little Huxley." We all stare at Juliet and she flushes. "What? I'm workshopping names."

Connor Li materializes beside us, phone in hand. "I just wanted you to know, I dropped Enzo the second Hunter gave the signal. The guy was always a snake. He tried to make me badmouth the other rookies to sponsors last month."

Shane nods agreement. "He tried to pit us against each other last year during contract negotiations. Good riddance."

One by one, other players drift over. Most are confirming they've terminated their contracts with Enzo and sharing stories of his manipulation and schemes. By the time they're done, it's clear Enzo won't work in Seattle again. His reputation is destroyed. His client list is decimated.

Thorne appears, massive and imposing in a suit that barely contains his bulky shoulders. "I heard you threw hands. Sorry I missed it."

"It was beautiful," Hunter says. "Silas went full caveman. Very romantic."

"It was assault," Juliet corrects, but there's approval in her voice. "Justified assault, but assault nonetheless."

I laugh, the sound bright and genuine. Somehow, everything feels lighter.

Later, back at the condo, I watch Silas ice his knuckles at the kitchen sink. His hand is swollen, definitely bruised, maybe worse. I fuss over him, overwhelmed at what he did for me.

"You're going to get fined," I say. "Or suspended. Cross is going to kill you."

"I don't care."

"Silas."

"I don't care." He moves to sit beside me on the couch. "You're more important than any fine, any suspension, any career consequence. You hear me? Plus, the guy is oily as fuck. He deserved it. I did the world a service tonight."

I nod, my throat too tight to speak.

Then he moves to kiss me deeply, his hands fisting in my hair, claiming my mouth the way he claimed me in front of that whole ballroom.

When we finally come up for air, I'm flushed and breathless. "Bed?"

"Bed."

He carries me down the hall, into the bedroom, where he lays me down with a reverence that makes my breath catch. We fuck, then after we slow it down and make love. I come so many times that I'm pretty sure there's not a drop of dopamine left in my brain.

Later, wrapped around each other in the dark, I trace idle patterns on his chest.

"Thank you," I murmur.

"For the sex?" He smiles slyly. "Or for punching your ex-husband?"

I kiss him gently. "For defending me."

"I'm choosing you," he says firmly. "Every time. Forever."

I kiss him over his heart. "Forever sounds perfect."

We fall asleep tangled together, and my last thought before sleep takes me is that I'm not afraid anymore. Not of Enzo, not of being too much, not of wanting things.

Because I stood up to my abuser and lived through it. Because Silas sees all of me and chooses me anyway. Because I finally understand that the problem was never me.

It was always him.

And now he's gone. In his place is a quiet, serious man who treats me like the Queen of Sheba. He loves me. I love him. And that's all she wrote.

Chapter Thirty-Four

Silas

Scout's been quiet since we got home from the arena. She's curled up on the couch with her laptop, working on something that has her brow furrowed in concentration. I've been watching her for the past twenty minutes, trying to figure out what's wrong.

"Okay," I finally say. "What's going on?"

She looks up, startled. "What?"

"You've been weird all day. Talk to me."

Her fingers still on the keyboard. She chews her bottom lip, that tell she has when she's trying to figure out how to say something difficult.

"I've been thinking about the mobility studio," she says finally.

"Yeah? Juliet said she's ready to move forward with the proposal. You excited?"

"I am. But..." She closes the laptop and sets it aside. "Juliet mentioned you offered to help fund it."

"I did. Is that a problem?"

"Kind of." She pulls her knees up to her chest, looking small and uncertain. "Silas, I don't want you paying for everything. The studio, this condo, groceries, dinners out. I know you say it's fine, but it makes me uncomfortable."

"Why?" I move to sit beside her. "I can afford it, Scout. It's not a big deal."

"It is to me." Her voice gets firmer. "Enzo took care of everything too. He paid for the apartment, the car, everything I needed. And it felt nice at first. But then it became this thing where I owed him. Then I couldn't leave because I didn't have my own money or my own place or my own anything."

Understanding hits me like a body check. "You think I'm doing the same thing."

"I don't think you're doing it on purpose. But the pattern's the same, Silas. You're taking care of me and I'm letting you and eventually I'll wake up and realize I'm trapped again."

"You're not trapped." I reach for her hand. "Scout, look at me."

She does, those green eyes full of worry and something that looks like fear.

"Enzo made you dependent on him," I say. "That's not what this is. You have your own job, your own income. You could leave tomorrow if you wanted to."

"Could I? I'm living in your condo rent-free. You pay for everything."

"Because I want to, not because I'm trying to control you." I squeeze her hand. "Do you know how much Enzo made me in endorsements this year?"

She blinks at the subject change. "What?"

"One point two million dollars. That's just endorsements. My actual salary is eleven million a year. Most of which I save because I don't know what else to do with it." I pull out my phone, open my banking app, and show her the balance. "This is my checking account. I could buy you ten mobility studios and not notice the dent."

Her eyes go wide. "Silas, that's..."

"A stupid amount of money, I know. But here's the thing, Pretty Girl. I'm going to keep making money whether you let me spend it on you or not. I'd rather spend it on things that matter. Things like your studio. And our life together. I love making sure you don't have to worry about rent or groceries or any of that bullshit."

"But I don't want to be taken care of."

"That's not what I'm doing." I turn to face her fully. "Taking care of you would be paying your bills without telling you, and making decisions for you, and expecting something in return. Is that what I'm doing?"

"No," she admits quietly.

"I'm investing in us. In our future. I'm not keeping score and I'm not expecting you to owe me anything." I cup her face in my hands. "Scout, I'm going to keep pushing our relationship forward. I'm going to keep taking care of you. Not because you need it, but because I want to. Making you happy makes me happy."

"What if I'm not ready for that?"

"Then you tell me to slow down and I will. But don't ask me to pretend I'm okay with you struggling when I could help."

She's quiet for a long moment, searching my face. "You really have eleven million dollars?"

"No. I have twelve-ish times the number of years I've played professionally, minus taxes, plus interest on some smart investments. However that math works out, give or take. Why, you gonna rob me?"

That gets a laugh out of her. "Maybe. I could use a new yoga mat."

"Baby, I'll buy you a hundred yoga mats." I pull her into my lap. "I'll buy you the whole damn store if it makes you smile."

"That's excessive."

"So? I feel *excessive* about you." I kiss her forehead. "Let me help with the studio. Not because you can't do it yourself, but because we're partners. Partners build things together."

She leans into me, her breath warm against my neck. "Partners."

"Yeah. Partners." I tilt her chin up. "I'm only using that term because I know that talking about the future and changing our labels freaks you out."

"Oh god." She pulls back slightly. "You have that look."

She's so adorable and sexy. I bite my lip to hold back a smile. "What look?"

"The look that says you're about to say something that's going to make me want to head for the hills."

She knows me too well. "Well, I do want to marry you."

Her eyes go wide. "Silas..."

"I'm not proposing right now. But I'm telling you where my head's at. I want to marry you, Scout. Sooner rather than later."

"We just got back together a few weeks ago."

"I know. That's why I'm not proposing today. But I'm not going to pretend I don't know what I want." I brush a curl behind her ear. "I'm all in on this. I can see the future, Scout. I'm going to keep pushing forward toward that. If you need me to slow down, tell me. But don't expect me to stop wanting to get there with you."

She's quiet for so long I start to worry I've pushed too hard. Then she says, "Marriage."

"Yeah."

"Like, wedding and rings and forever."

"That's generally how it works."

"Silas, we're still figuring things out. We're still learning how to be honest with each other. We're still..." She stops, frustrated. "I need more time."

The words sting but I swallow it down. "Okay."

"Okay?"

"Yes, sweetheart. You need time, I'll give you time." I pull her closer. "But that doesn't mean I'm changing my mind. When you're ready, I'll be here. Waiting."

"You're really okay with that?"

"No. I want to marry you tomorrow. But I'm okay with waiting because you're worth it." I kiss her softly. "Take all the time you need, Pretty Girl. I'm not going anywhere."

She kisses me back, slow and deep and full of something that feels like promise. When we break apart, she's smiling.

"You're ridiculous."

"You love it."

"I really do." She loops her arms around my neck. "Thank you. For understanding. For not pushing."

"I'm pushing a little bit."

"You're pushing a lot, actually. But I appreciate that you're trying." She grins. "Eleven million dollars. That's insane."

"Want me to buy you something expensive?"

"No. But you can take me to bed and remind me why I'm putting up with your grumpy ass."

Heat flares through me. "Yeah?"

"Yeah." She slides off my lap and holds out her hand. "Come on, big guy. Let's see if we can check another item off my Naughty Girl Scout List."

I'm on my feet before she finishes the sentence. "Still have items on that list?"

"Several. But this one's new." She walks backwards toward the bedroom, pulling me along. "You remember when we talked about me being in control?"

My mouth goes dry. "Yeah."

"Tonight's the night." She pushes me onto the bed and climbs into my lap, her curls falling around us like a curtain. "You're going to lie there and let me have my way with you. Think you can handle that?"

I groan, already hard just from the thought. "Pretty sure I can manage."

"Good." She leans down, her lips brushing my ear. "Because I have plans for you, Silas Huxley. And you're going to love every second of it."

She kisses me hard, all teeth and tongue and pure demand. My hands go to her hips automatically but she catches them, pinning them above my head.

"No touching unless I say so."

"Scout..."

"That's the rule. Break it and I stop." She rocks against me, making me see stars. "Can you follow the rules, big guy?"

I nod, not trusting my voice.

"Good boy." She grins and starts unbuttoning my shirt. "Now let's see how long you can behave."

Turns out, not very long. But Scout doesn't seem to mind.

Later, we're tangled together in bed, both of us sweaty and satisfied and completely wrecked. Scout traces lazy patterns on my chest while I try to remember how to form words.

"So," she says eventually. "That was..."

"Fucking perfect."

She laughs. "Yeah. It really was." She props herself up on one elbow. "How many items are left on your list?"

"My list?"

"The things you want to try with me. I know you have one."

She's not wrong. "It's a mile long, Pretty Girl."

"Tell me."

"I want to take you on my kitchen counter."

Her breath hitches. "Okay."

"I want you in my shower. Up against the tile."

"Keep going."

"I want to wake you up with my mouth between your legs." I roll her onto her back, settling between her thighs. "I want to hear you scream my name so loud the neighbors complain."

She's breathing hard now, eyes dark with want. "When?"

"Right now." I kiss down her body. "Unless you need a break."

"I don't need a break." Her fingers tangle in my hair. "I need you."

"That's another one off your list," I murmur against her throat.

She laughs, breathless. "Best list ever."

The Naughty Girl Scout List can wait. Right now, I'm working on my own list. And Scout's name is at the top of every single item.

Chapter Thirty-Five

Scout

My phone buzzes at six AM with a text about Dad's move. And for once, the familiar weight doesn't settle on my shoulders. Silas sleeps beside me, one arm thrown over my waist, his breathing deep and even. I read the message in the dim morning light.

Dad: Movers delayed until afternoon. I need help packing the kitchen and garage up.

Six months ago, I would've immediately started planning how to handle everything myself. Today feels different. I send back a new kind of response.

ME

I'll be there at 8. I'm bringing reinforcements.

DAD

Reinforcements?

ME

You'll see.

Silas stirs when I slip out of bed, his hand catching mine before I can get far. "Where're you going?"

"Dad's move got complicated. I need to head over early."

He sits up immediately, shoulders rolling as he shakes off sleep. "I'll come."

"You don't have to..."

"Scout." His voice is gentle but firm. "I'm coming."

I lean down and kiss him, morning breath and all. "Thank you."

By the time we arrive at my childhood home, cars already line the street. Juliet's SUV sits in the driveway next to Sable's hybrid. Mollie's distinctive yellow bug is parked crooked against the curb, and Hunter's truck pulls up behind us as we're getting out.

"Did you call everyone?" I ask Silas.

"I mentioned it to Hunter. Juliet probably handled the rest."

The front door stands open. Voices and laughter drift out from inside. We walk into organized chaos that somehow feels exactly right. Sable has commandeered the kitchen, wrapping dishes in newspaper while giving orders like a general. Juliet and Mollie work on boxing books in the living room, and Jett and Hunter are already hauling furniture toward the door.

"About time you showed up," Jessa calls from the hallway. "We've been here for twenty minutes."

My throat tightens with emotion I wasn't expecting. "You all came."

Ivy appears with a roll of packing tape, raising an eyebrow at my surprise. "You think we'd let you do this alone?"

Dad emerges from his bedroom looking bewildered but pleased. He's wearing his lucky moving day t-shirt, the one

Mom bought him twenty years ago that's more holes than fabric now.

"Scout, you didn't tell me you were bringing an army. I would have paid to have movers come. These professional athletes probably have way better stuff to do than be here."

"I said that to Silas and he acted like I was being crazy!" I hug him carefully, mindful of his bad back. "Everyone, this is my dad, Tom. Dad, this is... everyone."

The introductions happen in a blur. Dad shakes hands and makes his dry jokes while my two worlds merge without friction. Beck shows up with coffee and donuts, followed by Thorne with more boxes and terrible music that Mollie immediately vetoes.

"No oldies while we pack," she declares. "It's scientifically proven to make people slower."

"The fact that you think The Postal Service qualifies as an oldie means you're disqualified from having an opinion," Thorne argues.

Mollie sticks her tongue out at Thorne, who cranks the music up another notch.

They bicker good naturedly while working. The sound fills the house with warmth it hasn't had in years. This place has been quiet for so long, just Dad and his memories rattling around too many empty rooms.

Silas and I work in the garage, sorting through tools and holiday decorations that haven't been touched in years. Every box holds some piece of family history. Mom's old camping gear sits in one corner. My first hockey skates, tiny and rusted, are wrapped in a beach towel. Report cards and art projects fill a box labeled *Treasures* in Mom's handwriting.

"You okay?" Silas asks, finding me frozen over a photo album.

"Yeah. It's just... a lot."

He doesn't try to fix my mood or rush me through it. His hand settles on my lower back, steady and present, while I flip through pages of birthday parties and Christmas mornings and family vacations to places I barely remember.

"Your mom?" he asks, looking at a photo of her laughing at something off camera. "She was beautiful."

"Yeah. She would've liked you, I think."

"You think?"

I lean into his side. "She had a thing for grumpy men who were secretly soft. Why do you think she married Dad?"

From inside the house, someone drops something that shatters. Multiple voices shout at once, followed by laughter.

"I should check on that," I say.

"They're fine. Hunter probably just met his match trying to carry too much at once."

Sure enough, when we head inside, Hunter's standing over a broken lamp looking sheepish while Juliet lectures him about physics and grip strength.

"It was ugly anyway," Dad declares. "I never liked the thing."

Sable looks at me and I raise my brows. She just gives her head a tiny shake. Guess we'll deal with that one later.

The work continues in shifts. People break for water and snacks, rotating through tasks with an efficiency that comes from genuine care rather than obligation. Sable and Jessa develop an elaborate labeling system that involves color coding and subcategories. The hockey players compete to see who can carry the most boxes at once, which ends when Beck points out they're professional athletes acting like teenage boys.

"You're just mad cause you're old," Jett says cheerfully, balancing four boxes. He ducks when Beck whips a towel at his head.

Around noon, Sable orders pizza for everyone. We eat sitting on the floor of the empty living room, paper plates balanced on our laps, too many bodies crowded into the space. It's chaotic and perfect and makes my chest ache with belonging.

"This is nice," Dad says quietly beside me. "Seeing you with all these people who care about you."

"They're good people."

"That Silas seems solid."

I glance across the room where Silas is helping Sable move a bookshelf, taking directions without complaint. "He is."

"Definitely different from Enzo."

The comparison doesn't sting like it used to. "Very different."

Dad pats my knee with his weathered hand. "Good. You deserve someone who sees you, sweetheart."

After lunch, the professional movers finally arrive. We shift into high gear, everyone forming an efficient chain to load the truck. Years of belongings flow from house to truck in a stream of boxes and furniture.

By four o'clock, the house stands empty. Sable looks around, taking a deep breath. Watching my sister grieve this house is unbelievably hard. I stand in the bare living room, staring at the scuffed patch of wall where the couch used to be.

"Remember when Mom swore she could fit a Christmas tree in that corner?" Sable says from behind me. I hear the smile in her voice.

I huff. "She absolutely couldn't."

"She blamed the ceiling," Sable adds. "I believe the words *architecturally hostile* were thrown around."

"That tree leaned like it was tired," I say. "Every year."

The silence stretches, familiar but not sharp anymore.

From the doorway, Silas clears his throat gently. "You need a minute?"

I consider it, then shake my head. "Maybe just… a short one. Is that okay?"

"Take all the time you need," he says, and doesn't move.

Sable bumps her shoulder into mine. "We're almost done. I color-coded Dad's things. It should be a snap when we unload."

I smile despite myself. "Of course you did."

The memories don't grab me the way they used to. They sit there, warm and intact, but they don't pull me under. I slip my hand into Silas's and lean against him. "I think I'm ready."

At Dad's new apartment, controlled mayhem reigns. The space is smaller but nicer, with good light and no stairs for his knees to protest. It's part of a retirement community. Independently of me, Silas searched for the best living citation that would meet Dad's needs. This is what we came up with. On moving-in day, there are people coming and going in golf carts, a note of Dad's door about tonight's 70s dance party in the rec center, and no less than three cute older ladies have stopped by with baked goods. My dad is going to be a ladies man before he knows it.

Inside his apartment, everyone works to transform boxes and furniture into something resembling home.

Juliet and Ivy arrange the kitchen with ruthless efficiency. Sable sets up Dad's bedroom exactly how he likes it, down to the angle of his reading lamp, while the hockey players rebuild furniture and hang pictures. Only a few dishes break in the process, which feels like a victory.

"I need a beer," Thorne announces around six. "Who's with me?"

"You're not abandoning us now," Mollie says. "We're almost done."

"Beer would help us work faster."

She gives him the stink eye. "That's absolutely not true."

They're still arguing when Hunter returns with a couple cases of beer and a ton of empanadas. We eat standing up or sitting on boxes, too tired to care about proper dining arrangements. Dad holds court from his new recliner, telling embarrassing stories about my childhood that have everyone laughing at my expense.

"She used to practice her stretches everywhere," he says. "Grocery store, bank, middle of restaurants. Just drop into a split like it was normal."

"Dad, please stop."

"One time she got stuck in a backbend at Target. The fire department had to come."

"That's not even true!"

"Close enough to the truth," he says with a grin. It reminds me why Mom fell for him all those years ago.

As the sun sets, people start filtering out. Hugs and promises to check in soon get exchanged at the door. Jessa and Ivy leave together, debating the best route home. Mollie drags Thorne out, still somehow bickering about music choices. Beck heads to the gym because apparently moving furniture doesn't count as a workout.

I'm pretty sure he's insane.

Finally it's just family. Sable braids my hair while we sit on Dad's new couch, her fingers gentle and familiar. Silas, Jett, and Hunter break down empty boxes in the kitchen, their voices a low rumble of conversation. Dad dozes in his chair, worn out from the day but smiling even in sleep.

"You did good, Scout," Sable says quietly. "Letting people help. That's growth."

"It doesn't feel like sacrifice anymore. Taking care of Si, I mean. It feels good."

She hugs me from behind. "That's exactly what it should feel like."

Hunter and Jett leave first, clapping Silas on the shoulder with some brotherly comments I don't catch. Sable follows soon after, promising to bring dinner by for Dad tomorrow.

"We should go too," I tell Silas. "Let him rest."

Dad wakes when I kiss his forehead goodbye. "Thank you, sweetheart. For everything."

"I love you, Dad."

"Love you too." He looks at Silas. "Take care of my daughter, Silas."

"Always."

In the car heading home, I let the day wash over me. My body aches from lifting and carrying, but my heart feels fuller than it has in years.

"Your brothers are good people," Silas says, taking my hand over the center console.

"Our people," I correct. "They're ours now."

He squeezes my fingers. "I like the sound of that."

Back at the condo, we collapse on the couch. I curl into Silas's side, breathing in the scent of pine mixed with moving day sweat.

"Thank you," I say.

"Of course, baby."

The word *baby* settles over me like a warm blanket. I'll never get enough of Silas calling me pet names.

My phone buzzes with photos from throughout the day. Mollie caught a shot of Dad laughing at something Hunter said. Ivy snapped one of Silas and me working in tandem, not looking at each other but perfectly synchronized. Sable orchestrated a group shot with everyone crowded into frame, sweaty and tired and genuinely happy.

This is what belonging looks like. Not the desperate kind where you earn your place through service, but the real kind where people choose to show up because you matter to them.

"I love our life," I tell Silas, meaning it completely.

"Me too," he says, pressing a kiss to my temple.

Chapter Thirty-Six

Silas

The sound of my fingers drumming on the conference room table is too loud. Scout reaches over and stops my hand, shooting me a look. *Behave*, she tells me with her eyes.

I swallow and nod at her. This is the least comfortable I've ever been. I'm offering myself up to HR as a sacrifice. My career here is on the line. But it's worth it to protect Scout, if that's what needs to be done. I squeeze her hand and she smiles at me.

Those moss-green eyes and dark honey brown waves could get me to do anything. If she asked, which I doubt she would.

There's a reason I begged her to let me do all the talking in this meeting.

We sit across from the team's general manager Jared Duke, the head of HR, and the team's legal counsel. I try not to fidget with the water bottle they've placed in front of me. My suit feels too tight even though I had it tailored last month. I tug at the collar, feeling constricted in dress clothes. I'm used to hoodies and joggers, not this corporate armor. My dirty blond hair is pulled back in a low bun, trying to look professional, but I can feel strands falling loose. This isn't a disciplinary meeting, but it feels like one anyway.

"We appreciate you coming to us directly," Jared says. He's got that politician smile that could mean anything. "Why don't you tell us what this is about?"

I straighten my shoulders. "Scout Nash and I are in a relationship. It's consensual, it's serious, and I want everything documented properly so there's no question about propriety or her position with the team."

The HR director, a woman named Patricia who always wears pearls, makes a note on her tablet. "How long has this been going on?"

Scout's eyes find mine. I squeeze her hand again.

"Officially? About two weeks. Unofficially? We've had feelings for each other longer than that."

"And Ms. Nash, you work as a gopher, correct?" the legal counsel asks. His name is Marcus and he looks like he bills eight hundred dollars an hour just to frown at people.

It's hard not to scowl at him. "Scout runs the Mobility Monday program now. She also assists with player wellness and recovery protocols."

"We're just gathering all the information." Patricia pulls something up on her screen. "It says here, Ms. Nash, you were assigned as Mr. Huxley's temporary caregiver after his surgery?"

"That ended before we got together romantically," I say quickly. It's mostly true. We were already involved through the app, but they don't need those details.

Jared leans back in his chair. "Silas, I'm going to be direct. This creates some complications. Not insurmountable ones, but complications nonetheless."

"I'm aware." I resist the urge to pull at my collar.

"Are you?" Marcus interjects. "The optics alone could be problematic. Professional athlete and team employee. There's an inherent power imbalance."

My jaw tightens. "She doesn't work for me. She doesn't report to me. Her job has nothing to do with my performance or position on the team."

"But you have influence," Patricia points out. "Your status with the team. Your relationship with management and other players. These things matter."

"That's why I'm here. I want everything above board. Whatever paperwork needs to be filed, whatever disclosures need to be made, I'll do it. If there are problems, I want to handle them properly."

Jared studies me for a long moment. "And you, Ms. Nash? You agree to disclosure?"

"Yes." She nods. "We discussed it together."

"And if we determine that one of you needs to change positions or departments?"

The question lands like a check against the boards. "Then it better be me. Scout's worked too hard to establish herself here. She's got the Mobility Monday program running perfectly. The players respect her. If someone has to make a sacrifice, it won't be her."

Patricia and Marcus exchange glances. Jared drums his fingers on the table.

"That's not usually how these conversations go," Patricia admits.

"Usually the athlete expects us to make the problem disappear," Marcus adds. "Transfer the employee, create distance, minimize exposure."

"I'm not asking you to make anything disappear. I'm asking you to protect Scout while we handle this professionally."

Jared stops drumming. "You're serious about her."

It's not a question, but I answer anyway. "Dead serious. This isn't some fling or convenience thing. I plan to marry her."

As soon as Scout is ready to be a hockey wife, I'll have a big ring waiting for her.

"Silas." Scout chides me softly.

I slide her a look. "What? It's the truth."

"Well," Patricia says after a beat of silence. "That changes things somewhat."

"Look," I lean forward, needing them to understand. "Scout's finally finding her confidence, her place here. If this relationship costs her that, I'll walk away from her before I let that happen. But I'm hoping you'll help us find a way to make this work."

Marcus makes more notes. "There are precedents. Other teams have dealt with similar situations."

"The Sharks had a player marry their nutritionist," Patricia offers. "They created clear boundaries and reporting structures. It worked fine."

Jared nods slowly. "Here's what we can do. Scout maintains her current position but reports directly to the head trainer instead of through the general player services hierarchy. That removes any perception of influence from your end. We'll file formal disclosure paperwork that protects both of you. If any issues arise, they get addressed through HR, not team management."

"And her job is safe?" I press.

"As safe as anyone's job ever is in professional sports," Jared says. "Her performance determines her position, not her relationship status."

I don't miss Scout's relieved sigh.

"What about public perception?" Marcus asks. "If this becomes public knowledge?"

"When," I correct. "When it becomes public knowledge. We're not hiding."

Patricia smiles slightly. "Then we recommend a simple approach. If asked, you confirm you're together. No details, no timeline, just acknowledgment. The less dramatic you make it, the less the media will care."

"I can do that."

"There's one more thing," Jared says. "The other players. Have you considered how this might affect team dynamics?"

"Most of them already know. Nobody's made it an issue."

"Good. Keep it that way. Professional at the rink. Do whatever you want on your own time."

Marcus slides a stack of papers across the table. "These are the disclosure forms. Both you and Ms. Nash need to sign them. There's also a conduct agreement that outlines acceptable behavior in professional settings."

I scan through them quickly. Standard stuff mostly. No public displays of affection during team events. No preferential treatment in either direction. No discussing team business outside of appropriate channels. All things we're already doing.

"I'll get these back to you by tomorrow," I say.

The meeting ends with handshakes and promises to process everything quickly. Leaving the executive floor, I feel lighter than I have in weeks. Not because the conversation was easy, but because it's done. We're official.

At practice, nothing seems different on the surface. The guys run drills, coaches yell corrections, equipment managers hustle between tasks. But I catch Scout watching from the tunnel. When our eyes meet, she doesn't look away. Neither do I.

"Get your head in the game, Huxley," Cross barks, but there's amusement in his tone.

After practice, I find Scout in the recovery room setting up for tomorrow's mobility session. She's got her honey blonde hair pulled back in a ponytail, loose waves escaping to frame her face. She's wearing black yoga pants that hug her slender frame and a tight Havoc tank top. Those moss-green eyes are focused on arranging resistance bands with careful precision. She looks confident, competent, completely in her element. Beautiful doesn't begin to cover it.

"Did you mean what you said earlier? About wanting to marry me?"

"I probably should've run that by you first." I rub my hand over the back of my neck. "But I meant every word. I'd marry you tomorrow if I thought you wouldn't run screaming into the sunset."

She turns to face me, expression unreadable. "Are you proposing?"

"No. When I propose, you'll know it. This is just intention. Direction. Whatever you want to call it."

Scout reaches up and cups my face with both hands. "I want to call it perfect."

The kiss she gives me is soft but thorough, and when she pulls back, we're both breathing harder.

"We should probably avoid doing that here," she says, but she's smiling.

"Probably."

Beck walks in, takes one look at us standing too close, and immediately backs out. "Nope. Don't want to know. Didn't see anything."

We break apart laughing.

"I should finish setting up," Scout says.

"I should shower."

"You really should. You smell like hockey gear and bad decisions."

"You love my bad decisions."

"No, I love you despite your bad decisions."

I head for the showers feeling that same settled warmth that's been constant since we figured our shit out. This is what being chosen feels like. Not the dramatic movie version with grand gestures and perfect moments, but this quiet certainty.

Chapter Thirty-Seven

Scout

My presentation materials are arranged perfectly on the table in front of me, color coded and laminated because apparently I cope with stress by becoming aggressively organized. The conference room is set up for this meeting. Three months have passed since the studio opened and Mobility Mondays has been running smoothly. I'm wearing my most professional outfit, a navy blazer over a white blouse and black slacks, my dark blonde curls pulled back in a sleek ponytail.

Juliet sits across from me, reviewing her notes while we wait for the others to arrive. She's been instrumental in helping me prepare this formal proposal to make the program permanent.

"Are you ready for this?" she asks.

I straighten my shoulders. "Absolutely."

She smiles and squeezes my hand. "It's gonna be great."

Coach Cross enters first, followed by Beck, the head trainer, two assistant coaches, and someone from the front office whose name I can never remember. They settle into chairs with the kind of efficiency that says they have twelve other meetings today and limited patience for anything that wastes their time.

"All right, Scout," Coach Cross says. "Show us what you've got."

I stand without hesitation. My hands shake a little as I pull up my first slide on the screen. The old version of me would've started with an apology, some variation of 'I know you're busy' or 'this won't take long.' Instead, I dive straight into the data.

"Mobility Mondays has been running for three months. Here are the results." I click to the next slide, showing injury rates, recovery times, and player feedback scores. "We've seen a thirty percent reduction in soft tissue injuries, improved range of motion in eighty percent of participating players, and consistently positive feedback from both players and trainers."

Beck leans forward. "It's been helpful. A lot of the players have been eager to participate."

"What about the cost?" asks the front office guy. "Do you have an estimate?"

"Going forward, the program requires two hours of dedicated studio time per week plus four hours of training time where I can correct posture and be hands-on. Based on the reduction in injury related missed games, you're looking at a return on investment within the first month."

The front office guy frowns. "Is this really necessary? Players can stretch on their own."

The old reflex rises, the urge to soften my stance, to offer compromises I don't mean. I swallow it down and meet his eyes directly.

"They can. But they don't. Not correctly, not consistently, and not with proper form." I pull up a video showing before and after flexibility assessments. "This isn't about adding another obligation to their schedule. It's about protecting your investment in these athletes. Every game missed to preventable injury costs the organization thousands of dollars and potentially playoff positioning."

Cross nods slowly. "What about players who don't want to participate?"

"It's optional but incentivized. Players who attend consistently get priority PT scheduling and first choice of recovery modalities." I click to my final slide. "This isn't about forcing anyone. It's about creating infrastructure that supports long term athletic performance."

Silence fills the room. My chest tightens, but I don't fill it with nervous chatter or additional justifications. I stand there and let them process, trusting that my work speaks for itself.

"I like it," Beck says finally. "The injury reduction alone makes it worthwhile."

Sam, the head trainer, speaks up. "We've been seeing really positive improvements. This seems like a no-brainer to me."

Cross looks around the table. "Anyone have serious objections?"

The front office guy shrugs. "If the numbers hold up, I'm convinced."

"Then we're approved for full implementation," Cross says. "Congratulations, Scout. You've created something valuable here."

The words land like sunshine after a storm. I thank them professionally, gather my materials, and manage to hold my composure until I'm alone in the elevator. Then I slump against the wall and exhale every ounce of tension I've been carrying.

I did it. I stood in my authority and claimed space for my

ideas. The program's permanent. The studio's real. My career is actually happening.

When I get back to the condo, Silas is on the couch with his laptop. He looks up when I walk in, and the smile that spreads across his face makes my heart do something stupid.

"How'd it go?"

"They approved it." I drop my bag and practically run to him. "Full implementation. Permanent program. It's official."

He catches me when I launch myself at him, pulling me into his lap. "I knew they would. You were brilliant."

"You didn't even see the presentation."

"Didn't need to. I know you." He kisses me, slow and thorough. "I'm so proud of you, Pretty Girl."

We celebrate with takeout and champagne on the couch. Silas keeps looking at me with this expression I can't quite read. There's something intense there, something that makes butterflies erupt in my stomach.

"What?" I finally ask.

"I've been thinking," he says.

"That's dangerous."

"I know we've only been officially together for a few months. I know you're still recovering from Enzo. But I also know what I want." He takes my hand. "I want you. Forever. I want to wake up next to you every morning. I want to support your career and have you support mine. I want kids eventually, if you want them. I want everything with you."

"We already talked about this." I smile and pat his arm. "My answer is the same. Eventually, I do want to be Mrs. Huxley."

"I like the sound of that." He hesitates. "Am I pushing too hard again?"

I think about it. Really think about it. A year ago, the idea of remarrying would have sent me into a panic spiral.

Marriage meant losing myself, meant becoming small and accommodating and disappearing into someone else's needs.

But with Silas, it doesn't feel like that. He's seen me at my worst and stayed. He's supported my career without trying to control it. He's done the work in therapy, been honest even when it's hard, shown up for me consistently without expecting me to shrink.

"Si." My eyes get wet. "I love you so much. And you're being so patient."

"I love you too." He kisses my forehead. "Even if you're making me wait to put a ring on it."

"You can still buy the ring. Just don't propose yet."

His eyebrows lift. "You want me to buy a ring?"

"I want you to be ready when I am." I grin at him. "Plus, I have opinions about what kind of ring I want. We should probably discuss that."

"You have opinions about your engagement ring?"

"Obviously. It's going to be on my hand forever. I should like it."

He laughs, the tension breaking. "Okay. Tell me about this ring."

Grinning at him, I lean my head against his chest. I'm not ready yet, but Silas's excitement pushes me that much further along.

Chapter Thirty-Eight

Silas

The locker room buzzes with pre-game energy. We're playing Colorado tonight. Playoff implications, national broadcast, the whole deal. Coach Cross stands at the whiteboard, marker in hand, running through the game plan one more time.

"Silas, you're shadowing their first line all night. I don't care if Rzeznik takes a shit, you're in the stall next to him. Got it?"

"Got it."

Hunter grins from across the room. "Defense Daddy's gonna shut them down."

"Shut up," I mutter, but there's no heat in it. The guys have been calling me that since some TikTok went viral last month. I hate it. Scout thinks it's hilarious.

My phone buzzes. I check it even though I shouldn't.

SCOUT

Good luck tonight, baby. Sable and I will be in our usual seats, wearing your jersey, cheering on the most amazing d-man in the league. Go be intimidating.

ME

You're wearing my jersey, huh?

SCOUT

#12. With your name on the back.
Everyone's going to know I'm yours.

Heat flares through my chest. Three months ago, Scout wouldn't have been caught dead advertising that we're together. Now she's sitting in the family section wearing my number like she's proud of it.

ME

You're perfect. Love you.

SCOUT

Love you too. Now go win this game.

I pocket my phone and finish taping my stick. The ritual settles me. Heel to toe, no gaps, perfect spiral. My shoulder's been feeling good lately. Scout's mobility work is actually helping, though I'd never admit it to her smug face.

"Five minutes!" someone shouts.

We huddle up. Beck leads us in some ridiculous chant that Thorne started last season. Something about blood and ice and brotherhood. It's corny as hell but it works. By the time we break, we're ready to run through walls.

The tunnel smells like rubber and sweat and possibility. The crowd roar builds as we approach the ice. When my name gets called, the sound is deafening.

"Anchoring the blue line for your Seattle Havoc, six-foot-eight of pure shutdown power. Give it up for number twelve, Silas 'Ice Man' Huxley!"

I skate out and scan the crowd. There. Section 108, row 5. Scout in my jersey, curls piled on top of her head, grinning like she's never been happier. Sable and Juliet are beside her, and the rest of the Coven too. My girl brought her whole squad to watch my team play.

Something in my chest goes tight and warm.

The puck drops.

Colorado comes out flying. Their first line is fast, skilled, and dangerous. Rzeznik's got hands like silk and a shot that could punch through steel. Normally, trying to shut him down for sixty minutes would make me nervous.

Tonight I feel locked in.

First shift, Rzeznik tries to blow past me on the outside. I angle him to the boards, pin him there with my body, and steal the puck clean. Hunter picks it up and we transition the other way. No goal, but we controlled the play.

Second shift, I break up a passing play in the neutral zone. Simple stick lift, nothing fancy. Beck gets the puck and carries it deep. Still no goal, but we're dictating pace.

Third shift, Rzeznik finally gets a step on me. He's flying down the wing, Beck chasing after him but too far from the crease, my goalie Jett exposed. I dig deep and somehow catch Rzeznik at the hash marks. Poke check, perfectly timed, and the puck squirts past the goal, missing the net.

That was close.

Coach Cross nods at me when I hit the bench. That's high praise from him.

The game settles into a rhythm. Colorado's good, really good, but we're better tonight. Thorne scores first, a ridiculous tip that Jett would've had no chance on if it came from the other team. Hunter gets the second, crashing the net and jamming home a rebound. Beck adds a third period goal that makes the building shake.

And me? I play the best defensive game of my career.

Every gap sealed. Every passing lane covered. Each time

Rzeznik thinks he's got space, I'm there. I'm not playing dirty, not aggressive. But I have smart positioning and an active stick.

With five minutes left, Colorado pulls their goalie. It's not the unusual this late in the game if they know they're not going to win. Instead, they put in another enforcer. Six attackers against our five.

This is how games get lost, where one mistake costs you everything.

Coach Cross looks down the bench. "Silas. You're out there until the horn."

I nod and hop the boards.

The next four minutes are pure melee. Colorado throws everything at us. Shots from everywhere. Scrambles in the crease. Jett makes two incredible saves that have the crowd on their feet.

Then Rzeznik gets the puck at the point. He winds up for a one-timer, the kind of shot that beats goalie more often than not. I read it coming and step into the lane. The puck hits my shin pad, deflects wide, and I'm already moving. I scoop it up, spot Thorne breaking free, and hit him with a perfect pass.

Thorne goes in alone on the empty net. He scores and the building erupts.

We win 4-1.

The celebration on the ice is controlled insanity. Gloves fly, helmets come off, everyone's screaming and piling on Jett. I hang back, not big on the group hug thing, but Hunter finds me anyway and nearly tackles me into the boards.

"Defense Daddy!" he yells. "That's my fucking brother!"

Jett skates over, grinning ear to ear. "Dude. You were unreal. Rzeznik had like two inches of ice all night."

I can't repress a smile. "I was just doing my job."

"Bullshit." Beck joins us. "That was a shutdown clinic. You should teach a master class."

The reporters swarm after we get off the ice. Microphones and cameras and questions coming from every direction.

"Silas, incredible performance tonight. What was working for you out there?"

I think about Scout in the stands, therapy with Dr. Max, and finally feeling like I have a life outside of hockey.

"I got my priorities straight," I say. "I found something more important than hockey. It's helped me relax and just play the game."

"Can you elaborate on that?"

I have to try not to roll my eye. "Not really. But it's made all the difference, as you can see."

I shower quick and change fast. The media obligations can wait. I need to see Scout.

She's waiting outside the family room, still wearing my jersey, bouncing on her toes with barely contained energy. The second she sees me, she launches herself into my arms.

"That was amazing!" She kisses me hard, not caring that we're in public with cameras probably pointed in our direction. "You were incredible, Si. I've never seen you play like that."

"You inspired me."

"I was just sitting there eating nachos."

"You were wearing my jersey." I pull her closer. "Everyone in that building knew you were mine."

Her eyes soften. "I am yours. Completely."

"Good." I kiss her again, slower this time. "Because I'm not letting you go."

"Silas! Scout!" Reporters are approaching. "Can we get a quote about your relationship?"

Scout looks at me, questioning. This is it. The moment we

go fully public. No more hiding. No more protecting her from speculation or criticism.

I take her hand and turn to face the cameras.

"Scout Nash is my girlfriend," I say clearly. "She's also the best thing that's ever happened to me. Anyone who has a problem with that can take it up with me directly."

The questions explode. How long have we been together? Does the team know? Is there a conflict of interest?

"Guys," Juliet cuts in. "You know the rules. Be respectful of the players. Do you really think they would be dumb enough to announce their relationship if they didn't have all the paperwork cleared? Like I would ever let that happen on my watch."

"It's true." Scout takes it from Juliet like a pro. "We disclosed our relationship to HR months ago. The team's been supportive. And if you want to know more about my work with the Havoc, you should come to a Mobility Monday session. I'd love to show you what we're building."

She turns the conversation from gossip to her program without missing a beat. Pride surges through me. She's not hiding behind me or shrinking herself down. She's standing tall and claiming space and reminding everyone that she's more than just my girlfriend.

Later, after the media obligations are done and we're finally alone in my truck, Scout leans over and kisses my cheek.

"Thank you," she says.

"For what?"

"For not making me your dirty secret. You stood up there and told everyone I'm yours." Her voice gets quiet. "Enzo never did that. He always kept me separate from his career. I was something that he was ashamed of."

"I could never be ashamed of you." I thread my fingers

through hers. "You're the best thing in my life, Scout. Everyone should know it."

We drive home with her hand in mine, both of us grinning like idiots. The radio plays highlights from the game. The announcers are calling it a statement win, proof that the Havoc are legitimate playoff contenders.

But all I can think about is Scout in my jersey, smiling at me from the stands like I hung the moon.

My shoulder holds up better than expected. The PT work, the icing, the careful management pays off.

"You might have more years than you thought," the doctor said last week.

More years means more hockey. More Scout. More of this life that stretches beyond just the game. I could live with that.

Hockey's still important. It probably always will be. But it's not everything anymore.

Scout is.

Chapter Thirty-Nine

Scout

The condo smells like garlic bread and marinara sauce. I've been cooking all afternoon, prepping enough food to feed a small army. Which is good, because that's basically what's coming over tonight.

"How many people did you invite again?" Silas asks from the kitchen doorway. He's wearing jeans and a Havoc hoodie, hair still damp from his post-practice shower.

"The Coven, Hunter and Juliet, Ryan and Wren, Beck, Jett, Thorne and Mollie..."

"Thorne and Mollie aren't dating."

"They're not not dating either." I stir the sauce. "She's coming. He's coming. If they happen to arrive at the same time and spend the whole night bickering like an old married couple, that's not my business."

Silas grins and wraps his arms around me from behind. "You're meddling."

"I'm facilitating." I lean back against his chest. "There's a difference."

"If you say so." He kisses my neck. "Need help with anything?"

"You can set the table. We're doing buffet style so people can just grab what they want."

We work together in comfortable silence. Silas sets out plates and silverware while I finish the salad. The garlic bread goes in the oven. Wine bottles get opened and left to breathe. Everything's ready by the time the doorbell rings.

Hunter and Juliet arrive first, as predicted. Hunter's carrying a case of beer and Juliet's got a bottle of expensive wine.

"We brought provisions," Hunter announces, heading straight for the fridge.

"Make yourself at home," I say dryly.

"Already did."

The rest of the group trickles in over the next twenty minutes. Ryan and Wren, her hand resting protectively on her small bump. Beck with a bottle of whiskey that probably costs more than my car. Jett with his easy smile and terrible dad jokes. Jessa and Ivy together, already gossiping about something.

Thorne shows up last, looking grumpy. Mollie arrives thirty seconds later, flushed and apologizing for being late.

"Traffic was terrible," she says breathlessly.

"I just drove here. Traffic was fine," Thorne says.

"Well, maybe you drive like a maniac and I drive like a normal person."

"I drive the speed limit."

"The speed limit is a suggestion, not a challenge."

They're still bickering when I hand them each a glass of wine. Juliet catches my eye and smirks. I mouth "told you so" and she rolls her eyes.

Dinner is chaotic in the best way. We're crowded around the living room, plates balanced on laps, conversation flowing. Hunter tells embarrassing stories about Silas in juniors.

Juliet shares horror stories from dealing with difficult sponsors. Wren glows while talking about baby names. Beck and Ryan debate defensive strategies while Jett makes increasingly elaborate plans to prank the entire coaching staff.

Silas sits beside me on the couch, his hand resting on my knee. Every so often he squeezes gently, like he's reminding himself I'm real. I lean into him, feeling settled and happy in a way I didn't know I could be.

"This is nice," Jessa says, refilling her wine glass. "We should do this more often."

"I'm down," Ivy agrees. "I have a pizza dough recipe I've been itching to try out."

"We could do it at our house," Juliet offers. "We have that huge dining room we never use."

"Only if Scout cooks," Hunter says through a mouthful of garlic bread. "This is incredible."

I smile. "Silas helped."

"I opened wine bottles," Silas specifies. "And chopped all the vegetables. Scout did everything else."

The conversation shifts to upcoming games, then to holiday plans, then to Mollie's ongoing campaign to get the team more active on social media. Thorne argues that social media is a waste of time. Mollie argues that brand engagement is crucial for fan retention. They're both getting increasingly heated when Juliet leans in and whispers something to Jessa.

Jessa's eyes go wide. She nods, then whispers something back. They're both looking at me with barely contained excitement.

"What?" I ask suspiciously.

"Nothing," Juliet says innocently.

"You're terrible liars."

"We're excellent liars," Jessa protests. "You just know us too well."

"Spill."

Juliet and Jessa exchange glances. Then Juliet grins. "We've been asked to help someone shop for something big and shiny."

My stomach flips. "Big and shiny."

"Very big. Very shiny." Jessa's practically bouncing. "And we have opinions."

"Strong opinions," Juliet adds. "About cut and clarity and setting style."

I glance at Silas. He's suddenly very interested in his beer bottle, avoiding eye contact. His ears are red.

"I don't know what you're talking about," I say primly.

"Sure you don't." Juliet winks. "Just saying, when the time comes, we've got your back."

"And we have excellent taste," Jessa adds.

"The best taste," Juliet agrees.

Before I can respond, Beck's phone buzzes. He glances at it, then his eyebrows shoot up. "Holy shit."

"What?" Ryan asks.

Beck looks up, his expression stunned. "Enzo Morelli just got arrested."

The room goes silent. Everyone turns to look at me. I feel Silas tense beside me, his hand tightening on my knee.

"What for?" I ask. My voice sounds strange to my own ears.

"Betting scandal. Federal charges. Apparently he's been taking bribes to tank games for years." Beck scrolls through his phone. "Says here he could be looking at serious prison time. Multiple counts of fraud, conspiracy, racketeering..."

The words wash over me. Enzo. Prison. All those years he

spent building his reputation as a successful agent, and this whole time he was dirty.

"Scout?" Silas's voice is gentle. "You okay?"

"Yeah." I realize I'm smiling. "I'm actually great."

"You're smiling," Jessa points out.

"I know. Is that bad?"

"Hell no," Hunter says. "That asshole had it coming."

Juliet raises her wine glass. "To karma being a bitch."

"To karma," everyone echoes, raising their glasses.

I clink my glass against Silas's. "I should feel something, right? Like, shocked or upset or vindicated or something."

"What do you feel?" he asks.

I think about it. Really think about it. Enzo's arrest should be this huge moment. The man who made my life miserable, who made me feel small and worthless, who controlled every aspect of our relationship, is finally facing consequences.

But all I feel is... relief. And maybe a little bit of satisfaction.

"I feel free," I say finally. "Like this is the final proof that leaving him was the right choice."

"It was the right choice," Silas says firmly.

"I know. But now everyone else knows too." I lean into him. "Everyone's going to see him for what he really is. Not the charming agent. Not the former hockey star. Just a criminal who was willing to destroy people's careers for money."

"You think any of his clients knew?" Beck asks.

Silas shakes his head. "No way. Enzo was too smart for that. He kept everything compartmentalized."

"Well, he's screwed now," Ryan says. "Federal charges? He's going away for a long time."

The conversation shifts to speculation about the case, about which games might have been affected, about whether any current players were involved. I tune most of it out, focusing instead on the feeling of Silas's arm around me, the warmth of friends surrounding us, the life I've built that has nothing to do with Enzo anymore.

"You really okay?" Silas murmurs in my ear.

"Better than okay." I turn to look at him. "A year ago, this news would have destroyed me. I would have spent weeks obsessing over it, wondering what I could have done differently, blaming myself somehow."

"And now?"

"Now I'm just grateful I got out when I did." I kiss his cheek. "And grateful I found you."

His eyes soften. "Pretty Girl..."

"I mean it. You helped me remember who I am. You never tried to make me smaller or easier to manage. You just..." I struggle to find the words. "You just loved me. The real me."

"That's the only version worth loving."

We're interrupted by Thorne and Mollie arguing about something. She's gesturing wildly with her wine glass and he's got that stubborn set to his jaw that means he's not backing down. Juliet's filming them on her phone while Hunter provides commentary.

"They're going to kill each other or sleep together," Jessa observes. "Fifty-fifty odds."

"I've got money on sleep together," Ivy says.

"Same," Wren agrees.

"You're all delusional," Mollie calls out. "I would rather die."

"Noted," Thorne says flatly.

The party goes late. People start filtering out around eleven, promising to do this again soon. Hugs and goodbyes and tipsy declarations of friendship fill the doorway. Finally it's just me and Silas, surrounded by empty wine bottles and dirty dishes.

"I'll help clean up," he offers.

"Tomorrow." I'm too tired and content to care about the mess. "Let's just go to bed."

We brush our teeth side by side at the bathroom sink. He makes faces at me in the mirror and I flick water at him. It's domestic and silly and perfect.

In bed, Silas pulls me against his chest. His heartbeat is steady under my ear.

"Today was good," he says.

"It really was."

"I like having everyone here. Felt like family."

"It felt like home." I press a kiss to his chest. "Our home."

"Yeah." His arms tighten around me. "Our home. Our family. Our life."

I think about Enzo in a jail cell somewhere, finally facing consequences for his actions. I think about the girl I used to be, trapped in a marriage that was slowly killing her spirit. I think about how far I've come, how much I've built, how happy I am.

"I have everything I want," I whisper into the darkness.

"Me too, Pretty Girl." Silas kisses the top of my head. "Me too."

We fall asleep tangled together, surrounded by the evidence of a life well-lived. Good friends. Meaningful work. A love that doesn't require me to disappear.

Enzo's arrest doesn't change anything about my life. That's the most beautiful part.

I already won. I've been winning for months now.

And I'm never looking back.

Chapter Forty

Scout

SEVEN MONTHS LATER

The sign above the door reads *Sage & Stone Yoga* in clean, modern lettering. I stand on the sidewalk staring at it, still not quite believing this is real. It took Silas's financial backing, Ivy's connections in the real estate world, and a signed contract from the Seattle Havoc for Mobility Mondays for the next two years. But with all of that, I managed to get the perfect location, mere minutes away from the Rainier Bank Center where the guys play.

It's been a stressful six months, getting this project off the ground. But now it's all come together. I suck in a breath, swearing to myself that I won't cry.

"Are you going to go in or just stand there all day?" Silas asks from behind me. His hand rests warm on the small of my back.

"I'm going in. I'm just..." I trail off, not sure how to finish that sentence.

"Proud? Excited? Terrified?"

"All of the above." I turn to look at him. "What if nobody shows up?"

"Baby, half the team is already inside. Hunter texted me ten minutes ago asking where the coffee is."

"There's no coffee. Why would there be coffee at a mobility studio?"

Silas grins. "Exactly what I told him. He called me a monster."

That makes me laugh, which was probably his intention. Taking a deep breath, I push open the door.

The space is perfect. Better than I imagined when Ivy first texted me about this location four months ago. Hardwood floors, floor-to-ceiling mirrors, cubbies for personal belongings along one wall. Yoga mats rolled and waiting in neat rows. Resistance bands hanging from hooks. Foam rollers stacked in the corner.

And people. So many people.

The entire Havoc roster is here. Thorne and Beck stretching in the corner. Jett and Connor comparing hamstring flexibility. Shane showing Theo some hip opener I taught him last week. Hunter doing absolutely nothing productive, just standing around with a protein shake like he owns the place.

The Coven's here too. Juliet in full PR mode, taking photos for social media. Jessa and Mollie setting up a snack table that nobody asked for but everyone will appreciate. Wren chatting with Coach Ryan, her hand resting on her barely-there baby bump while she beams. She's the cutest pregnant person I've ever seen.

Sable stands near the front, talking to Dad. My dad, who drove over from his assisted living facility with Sable this morning specifically for this. He's using his cane but standing tall, looking proud and healthy in a way I haven't seen in years.

And it looks like he's brought a few friends with him, as well. A bunch of ladies from his retirement community are clustered around Dad, seeing to his every need. I don't quite understand the nature of their relationships, but my Dad seems to be fitting in well in the community. He's *thriving*.

"Scout!" Juliet spots me and waves. "Get over here. We need to cut the ribbon."

"There's a ribbon?"

Her eyes widen a fraction. "Of course there's a ribbon. I'm a professional."

She drags me to the front entrance where someone has strung up an actual ribbon across the doorway. Silas produces a pair of giant gold scissors from somewhere. The team gathers around, phones out, recording.

"Speech!" someone yells. Probably Jett.

I flush. "I didn't prepare a speech."

"Good," Beck calls out. "Keep it short. Some of us are old and need to pee frequently."

That gets a laugh. I look around at all these faces, these people who showed up for me on a random Tuesday morning. My throat gets tight.

"Okay. Um." I clear my throat. "A few months ago, this was just an idea. A hope that maybe I could help you guys stay healthy and keep playing the sport you love. And then Juliet helped me turn it into a proposal. And then Silas..." I glance at him. He's watching me with that expression that makes my insides go soft. "Silas helped make it real. But this isn't just my studio. It's ours. All of ours. This is a space for the team, built by the team, to support the team. So thank you for believing in me. Thank you for showing up. And thank you for letting me do what I love."

"Cut the damn ribbon!" Thorne shouts. "We've got places to be!"

I laugh and cut the ribbon. It falls to the floor in two neat pieces. Everyone cheers. Someone pops a bottle of champagne that sprays everywhere and makes Juliet shriek about the hardwood floors.

The first official Mobility Monday class in the new studio starts fifteen minutes later. Twenty players show up. That's more than half the roster, more than I ever expected for a voluntary session.

They sprawl across mats, some confident, some looking vaguely terrified. Shane's done this enough times that he knows the routine. Hunter's here purely to support me, which is sweet even if he's going to complain the whole time. Thorne's in the back corner looking grumpy. Mollie's hovering near him with a foam roller, trying to explain how it works while he ignores her.

"Okay everyone," I call out. "We're starting with cat-cow to warm up the spine. On all fours, please."

The room fills with the sound of grown men trying to figure out how to arrange their massive bodies into a tabletop position. It's crazy and perfect.

I move between mats, adjusting postures, offering modifications. Connor needs help with his hip alignment. Theo keeps forgetting to breathe. Shane's got it down but I praise him anyway because positive reinforcement works.

When I reach Hunter, he's doing the movement completely wrong.

"You look like a dying giraffe," I tell him.

"I'm trying, though," he grumbles. "That counts, right?"

"Absolutely. This stretch is helping your body recover from getting checked into the boards three times a game." I press gently on his lower back. "Arch here. Good. Feel that stretch?"

"Yeah," he admits grudgingly. "It feels nice."

"That's because I'm a genius."

His lips twitch. "Don't let it go to your head."

I move on to the next player, then the next. The room settles into a rhythm. Breathing and movement and the occasional grunt when someone discovers a tight muscle they didn't know existed.

Silas watches from the doorway. He's not participating because his shoulder is on complete rest, but he shows up anyway. He's supporting me. Not just that, he's proud of me. And he's making sure that everyone knows today is a big deal.

After class, players linger. They don't rush off to showers or meetings. They stay, asking questions, wanting to know when the next session is, thanking me for teaching them. I'm absolutely *glowing* from within.

Beck approaches while I'm rolling up mats. "This is good, Scout. Really good. The guys need this."

"Thanks, Beck."

"I'm serious. We're getting older, staying healthy is getting harder. Having someone who actually gives a shit about our long-term wellbeing?" He shakes his head. "That's rare. Don't let anyone make you doubt your value here."

The words land heavier than he probably meant them to. I think about Enzo, about all the years he made me feel like my work didn't matter. He had a way of making it seem like I was playing at having a career instead of actually building one.

"I won't," I promise.

After everyone leaves, it's just me and Silas in the empty studio. Afternoon light streams through the windows, making the hardwood floors glow. I sit in the middle of the room, legs crossed, just breathing it in.

Silas sits beside me. "You did it."

"We did it." I lean against his shoulder. "I couldn't have done this without you."

"Bullshit. You would've found a way." He kisses the top of my head. "But I'm glad I got to help."

"You paid for half of it."

"So? It's still yours." He tilts my chin up to look at him. "I don't need my name on everything I care about, Scout. Watching you teach today, seeing how much the guys respect you, knowing you built something that matters? That's better than any plaque or sign."

My eyes get wet. "You can't just say stuff like that."

"Why not?"

"Because it makes me want to kiss you in front of everybody. And we agreed to limit our PDA in work settings."

"There's nobody here right now." His mouth curves. "I'm just saying."

Leaning in, inhaling a deep lungful of his scent, I kiss him. Slow and deep and full of gratitude and love and the overwhelming feeling of having built something real. It's not just the studio.

This relationship almost didn't happen because we were both too scared to be honest. I'm so fucking glad we both took a chance on each other.

When we break apart, Silas rests his forehead against mine. "I'm so proud of you, Pretty Girl."

"I'm proud of us."

"Yeah." He smiles. "Me too."

My phone buzzes and I see that Dad's texted a photo. It's me cutting the ribbon, Silas beside me, both of us grinning like idiots. The caption reads: "My daughter, the business owner. Your mother would be so proud."

I show Silas the text. He squeezes my hand.

"She would be," he says. "I'm sure of it."

For the first time in my life, everything feels like it's exactly where it's supposed to be.

Chapter Forty-One

Silas

I wake up happy.

Not the manic happiness that comes from winning or the desperate happiness that comes from avoiding loss. This is something quieter, steadier. Contentment maybe, though that word feels too small for the warmth that's taken up permanent residence in my chest.

Scout's already up, because of course she is. She's probably in the kitchen making one of those green smoothies she swears taste good but definitely don't. Her yoga clothes are laid out on the dresser, which means she's teaching the early class at her studio. One year in and those words still make me stupidly proud.

I force myself out of bed and find her dancing to music only she can hear through her earbuds, adding spinach to the blender. She's wearing one of my t-shirts and nothing else, honey blonde waves piled on top of her head in a messy bun that defies physics. Her slender frame moves unselfconsciously to whatever she's listening to, fair skin with those olive undertones glowing in the morning light. She looks beautiful and ridiculous at the same time, which is exactly how I love her.

"Morning," I say, loud enough to be heard over whatever she's listening to.

She jumps, then laughs, pulling out one earbud. "You're up early."

"You're up earlier."

"I have the sunrise class. What's your excuse?"

"Watching you dance badly in my kitchen."

"Our kitchen," she corrects. "And my dancing is perfectly adequate."

I move behind her and settle my hands on her hips. "Your dancing is terrible. Good thing you're pretty."

She leans back into me, her smile wicked. "Good thing you're easy."

"Only for you."

The moment stretches warm and comfortable. A year of mornings like this have changed me, made me comfortable in ways I didn't know were possible to feel. Scout fills our space with plants and laughter and the kind of easy intimacy I never thought I was capable of.

Plus, she keeps me on my toes with a near-constant supply of new yoga pants. Whenever I see charges from Lululemon and Alo on my credit card, I get a spontaneous erection just thinking about her showing off her new outfits for me.

"Are you okay?" Scout wrinkles her nose at me. "You went away somewhere, and then you started looking horny."

She knows me too well.

"Yeah, Pretty Girl. I'm more than okay. By the way, I have something to show you later," I tell her. "After practice."

"Another surprise? The last time you surprised me, we christened a coat closet at a gala."

"This is different."

She turns in my arms and studies my face. "Is that a good thing?"

"I think you'll be pleased."

Before she can interrogate me further, her alarm goes off. "Shit, I need to go. My class starts in forty minutes."

I sigh and get moving. My brain is more interested in what will happen tonight, but I slog through dryland training anyway. After a shower and video review and all the normal rhythms of professional hockey, I text Scout.

ME

Meet me at the rink. Main entrance.

SCOUT

Why?

ME

Trust me.

SCOUT

Those words have gotten me in trouble before.

ME

Good trouble though.

She sends back a laughing emoji and I catch myself grinning.

The arena is mostly empty by the time she arrives. A few maintenance staff and security are doing rounds, but the public spaces are deserted. She finds me by the doors to the main rink, curiosity written all over her face. She's wearing yoga pants and a tight Havoc tank top under an open hoodie, her honey blonde hair falling in loose waves around her shoulders. Those moss-green eyes search mine, trying to figure out what I'm up to. Beautiful doesn't even begin to cover it.

"What are we doing here?"

"Patience, please?"

She gives me a look like she's trying to figure out what I have up my sleeve.

I lead her through the doors onto the concourse and take her down to rink level. The ice stretches out before us, pristine and perfect, Zamboni tracks still visible. The overhead lights are dimmed to maintenance levels, giving everything a twilight quality.

"Are we allowed to be here?" Scout asks.

"I cleared it with management."

"For what?"

Instead of answering, I grab two pairs of skates from the bench. Mine and a pair I borrowed from equipment that should fit her.

She eyes them with amusement. "You're making me skate in street clothes?"

"I've seen you skate in worse."

"Fair point." She sits down and laces up with practiced efficiency. "This better be worth missing dinner."

"It will be."

I step onto the ice first and reach back for her hand. She takes it, gliding onto the ice with easy confidence. Her movements are smooth and natural, the way they always are when I catch her skating between sessions at the rink.

"Show off," I mutter as she does a little spin.

"You're dating an athlete, remember? We do coordination for a living."

"Don't let go," I say anyway.

"Never." I look at her, my heart rate speeding up. "Not ever, Scout."

She tilts her head to the side. "You're being both extremely weird and extremely sweet tonight."

I say nothing, just wipe my spare hand on my pants. It's sweaty and gross. Scout doesn't seem to mind though.

We move slowly, me skating backward while Scout matches my pace with the kind of grace that comes from regular practice. She's not a hockey player, but she's spent enough time on the ice that it's second nature now.

"Look at you," I say. "Making this look easy."

She smirks. "I was born in skates. Same way I bet you were."

"Jett has some polaroids of me in a hockey uniform at four. They're... pretty cute, I guess," I admit grumpily.

"Oh. Now I have to see those."

I grunt. We make it to center ice and I stop. Scout raises an eyebrow at me.

"Why are we stopping? Are you going to make me do bag skates?"

I shake my head slowly, my heart pounding harder than it should. Enforcers twice my size have given me less nerves than this moment.

"This place taught me a lot of things," I say. "Discipline. Focus. How to take a hit and keep going."

"Okay..."

"But it also taught me to never show weakness." I brush a loose wave away from her face with one hand while keeping her steady with the other. "You taught me something different."

Scout's expression softens. "Silas..."

"You taught me that strength isn't about walls. It's about choosing to stay open even when it's scary. It's about letting someone see all of you, not just the parts that are easy to love."

Her eyes are bright with tears that don't fall. "If you're about to make me cry on ice skates, I'll never forgive you."

"Too bad."

I drop to one knee on the ice, which is exactly as uncomfortable as it sounds. Scout gasps, one hand flying to her mouth, the other reaching for my shoulder instinctively.

"Scout," I say, pulling out the ring I've been carrying for months, waiting for the right time. "You see all my sharp edges and choose to stay anyway."

"Baby, of course I do."

"I love your terrible dancing and your aggressive morning energy. I love how you take care of everyone but still protect your boundaries. I love that you turned my cold condo into a home just by being in it."

Tears stream down her face now. Definitely crying.

"Will you marry me?" I ask. "Keep teaching me how to be better? Let me watch you heal hockey players? Be my partner in absolutely everything?"

Before I even finish, she says yes. She brushes away a tear. "Yes to all of it. Yes, I will."

The ring slides onto her finger while my hands shake. It's huge, an exquisite yellow diamond. She'll have to take it off when she does yoga or Mobility Mondays. But I need other people to look at her and realize how very married she is to someone who cares enough to get her a rock the size of a small moon. For a moment she just stares at it, then launches herself at me.

Both of us go down hard.

Freezing ice presses against my back while Scout's on top of me, laughing and kissing my entire face. I'm mainly concerned about protecting us from skate blades.

"We're going to die," I point out between kisses.

"Worth it."

"Your engagement story is going to be that I proposed and then you ended up with a concussion."

"Still worth it."

I somehow manage to get us vertical again, though Scout's laughing too hard to skate properly now. I keep her steady as we make our way to the boards, both of us grinning like idiots.

"I can't believe you proposed on the ice," she says.

"Where else would I do it? This is where I learned to be tough. You're where I learned to be soft. It felt right to finish my story as a bachelor here."

She kisses me again, slower this time, and I can taste her happiness mixed with tears.

"I love you," she whispers against my mouth.

"I love you too."

We sit on the home bench while Scout immediately pulls out her phone to look at the ring in better light. "How long have you been planning this?"

"Bought the ring months ago. I've been carrying it around like an idiot ever since."

"Why tonight?"

"Because this morning I woke up happy. And I realized I get to keep waking up like that as long as you're here."

She leans into my side and smiles. "That might be the most romantic thing you've ever said."

"Don't get used to it."

"Too late. You're soft now. No taking it back."

Quiet fills the arena around us, empty seats and dormant dreams surrounding our moment. In a few days this place will be packed with screaming fans while I'm out there throwing hits and protecting my teammates. Scout will be in her studio, teaching people to move without pain, building her business one body at a time.

And someday soon, I'll have to retire. My body still has a clock on it, even if I'm more flexible from living with Scout.

But right now, it's just us. A woman who teaches flexibility and a man who's learning to bend. A ring that promises permanence and a life that finally feels worth keeping.

"Hey," Scout says suddenly. "We're getting married."

"We are."

"Scout Huxley sounds right to me. I'm going to be Scout Huxley."

"If you want. You can keep Nash. It's whatever you want."

"Are you kidding? I just want you, big guy."

God, I'm so gone for her. "You have me. Forever, apparently."

"Forever," she agrees.

And the word doesn't scare me at all.

Chapter Forty-Two

Thorne

The end of season party thumps through speakers that rattle the walls of the private venue. Players pack the room shoulder to shoulder, finally loose after months of grinding through games. Sponsors hover with drinks they'll never finish. Photographers float between groups, hunting for smiles that look genuine enough for social media.

I'm not looking for her. I made a promise to myself that I'd behave tonight. Behaving means not seeking her out or staring at her like a stalker from across the room.

I claim space near the bar. People automatically give me room the way they always do for the captain. I'm also a big guy. Six foot four, six four and a half on the weekend. Not as husky as Hunter or Silas, but a hell of a lot faster on the ice. Plus, I'm the fucking center.

That counts for a lot around here. Especially with the bunnies. A cluster of them stand nearby, making eyes at me. But I'm being good. So not only am I not looking for her, I'm not looking for anyone to keep my bed warm tonight. Just me and my hand.

Across the room, Silas stands with Scout near the dance floor. She says something into his chest and laughs, head tipped back with waves bouncing. His hand rests at her waist like it belongs there. He looks settled in a way I never see during games. Not loose exactly, but comfortable in his skin for once.

Watching them creates an itch I don't want to examine.

Discipline makes sense to me. Focus and control are languages I speak. Building something through repetition is how you survive this league. What doesn't compute is believing in permanence when hockey eats relationships alive. Recently, two of the meanest, baddest guys on our team have settled down.

They didn't just find girlfriends. Hunter is married. Silas is engaged. If I ever felt some kind of solitary brotherhood with my fellow hockey players, I sure as hell don't anymore.

Marriages crack under the schedule while divorces play out in headlines. Women who used to wear team jackets like armor end up flinching at the sound of skates.

Yet Silas looks happy anyway.

A photographer waves me over before I can look away. My feet carry me to the designated spot and I arrange my face into the expression they want. Neutral works best for these things. Some nameless guy in a suit shakes my hand while saying my name like they own part of it. Another person claps my back and calls me a natural leader. Someone else thanks me for a season I haven't processed yet.

The glass of beer in my hand stays untouched. Can I go yet? I check my watch, feeling my impatience growing. Since I can't take out my aggression the normal way with two pretty brunettes who writhe and gasp my last name like I'm a fucking god, I'm more wound up than usual.

That's when I find her. It's not my fault. Mollie catches my sleeve when I'm looking for an exit.

"TikTok?" she begs, already holding her phone between us. "Thirty seconds. Please? It'll make the fans so happy."

Confidence radiates from her in waves that throw people off if they don't know her. Tonight she's wearing lipstick bright enough to stop traffic, a black geometric print dress that hits mid-thigh, and black Converse. Her long copper hair is styled straight and shiny, catching the light as she moves. She's always like this, matching something she's wearing with one of a seemingly infinite number of pairs of shoes. It's annoying. I know that hair won't stay straight for long in this humidity. Give it twenty minutes and it'll start curling gently at the ends.

I scowl automatically. Her grin says she expected this reaction.

"I don't have time."

"You're literally going home to fuck some drunk chick. She can wait ten minutes. In fact, you can probably tell her that it's foreplay. So really, I'm doing you a favor."

I growl at her teasing expression. "Don't talk about foreplay. Jesus, Squeak."

"Don't call me that." Mollie glares daggers at me. "Just say the line. You don't even have to smile."

"This is my smile," I tell her.

"That's a hostage situation pretending to be an expression," she counters, adjusting the phone angle. "Try again."

The video takes less than a minute. Mollie prompts me when I stall and laughs when I deliver the last line like I'm reading tax code. After she lowers the phone, she rolls her eyes. "Was that so bad?"

"Counterpoint." I raise my eyebrows. "Why does TikTok even exist?"

She waves her hand to indicate all of me. "You're the worst."

She spins on her Converse, flipping her hair over her shoulder and moving away. Good. I've been avoiding her all night. Now I can go back to dodging her and make my way to the door. My eyes skim down her dress. When I see how short it is, my jaw tenses. She used to wear these colorful tights under her dresses.

But lately, Mollie has been playing at being a grown up. Part of that apparently is wearing dresses that skim her thighs. Where is Beck? Her older brother needs to be policing her outfits so that I don't have to.

Across the room, Mollie nearly collides with a rookie I don't recognize immediately. Young kid, too new to know better, carrying confidence that hasn't met consequences yet. Whatever he says makes her cheeks go pink and she laughs, surprised and pleased. Flirting comes naturally to her because everything does.

Before my brain catches up, my body moves.

Three steps put me between them, close enough that the kid has to crane his neck to meet my eyes. Volume isn't necessary and contact isn't required. He reads the situation fast enough to stammer an apology.

"S-sorry, Thorne. I'll just, um..." He jerks his thumb over his shoulder, his face as red as a cherry tomato. "Yep."

I unclench my fists and force my shoulders to relax. But when I look, Mollie's glaring at me again. It's the facial expression I deserve.

"You can't do that," she says. "He was just being nice!"

"I already did it."

"God, Thorne." She crosses her arms and cocks her hip. "I wasn't asking for protection."

When she looks all angry and huffy like that, I can't help but goad her.

"You didn't need to, Squeak. Besides, I probably saved that kid from an ass beating. You and I both know how temperamental Beck can be."

"You let me deal with my brother." Her jaw tightens. "I'm not fragile, you know."

"Hm." I cast a skeptical gaze down her body. "You're injured, Squeak."

"Just because I can't skate anymore doesn't make me off limits."

Arguments sharpen fast between us. They always have. I slide my gaze around, smirking when I see that no one is listening to our conversation. Unable to help myself, I slide closer until I feel her breath against my chest. My body leans in without my permission.

Asshole.

"You chose to work for the same team as your big brother, darling," I say, dropping my voice. "At this point? You're pretty much going to die a virgin."

Color drains from her face while her expression hardens to something very close to rage. "I hate you."

Her voice doesn't wobble. The words hold no hesitation. I'm used to her barbs, but this one nettles me, burying itself deep under my skin.

"I know." I give her a cool little smile.

Before either of us can say anything else, Beck appears. His hand lands on my shoulder with easy familiarity.

"All good here?" he asks. His eyes catch on her short dress. "Good god, did the dress store run out of fabric or something?"

My lips twitch. "I just chased off a farm team kid who thinks your little sister is fair game."

"Fuck. Really?" He glances at Mollie, then back at me, and nods. "Thanks for watching out for her."

"Of course." The assumption sits between us like an established fact. This is a role I've accepted without question for a long time. I hold out a fist and he bumps it. This works for us.

"I'm not going to stay here and listen to you two meatheads," Mollie says.

Mollie stalks off while Beck talks. After a few seconds, someone calls Beck's name, and he gravitates toward the bar. Right. This is my chance to leave.

My eyes track Mollie across the room. She films something with other players, laughter bright and effortless again. When she bends and then straightens, she winces. She stands still as she rolls her ankle, biting her lip. I assume she's trying to relieve some of the lingering nerve pain she's struggled with ever since she tore a ligament and fractured her ankle when she was skating.

She went from a national figure skating champion to a girl so scared of being hurt again that she won't even get near an ice rink. So yeah, maybe it makes me a little protective. So what? Mollie could use a little safeguarding.

Silas appears at my shoulder without warning. He doesn't crowd me, just follows my gaze to where Mollie stands, then looks back at my face.

"You all right?" he asks.

I shrug, turning away from Mollie. "Why wouldn't I be?"

He narrows his eyes and jerks his head. "You're not hiding it well."

"Hiding what?" I can feel a flush creeping up my neck.

"Beck's sister."

"Mollie?" I keep playing dumb, even though he obviously knows something's going on. "What about her?"

"He trusts you."

My jaw clenches. "Sure. I know."

Silas watches me for another beat. "I spent months hiding behind a screen because I thought Scout would reject the real me. Lying hurt us both more than honesty ever could."

"Fuck off, Silas." I roll my eyes. "I've got it under control."

"Mhm." He looks at me for a second and sucks his teeth. "You're playing a dangerous game, Thorne."

He walks away before I can answer. Me? I go back to watching Mollie like she's magnetic north.

Chapter Forty-Three

Thank you for reading ***Dear MVP, You're Ice Cold***. I loved every second of writing this book and I'm so thankful to you for being a reader! As a special token of my gratitude, I've written a bonus epilogue. It features your favorite characters – Silas & Scout.

Here's a list of all the couples in this series!

Dear #47, You're the Worst - Hunter & Juliet - Enemies to lovers, fake fiancé

***Dear MVP, You're Ice Cold*-** Silas & Scout - Enemies to lovers, grumpy x sunshine
Dear Hotshot, I Hate You - Thorne & Mollie - Hate to love, teammate's little sister
Say Yes to the Nemesis - Ryan & Wren - Enemies to lovers, brother's best friend
The Accidental Honeymoon - Jay & Calla - Accidentally married, road trip hilarity

If you loved this book, please consider leaving a review. It's the best way to let me know that you want me to write more books like this one!

I'm so excited for what's next. I know that if you liked this, you'll love ***Dear Hotshot, I Hate You***... It's Thorne & Mollie's story. It's time to head back to Seattle to find out what Thorne and the Seattle Havoc hockey team are up to! (Hint: it's dirty.)

Forbidden love is very close to my heart... and I am very excited to be able to present this combination of some my favorite tropes: sports romance, teammate's little sister, hate to love, forbidden romance, workplace romance, touch her and expire, forced proximity, bad boy player x good girl, spicy romance

The team's hotshot just fell for the one girl who hates his guts.

Mollie Tate just wants to do her job, build her career, and stop getting introduced as *Beck Tate's little sister* like it's her full legal name. Working for the Seattle Havoc is a dream. It's also a daily reminder that hockey players are all walking red flags with great abs.

Her ground rules are simple: don't date, flirt, or even think about hockey players. Especially not Alexander Thorne, the team's golden boy who's charming in interviews and friendly with fans but somehow reserves all his grunts and attitude just for her. He's hot, but he's *such* a jerk.

Thorne knows he's being a dick. He also knows it's the only way to keep his hands off his captain's little sister. She drives him crazy, and the only cure is kissing her until that sharp little mouth finally shuts up. Except his teammate would absolutely murder him for it.

Because the alternative is admitting that every time Mollie rolls her eyes at him, he wants to push her against a wall and find out if good girls actually taste as sweet as they look.

Tropes: sports romance, teammate's little sister, forbidden romance, workplace romance, touch her and expire, grumpy-only-for-her, forced proximity, bad boy player x good girl innocent, high heat spicy romance

Grab *Dear Hotshot, I Hate You* right now!

Acknowledgments

This book would not have been possible without with my awesome beta readers Lizzy, Patricia, Blake, and Shea. Thank you all for bearing with me as I tried to figure out how much sexting is too much. (The limit DOES exist!)

About Vivian Wood

Vivian likes to write about troubled, deeply flawed alpha males and the fiery, kick-ass women who bring them to their knees.

Vivian's lasting motto in romance is a quote from a favorite song: "Soulmates never die."

Be sure to join her email list to keep up with all the awesome giveaways, author videos, ARC opportunities, and more!

Vivian's Works

Seattle Havoc
Hockey Romance
Dear #47, You're the Worst
Dear MVP, You're Ice Cold
Dear Hotshot, I Hate You

Wildflower Lane
Small Town Rom Com
The Accidental Honeymoon
The Always Bridesmaid
Say Yes to the Nemesis

Cape Simon
Small Town Romance
The Grumpy Boss Agreement
The Fake Fiancée Proposition

Sinfully Rich
Steamy Billionaire Romance
Sinful Fling
Sinful Enemy
Sinful Boss
Sinful Chance
Sinful Teacher

Billionaires Ever After
Steamy Bad Boy Romance
His Best Friend's Little Sister
Claiming Her Innocence
His Fiancé To Keep
His Lovely Virgin

Hush Hush Club
Forbidden Billionaire Romantic Suspense
Such A Good Girl
Such A Spoiled Brat

Married At Midnight
Forbidden Billionaire Romance

Deal With The Devil
Wed to the Devil
Vow to the Devil

Ruined Castle Trilogy
Forbidden Billionaire Romance
The Single Dad
The Nanny
The Caress

Broken Slipper Trilogy
Forbidden Billionaire Romance
The Patron
The Dancer
The Embrace
Possessive

Fifth Avenue Villains
Fifth Avenue Devil

Royally Rich
Forbidden Royal Romance
Cruel Heir
Sinful Princess
Pretend Princess

King's Capture Duet
Dark Billionaire Romance
King's Capture
Queen's Sacrifice

Addiction Duet
Angsty Dark Romance

Addiction
Obsession

Other books
Wild Hearts

For more information….
vivian-wood.com
info@vivian-wood.com

www.ingramcontent.com/pod-product-compliance
Lightning Source LLC
Chambersburg PA
CBHW070303310726
48976CB00005B/1543